RESTITUTION!

NICKIE --

Thanks & Enjoy the Ride --- of Life!

www.Restitution-the-novel.com

RESTITUTION!

A HEEP [URIAH] OF REVENGE BY THE ROAD ROGUE

K.W. Clark

CONTENTS

PREFACE

I am not a leader, but I will not follow. I would rather seek solitude than be subject to servitude ... I am an independent individual ... I will choose my own road.

I sincerely desire that you will find value in this literature, even if you find that literary rules have been broken in its creation. That was intentional. The story itself includes broken rules, promises, hearts and dreams. Enter into a three-dimensional world of fact, fiction, and fantasy—of past, present and possible. You may think you are being taken for a ride. That, too, is intentional. My expectation is that interactions will occur between the characters, the author, and the reader. You might love the music, or you might hate the music. You might love what is written, or you might hate what is written. However, as long as you hate to set the book down, I win my restitution.

A complete copy of the United States Constitution is included as a gift and as a reference. I pray that you will at least read and retain that valuable document. Every American should read it without interpretation. You are an individual. Your own individual existence, beliefs, desires, and dreams are intended to be protected by the Constitution.

Final Note: Three dates are significant to this work:

1. February 27, 2001, when I decided that this story must be told.
2. July 4, 2001, when I began the project.
3. September 11, 2001, when I stopped the project, nearly completed, and thereafter gradually decided, based upon the government's responses to September 11, to finish utilizing a major revision.

Unfortunately I was unable to receive permission to reprint the complete lyrics from Uriah Heep on the songs referenced in this book. For complete lyrics please refer to: www.uriahheep.com.

FOREWORD

Once upon a time in the not-too-distant future...

There was a small traveling circus, one of the last of its kind, with a long history filled with the joy of entertainment, adventure, and pride. However, the times had changed and the circus was smaller than ever, with only one quality, crowd-pleasing act—the elephants.

Only two elephants were left. Mary was the female (about 29 years old). Joseph, or Mighty Joe (current billing name), had been born into the circus and was entertaining in his fifth decade. He had been billed under many names, including Jumbo or whatever was popular, to help the gate. He simply responded to the J as grunted by the trainer. Always there was trouble with the use of a copyright or other such infringement, but Mighty Joe instinctively knew how to wow the little boys and girls, as he had for generations.

New trouble was brewing for the little circus, this time far more diffi-cult than ever faced in its history. The animal rights people were protest-ing the use of elephants, and this little circus was an easy target. With pressure on politicians, a coming election, and three canceled Saturday night performances (due to the protesting), Congress acted. They wrote and passed another convenient law violating the Constitution's purpose of limiting the size and power of the government. Yet again politicians ad-vanced, overreaching authority to further empower government at the ex-pense of the individual, be it one or one little circus.

The little circus's owner took the news hard. The decision was made reluctantly. With those three canceled Saturday night performances, no money was left. The employees were told in a tearful meeting. The little circus could not operate without the elephants. The "show" must end. Good-bye and farewell!

Everything was sold, from the antique pipe organ and hand-carved carts to Mary. There was one last problem. Old Mighty Joe was soon to be 60 years old, and no zoo wanted to risk him dying upon entering into their care. Animal rights people were after zoos, too. The little circus owner held out as long as he could, but Mary was sold without Mighty Joe.

Days and weeks passed by, and Mighty Joe had lost his world. Even the trainer of the last 10 years was gone. Now a young teenage boy fed and cared for Mighty Joe while the little circus owner desperately searched for a buyer.

Mighty Joe just stood there, day after day, with the sides of his massive face wet and stained from the weeping of his eyes for his lost world with Mary (now in a zoo halfway across the country)—no more performances, no duty, and no reason to live.

Mighty Joe turned rogue 60 days after Mary was sold. His first victim was the young teenage boy. Without warning, the young boy was thrown like a rag doll against the electric pole Mighty Joe was chained to. The little circus owner heard the noise from his trailer, and upon viewing the scene, he called 911. He then approached the mad elephant, his old friend, to attempt to calm him. That was impossible now. The rogue crushed the life from the old man moments after throwing him to the ground with his trunk.

Two patrol cars, each with two officers, arrived within minutes. Upon observing the two motionless bodies and the rampaging elephant, pistols were drawn. Volley after volley of insufficient caliber bullets struck Mighty Joe's flesh. He screamed in agony. Then standing on his hind legs, trunk pointing skyward (as he had on so many Saturday nights), exposing his soft tissue underbelly, he trumpeted his charge with a haunting squeal of bloody spray emanating from his collapsing lungs. Breaking the chain on his hind leg and the leg itself, he reached one of his tormenters and fell upon him. Mighty Joe's last performance was over.

Do you, reader, know why the elephant became mad? Of course, you do. It was his broken heart and the power of hate created by the broken heart. The elephant has no understanding of government, laws, finances, or why he should or should not perform. He is only a "beast of burden," with a willingness to do the tasks asked of him.

Come with me now, if you understand, with another rogue, a human beast of burden with a broken heart. It is a 5-million-mile ride on the highway to heaven, with stop offs inside the gates of hell. Beware, my friend, because this highway may run right by your town and into your own heart.

CHAPTER I

Sunrise

February 2001

As he rolled over onto his side, placing his feet onto the floor next to the sleeper bunk, he could feel every aching muscle. His head was pounding . . . ! He was cold . . . but sweating profusely . . . and his left side felt numb. It was dark or dark again, he did not know which. Forcing himself into the driver's seat and to the door, he attempted to climb down out of the cab . . . but his muscles would not move correctly . . . The left side of his chest now burned, and his left leg was not able to hold the dead weight of his large body . . . He fell hard onto his left shoulder, luckily not breaking his collarbone. Painfully, he struggled to his feet and stood at the back side of the fuel tank in front of the tandem drives and emptied himself.

Using what little strength his iron will could summon, he climbed back into the cab, moaning from the effort of it. He sat in the driver's seat and leaned heavily on the wheel. Reaching behind the seat, he found the coffee thermos . . . It was filled with cold, bitter poison . . . . Straining further, he was able to grab the cooler handle and pull it close enough to open it. Fumbling, he found a can of beer. He managed to open the can, only to taste warm, ugly foam. "How is it possible for coffee to get cold and beer to get warm at the same time?" he cursed to himself.

He next attempted to get a pack of Winstons from his coat pocket, but all he found was that tiny brown bottle containing the nitro that had been prescribed 2 years ago. He put two of the tiny pills under his tongue. With a long sigh of exhaustion, he settled his head, chest, and shoulders onto the wheel . . . Slumbering, with eyes closed and breathing irregular and labored, his right arm instinctively grabbed the gear shift . . . his left foot pushed in the clutch . . . the left hand somehow found first the key . . . then the start button . . . While completely unconscious, he checked for neutral and pushed the start button . . . Five hundred horsepower of Caterpillar diesel engine sputtered, shook, and came to life . . .

The engine's massive size vibrated the entire rig, and the vibrations sent the engine's own life force through the wheel, into the chest cavity and heart of its master . . .

As the big Cat's cylinders, pistons and internal metal components were being massaged with their lifeblood oil, smoothing out the vibrations, evening the flow of diesel into the injectors and gradually bringing the legendary motor to normal's operating temperature, so were the blood circulation and heart rhythms evening in the driver's body. Muscles relaxed to normal . . . breathing was no longer labored . . . Engine, body, mind, mechanics, and the entire combination of man and machine were reaching perfect harmony . . .

His eyes struggled to open with the day's dawning. The first real light helped clear his mind, and he began to recognize the area around him. He started to have a remote understanding of where he was. In the far distance to the sunrise side directly in front of the windshield, he could make out the outline of mountains. They were majestic! Just like what is written in the song "America the Beautiful." Between him and the mountain's purple outline was a vast white valley. It was the salt flats, *Bonneville!*

His rig was sitting on an entrance ramp just outside of Wendover, Nevada, with an absolutely stunning panorama before him. It was a perfectly clear, winter desert morning—the kind in which one can "see as far as the eye can see." In his world, with an absolute dream truck under him, a clear desert winter morning, and an engine now calling him, he pushed the gearshift into first and released the air brakes. Just as he pulled onto the pavement, a small flash of glare appeared in the driver's side mirror. Its outline was familiar to him. It was the shining grill of a Kenworth W-900, and that truck was rolling fast.

The W-900 moved into the hammer lane to allow his black Peterbilt onto the freeway. In the frozen instant as the KW W-900 passed, he could see the other driver's face. He was a younger man (probably in his early thirties), with determined pride etched in that face; indicating that this bright yellow, chromed-up, studio sleeper KW was that man's ultimate truck. He could hear the whining turbo of a big block Cummings under the hood.

The black Peterbilt moved into the main driving lane and then moved into the hammer lane, just as the yellow W-9 pulled back to the right. At the very moment that the black Pete's driver knew the other driver would be checking his shoulder view, he pushed the gearshift into the highest gear and stepped down hard on the Cat's tail, signaling with billowing clouds of black smoke that the W-9's driver had not seen the last of this classic black and chrome Peterbilt. Returning to the driving lane, he put the motor back into its proper gear at this speed, and worked the transmission and motor perfectly to build speed . . . The yellow W-9 was distant now and getting smaller and smaller. When the Pete reached its top gear, the distance between them stopped growing . . . Then the Pete started gaining as the big Cat's RPMs were reaching maximum power range.

The heat flow from the clean burning stacks of the yellow KW changed, ejecting just a little more smoke into the rushing air, and the Pete's driver knew the other driver was now ordering the computerized big block Cummings to release all 600 horses.

Gaining . . . gaining . . . with plenty of RPMs left, the black Pete's old-style mechanical Cat 3406 stalked its prey. The black Pete's driver decided to just let it go with less than a quarter of a mile of distance remaining between, blowing by the yellow KW W-900 by 15 miles an hour at the Pete's top geared rolling speed of 108 miles an hour. He left the other driver in a disappointed bewilderment.

With the race over and joyful pride flushing his ego, the black Pete's driver punched up "Sunrise" by Uriah Heep, to hear words that he had memorized decades ago. The 12-disk CD changer with its Concert 2000 system was blasting:

> Sunrise . . .
> The morning of another day without you
> And as the hours roll by . . .
> There's no one to see me cry . . .
> (Ken Hensley)

Thoughts of the last race were gone now, replaced with darker, sadder memories. His mind wandered . . . The Pete was now being driven on instinct . . . Then thirst and hunger set in, and he pulled into a truck stop just west of Salt Lake City.

With Bonneville behind him, and sitting at a table, the big yellow KW pulled into the parking area. Its driver purposely drove by the black Pete with its highly polished grill and West Coast custom bumper smiling at him. The yellow dream truck's driver wanted to talk to the black Pete's driver, but he knew that the driver was already inside. Disappointed, he parked next to the victorious machine and studied it. "Damn! What a truck," he said audibly to himself.

This was no standard factory truck. This Pete was painstakingly detailed; it had chrome everywhere it should be, including chrome antique headlights. Its black color was not just black, it was deep; like looking into a demon's soul. No markings touched its paint. Half-inch thick Plexiglas was bolted onto the sleeper sides, low, subtly placed, and a half inch away from the surface with special chrome bolts. All markings as required by law were on the Plexiglas rectangle 10 inches high and 24 inches long. There also was a small, 3-inch by 5-inch gold plaque on the driver's door just below the window. It read:

This Unit Custom Built For:
THE WORLD'S GREATEST TRUCK DRIVER.

CHAPTER 2

Wonder World

He was born 50 years ago. A breech baby, he nearly caused his mother's death. And he followed his own independent way from that first day.

His given name, after his grandfather, was Bartholomew Levi Williams. Of course, in his life he was called many nicknames, but never Bartholomew. He was Bart, Barty, Lee, Barry, and Billy. But upon reaching adulthood and acquiring an acute taste for beer, the name was combined and shortened to Barley Bill by his closest friends, and it stuck.

His personality was patterned after his favorite character and legend, Babe Ruth (not for hitting baseballs). He usually bragged that he could drink more draught beer than any man alive, and he thought of himself as the world's greatest truck driver. This to some may sound like being the world's greatest dishwasher. Anyone of reasonable strength, reason, and ambition can learn to drive a semi truck. Hell! Even women do it now. [Whoops! With that line, my bartender just cut me off!]

But he *was* the best; the best there has ever been. Not because he could drive without ever missing a gear—and he could. Not because he could back a trailer into impossible spots—and he could. Not even because he could get from load point to delivery point faster than any other driver—and he could. No, it was his mind and its development over 5 million miles.

Like when a temper tantrum–throwing, upset little boy will try to hold his breath (intending to die) to exact some revenge on his loving parents, he cannot stop his subconscious mind from taking over when he passes out, restoring normal breathing. The little boy is protected by the subconscious mind. Barley Bill's driving mind developed into the physical side of driving a semi truck controlled by an instinctive subconscious with a separate thinking personality, allowing his conscious mind to leave the trappings of boredom and the endless white line fever, daydreaming without making any mistakes. His mind could be anywhere. He could daydream himself into the world's greatest anything. He also could *relive,* in actual feeling, the painful details of all his life that had brought him to this morning's sunrise (just outside Wendover, Nevada, with the salt flats of Bonneville and the spectacular view).

He consciously knew he had made many mistakes in his life, but had never intentionally hurt anyone, ever. His subconscious mind protected him though and would not allow him to blame anything on himself. No, he blamed the government—the ever-increasing government—its taking of individual freedom, its attack on the individual for the sake of the group, its constant tactics to gain power and authority by cunning politicians winning elections by throwing bones to group causes.

And there was more than just this eternal battle of right versus left. There was *much more personal conflict* between government, its ridiculous Justice Department, and Barley Bill.

In his early days after buying his first semi truck at 21 years of age, the conflict began with the 55-mile-per-hour speed limit and the continual game of truck versus cop or bear, AKA Smokey the bear, full-grown bear, county mounty, plain white wrapper, or as he thought, bandits (bandits in the sense of WWII German fighters attacking a B17 flying fortress from all angles).

In those days, with his plain Jane GMC Astro, speeding tickets were just inconvenient and a business expense. Truckers and trucking were respected back then. It was an honorable profession that required much more of a driver—no power steering and rough living conditions in truck stops and such—but always respect and admiration from the public.

For Peterbilt's sake! There were trucking theme shows on TV ("Moving On," "BJ and the Bear"), movies about trucking, and most of all the constant flow of country music calling men to a noble trade. Those were the days for Barley. He was probably the happiest man on earth. Although he was not handsome, he was strong—very strong—and full of confidence, dreams, and optimism. He loved having the opportunity to be an independent businessman, doing exactly what he enjoyed.

He worked harder than anyone and partied harder than anyone, too. He had to sleep but not much. He was never more than a little white pill away from pulling all night, be it trucking or drinking draught beer at a little workingman's bar.

As a teenager, he was scared to death of girls and never could understand them. "Why do the pretty girls always go for the bad guy, the scoundrel?" he wondered. That fear left after buying his first truck.

Barley now had a new love: trucks, the road, adventure, seeing, doing, and most of all the pure freedom of all aspects of trucking—that ability to escape authority and just dream on his own schedule. He loved the entire country: the scenery, the people, the dialects, and the food.

All of this brought that confidence that attracts a woman's soul. By the time he traded the GMC for his first dream truck, he was a master—in complete control, indestructible, picking up women and passing to the next as easily as passing cars on the freeway.

The first dream truck was a wonderful experience for Barley. By keeping the GMC until it was paid for, he was able to order a truck that he specifically specked out for himself: type of model, engine, transmission, gear ratio, wheels, and interior detailed in leather down to the buttons in the upholstery. Every possible gauge, switch, and option was included. Never mind the stereo. He would install his own kick-ass system upon taking delivery.

He had only one problem, that being the length laws of the day. So he chose a cabover Aerodyne KW. This was the first truly great production sleeper truck made. Kenworth designed it for the Bicentennial in 1976. (Soon after that the TV show "BJ and the Bear" used one.) Barley would rather put together a conventional Peterbilt, but that length law would cause him problems. Damn government!

The Aerodyne was Barley's first experience with the legendary 3406 Caterpillar that ruled the road for decades. It was truly the king-of-the-hill motor, and its horsepower was measured on the ground, not at the flywheel (or so the legend stated). Having a "four and a quarter" (425 horsepower) Cat represented first class pride and satisfaction. The Cat made a statement in the world of the owner operator and greatly increased the value of any truck. Barley had chosen a 13-speed transmission with a tall top overdrive. Yes, she had long legs that Barley showed off daily.

No woman could compete with Barley's truck for his love, dedication, or commitment. He just felt so strong, so indestructible, and so full of pride at being the best there has ever been.

For years he did not even need close friends. He easily could arrive at any small workingman's tavern and quickly have buddies guzzling beer, laughing at a national collection of jokes, and marveling over his beautiful truck and its sound system.

He had reached a nearly instant, small-environment, celebrity status. If he just could have stayed 25 years old for the rest of his life, that would have been heaven. But storms, endless sunrises, sunsets, mountain roads, cities, towns, people, his quest to see and do it all, needing to always be the best, and always burning the candle at both ends—were taking their toll on him.

Along the journey he also had built a reputation with all of the companies that he pulled for, to such an extent that sometimes he would leave a company and lease on with someone else just to save that reputation. Any hot load was best serviced by Barley, and he loved the challenge. Dispatchers who worked with Barley always had that ace in the hole, and they played it often.

He also wanted new challenges. He didn't just change companies; he would try different types of freight and rig combinations. He had hauled and could haul anything from box trailer, reefers, and flat beds to tankers and even livestock.

Always seeking new adventures, he explored the entire country of the continental 48 states and most of Canada. He visited all of the ballparks of major league baseball, and reviewed the box scores daily throughout the seasons. He knew baseball players and their individual statistics as well as anyone. Much of the time he included baseball in his conversations in the many taverns he found. Then there were the amusement parks and various tourist attractions. He did them all. He just loved his life, his country, and his freedom. He would never give it up.

There were some problems, however, the most threatening being his accumulation of speeding tickets on the various state driving licenses he carried. The government was pushing hard on a supposed national problem with truck drivers, and the 55-mile-per-hour speed limit was creating nasty-looking driving records. A new term was developed: *habitual traffic offender.*

Barley was never in any kind of accident. He had not even hit a deer or any other animal on the road—only those damned speeding tickets. Generally the tickets were acquired while he was listening to his favorite music by Uriah Heep. He always played Uriah Heep loud and was not able to hear bear reports on the C.B. radio.

Additionally, the country was so much smaller now for Barley. He was running out of new things to do.

Barley decided that the constant threat of license suspension and the government's full intention to invade his world with its compliance enforcement must cause a change. "I will hire a codriver, damn it!"

This would give him time to clean up his driving record. This also would allow someone to get close to him and learn more than just his one-day or one weekend beer and truck personality. But who could he allow into his world, and who could he let drive his dream truck?

The answer came just as he had been suspended and had returned to his original hometown to face yet another courtroom to explain: "I'm a cross-country truck driver. I drive 200,000 miles a year. To pick up a couple of speeding tickets a month should be expected with all these speed traps and new police technology." Individual judges generally understood, but new pressure was coming from the federal government, and the public was being receptive to all the hype about dangerous truckers. In this court, Barley had to submit his plan to hire a codriver in order to get the judge to lift the suspension.

An old friend from his childhood days saw his truck, and Earl invited Barley to an outdoor bonfire and keg party that very night. Earl and Barley had grown up together and always partied whenever Barley came back to town. It was going to be a wonderful party. A local rock band was going to play in the big backyard of a farm, using a large red barn as the backdrop for the makeshift stage.

This was a small farming community where everyone knew everyone. The area farms, however, could no longer support families as they had for generations. Government policies were destroying this way of life. Barley just could not understand why small farmers could accept the government's intrusion into their lives. In Barley's mind, as was soon to be stated by Ronald Reagan: "Government is not the solution to the problem, government *is* the problem! ..."

Earl was like every farmer there. He could hold a regular job and give up his dreams, or try to keep part of his dream alive by farming in his spare time like a hobby. The local town had a factory that was shutting down because of foreign competition created by some government politicians allowing unfair trade. "Can you spell *contribution?*" Barley asked as Earl and others explained that this party was more of a wake because they had lost their jobs and benefits.

The party ...

CHAPTER 3

The Wizard

Barley left the Salt Lake truck stop and drove through the city area of the Interstate 80, still marveling at the clear view of this crisp, arid morning. While listening to a local AM station, even Rush Limbaugh's liberal bashing could not compete for the excitement of climbing the grade on the way to Utah's heights. The mountains just kept presenting more spectacular views as the elevation increased.

The road there is a remarkable achievement of man's ability to conquer natural barriers, and its grade provided more ego enhancement for Barley from the big Cat as he passed truck after truck on the way to the Park City Skiing Area. Heading east he reached The Sisters—the rolling mountains of Wyoming before the flat land.

Barley just listened to that mighty engine work, loving its song. As the road flattened out, he sighed, "Wow, that is what it's all about." He then punched up "Look at Yourself," went into a dream, and his subconscious Roy Hobbs (i.e., the Robert Redford character *The Natural*) of a codriver took control. He began to reminisce about the party . . .

His small hometown was the only place where Barley was known then, at least without his road persona. He had never really even dated anyone from there. The day he pulled his KW Aerodyne into the yard near the barn and its makeshift stage was an uplifting experience. It also was the first time he felt like he was able to let "home" know who he had become, even Earl. Something about the plight of these hard-working people made him wish he could be like his fantasy friend "The Wizard" (Uriah Heep).

> . . .*And when he spoke I felt a deep desire*
> *To free the world of its fear and pain*
> *And make the people feel free again.* (Ken Hensley/Ian Clarke)

Barley laughed and drank and told road stories well into the night. He smoked some pot, but he really only smoked socially these days. Pot had opened his teenage mind. He had discovered Uriah Heep while buying his first pot from a man who was an "underground following" listener. That was before any Heep was even heard of in America. Now the pot use tired him, and he avoided using it whenever trucking.

During this evening of fun, food (wonderful, homemade potluck dishes brought by the young families there, as well as a pig roasted over an open fire), and pretty damn good bluesy rock 'n' roll, a dark-eyed beauty was beginning to catch Barley's eye. She seemed a little mysterious and was obviously cautiously following Barley around the campfire, keg, and food areas. Barley had seen this look before. She was interested in his confident manner, and she knew he was not local. To her he was a rugged character. Lines were already showing around his eyes, suggesting experience. All the while, he was laughing and thoroughly enjoying himself. He was not attached, she was sure of it. Barley had not seen that look before in *this* town, and had never been attracted to dark eyes before.

The band stopped playing when the beer ran out, but Barley and Earl were having such a good time that Barley offered a ride in the KW to bobtail to the rural party store 2 miles from the farm. Earl asked if there was room for his girlfriend, and Barley nodded "Yup." Then he turned to the dark-eyed girl, saying, "We're gonna make a beer run. Want to come along?"

The cab design was well suited to accommodate four, with the front two air-ride seats separated by the "doghouse" that extended back to the bottom bunk. The top bunk was folded up against the back wall and had never been in the down position before. The girls sat in the bunk with legs and feet dangling down on each side of the doghouse. Barley was somewhat concerned that he could be pulled over even in this rural area (and even back in those carefree days). Barley also was remotely aware that small groups of people were running off and returning to the party later in greatly different moods.

"Sort of like running off to smoke a joint," he thought to himself. "But that can't be because joints were floating around all over the yard. Maybe it was just some real quality stuff?" He was about to find out.

"Well, we've got beer. Anyone have any pot?" he said upon jumping back into the cab after buying a case of Blue Ribbon.

"Barley, I don't even smoke that stuff anymore. I haven't in over 2 years!" Earl said. "And by the way, nobody drinks PBR anymore!" Earl jumped down and returned with Miller and a Styrofoam cooler with ice. "I've got some magic powder; do you have a mirror?"

Barley just watched as the lines were drawn. He had seen the cocaine routine in the movies, but had never seen or done it in person. He snorted up his line in turn, and somewhat fearfully waited for the resulting effect. "Wow! Let's go for a real ride!" said Barley. The coke was not what he expected. It was much like chewing up a truck stop speeder; only a lot quicker, more exhilarating, and much more than just becoming wide awake.

The girls had been looking through the cassette tape collection, and with ZZ Top blasting, they were off.

After what seemed like an hour, Earl suggested Quarter Moon Lake and a drink until sunrise. Without so much as an introduction between Barley and the dark-eyed girl, they arrived at the west side of Quarter Moon Lake, the music was turned down low, and the talking and laughing began. They did more lines and beer. Then Earl's girlfriend played "Desperado" (an Eagles tune) on the system and figured out the top bunk. After pulling it down, she remarked to Earl, "You can see the stars from these roof windows." Earl jumped up and the curtain went down. This was a little uncomfortable for Barley, so he turned up the music with some Uriah Heep and stated that it was his favorite. Neither he nor she wanted to talk, and into the bottom bunk they went .... No air was left in the suspension when all four returned to the spellbinding windshield view of the sunrise on Quarter Moon Lake.

The lake was completely placid, with the opposite shore reflecting perfectly as the first light grew. There were only woods over on that side because it was a wetland area. Their view could have been the same a century ago. The music was off and the windows were down. They could hear morning birds making their first sounds. "The peace of this place is ... what would be the current cool word, Earl?" No answer came.

"How about *surreal*?" Barley suggested. "Just another of God's paintings, and I've seen thousands of sunrises and sunsets. Sunrises are my favorite. But I always feel best when I'm heading west." None of Barley's passengers were saying anything. All of them were totally immersed in the scene.

"Hey!" The silence was broken by two men over 40. "We want to launch our fishing boat. Can you move this monster?"

With that, Barley started the motor and said, "Just give me a couple of minutes to build up the air to release the brakes." The foursome bobtailed to a small town nearby that had a Big Boy Restaurant. They all went in for much-needed replenishment and to recover from a night they would never forget.

After eating and getting "coffeed up," they returned to the tractor. The still-unintroduced, dark-eyed girl took the shotgun front seat, and Earl and his girlfriend took the back. Before Barley started the motor, he quickly blurted out: "Earl, I need a codriver. Do you want to go and see America?"

Earl was stunned momentarily and then responded, "I've got no job, and I've not been outside this state ever. The farmland has been rented out. My family doesn't even own a tractor. My unemployment check will run out in 6 weeks. Hell yes! When do we leave?"

"Tomorrow morning," Barley replied.

Earl's girlfriend sat silent and stewing, signaling that she was about to erupt violently. Barley could see her out of the corner of his eye. She was a beautiful girl with perfect teeth, a silky complexion, and definitely some hot-blooded Italian in her (he would not dare to say). The dark-eyed girl shattered the silence, divulging information as she excitedly inquired, "I'm from Nevada. How often do you go through Nevada?" She probed his eyes with hers.

Barley sighed heavily and paused. Then, using his best John Wayne imitation and voice, he informed her, "Well, Miss Nevada, I'll give you this. You scare me. I love what I do and who I am. I love my truck and my carefree life exploring America. You're so damned pretty. My life will change the moment I see you again. So I never want to see you again. I just wouldn't feel right about it."

Her eyes—her eyes darkened, and what she said was absolutely foreign. It was not like French or Spanish or German, but was a chant, an ancient chant. Then she hastily opened up the door, jumped to the ground without using the ladder or steps, and ran through the parking lot. She stopped at a pickup with a young man inside, quickly said something to him, hastened to the passenger side of the pickup, and was gone. Barley would never see her or Quarter Moon Lake again. Barley could not believe what had just happened. He had had time enough only to climb down and place one foot on the ground before the pickup was out of sight. He got back into the cab, looked at Earl, and asked in a continuing John Wayne imitation, "Was that Apache? I think I've just been cursed or had a spell cast on me. Last time a woman put a spell on me was outside of Boston. I took a run to Seattle and Mount St. Helens blew up. The ash got through the filters and destroyed my motor, just after going over the warranty mileage. That damn near put me into bankruptcy. 'Wolf, if they ever get the vote, Lord help us' [quote from *Rooster Cogburn,* the movie with John Wayne and Katherine Hepburn]."

Earl would face his own volcano later, after Barley dropped them off.

CHAPTER 4

Easy Living

Barley snapped out of his reverie when he noticed the sign for a Little America Truck Stop. It was one of his favorites. They were expensive, but they had great food and a good place to get cleaned up. He was planning to push on hard through the night without regard for compliance, weather, or anything. He needed to get home. There was trouble at home. He knew it and had called the company he was leased to when he loaded. "I've got domestic problems, and after I deliver I have to go home. I might need a week, or I may call back right after I get there. I sure hope you guys understand. This isn't negotiable."

Barley listened to music differently since buying the CD player. He still had a tape collection, but the CDs allowed for him to listen to one song to set the mood and then drift off into another world while his imaginary codriver took over. Those two independent controlling parts of the brain, one voluntary, one involuntary, were mirror images. They certainly were not Jeckel and Hyde, but more like Babe Ruth (a real person considered the most gifted phenomenal athlete ever) and Roy Hobbs (the movie character in *The Natural* who had enough talent to rival Ruth), mysterious and with dark secrets. The Ruth side of his mind was aware of Hobbs only in the respect of driving across a state but not remembering much of the trip. When Barley ran hard and some dispatcher or shipper would ask how he did it, Barley would say something like, "I'm the Babe Ruth of trucking, and my codriver is Roy Hobbs." Those who hadn't seen the movie, or had forgotten, actually thought he had a codriver named Roy Hobbs. The physical and emotional toll of Barley's life was changing the way this talent was working. Barley's voluntary Babe Ruth ego and personality had used up his energy, body, and youth carelessly. He held on to what he was, "The Best," even if it had sent him to the hospital with heart trouble. The involuntary Roy Hobbs protected Barley and was aware of all the physical deteriorations that had been created by age, abuse, and overworking. Hobbs was getting stronger and controlling more and more of the voluntary thought processes. Ruth was getting weaker and unaware of what Hobbs was doing. There was a tumor, a cancer eating away at Ruth. Hobbs knew about it and was learning how to use it.

After Barley was finished with fueling, showering, and eating, he returned to the road with the Ruth ego ready to roll on and get home fast.

He was ready to drive all night without sleep as he had so many times. Hobbs simply put a little suggestion of "Easy Living" (Uriah Heep) into his mind, and Barley was drifting back to the past right where he had dropped Earl and his girlfriend off. Barley tried to concentrate on the road. The weather was deteriorating quickly, with drifting snow blowing across the ever-flattening road heading eastbound. The open tundra of eastern Wyoming offered no resistance to the ever-increasing wind. A frozen tumbleweed danced across the highway as nightfall was engulfing the view. The gauges began to glow brightly, and Hobbs was now in control. Barley's Ruth slipped back in time . . .

Barley had pulled the Aerodyne and trailer onto Earl's road and realized that he would simply have to block one of the two lanes of gravel. With the four ways flashing and a quick pull on the air horn, he jumped down and walked toward the old farmhouse. He was surprised to see Earl exit out the side door with a large military duffel bag over his shoulder. His girlfriend was following about four steps behind. Earl was walking fast, and his familiar smile showed that he was beaming with excitement. He turned to her and said, "I'm off to sea." She stood rigidly and then stared at Barley with eyes of cold steel.

Barley drove a short way out of town and entered the freeway with only the comment of: "I hope your night went better than . . ."

"She has ambitions that I cannot fulfill," Earl interrupted.

"She is a beautiful girl. Are you sure that you want to do this?" Barley responded.

"Yes!" Earl stated almost defiantly.

Barley sighed. "We'll try it for 30 days, and if you like it I'll qualify you. We'll try to make some money and see America."

Barley pulled the truck into the first rest area and asked, "Are you ready?"

"You mean to drive?" Earl asked. "I've never driven a truck."

"Well, let's look her over. Get out." Barley then walked Earl around the rig, pointing out first the wheels and tires, then the air lines and lights, then the fifth wheel. After opening the side box to grab the small pipe used to jack up the cab, he showed Earl how to raise the cab manually. Then he said, "This is a pretty fancy truck. As long as the air pressure is built up, you can jack her cab with this button and not bother with the manual jack. But I wanted you to know how to do it manually, because chances are that if you want to get to the engine, something is wrong and you won't have air." Barley then jacked the cab all the way over to demonstrate the impressive engineering of this state-of-the-art design. With the windshield pointing straight down, the massive Caterpillar diesel engine was fully exposed. Earl had never even seen such an engine! It was much larger than that of a farm tractor.

"Okay," Barley explained. "This engine looks big, but compared to the size of the rig, it is much smaller than the ratio of your car engine to your car. Driving a semi truck is very much like riding a 10-speed bike, with limited horsepower requiring many gears. You can't take off in tenth, and you must drop gears when climbing a hill. It really is that simple. The only thing that you will need to learn is the difference in shifting a diesel instead of a gas-powered vehicle. Of course, the size will take getting used to, but your vision is much better in a truck because you are sitting so much higher. The trailer will follow, just leave room. Always leave room. The sharper you turn, the more the trailer will cut off—you know, curbs and other obstacles."

The cab settled back into driving position, and Barley got in on the passenger side saying, "Let's go." Earl was excited. Barley showed Earl each control on the dashboard and carefully explained the basic principles. "Go ahead. Turn the key on, check for neutral, and wake up the Cat. Don't worry, the air brakes are locked. We're not going anywhere yet." Barley told Earl to rev the motor and look at the tachometer. "Unlike a gas engine, a truck diesel engine has a limited range of power. This Cat will not exceed 2,100 and has power down to about 1,400. Peak power is from 1,600 to 2,000. When I say *power* I mean *torque*. Push the air buttons in and release the brakes. If it moves, pull down on the trailer valve until you get into gear. Now it's just a glorified four speed, really."

"Yeah, 13 is just a glorified four," Earl mused.

Barley showed him the pattern and said, "For now, you are not going to need granny, so put it into first [i.e., second speed] like a car's four-speed H pattern." With that, the brakes were released, and to Barley's surprise Earl went through the first four gears without trouble. Then he showed Earl the high-range button and the overdrive for each of the top four gears.

When Earl reached 11th gear he was rolling at 50 miles an hour and said, "It just feels comfortable here." Barley then opened his briefcase, pulled out a piece of paper, tore it to the approximate size of the speedometer (4-inch diameter), and taped it over the speedometer. Barley lit a cigarette, and after looking over the road, told Earl to pull the gearshift down into the big gear (12th speed). Shortly after, Earl said, "Well, it just feels comfortable about here."

"Okay. Now flip it over into overdrive. Now you're in the top gear. Are you feeling comfortable?"

"Yep."

"Now pull off that paper."

"Oh man, we're going 75 miles per hour!"

"And my guess is your tach reads 1,650, correct?"

"Yep."

"Now you should get it. The motor's limited range has an optimum cruising RPM, and that is where she is comfortable, no matter what gear you're in. At 1,650 you have plenty of RPMs to accelerate or decelerate in the power range. Now downshifting might be a little strange. Give it just a little throttle to remove pressure, then release the throttle and move the gearshift into neutral. Raise the RPMs up past where you were, about 400, and put it into the next-lower gear. Do it right, and it will fall right in. You don't need to use the clutch pedal, but you can if you need to. It will give you a little more leeway. The method is called double clutching, and you need to know how to do it for driver testing during qualification. But I think you will agree right away that it isn't necessary once you learn the proper RPM range. First, you will do it by tach, then motor sound, and finally by instinct and habit."

After a few gears were ground, Earl quickly caught on. In fact, he was having little trouble at all, and was relaxed and smooth.

Barley was thoroughly enjoying this. It was as if they were young kids again, with Barley being a big brother. Earl was nearly 2 years younger but only one grade below in school due to birthdays. They grew up in houses right next to each other and had been teaming up on life's offerings until Barley bought that first truck 8 years and before more than a million miles of adventures. He was now 29 years old.

"Well," Barley yawned. "Don't worry. We'll work on the backing and parking as we go. If you like it and can handle road life, you'll be ready to be qualified as soon as we arrange to go to Capital City. I'm going back to the bunk. Holler if you need help. Look for Smokeys, and don't try to cross any scales or state lines." Barley did not intend to sleep until Earl became accustomed to driving the semi truck; he just wanted Earl to relax behind the wheel without experiencing the feeling of being watched.

They delivered a load to Boston and started making pickups until Saturday morning, where they were forced to wait in Utica, New York, to finish loading on Monday. They were heading for Texas. After cleaning up (Earl's first truck stop shower of the old locker-room style), Barley dropped the trailer and headed for a local honky-tonk he knew of that he thought Earl would enjoy.

Earl couldn't believe it at first, but before the second beer, a pretty good-looking girl came up to Barley and obviously knew him. And she had a friend. They all drank and listened to the band, even danced a little bit. But Barley didn't like the music—too much disco. Actually, he hated it.

Barley had a small quantity of pot and offered a trip to the truck, and Earl had just enough of the coke to offer a toast to life. They did not return to the bar.

Such were the social times of the seventies. Earl was hooked. "Is it always this easy?"

Barley just laughed and said, "Well, you look like the Marlboro man and have that magic snow that the girls of today seem to crave. I guess for you it will be."

Earl was a much better-looking guy than Barley, slimmer and taller with that Marlboro mustache and shoulder-length brown hair. He could pass for a rock star. Barley, on the other hand, looked like Dan Hagarty of the TV show "Grizzly Adams." He finally used Grizzly as a CB handle because of all the references. He had broad shoulders, a barrel chest, and outweighed Earl by 50 pounds. This was helpful to Earl in the singles bar scene where his natural good looks attracted women and their men didn't like it. Barley just didn't look like anyone to mess with.

Barley and Earl became a natural team. They got along well, loved to party together, and wanted to explore the whole country. Earl was qualified in his second week, and the first 30-day trial lasted more than 3 months. "You'll just lose all track of time out here on the road," Barley said that first week.

They also were a complement to each other in driving habits. Barley liked to get up early, drive through sunrise until mid morning, and have breakfast. Earl was a sunset man, driving well into the late-night hours. The afternoons were spent listening to music, talking, joking, and enjoying the ride and scenery. They ate up miles, and could cross the country coast to coast in record time every time. For Barley, having his lifelong friend sharing what his life was in a little brother role—these were the happiest, most carefree days of his life. But something like this can only last as long as circumstances will allow. And there would never be another team partner in Barley's world. Again, the government's intrusive lawmaking would help to force a change, including a change in the public's perception of trucking. This would be accomplished by use of a willing liberal partner, the media.

CHAPTER 5

Poet's Justice

Barley had driven a long way since the morning's sunrise at Wendover, Nevada, and pulled into the truck stop at Ogalala, Nebraska, for a break and a late supper. He chuckled to himself because all the truckers called this town "Oh my golly," Nebraska. Although his Ruth ego still wanted to push further, he realized that he had not read the day's newspaper, nor even listened to Rush Limbaugh (or any other news program). Rush was Barley's favorite 3-hour break from driving, while driving. He bought a *USA Today* that was still available, noticing a side content headline: Bush's Cabinet Choices: Who Are They, And Are They Effective?

Barley laughed to himself, because only a few days ago he had been having a "sitting-at-the-bar-talking-politics-when-you-know-you-shouldn't" conversation comparing the new president with the previous scoundrel and scandalous low life, Bill Clinton. "Just look at it this way," Barley had emphatically stated. "Ross Perot [whom I am ashamed to say I voted for in '92] said it best. He was on 'Larry King' and endorsed George W. by saying that as he did in Texas, he will 'surround himself with the best-qualified people, and will not disgrace The Office' [or something very similar]. Now understand. Ross Perot is the reason we ended up with Clinton instead of a second term of Bush's father. Me and 20 million thinking Americans voted for Ross looking for a boost. Instead, we got Clinton because of the rock-solid Democratic base of people who are not informed enough to even know how the government works. But just compare Clinton's administration with Bush's like two World Series baseball teams: position by position. Clinton chose people only to be politically correct and to exalt himself. You know it. We all know it. Bush's team has highly qualified people . . . ."

Barley would now have a chance to see the subcabinet White House staff and how the liberal press was evaluating them. He began reading just as the food arrived, and after another attempt to reach home without success (he hadn't had contact In 2 weeks), Barley choked when he came across *that name*—that awful name.

"No, it can't be!" George W. Bush had promised to bring dignity back into the White House. Barley had felt so strongly that "W" was the next "Reagan" and would end the disgrace of Clinton and his cronies. But there it was—in the *USA Today* story—the name of the man who Barley associated with causing all of the pain in his life. This was not politics, this was personal—the personal destruction of Barley's previous life, dreams, and love by a man he had never actually met, a man whose face Barley vowed never to look at for fear it might provoke a violent vengeance of rage and attack if he ever was able to get near him. He had prayed to God Almighty for justice and election defeats for this man, his focus of hate. And now he would be working in the White House of George Bush.

Barley hastily stood up and with the waitress staring at him, he said, "I have to leave now. Here's a 20 to cover the food and tip. Keep the change." He turned, with every muscle flexing, feeling even his hair, and walked as stiff and deliberately out the door as a 1950's movie monster (and at this moment, he was). Outside he stopped with fists clenched, looked to the stars, and with a voice from the deepest pits of a fiery hell, he screamed, *"RESTITUTION!"*

He was visibly shaking, and the left side of his chest was burning again. The Ruth of him wanted to use this adrenaline rush of energy to get home. He must get home. The tractor was not locked, and he jumped up and into the cab like a cowboy jumping onto a horse to go and chase the bandits in an old western movie. Once reaching the interstate, he was accelerating as fast as the icy road would allow without losing traction. He reached the big gear and continued to gain speed. Hobbs wanted control— to protect—but Barley's conscious mind, the Ruth ego, was stimulated and determined. The C.B. and radar detector were on, but he was oblivious to any sound. He rolled by the hiding bear at 80 miles per hour and still gaining speed.

The officer was a well-trained veteran truck speeder bandit working a little overtime, and he called in to dispatch as he entered the interstate with lights flashing. "Got one. Heading east in pursuit."

The flashing disco lights quickly caught Barley's eye in the shoulder view, and he checked his speed. "Oh God! I'm doing 85 miles per hour. They'll take my license this time for sure." Then the feeling of panic was replaced with a throbbing, pounding pain deep inside of his head—intense. Hobbs was sending impulses to the cancerous tumor. The pain intensified, and Barley closed his eyes. His chest ached. Hobbs seized control of the wheel and instinctively knew exactly where the patrol car was. The cop had positioned himself close behind the trailer, half into the driving lane, with the lights flashing off the mirror into the trucker's face. In a deft maneuver, Hobbs eased off of the throttle, drifting to the right to expose the bandit. Then he pulled the trailer brake handle all the way down and hit the hammer while driving hard to the left. The swatting motion of the 53-foot trailer resulted in the tandem striking the patrol car on its passenger side just as its driver had swerved left in a vain attempt to avoid the attack. The car was sent airborne across the median ditch with "Ruthian" force and into the westbound side rise of the median onto the driver's side window, killing the officer instantly. The car then bounced up airborne again, with its disintegrating body spinning, until being struck by an oncoming semi truck head on. The flying debris through his windshield struck the westbound truck driver. The collision sent the truck into a jackknife and then into a roll into the center median. Parts, wreckage, and freight scattered for 200 yards. Two human beings, each with dependents, were gone in one violent moment.

The momentous force of the trailer swat had thrown Barley's rig into the hammer lane's shoulder, shocking Barley's conscious mind into an instantaneous reaction to correct the out-of-traction trailer. He caught it before leaving the pavement, bringing the rig under control and back into the driving lane, and settling into the groove at 70 miles per hour.

"Holy Jesus! I must have nodded out." Barley's Ruth was completely unaware of what had just happened. Hobbs had replaced the impulses causing pain with body chemicals that create the effect of a sexual climax. Barley poured himself a cup of coffee and lit a cigarette. He was completely relaxed, feeling no more pain or anger, and Hobbs regressed into the hidden subconscious. "I guess I need a little stimulating music if I want to get very far tonight," Barley casually thought to himself. "Let's see. How about a little Uriah Heep, 'Love Machine'?"

Only one living eyewitness existed. He was carefully driving eastbound in a pickup and had been passed first by the fancy Peterbilt, then by the patrol car. He had had a full view of the event, but he had a prior drunk driving arrest, no license, and was already more than halfway through a 12 pack. He was too frightened to stop or to report what he had seen. He pitched the remaining beers and got off the interstate at the next exit. He pretended that this carnage was just a nightmare—one secret that he would carry to his grave.

Barley drove into the night. Hobbs knew that distance was protection tonight. Upon crossing over into Iowa, even Barley's Ruth had to lie down. He reached a state of deep sleep just before sunrise.

CHAPTER 6

More Easy Living

Between sunrise at Wendover, Nevada, to sleeping through sunrise at Council Bluffs, Iowa, Barley had driven 1,400 miles. He had taken just three stops (Salt Lake City; Little America Travel Center, Wyoming; and Ogalala, Nebraska), totaling 1.75 hours. He had averaged more than 63 miles per hour, regardless of the natural and unnatural obstacles—an amazing feat. Barley woke up pleased with being in Iowa, but he had a strange feeling, a vague and incomplete memory of a weird dream.

"Did I eat pizza before I laid down?" he thought to himself. "Oh well, yesterday was quite productive. I haven't been able to put that many miles behind me in one day for a long time. I guess I'm still the Babe Ruth of trucking!"

Barley walked into the truck stop, showered, and sat down for an early afternoon breakfast. *USA Today* was already sold out, as was the Omaha, Nebraska, paper, so he settled for the *DeMoine Register*. He was very hungry and ordered two "Monica Lewinski omelets." The waitress had few customers and was curious.

Barley explained: "During the whole impeachment mess with Bill Clinton, the power broker lawyer, that colored fella, denied meeting with Monica Lewinski in an attempt to protect Clinton. But Monica had given information about an omelet purchased by this Vernon Jordan, an egg white omelet. The investigation's lawyers produced a credit card receipt signed by Vernon Jordan, thus strongly implicating the obstruction of justice and abuse of power being carried out by Clinton and his friends. It wasn't the blue dress, but almost."

"Oh, you're a Clinton hater, eh?" she asked.

"Yep," he responded. Actually, with this type of omelet, Barley was attempting to address his heart problems without giving up the road, eating as close to fat free as possible. It wasn't working.

The *DeMoine Register* had printed a repeat of the previous day's Bush cabinet and subcabinet members. But Barley wasn't angered, just disgusted as it was mentioned that the former mayor and tough prosecutor had been chosen. "If America only knew!" Barley first thought, and then realized that it wouldn't matter. "Who cares if one lowlife truck driver has been stepped on along the way," he thought. "Today's media surely would not care unless I were a gay, liberal, vegetarian tree hugger just trying to save the planet . . . *planet.* I hate anyone who uses the word *planet* as if they are on an equal plane with God Almighty looking down at an environmental abuser [i.e., independent trucker] as a behemoth polluting monster. All politicians are elitists. Damn, I thought Bush could be better."

Having finished eating his one meal for this day, Barley jumped back into the Pete and continued pulling hard to get home, all the while dreading what he would find. Iowa's rolling farmland provided an easy-to-handle backdrop for a return to memories of just how it all happened that Barley's life would cross with the politically ambitious "Golden Boy Prosecutor," who was now a cancer in this previously promising new president's administration. But Barley needed happier thoughts, and he wished that it were summer with these rolling hills covered with tall corn like a late July morning. With that thought, Barley was back in the Aerodyne riding with Earl. Hobbs took the wheel, with intentions of setting a protective pace to avoid bandit battle.

More than 2 decades ago, Barley and Earl were riding east and heading back home in Michigan on these same rolling Iowa hills. Barley brought up the subject of the party and asked, "The seventies are almost over, and I'll be 30 years old soon. You quit smoking pot. What really caused that? You used to smoke it a lot."

"Yeah, I did. But one day I had smoked enough that I couldn't feel the water in the shower. I never wanted to get high again." Earl spoke using an experienced teaching tone that was refreshing for him, because this first 3 months he had been in constant learning status. "Besides, everybody is into the coke now." Earl shook his head and sighed. "But coke is so expensive, I don't think I can afford it with what you're paying me," he said chuckling.

"Well, you know, pot, pot opened my eyes and changed my perspective on everything. I never really 'heard' music before—the feeling of it. Everything I see now—trees, sunrises. I see all the detail that I used to overlook. It's a love of giving thanks or something. And I don't need much at all now. One hit off my little pipe in the morning, and I don't even think of it the rest of the day. Of course, I've always used pot in looking for love when I'm out partying. The whole idea of meeting someone and going to the truck to enjoy a high has worked pretty well for me." Barley then slowly shook his head. "Everything is changing. Mostly the women, they all seem to be getting this liberated attitude. But I sure notice that attitude disappear when coke is mentioned."

Earl nodded. "I know just what you mean. I've used coke just like you use pot."

"I just don't see the value of it. The high only lasts a few minutes," said Barley.

"But what a high!" Earl was smiling.

"Well, I guess we should have a little for road partying if we ever want to get laid. I suppose you have contacts at home. I'll split the cost of the white stuff, and get me an ounce of pot too, if you can. I haven't stopped loving her—'sweet leaf'" (referenced from a Black Sabbath song).

"How long are we going to stay home?" Earl asked.

"I guess until we run out of money, probably a week. I'd get bored if we stayed longer. But I never even asked. Do you still want to truck?" Barley asked.

"Are you kidding? I love it! And the stories I have already. You know I have to talk about Dallas," Earl responded.

"Oh, you mean about Harry Hines Street, or about the mud wrestler?" asked Barley, while Earl and Barley laughed until the tears formed.

That first trip into Dallas was typical of the fun times they had on the road when they were laid over for a weekend and doing a town. After getting empty (i.e., unloaded), Barley rented a double room in a Day's Inn with the following agreement. If one gets lucky, the other sleeps in the truck. If neither gets lucky, they both stay in the room. If they both get lucky, flip a coin.

Barley offered Earl some explanations of Dallas. "This town is weird; local laws dominate the area. On that side of the beltway, you can't even get a beer in a Pizza Hut. But over here, down on Harry Hines Street, you can get anything you want."

The motel was just one block away from the notorious street. After showering, Barley dropped the trailer and they drove down to a place to park within walking distance of two bars. One was featuring live bands at night, and the other was featuring live girls dancing down to G-strings in a not-so-typical strip club atmosphere.

This second bar was dominated by pool tables and not the stage show, which allowed for a relaxed club with a workingman's tavern feel, only larger. Barley and Earl played some eight ball and casually looked at the dancing girls, trying not to get caught up in their game of collecting dollars. One dancer, however, must have been convinced that Barley and Earl were carrying money that she could entice from their pockets. She kept coming by when she was not on stage. She was a real looker and called herself Misty Blue. Barley and Earl had developed a code of communication for use in situations like this, which involved the use of lines and voice imitations from Gene Tracy comedy tapes.

Gene Tracy was the raunchiest, most foul-mouthed comedian of his time and was known as Mr. Truck Stop. Gross as gross can be, his humor was full of accents, ethnic slurs, and stereotypes. For some, he was absolutely the funniest man ever alive. Gene Tracy tapes continue to sell in truck stops by the millions. Barley and Earl had the entire collection and had memorized most of the party jokes.

Misty Blue first tempted Earl, then Barley, then went back to Earl. Finally, she stood between them and the pool table, and with a good amount of cleavage showing, asked, "Come on boys, what'll it be?"

"Oh, what the hell," Barley sighed. Then using a line from a Gene Tracy joke about "A dumb truck driver, so dumb he had never had a piece of ass," Barley pointed over to the small table dance area and said with his best imitation of a Gomer Pyle voice: "We have one of them, there, whatever them be." Barley, Earl, and the girl all chuckled with that line.

The routine was for the girl to dance two songs (from whatever was playing on the main stage), using the first to strip, and the second to get real suggestive (in hopes of luring away more money). The first song was a disco number that neither Earl nor Barley liked, but Misty was talented, very talented, and they both donated. Misty had gotten down to the bare minimum (i.e., nothing but a G-string) by the time the second song started. (It was a Bob Seger tune that was much more to Barley and Earl's liking.) She was trying very hard now, doing suggestive moves that must have been learned in gymnastics and a bedroom, finally ending up with her feet flat on the table on each side of Earl with her back arched, belly up, hands down on the table, like she was going to crawl back under herself—all the while shaking the "center of the universe" in time with the music about 6 inches in front of Earl's nose. Barley was sitting within 2 feet of this. Both were in awe when they saw it—the telltale little string of a Tampax sticking out of that G-string 2½ inches!

Earl turned his head to meet Barley's eyes, and using a Gene Tracy "hair lip boy" voice, said, "Say, you s'pose she wants me to pull that there?"

Barley exploded into laughter at the same time as Earl, but he had just taken a gulp of beer, thus spraying foam through his nose and causing Earl to lean back and tip his chair over backwards. Laughing so hard that he actually fell forward, Barley hit his forehead on the table hard enough to leave a welt. He was unable to stop laughing, and ended up on the floor on his hands and knees. Misty was outraged and unaware of what had caused the eruption. Barley and Earl were still laughing and couldn't risk looking at each other as the bouncers were escorting them out of the building.

Without losing stride, Barley and Earl walked past the tractor, across the street, and 100 yards south to the next bar. This bar would have a live band. They were still giggling about the dancer when they walked into the ID checkpoint and paid the cover charge. "Why the $5 cover?" Earl grumbled.

"There's a special act tonight. Trust me, you'll like it," was the door-man's response. "What the hell happened to your head, fella? We won't tol-erate any fighting in here."

Barley tried to keep a straight face. "I fell into a table." Earl laughed hard all over again. "It wasn't a fight sir, I fell while dancing." Earl was hav-ing a ball with this whole conversation.

Once inside and seated, they started checking out the scene. Barley stated, "With a bump on the noggin like this, I guess I shouldn't worry about getting lucky, so I'm going to drink and have 'a wild time tonight'" (reference to Gene Tracy). They laughed. "You drive us back to the motel, okay?" The motel was less than a half mile from where the tractor was parked, so neither of them was overly concerned about being stopped by the police. The tractor was parked in a strip mall away from the two bars.

"Hey Earl, you ever heard of this band that's playing tonight? Are they recording stars or something? I mean, $5 dollars just to get in."

"Nope," said Earl.

"Well, you being more in tune with the current times than me, just thinking. Hey, what the hell is that? I've been here before. That's where they used to have the electric bull riding." (Bar bull riding of *Urban Cowboy* fame was waning out, even in the Southwest.)

In the former riding area was what looked like a shallow backyard swimming pool filled with slick, greenish-brown goo. That special act was a female mud-wrestling show, the waitress explained. Barley and Earl were in for a treat. Because they were early, they moved to a table close to the mud pool. The costumes worn by the participants were made of tight-fitting cotton, and the wrestlers wore various sunglasses or safety glasses that were decorated in the styles of big time wrestling, as seen on TV.

This show was hilarious. The costumes were transformed into com-pletely revealing wet T-shirts as soon as the goo soaked in. The matches were hard-fought catfights with real anger between these girls, or so it seemed. An announcer continually described and encouraged the action, providing the audience with endless humor and belly laughs.

"Wow! What a night," Earl laughed, after the lights on the mud pool were turned off. "You know, it's still early. The band is just getting ready to play."

As the band went through its warm-up routine, Barley surveyed the club and realized that it was now standing room only. If they wanted to have a seat, they had to stay at this table in front of the mud pit. Earl was enjoying the band's music, which was hard rock of the kind that killed the disco fad, when a beautiful girl in her early 20s walked up and stood right in front of him. Barley thought that she must like Earl's Marlboro man mustache and smile. Barley tapped Earl on the shoulder and pointed to her. The music was so loud that talking would be fruitless. She just stood there, dressed somewhat conservatively, looking quite innocent and wholesome. Earl finally motioned for her to sit down and pointed to his beer, asking if she would like one. She nodded "Yes." Between the end of the song and the start of the next, she asked, "Well, how did you like the show? I was in the lavender costume."

Barley stayed in the truck that night and the next.

And so life on the road for two lifetime buddies continued. Barley truly loved this country and sharing adventures. They tried to take it all in— baseball stadiums, amusement parks, and the ongoing girl hunting. They both knew this could not last forever, and they wanted to see and do all that this beautiful country had to offer. The truck driving was no real work at all. Many times they would race like little boys to see who could get to the driver's seat first. Barley was enjoying life too much, however, and he was missing—something.

If there was a drawback that Barley could put a finger on, it would be that since Earl joined him, he had lost interest in news and politics. Deregulation came without his knowledge of it. Of course, it was not true deregulation of trucking. No, it was called deregulation by the politicians, but it actually was war on the independent trucker. Rates were dropping. The government published statistics and propaganda to demonize the independent trucker and trucking in general. Its always-willing partner, the media, eagerly pushed the government's game plan. Will and Sonny ("Moving On"), and "B.J. and the Bear" joined the westerns of white hats and black hats in the forgotten times of judgmental behavior, being replaced by shows that always put evil into the gray area. The government and media had aggressively launched an attack on all moral institutions. John Wayne was no longer a hero, and there was no icon to replace him. America suffered. Reagan was elected but into a sea of liberals. Reagan reminded people of John Wayne's moral symbolism and made Americans proud again. But Congress and the liberal media hated him. In the end it was just rhetoric, government continuing to grow and continuing to take away freedom.

CHAPTER 7

Wake Up

(SET YOUR SIGHTS)

At the Washington, D.C., headquarters of the F.B.I., 36 hours after the crash in Nebraska, agent William (Bill) A. Jackson was called into the assistant director's office.

"Mr. Jackson," greeted the assistant director.

"You can just call me Bill." William Jackson, an African-American of tall, sturdy build, was a proud man who objected to being called "Willie," as most people of authority over him had done in the past.

"Okay, Bill," the newly appointed "political calculation" aristocratically replied. "I've been told you have special expertise in the trucking business."

"Yes," Bill nodded. "My father owned several trucks, and I drove trucks to earn my way through college."

The assistant director had assumed that because this man was black, he had been put through school on some government program. Nothing could have been further from the truth. Bill's father was a fiercely independent and proud man who "wouldn't take nothing from nobody." He had started with one old used truck and ended with more than 20 late-model power units operating under his own authority. He would give no money to his son without Bill "pulling" for it.

"We have been notified by the local boys of a real messy crash in Nebraska. I want you to go out there and investigate. It has some potential for embarrassment for the bureau. A patrol officer was killed, and his sister is a local TV reporter. Be careful of what you say. You'll meet the regional director of D.O.T. He's handling the case."

"I'll just gather information and report back to you," Bill reassured.

Bill Jackson was a well-trained investigator. He had some preliminary information given to him to study on the flight out. He didn't like the look of this case. All investigators (D.O.T., patrol officers, and insurance adjustors directly involved) would meet in Lincoln, Nebraska, at the state office building to discuss any available information and theories of explanation of what had happened. Bill's main concern was the lack of witnesses.

At 2 P.M., the meeting came to order. The photos, diagrams, and measurements were well prepared, and the lead D.O.T. representative provided narrative analysis. He was a former state patrol officer and had risen to regional director of the Department of Transportation of the Federal Highway Administration, with a respected, thorough work record. Yes, Arnold (Arnie) Benson was thorough and would normally be beyond reproach, except in this case. He personally knew the slain officer and the TV reporter sister, Linda (Cooper) Wright. Arnie had made a promise to find the culprit and to keep her completely informed. She was in the meeting room. Bill Jackson recognized her as soon as he entered the room and would say nothing until he could meet one on one with Arnold Benson.

Arnold Benson's narrative began: "Based upon the available information that we have gathered, and with no eyewitness coming forward, we believe that officer Cooper was struck by an eastbound semi truck while attempting to pull the driver over for speeding. The skid marks, please notice the measurements and photos [pointing to the projection screen], suggest that the driver was probably startled and hit his brakes too hard, causing the truck to partially jackknife. The road conditions at the time were fairly good, but there were patches of black ice in areas where snow was blowing across the pavement. As you are all aware, that driver did not stop, creating this hit-and-run crash scene. It is doubtful that any serious damage was done to the truck. The trailer tandem tires struck the patrol car, and there was no sign that even a flat tire was sustained. That driver knows he hit the patrol car. We need a witness or for that driver to confess to someone. A reward will be offered and televised."

Bill Jackson met Arnold Benson in his office after the meeting and carefully offered, "I think that your report is missing something."

"Arnie. Just call me Arnie."

"Okay, Arnie. Look here at these skid marks. There are no skid marks left by the tractor, only by the trailer. If the driver was simply in a daze and was startled, he would have hit the foot pedal. Clearly, he pulled the trailer hand valve."

"My God! Are you saying this was murder?" Arnie's anger was intensifying.

"Well, I've looked all this stuff over, and I just get the gut feeling that this driver attacked the patrol car. Like a rogue elephant. If that driver was afraid of losing his license or job ... well, I think you understand that there is no love lost between cop and truck driver. I know, I used to drive truck. My father drove truck and owned trucks all of his life. He hated that I went into law enforcement."

"Hated it, or you?" Arnie quizzed.

"Well, let me say this. He once said to me: 'If you try to pull *me* over, I'll trailer swat you off the road.' He was disappointed. I think that he always expected me to take over his trucking business. He worked very hard.

Damn! Look again at the skid marks; this looks like a trailer swat. I've never been a patrol officer, but to my father, I had joined up with the enemy. This driver, like I said, maybe he's an old dinosaur antiauthority type who is in trouble and can't risk being pulled over. No more tickets or something."

"Then he'll strike again. And we have *nothing* by which to recognize who he is." Arnie shook his head and clenched his fist.

"Washington is waiting, if you know what I mean. Call me with anything new and I'll do the same." Bill shook hands with Arnie.

After Bill Jackson left to return to Washington, Arnie Benson met Linda Wright for dinner at a local Holiday Inn. "Did the Washington agent have any information on who that other driver is or might be?" Linda was anxious for anything.

"Now you know I can't tell you anything that I discussed with that F.B.I. boy. Excuse me, I need to use the rest room." Arnie stood up and deliberately dropped a pocket dictation recorder on the tablecloth.

Linda, without speaking, picked it up, pulled the micro tape out, and set the unit back on the table next to Arnie's drink. Upon returning, she mentioned to Arnie that he had dropped his pocket recorder.

"Thanks," Arnie replied.

"And thank you," Linda smiled.

They did not speak of the crash again that evening, except regarding the reward for a witness.

Linda Wright provided an exclusive news break with the offer of a reward. The footage taken of the crash scene with the focus on the wreckage of the patrol car provided an excellent backdrop for Linda's message of a rogue driver. Competing stations were using the term *Road Rogue* in printed graphics, with news anchors' commentary, which in turn was used by area radio affiliates. Linda Wright was contacted by the network for a piece to be shown on a news magazine show.

Trucker talk on the C.B. radio was dominated by the crash, and as the term *Road Rogue* was aired, the stories became exaggerated. AM talk radio was swamped with calls.

Only there were some strange reactions. Truckers started venting frustrations of years and decades of alleged abuse of power by police. Reactions came from other citizens of the working class who had experienced conflicts with police and government authority in general. The calls usually started, "I think I understand why the Road Rogue attacked. Let me tell you what happened to me." No calls came from anyone who could identify this Road Rogue or his truck though.

A small-time traveling country music band with a lead singer/songwriter who desperately wanted to become a recording star was playing in the Lincoln, Nebraska, area when this buzz about a Road Rogue hit the airwaves. Bobby Long had some talent, and the Long Riders had been playing together for 2 years. It had cost more to record their one CD than they had made off of it.

"Hey boys, let's see if we can do something with this Road Rogue and Smokey the Bear. Anybody remember Jerry Reed and 'Eastbound and Down' (*Smokey and the Bandit* movie theme)?"

Bill Jackson arrived at his metro Washington, D.C., home and went straight to his liquor cabinet. He poured a double shot of bourbon, drank it with one gulp, and then focused his eyes on his loving wife. She didn't say a word. She didn't have to. "I don't like it. I don't like it at all—this new case I have been assigned to. I feel like I have to track down the ghost of my father."

CHAPTER 8

July Morning

It was still daylight of the first day after the crash when Barley pulled into the Iowa 80 truck stop near the eastern border of Iowa. His mood was changing. Fear of what he would find at home was now setting in. He feared that he might have lost his second chance at life, love, and rebuilding his heart. He needed something in order to gather the courage and determination to finish this run. He remembered one of his favorite bar quotations:

> *If trouble is brewing with your wife*
> *And you know there's going to be a fight*
> *In which you will lose your home,*
> *Save your life*
> *Just tell her she's right*
> *And go out and buy a new piece of chrome.*

He bought a new chrome hood ornament, replacing his swan with a flying goddess. "Well, if she tells me to take a flying fuck, I'll just get back in the truck and leave." Barley's thoughts were actually defensive. He was worried sick. This fear and dread hung heavy. Hobbs punched up "July Morning," knowing the mood would change, allowing Ruth to abandon the wheel.

The song's opening organ solo is a hypnotic prelude to Barley's one special moment in life . . . that only one special moment of a lifetime . . . God only grants one . . .

> *. . . I was looking for love in the strangest places, . . .*
> *. . . Not one was aware of the fire that burned*
> *In my heart, in my mind, in my soul.*
> (David Byron/Ken Hensley, Uriah Heep)

Barley was back in time again . . . back in the Aerodyne with Earl. They had been together for 2 years. So many adventures they had had! But on a July morning, at the home office terminal in Capital City, the end of the adventure would begin.

Over the 2 years Barley and Earl were together, Barley was changing—getting older and realizing that the frolic of the seventies was gone. After their first year together, Barley ran head on into the new decade's changing society. Heavy metal had killed that awful disco junk, but this heavy metal wasn't Uriah Heep, or The Doors, or anything meaningful—just ear-busting guitar. Barley drifted into country music (Hank Jr.) and some of the classic country music. Sometimes, while both were awake, Barley would put in some Hank Jr., or even Hank Sr., crank it up, and they would sing those old songs. The music had to be loud though, because neither of them had a voice.

"People don't like country until they have some of their life behind them, because country music is about life," Barley would say.

In Denver, Earl had found a two-level bar, with one level playing country and one level playing rock. Barley drank at the country bar while Earl explored the rock level. They both were looking for sex. The evening ended up a drunk—a flat-out "don't remember." At daylight, Barley woke up on the bottom bunk, with the tractor parked at the back edge of the two-level bar's parking lot right where they had originally parked it the night before. A young woman was sleeping in the passenger's seat. Barley woke Earl, who was in the top bunk. He had no idea, and neither did Earl, why this woman was here. Barley woke the woman, who was startled and said, "Oh my God, it's morning! I have to go." With that she jumped down and was gone. Seventy-two hours later, in Salt Lake City, Barley was in a health clinic getting a cure for gonorrhea. That experience ended the reckless, promiscuous lifestyle. Barley had been lucky. New diseases arrived with the new decade, ones that penicillin had no effect on. The new ones spelled life or death.

The business began suffering, as well. Deregulation was cutting into already-slim profits. Earl was disappointed with available pay, and Barley began to realize that it would be increasingly hard to keep Earl long enough to clean his license. They held on through the winter, and in early July, on a hot, humid Midwest day, Barley pulled into the home terminal to demand better paying loads to keep the team running.

Barley stopped at the mail room to get his latest statement for evidence. He leaned into the opening over the counter to get someone's attention.

Time stopped as his eyes met hers—her eyes . . . Her eyes looked into his, and into his very soul . . . He was absolutely stunned. He stepped back, desperately looking for a drinking fountain, and had trouble walking to it. He drank long, sucking as much of the water into him as he could. Barley felt as nervous as he had ever felt in his life. He was shaking, visibly shaking, "like a dog passing a bone," he would say later.

Barley walked back outside the building and lit a cigarette while collecting his thoughts. "What is it about her? I've seen beauty before. There is something else . . . I've never seen eyes like that. Those eyes and face . . . almost holy . . . like a medieval painting of the Virgin Mary!"

Ten minutes passed, but it seemed like hours. Barley walked back inside and somehow found the courage to look at her again—to meet those eyes again. She smiled, and the room just got lighter. Barley was so focused on her that he forgot to ask for the mail.

"Could I buy you a cup of coffee or something in the cafeteria?" Barley asked.

"I don't drink coffee," she said playfully.

His heart and face just sank.

"But I'll have a Coke," she replied.

Barley's mind was a mess. He couldn't think of anything to say except, "Let's party."

At a table in the cafeteria, Barley just couldn't think straight. He was not able to make any small talk. "Are you married?" he inquired.

"Yes," she answered, again with playful, warm eyes.

His heart sank again, and his face showed his disappointment.

She smiled again, lighting up the world. "But I'm going through a divorce."

Barley started to gain a little control of himself and asked, "Could we . . ."

She stopped him with, "I have a child, and I'm not dating—yet."

Barley walked back to the truck after picking up a phone to get his next load. He did not talk about money or the lack of it to anyone. The Aerodyne didn't look right. Maybe it just needed to be waxed. Earl was in the driver's seat, rocking to music, tapping his fingers, and was ready to run. Barley climbed into the other side, lit a cigarette, and exhaled long. The next drag on the cigarette was deep, and he held it as if it were pot.

"What the hell is wrong with you?" Earl quizzed, never having seen his friend with this expression on his face before. "You look like you've seen a ghost."

"I've just met the woman that I'm going to *mate!*"

"Yeah, sure," Earl scoffed. "Did you get a good load?"

"Yeah, it better be." Barley forced a smile. "Let's go to Florida and have a good time. I need to forget this day."

Earl smiled. "By the way, what is her name?"

"Damn!" Barley grabbed his forehead. "I forgot to ask."

"Mission accomplished!" Earl laughed, and then he put the truck into gear and said, "Let's head for the beach."

This was a good-paying load with several pickups and several drops. Before they headed south, after finishing the loading outside of Cleveland, Ohio, Earl was doing the driving into the night. In fact, he had been doing most of the driving through the 3 days of picking up shipments in the Midwest to be delivered throughout Florida. Barley just wasn't into it. The LTL (i.e., less than truckload) freight would allow for more profit than a long-distance truckload in a mileage comparison, but the time factor would not warrant a team operation. It took 3 days just to get loaded because this type of freight could be loaded only during business hours. The 3 days simply resulted in 2 nights of finding something to do. Of course, Barley and Earl usually had no trouble finding something to do. They took in a ball game at old Tiger Stadium in Detroit the first night, and a nightclub outside Cleveland on the night before finishing the loading.

The meeting of the mate was influencing all of Barley's thoughts and daydreams. Barley was analyzing, justifying, evaluating, and speculating. Everything within sight, sound, and feel was beginning to change his perspective. Just as the first highs of pot use had slowed down his senses, thereby allowing full absorption of sensations and surroundings, this encounter had shifted the gears in his perception of life's journey.

The ball game at Tiger Stadium was great. Barley and Earl drank beer, enjoyed the game, and had a foul tip hit right at them. Barley saw the ball coming as if it were in slow motion ... He put his left hand up as if he were playing first base like he used to do. But the ball slapped off of his palm, hit the concrete, and bounced up, to be snatched by a laughing Earl. "Damn! That ball was thrown by the Goose (i.e., Rich Gosage of the Yankees)!" exclaimed Earl.

The ballpark, Tiger Stadium, and the whole evening were surreal.

All during the next day, Barley calculated and wondered about his life, thinking things like the following. "I'm having a great time with Earl, being on the road with my best friend. This is something special, but where am I going? Where is Earl going? There isn't enough money. The government is attacking independents. The media and Hollywood are taking away the respect for the profession. All I have is this truck. There must be something in life more meaningful ... Family? Wife and child? Oh, no! Wake up!" [Pause.] "Damn it!" Barley voiced loudly to himself and Earl.

"What?" Earl asked.

Barley replied, "We've got time. Let's find a tavern tonight."

"Okay," Earl agreed. "But it *is* Wednesday night."

Earl had known Barley all of his life, from 4 years old onward. Only in the 8 years between when Barley left for the road at 21, and when at 29 Barley had asked him to join him, did Earl not have regular contact and knowledge of Barley's life. Earl could feel something was really bothering his friend. He knew it was that girl back in Capital City, but it didn't make any logical or practical sense. Earl wondered what Barley could be thinking.

They found a suitable tavern with a safe place to park the tractor and trailer. Earl had picked it out. This wasn't a large, pick-up-babe place, but more of a pool tables and workingman's bar. The suburb it was located in was south of Cleveland and within 10 miles of their final pickup the next morning. The building was of hollow concrete block construction, suggesting that it may have had prior use as a laundromat or small furniture store. It housed four pool tables, a row of dart machines, and two pinball games. Barley liked the idea of the pinball games because in most places these were being replaced with video-type machines. Barley was wanting to have a good time, and Earl was determined that Barley would.

After a couple of tries on the pinball, which demonstrated that Barley was no pinball wizard, Earl suggested some pool, but the tables were all taken.

"You're better than me, so go and see if you can get a table. I'm going to sit down at the bar and loosen up a bit," Barley said, smiling.

Earl mingled into the groups of patrons, leaving a couple of quarters on a table to challenge. The place was fairly busy, and Barley had to take a stool in the middle of the bar, in front of a long mirror with two rows of liquor bottles on display. Barley always hated sitting in front of mirrors at a bar; he never liked to sit alone and look at himself. After a shot of tequila and two tall draughts, Barley tuned out the noise of the bar, and the focus of the room changed. He was staring forward, but not at the mirror. His eyes focused on the glare of the liquor bottles ... the double row of liquor bottles ... He was entering something, a private world he had been to before. How many times had he stared like this into the bar light glare coming off of a row of liquor bottles?... In how many different places?... in how many years?... in how many miles?...

"Hey, Barley!" Earl startled Barley back into this world with a hand on the shoulder. "I've got two babes that want to play us in pool."

Barley got up, smiled a greeting, and joined them at a table near the back corner of the building.

Earl held out his left hand and said, "This is ...". (Their names weren't important. Barley didn't really hear them.) "And girls, this is Barley Bill, the World's Greatest Truck Driver."

The young beauty sitting nearest Earl questioned, "And what makes you the World's Greatest Truck Driver?"

"It's time for a story," Earl suggested.

"Well, I suppose it's because I'm the Babe Ruth of trucking. I once was a mover, and while I was out in the San Francisco Bay area, I got drunk. I mean, I partied hard. The next day I had to load, and when you're a mover you need a crew. So I popped a couple of aspirin and a cup of coffee to shake off the major league hangover, and picked up a four-man crew who all had to climb into my single bunk Jimmy Astro. Please understand, these four fellas had no idea who I was or what shape I was in. Anyway, the load was on the other side of the bay, so I had to cross the San Meteo Bridge. This bridge is two narrow lanes and is more than 5 miles long. As soon as the truck was over water, I lost it. I got sicker than a dog. With one hand on the wheel, I drove across that bridge while puking out the window, and I didn't stop or hit anything. On the other side, I pulled my head back in, wiped my chin off, and turning to those four terrified bastards in my bunk, I said, 'Is there any argument who the world's greatest truck driver is?' Damn, I'm lucky to have gotten through that day!"

They all laughed at the story, even though Earl had heard it several times. This should have been the start of a fun evening, with maybe even a chance to get lucky, but the other girl asked Barley, "Okay, Babe Ruth, that makes you the greatest, but who gave you the name World's Greatest Truck Driver?"

"Well, that's an entirely different story, a sad one." Barley's expression was serious. "You better have another drink to hear that one."

"Hell, I haven't even heard this." Earl smiled.

And with the table's interest, Barley began. "I was in Houston, stuck for a whole weekend. It was 1976, the year of the Bicentennial. I was still driving the first truck I had ever bought, and I was still leased to a moving company at that time. Movers are a real different breed of truck driver."

"You mean this happened before the bridge crossing with the world's greatest hangover?" Earl joked.

"Maybe we should just play a game of pool," Barley said, as he looked at the two young women.

"No, we can play pool anytime," the one closest to Barley said.

"Okay, like I said, movers are a different breed. You live in your truck for extended periods, or just live in the truck, period."

"Like we do now," Earl offered.

"Yes, only movers are always left with lots of time to kill on the road. Even though we are leased to a moving company right now, we aren't 'bed buggers.' We haul computers and special freight that requires air-ride equipment. More like—Earl, you'll know what I'm saying—more like when we haul for trade shows."

"Yeah, why don't we haul trade shows anymore?" Earl questioned with genuine interest.

"Because of the government's deregulation that is only one-sided deregulation. The rates have been cut in half, and they're not done. The government is hell bent on screwing up all of trucking."

"What are you guys talking about?" The impatience was showing in both of the women. "What about Houston?"

"Oops! I'm sorry, I'll get back to Houston," Barley acknowledged. "I was planning to go to a party, but I wanted to get some pot, so I got on the C.B. and, you must understand, in a major truck stop you can 'get anything that you want,' like Alice's Restaurant (reference to the Arlo Guthrie tune). I was expecting a marijuana salesman, but instead a pretty good-looking gal came up to the tractor. She was obviously a professional girl, if you know what I mean. Anyway, she offered the pot and asked if I wanted any company. I said, 'no, just the pot, Mame.'" Barley said this in Gene Tracy style.

"Oh yeah, sure," Earl chuckled.

"Well, she didn't want to hear the *no,* and she said, 'I'm not what you think. I'm the world's greatest, and my father always told me to be the best no matter what I chose to do.' Well, she got my interest. I let her up into the cab and we shared a joint. It was pretty good stuff, so I bought it. It was expensive, and to my surprise she wanted to know if I wanted to trade some of it back. All the while she was sitting in the jump seat, she kept showing more and more of those . . ."

"Titties," Earl interjected, with his own Gene Tracy impersonation.

The two women at the table were now quite interested in the story.

"Finally, I just couldn't take it any longer." Barley was again sounding like a Gene Tracy southern hick. "So I jumped back into the sleeper, and she taught me how a—what do you call those things? How to install a condominium in the proper, professional way."

"A rubber, you ass," the closest woman said. "And just how does the world's greatest whore install a rubber?"

"Well, she puts it in her mouth like chewing gum, and sort of blows a bubble in reverse," Barley said with a suggestive head move.

"Oh God, how gross," said the woman.

"Wait, wait, wait! That's not how I got the name. There's more. This gal was quite proud of who she was. She wouldn't be called a whore. She was a prostitute. She said she made $1,200 a night, take home. Let's see now, at $50 for half and half, you do the math. Anyway, after she left I got back into the driver's seat and watched her enter a cab two spaces to the right of my truck. She shook that cab. I rolled myself another joint and noticed that the driver of that truck hurriedly got back into his driver's seat, started his engine, put his truck into gear, and pulled out to leave. I could see that he was feeling self-conscious, and he was leaving in a rush. Just as his cab pulled in front of my windshield, I heard screaming, and then saw that prostitute holding on to the front axle of the trailer tandems with both of her arms. Her pants were down around her ankles, and she had just been run over by the front wheels of the trailer's tandems. She was being dragged between the tandems, screaming for her life. I blew the air horn at him. He slammed on his brakes, and I pointed to his trailer tandems. He must have panicked, and he put his truck in reverse and backed over the poor thing. He then pulled the parking brake. I jumped out of my cab and ran to her. Drivers from all over the parking lot came and were circling her and me while I tried to calm her and make her understand that she shouldn't move. All of those men were just staring at her in disbelief. I looked at the driver who had run over her, and motioned for him to come over to me and hold her head. I then ran back to my truck and grabbed a pillow, blanket, and that joint I had rolled. I came back, put the pillow under her head, threw the blanket over her, and gently tried to tuck it under her sides without moving her back. That other driver was kind of in shock, so I just looked at the circle of men and shouted for someone to call an ambulance. The woman was terrified and afraid she was going to die. Hell, she looked to me like she was going to die. The tires had run over her hips and thighs twice. There were broken bones and blood. I put my hand on her face and made her look into my eyes and face. I lighted that joint and held it to her lips. She inhaled deeply. And then again . . . deeply. Then, as calmness entered her eyes, she said, 'You're the world's greatest truck driver.' She passed out right after that, and then the ambulance arrived, along with the police. That other driver was a mess—shaking and crying. The police took him to a motel, and I was asked to repark his truck. I will, of course, never forget that experience. Every time I go to Houston, I try to avoid that place, that old 76 truck stop. But, one day about 2 years after, I had to stop there because I needed fuel. Guess what. There she was, back working that lot. How she survived, I'll never know, but to go back to it. Wow!"

"Hey, ah, we got to get out of here." With that, the two women left the bar.

"Damn! What did you tell *that* story for?" Earl looked puzzled. "You chased them right out of here."

"Maybe I wanted to," Barley said with a low, sad voice. "It's true, you know, that truck stop whore. Tough damn lady! I just want to have a few drinks and get a good night's sleep." Then with a final Gene Tracy hick voice he said, "Bet she never pisses under a trailer again."

On Barley's first shift of driving, Earl slept and Barley played his second-favorite tape of Uriah Heep music. He rewound "July Morning" to concentrate on the words, and then he did it again and again. Finally, Earl woke up, stuck his head out through the bunk's leather curtain, and said: "Hey, you've got over 300 tapes, can't we hear something besides Uriah Heep?"

"Sorry. How about REO Speedwagon, 'A Decade of Rock and Roll'?"

"Yeah, that'll work," Earl sighed.

"Hey, we'll be able to get rid of some of this load Friday in Jacksonville, and we'll have most of the weekend to kill. I'll keep my mouth shut," Barley offered.

"Sun and fun? Great! I'm going back to sleep."

CHAPTER 9

Blind Eye

... It was good for a while
I could laugh, I could smile
But I woke up one day
And the sun was gone. (Ken Hensley)

Barley drove on with first REO Speedwagon, then Bob Seger's "Live Bullet", and then to allow for more reflection upon his life, he put in the sound track of the movie *Easy Rider*. Barley was influenced by that movie's theme of looking for America. He had thrown his watch away like Peter Fonda's Captain America when he bought that first truck. How many miles ago was that? Two or 3 million? It seemed as if the time had passed in an instant. He snapped on a map light, pulled down the sun visor, and looked carefully into his own face. Age and a decade of sunrises and sunsets were starting to take their toll. A few gray hairs showed in his beard's sideburns. He shut off the light. "Damn."

And the white lines ... the white lines kept rolling by like waves on an endless voyage across an endless sea.

They drove straight through to Florida with only one fuel stop and began delivering on Friday in Jacksonville. Barley made phone calls to the consignees at the other Florida cities with drop-offs, but no one would take delivery until Monday. They dropped the trailer at the truck stop and found a reasonable motel near the beach. From 3 o'clock when they arrived until sunset, the beach was crowded with people. Barley was enjoying the scenery, not just the beautiful, tanned women in bikinis, but all of it—waves, sand, breeze, sailboats reflecting the brilliant setting sun, children and families frolicking in the sand and breaking waves. The sounds were as delicious as the pina coladas being served at an outside, palm-covered service bar sitting between the ocean shore and the main hotel bar and restaurant. One thing about a beach, Barley thought, "Everyone is wearing sunglasses. There are no windows to the soul. It's hard to get a read on anyone, but the beach is always full of joy."

As the sky darkened and stars began to shine in the distant east over the Atlantic, Barley went inside to the main bar. Earl had already met a blond beauty during an extended happy hour, and she had several friends. "Some kind of girls' night out," Barley thought.

The evening quickly evolved into a friendly and intriguing flirtatious adventure, quite usual compared to past encounters of the two trucking buddies, and this night Barley was intent upon freeing his mind of those penetrating eyes back in Capital City that had been dominating his thoughts. The blond seemed attracted to Earl. She invited Earl and Barley to her house for a party with fresh strawberry daiquiris. "It's strawberry harvest time around here," she pointed out.

Earl drove the tractor with the blond, and Barley rode in a car driven by a cute young woman whose "no-no's" were loosely covered by bib overalls. She was wearing a bikini underneath. Barley couldn't keep himself from looking right into the wide-open spaces, provided intentionally. Within 45 minutes of arrival, the house was filled with eager partyers, and the blender continuously produced a strong mixture of rum and fresh strawberries. There also was plenty of pot, coke, and music. This was a wild party.

Barley woke up well after sunrise and was sweating from the humid heat. He felt sick, very hungover sick. He was alone in the Aerodyne but noticed small bib overalls draped across the jump seat. Barley then climbed down out of the cab and staggered over to an alley behind the house to relieve himself. But he became violently sick, vomiting and defecating before he could even pull his pants off. "Oh God, I hope no one sees me like this," he thought. While on his knees and hands, he experienced the worst case of dry heaves imaginable. It felt as if he would turn inside out. When the attack was over, he pulled off all of his clothes, wadded them up, and put them in a barrel across the alley. Then, while hiding in the bushes, he checked for a chance to get back to the truck cab. Luck was kind, and he made it back, started the engine, turned the air-conditioning on, and fell back to sleep. Two hours later he was able to get up, get dressed, and walk inside the house to find Earl. It was nearly 4 in the afternoon.

Barley had folded the small bibs and was going to return them if she was there. But when he saw her, she sent him a stare that said, "Do not hand those to me." There was a guy sitting next to her, and they obviously were attached in some way. "No problem," Barley thought. "I can't remember much of last night." He walked to the kitchen and left the bibs near the sink. Earl was in the kitchen with the blond. Earl was smiling and excited. "Hey, I thought you were going to sleep all day. We're going to party again tonight!"

Barley stopped Earl and said, "I'm not. I'll tell you what. How about you stay here for a couple of days while I go empty out the trailer." Barley and

Earl had used this arrangement before when one of them had something special going on. The blond's eyes lit up, and she touched Earl affectionately.

"Okay," Earl replied, "but you're going to miss a heck of a party. When are you leaving? Now?"

"Yep. Why don't you get what you need from the tractor," Barley said matter-of-factly. "I'll be back by Thursday at the latest. I might try to get started loading."

Barley hit the road but only drove to the Jacksonville 76 truck stop. He was still very sick. He was a beer man, and the fresh strawberry mix had ravaged his system. With a good night's sleep and a healthy breakfast before dawn, Barley started the day with "Sunrise" (Uriah Heep), feeling really good about a trip alone. The ride to Miami would only provide a few good miles, however. Barley should have enjoyed this ride. The road was smooth, the traffic was light until afternoon, and the Florida scenery was pleasant. The mood changed when "July Morning" (Uriah Heep) began, and Barley could think only of her, back in Capital City.

Barley began to feel terrible; he had an aching in his gut. He knew what he must do. He must say good-bye to Earl. He wanted to get back to Capital City. His life must change. "It is changing," he said to himself. "The government is attacking trucking. This business does not warrant a codriver unless it is a wife." Barley was trying to justify what would be the most difficult task he had had to face up until this point in his life—to hurt his best friend. There would be no easy way to do it. "Well, I guess it will have to be like a mother bear chasing her cubs up a tree and not returning."

Barley unloaded, then reloaded the trailer with a three-stop shipment going to the Boston area for delivery no sooner than the following Tuesday. He arrived back in Jacksonville on Wednesday evening.

Barley went directly to Earl and said, "We have to talk. Come out to the truck." Earl was surprised to see that Barley hadn't dropped the trailer. "Earl," Barley began, "you're my best friend and I don't know how to say this except, it's over, you and me. I can't go on like this. We're having fun, but we're not getting anywhere. You're not getting anywhere. You have a trade now. You can drive for a company or buy your own rig."

Earl was stunned, hurt, and angry. "You're going back to that girl, and you don't even know her name."

"I probably will." Barley tried his best to be firm. "No matter what, the government is taking the profit out of trucking. They want to force independents off of the road. I can't pay you what you're worth." Barley sighed deeply. "How do you ... do you want to go home on a bus or plane? I owe you that."

"Nah," Earl rebutted. "I'll just stay here."

CHAPTER 10

Traveler in Time

Bill Jackson had been home less than 2 hours and was in the shower when the call came from the assistant director of the F.B.I. "Bill, get back to the airport as fast as you can. We've got another dead highway patrol officer in Kalamazoo, Michigan. Fax me what you have so far on your theories and find out if this is connected to Nebraska. They have the driver. You can read what we have discovered on the plane."

Abu Azmath was heading east on I94 in Michigan with a load of empty racks used to haul axles made in Detroit. He was coming from the General Motors plant in Janesville, Wisconsin. He had immigrated to the United States with his father's family, originally from Jordan, then Iraq. They had settled in the Arab community on the southwest side of the Detroit metro area. The family owned a small, run-down motel and convenience store. When Abu Azmath became 21 years old, he decided to try his hand at trucking. The family business could not support another adult. With the help of a government-subsidized loan and a government-subsidized truck-driving school, he hit the road with a brand-new tractor. It was of modern design, an aerodynamic mass of shaped plastic. After 6 months, it looked exactly like what should be expected of a truck driven by an overwhelmed, inexperienced, and frightened man. There were scrapes, scratches, paint skid marks, and punctures all around the unit. The side moldings were bent, with sections missing. Abu Azmath had never been in any major accident, but he hit things often. He had trouble backing. He never was able to relax behind the wheel. A 10-hour run was exhausting for him. He was exactly what the government wanted in a truck driver. He would do exactly as he was told and was willing to operate for no more than enough to make his subsidized loan payment and a road advance to eat on. He wore a turban and was on the satellite system Qualcom.

When the fast, fancy truck passed Abu Azmath and then pulled in front of him in the driving lane while slowing down, his muscles tensed even more than usual. Then the flashing lights of a patrol car coming by in the fast lane frightened him. The truck that passed him had slowed to 55 miles per hour, and Abu Azmath was within 50 feet of the rear of that trailer. He slowly realized that the policeman was after the other truck and watched in terror at what happened.

The police car pulled alongside the other truck. Then the trailer swerved, first to the right. The brake lights lit up with smoke from the trailer tandem tires as the trailer swerved violently to the left, hitting the police car and sending it directly into the concrete of the center support columns of an overpass. Then the trailer swung back, clipping the fiberglass driver-side fender and front-left-side bumper of his truck. Abu Azmath traveled nearly a half mile before he was able to regain enough composure to stop on the shoulder. His heart was racing, and he was frozen in fear.

Barley Bill's Hobbs had struck again, seizing the wheel while Barley's Ruth was vulnerable. Reliving the experience of saying good-bye to Earl was more than saying good-bye to his friend. It was saying good-bye to his youth and its carefree days. That memory created emotion. Hobbs acted without malice, without hatred, without emotion of any kind. Hobbs had no morals, no ethics, no respect. Hobbs had only instinctive animal survival intellect. Hobbs reacted to and controlled environmental conditions that created emotional turmoil in the Ruth ego. All emotion, love, hate, morality existed in the Ruth side, and the cancer was destroying that side. Hobbs grew stronger and took more control each day. Hobbs would kill a bandit in the same manner as a housewife stepping on an ant crawling across the kitchen floor invading her space. It was protection, instinctive protection. Ruth could hate; Hobbs could kill as a result.

Bill Jackson arrived in Kalamazoo, Michigan, 2 hours after Arnie Benson and his D.O.T. crew. Linda Wright had been in town 3 hours earlier, representing the network. She had access to quicker response transportation, and the Road Rogue would now become a national news story. Footage already was airing showing the destroyed police car and Abu Azmath's banged-up truck. Abu Azmath's face was a perfect fit for the misinformation and hunger being created. This man looked like a terrorist. The public *would* be fed.

Arnie's team gathered information. Bill Jackson went to the sheriff's department county lockup where the terrified Abu Azmath was being held. The local officers who had arrived at the scene first had arrested him. Bill Jackson was shocked when he entered the cell. Abu Azmath had been beaten badly. He was shaking. His lower jaw vibrated, as if he were sitting on a block of ice. He was terrified and could not remember much if any of the English words he had learned to be able to pass D.O.T. qualification. This was not who Bill Jackson was looking for. Bill Jackson was looking for or expecting an old veteran driver like his father. "Oh God, forgive us." Bill patted the man on the shoulder and said to the local sheriff, "I need an interpreter; he's speaking Arabic." As Bill Jackson turned to walk away, Abu Azmath forced out the English words: "Other truck, other truck!"

The following morning in a room hastily arranged as a conference room, Arnie Benson broke the news. "This is not connected to the Nebraska killing. We have the satellite Qualcom records. This truck has never been west of Illinois. The driver is on a dedicated run from Detroit to Janesville, Wisconsin, and return."

Linda Wright asked, "Then he is not the Road Rogue?" She knew what the footage being shown was implying and that the misinformation must stop. Linda Wright left the room to call the network.

Privately, Arnie and Bill studied the evidence. The photos, measurements, and wreckage did not add up. Abu Azmath's truck had been hitting things, but nowhere was any Michigan state trooper blue found. Bill and Arnie agreed that the local boys had jumped to the conclusion that the Arab driver was the cause.

"Did you see Azmath?" Bill asked.

"Yeah," Arnie sighed. "He looked like *he* hit the overpass."

"It's going to be difficult to keep a lid on this." Bill shook his head. "Lawsuits and embarrassment galore."

The interpreter arrived to confirm Bill and Arnie's suspicions. There was another truck. Abu Azmath could not provide details. He didn't know the difference between models, or the brand names of individual trucks. His father *did* know a good attorney. The only usable description was that it was a fancy new conventional tractor with dark paint.

And the Road Rogue rides on, and the legend begins. Where is he? Where is he going? When will he strike again?

CHAPTER 11

All My Life

A call back to the company Barley was leased to provided a detour on his trip home. He needed the detour. He was afraid of what was at home. He needed to think to somehow fight the feeling of dread. The company trailer was due to be traded in at the Wabash Trailer Factory in Lafayette, Indiana. Barley already had informed his dispatcher that he would be out of service for an extended period of time. The dispatcher sent him to turn in the trailer and then he could bobtail home. On the way, Barley replayed the song "July Morning" and drifted back in time . . .

After leaving Earl in Florida, Barley drove out of route, directly to Capital City. He finished the long ride in less than 24 hours. The ride was easy. He felt strong and excited. The beautiful views of the Appalachian Mountains and dense forest soothed the pain of good-bye. He felt and believed he was doing the right thing, following destiny.

Upon arriving in Capital City, he first checked into a motel close to the home terminal. "Not bad," he thought. "I can stay 2½ days and still make delivery on time." He showered, put on his coolest T-shirt, and wrote down the room number and phone number on the motel stationery. He then drove to the terminal, and with confidence walked up to the mail room door. She was there. The first gaze of recognition told Barley she was still interested, and she was. She had the advantage of knowing about him from having made inquiries with other truckers in the company. She knew his name and truck number. "He's wild, as wild as the west Texas wind," she had been told (in reference to the Marty Robbins classic hit "El Paso").

Barley noticed the other people, her coworkers, making teasing eyes at her. He caught her eyes again as she approached and quietly stated, "Let's party." He left the motel stationery note on the door counter and smiled before turning around to leave the building. Barley walked directly to the tractor and returned to the motel room. It was a Thursday afternoon, nearing 4 P.M. local time, when Barley laid down on his motel bed next to the phone.

She had been asking about him. She had walked into the dispatch area to ask a friend about him. "Oh, he's on his way to the East Coast—Boston area."

She realized that he shouldn't be here, unless? She walked briskly to the cafeteria phone and called. "Well, do you expect me to just come to your motel room? Or just what did you have in mind?"

Barley knew who had called instantly, although he still did not know her name. "I was thinking about asking you to dinner. I guess you didn't need the room number, but [he laughed] oh hell, whoops, excuse me, will you have dinner with me?"

"I, I wasn't expecting . . . . I don't know if I can make arrangements." She was quite curious. "Aren't you supposed to be somewhere?"

Barley smiled, because he knew for sure now that she would come. "Well see, you did need that room number." Chuckling, he then added, "If you can call me back, or I'll gladly meet you. There's a pretty nice Mexican restaurant close by. Anyway, I'll stay here for a while, at least until I get thirsty."

She called back within 20 minutes and agreed to meet him at the Mexican restaurant. She saw his fancy truck on the street when she pulled into the parking lot, and Barley was waiting for her in the entranceway. Barley waited until after ordering frozen margaritas to ask her name, not realizing he had the frozen concoction all over his mustache and beard when he finally got the words out. He was intrigued by her look, and then blushed with embarrassment when she smiled and motioned to the problem. "Why does this girl do this to me? I keep stumbling. Damn, she's pretty!" Barley mused to himself in thought.

"Erika, my name is Erika." She smiled and her eyes lit up playfully.

"Oh, like that soap-opera gal, the one who keeps getting married?" Barley returned with an equally playful gaze.

"More like her than you want to know." Erika smiled, lighting up the whole room in Barley's view.

The dinner was enjoyable, with flavors Barley had not tasted in this way for a long time. He was with *her*. He knew it. This girl *was* the one, the *you* of his "July Morning." Nothing she could say would bother him. Everything about her was perfect. He just loved the way she said it, anything that she said. She had problems. There was a divorce. The divorce was not yet final. Barley couldn't care less. "Compared to me, you've been a saint," he told her.

"Oh, I wouldn't say that." She lowered her head. "I have two daughters, and this is my *second* divorce."

"My God!" Barley was astonished. "You look so young. Well, I guess you're so pretty they just keep falling in love with you, how about it?"

"I'm 22."

The conversation went on into the evening. Barley rationalized that Erika was in need of stability in her life, and he envisioned himself as the provider of it. He had cheated himself of a real life, one with meaning, and he wondered how any man could walk away from this girl. "Must not have been men, must have been boys," he thought first. Then he realized how many women he had walked away from. It didn't matter; "None of them were aware of the fire that burned" (K. Hensley, Uriah Heep). Barley also was of the mindset that if Erika had not made the mistakes in her life she was referring to, then he would feel guilty entering into her life. She was young, and he would not want to cause her any pain.

Barley did not want the dinner and the evening to end, but he walked her to her car, which was an old-model pickup. "This is what you drive?" The pickup seemed to make a statement. A country girl, she just smiled with the most inviting look he had ever seen. Barley touched her long brown hair, looked once more into her eyes, and they kissed. Erika would not look back at him nor meet his eyes, until the moment when she turned out of the parking lot for a last look and a good-night wave. Barley just stood there for a moment, stunned by how good, how warm, how tender that kiss had been. The sound of her pickup with its V8 engine and glass pack mufflers echoing off the windows of the restaurant snapped him out of his daze. "Glass packs. She's after my heart," he thought.

A neighborhood bar and grill was located next to the restaurant, and Barley went inside and ordered a draught beer. There were other drivers sitting at the bar that he knew and more who knew of him. He should have had a good old time. But instead he focused on the glare, the glare of the liquor bottles in front of the mirror . . . Yes, she was the one . . .

The next day Barley went to the terminal building even though he did not want to be seen by dispatch. He just didn't care. He had forgotten to ask to see her, Erika, again. They went to lunch, and Barley asked to see her that night. "Hey, it's Friday!"

"Are you still in the motel?" she quizzed.

"Yes, I'll wait there." Barley was almost pleading, and he knew it. ("Damn, get your act together, you fool," he thought.)

"I don't know if I can."

"I'll be there. I have this weekend available, and if you haven't guessed, I'm here to see you." Barley just blurted that out without caring further. There would be no more trying to impress. "I want to get to know you."

Barley waited until after 6 o'clock. No call came. Anxiety set in, and he stood up and walked over to the door to leave. He would go to the bar. At the very moment his hand grabbed the doorknob, there was a knock. Barley opened the door, and there she was with her two children. There was a beautiful young blond girl of about 4, and to Barley's complete surprise a baby. Erika smiled with caution and said, "If you want to know me, you must know my girls."

"Well, come in." Barley tried to make the 4 year old feel at ease. He knew his size, long hair, and beard would be scary for her. "You ever see

Grizzly Adams before?" Barley laughed and smiled at her. "How about a big truck ride to a pizza parlor?" He waited for Erika's response.

"Yes, but if you don't mind, I need . . ." Erika motioned to him that he would need to hold the baby.

Barley was instantly nervous and sat down in the chair next to the window. Erika handed the baby to him, and he looked up saying softly, "I've never . . . I've never held a baby."

Barley held the precious bundle, looking at the tiny face. A tear welled up in the corner of his left eye. "How can this be? How could someone screw up so bad as to risk losing this precious little girl—this precious family? Barley was nearly overwhelmed with the emotion of this scene. When Erika picked up the baby, Barley looked at her, trying to understand. What trouble was she in? "You have two beautiful daughters," he barely managed to choke out.

Barley took them in the Aerodyne to a Pizza Hut and then stopped afterward in a small park until darkness began to set in. When they returned to the motel, Erika loaded the children and necessary bags into her truck and then turned to look at Barley. No words were needed. She gave a soft smile with eyes that emitted an underlying pain, and somehow an understanding of it in return.

Barley was completely surprised when Erika tapped on the door a short while later. The children had been taken to their grandmother's. Understanding became comfort. Comfort became passion, passion as Barley had never known. Barley had only known lust or physical need without caring. This was love. It must be. He could not have enough. *They* could not have enough. All the rest of the available hours were spent in passionate love. Two souls of destiny, each needing what the other was.

Barley had to leave on Sunday to make delivery on time and had checked out of the motel in time to return to the terminal before heading east. He was walking up to the driver's lounge to pick up some supplies when Erika and her two daughters approached from around the corner of the building. She was smiling and walking directly to Barley, who stood a few feet from the door. There was a bench just outside the room between the door and the corner Erika was coming from. A young man saw her, and she walked by him without notice. He saw that she was heading straight to Barley. He had a look on his face of longing, and he warned, "Erika, you can't be with him" (pointing to Barley as if he knew him or of him). "He's a wild man!"

"Well, maybe I'll just settle him down some," she responded, while looking directly at Barley and smiling. "Can you come to my place for dinner before you leave? There's a place across the street from my apartment where you can park."

Something sent warning signals into Barley's thoughts about the look of that young man. "Well, she sure is going to attract them," he thought.

There would be good reason for the warning signal, but it wasn't that Erika was attractive.

CHAPTER 12

Love Machine

Lovely little lady
You got me on the run
You're a love machine ...
(Ken Hensley/David Byron/Mick Box)

Still daydreaming ...
Barley pulled the Aerodyne and trailer into the vacant lot Erika pointed to. She lived in the large apartment complex across the road. The complex looked rather run-down. "Probably a lot of government subsidies living here," Barley thought. He had plenty of room to park though, just as she had said. She opened the door of the pickup for him to climb in. "I think that would be a little tight. Why don't I just walk over to—which apartment?" He walked up ready for a home-cooked meal ...

The thoughts of that night and the first home-cooked meal any woman had offered him in years brought Barley's remembering into an almost angry vocal response to no one except himself, "Oh God. How did it all happen so fast, and why? Why?" Barley's heart began to beat rapidly, too rapidly.

Barley was worried now, and he pulled over to an exit ramp, crossed the road, and parked on the side shoulder of the entrance ramp. He laid his head down on the steering wheel but not to sleep. It was time to face this memory and put it behind him before he faced going home. Going home could be another nightmare. He took a nitro.

He let the vibrations of the wheel enter and soothe his chest ... and his mind drifted back in time ...

The meal with Erika and her two daughters was special because of the setting of a home, however humble. Barley felt as if he could be part of this, or more importantly, that he could be needed by them.

Later that night, with a kiss of good-bye that seemed to mean much more, Barley left to complete his run. He had left himself very little extra time and would need to pull for the rest of the night. It was easy. He felt exhilarated. The weather was clear, and the highway was smooth. Without any reference to a map, Barley worked his way toward Interstate 80, intending to cross Pennsylvania. He wanted to avoid any tolls and enjoy this mountainous freeway ride by sunrise.

The line of trucks following him complimented Barley's ego. The C.B. radio talk of the drivers behind him reminded Barley of respect for an obvious veteran with a powerful horse on the "front door." This kind of respect and comraderie was becoming rare. Only during the wee hours of the night, the trucking hours leading to dawn, did he see it anymore. So much was changing in the world of trucking. Many of the great names of trucking were disappearing. Long-established companies were going broke or being bought out—Double Diamond, Campbell Express with its Humping to Please camel logo, and of course the legendary Monfort of Colorado. At one time the hammer lane was called the Monfort Lane because of that company's reputation for fast trucks. The government had busted them, Barley was sure.

The government and its willing ally, the media, were changing the very language of trucking. Cowboy lights (the extra lights put on trucks by owner-operators) became chicken lights, which destroyed the original concept. The first trucks lit up were long-distance cattle haulers who needed to get to their destination as fast as possible. These were the drivers who had freight that wasn't just perishable; it was live animals that would die if left in the trailer too long. At one time, out west in the desert nights, all truckers (and even Smokeys) would stay out of their way. The practice was similar to lapped cars in a Nascar race moving over to let race leaders go by. Not this new breed of driver, Barley thought, "These guys will line up two trucks, both incapable of 65 miles per hour, and tie up the Monfort [or hammer lane] for miles." Barley was sure this whole change was a persistent plot by the government to take the cowboy out of trucking, and not just the cowboy, but also the independent individual. "Where did this philosophy of everything and everyone must be the same, come from?" he thought.

Just before dawn, Barley put Uriah Heep into the tape player and revisited the words of "Sunrise" as the first light exposed the morning painting of God's splendor of mountain forest divided by man's reflecting pavement ribbon.

There is no one to see me cry
Except the sunrise
The sunrise and you (Ken Hensley)

Determination set into Barley's mind. He pushed on without breakfast (always his favorite meal), just grabbing a couple of hot dogs while fueling at a Bingo station. (Bingo stations are gone now. They were a symbol of independence.) Barley saluted the large American flag that all Bingo stations proudly displayed. "This is still a great country. No matter what I've done in my life, I can still find happiness." Barley rejoiced in the thought.

Barley emptied out in 2 days and reloaded by Friday morning, all within the Boston metro area. The load would end in Florida again, and he thought only about traveling out of route to spend at least some of his available hours with Erika. She was dominating his thoughts. He just had to get back to her. He was afraid that he would lose his chance at a real life—a life that must have been his destiny. Barley arrived back at Erika's door before noon on Saturday. He had driven straight through and had parked across the street in the vacant lot Erika had pointed out the previous Sunday.

Erika met him at the door with a welcome hug and embrace that acknowledged that she too was succumbing to a feeling of destiny. As soon as was possible (with the children being dropped off in the late afternoon), passion conquered time. By the eventual mandatory departure time, Barley was exhausted.

Barley put the Aerodyne into gear, heading south with the full intention to drive all night again, but he couldn't. He had to sleep and recover. The world's greatest truck driver was going to be late—late on delivery for the first time in his life. Dispatch was shocked. Barley could have said he was broken down. He didn't. He just said that he was tired and had pulled over in Chattanooga, Tennessee.

"What the hell are you doing in Chattanooga?" his dispatcher asked. "You're out of route."

"I'll be there tomorrow. I have nothing more to say." Barley refused to acknowledge any amount of submission to authority.

The dispatch department had been notified that Barley was no longer running with a codriver, but they knew something else was up. The Babe Ruth of trucking would not have admitted to just lying down. "He's got something going on in Capital City. We better get him out west or we'll lose him," the load planner stated to Barley's dispatcher.

Upon emptying the trailer on Thursday, Barley was looking to load before the weekend to somewhere, anywhere that he could stop in to see Erika. Dispatch had it all figured out by then. They knew of the pretty girl in the mail room who was asking questions about a certain truck number. The game plan was put into motion. A great-paying load was arranged, taking Barley from Florida to San Diego and Los Angeles, California. This was the type of load they thought would have tempted Barley beyond his infatuation with this mail room girl. From there they could send him north to Seattle, Washington, and maybe into Canada. Then they could route him to Texas. The plan was to keep him out of Capital City for months.

The original load would take 4 days just to put on—Thursday, Friday, Monday, and Tuesday—with a layover in Orlando, Florida, on the weekend. Barley jumped at it. He loaded on Thursday and Friday as planned. Friday afternoon he parked the rig in Orlando, hailed a cab, and flew to Capital City, arriving by 7:30 P.M. Erika was at the airport to pick him up, having arranged for the children to be watched for the evening by the grandmother.

They had a wonderful weekend full of love, family, and a feeling out of each other's personality. Erika was surprised by the traditional, conservative desires of this man who had seemed to be so wild. Barley was just infatuated with her. She was so down-to-earth natural. She loved animals, and during the weekend she found a helpless and obviously homeless cat.

"Uriah Heep is what we should call her," Barley stated. Uriah Heep music is my favorite. It's not the stuff dreams are made of; it's the stuff that allows you *to* dream."

Erika would have that damn cat (named Uriah Heep) for more than a decade, but she never would have anything to do with Uriah Heep music.

Barley climbed back into his cab on Monday morning thinking that he had fooled the world. One of the dispatchers had seen him in the Mexican restaurant with Erika, though, on Friday night. That same dispatcher was shocked to find out Monday that Barley was still in Florida, on schedule.

Sensing that this could be his last ride west, Barley concentrated on enjoying it. On Monday night, he had contacted the blond girl in Jacksonville, hoping to see Earl. Earl had left, presumably to go home to Michigan. "I wish he could make this ride, Florida to California, with me," Barley sighed to himself.

By Tuesday afternoon, Barley was finished loading, had had his Aerodyne washed, and was rolling west. There was no push by dispatch. The load would not start delivering until the following Monday. This would be a ride to say good-bye to freedom—freedom as a single man. Barley realized that now. He could not run irregular routes in the 48 continental United States and Canada and try to have a traditional life with Erika. These were his thoughts as he set out to indulge himself in his last great ride west. He wanted to see every blade of grass, every tree, every river, each city skyline, the opening of the tundra, the desert, the mountains, and the stars. He would soak up every view, every last breath of freedom on this ride.

And ride he did. The big Cat purred as he drove into the night. The white lines rolled by through the panhandle of Florida. The dawning of light was growing from behind as he entered Alabama. He had a good breakfast and then pulled over in Battleship Park (Mobile, Alabama) to walk the decks of the great ship once more. He remembered taking Earl there. And then he returned to the road, finding Interstate 10, and traveled out of route to pass through New Orleans, through the last stop of the Easy Rider buddies. More memories flooded his mind. Now onward to Texas.

Barley pulled over to sleep in the first rest area of Texas with a plan to wake up and race the sun across Texas on Interstate 10 the next day. When he entered the cab of the Aerodyne after a good breakfast and fueling, it was as if his damn truck understood its competition. More than just the damn truck, the road and the country itself understood. The trucks and traffic on the highway, the passing scenery, the cities; all were watching as if the great Ruth was rounding the bases for the last time. All was giving way in a salute. What a ride! Barley pulled into El Paso just as the setting sun's glorious colors faded to allow the stars' brilliant display across the enormous sky.

Barley pulled his sleeping bag from the bunk and laid down outside on the sand for a few minutes to wonder at the display, and to wonder if what he was planning was the right thing to do. Only the desert chill made him return to the bunk for a sleep that would be as restful as he had ever or would ever know. His decision had been made.

CHAPTER 13

Bird of Prey

The following day was a continuation of the realization that a change of life was destined. Barley immersed himself in his love of desert driving. New Mexico's scenery is as uniquely stunning as is any from the windshield of a dream truck. The border crossing into Arizona was without hitch, and Barley pulled on. He would finish this day at one of his favorite places: the Triple T Truck Stop of Tucson, Arizona (voted America's best in 1969).

At the Triple T, Barley wanted to take it all in. First, he was happy to see that the large, black bird that could say a few words was there in the chrome store. Then he just had to have their famous cherry pie à la mode. He then went out into the endless parking lot (trucks can just park on the desert floor past the paved section, allowing for unlimited parking). A party would be happening out there somewhere. Barley found some laid-over truckers planning a campfire and barbecue. These kinds of gatherings are spontaneous triumphs of America. Complete strangers gather for nothing more than a good time. Some of them are lonely, some are new, and some are old. Some, like Barley, will never return (at least not with their dreams). There is the fire under the stars, the beer, the exchange of jokes, and then the music.

One of the drivers had a codriver who brought out a guitar and could sing. Barley was astonished and honored that she knew how to play and sing "The Wizard." "You just don't hear any Heep anymore," she said. "It was great."

What a night!

Barley pushed on the next day, thoroughly enjoying the climb up and then down into California. Some of that area looks as if it is on some other planet. The rocks . . . the piles of rocks are just incredible. The Aerodyne and its big Cat handled the grade as if it were Kansas. California used to be a place Barley enjoyed, but no longer. California's liberal elitism and wacked out environmentalism convinced Barley that there must be something in the water. He guessed it was really just a lack of water. "Too bad, California has the overall best scenery and climate of the country, but I would rather live in a Midwest gray iron foundry than be with people willing and asking for their freedoms to be taken from them," Barley thought.

Barley emptied his trailer way ahead of schedule and called in looking for a load back to the Midwest. The offer was to Edmonton, Alberta, Canada.

"Wrong season. No hockey at this time of year," was Barley's response. Push came to shove, and Barley just let it out. "It's over Johnny. [The dispatcher wasn't named Johnny.] I'll just bring the trailer back empty from here unless you have something going that way."

"You can't."

"Yes, I can. I'm done. It's time for a change. I know what you're planning, and I can't live this way anymore," Barley stated without emotion.

"Give me a couple of days to put something together," the dispatcher pleaded.

"I'll be in Capital City on Monday to turn in the trailer."

With that final word, Barley put it into gear and headed east, never to talk to his dispatcher again. He drove back, taking 3 days to complete the trip. He arrived, checked in the trailer, went to Erika's door that evening, and asked her from the doorway, "Will you marry me?"

Like a bird of prey
You capture me . . . (Mick Box/David Byron/Paul Newton)

Erika held him tight. She knew he was coming and not just by having a connection in dispatch. She had felt it.

It was September 20, 1982. Ronald Reagan had survived the assassination attempt and was winning the battle of rhetoric with the Democrats. The media couldn't get him either. Ronald Reagan had core values, and he made Americans feel proud again. There was optimism. The American dream was *alive*. It lived also in the hearts of these two lovers meeting at a crossroad intersection from two different worlds. Barley would need a plan—a plan to provide without being a long-distance owner/operator.

The plan to provide . . .

CHAPTER 14

No Heep, No Hope

Barley lifted his head, chest, and shoulders off of the wheel 3 hours after pulling onto the entrance ramp shoulder. The engine was still idling, and he was angry with himself for not shutting it off or turning it up to fast idle. He might have hurt her, the big Cat. He felt better now, without the pain of a racing heart.

Daylight was dimming fast, and Barley wanted to complete the task of turning in the trailer so he could bobtail on home to whatever awaited. He arrived at the trailer factory and was rushed through the check-in inspection, then given the papers showing delivery of the trailer. The security guard instructed him to go to the fourth gate and drop the trailer where the yard dog could move it to its final parking space. (A yard dog is a tractor equipped with an airlift on the fifth wheel, designed to allow trailer moving without having to crank up the dolly wheels. These are specifically designed cabs not intended for road use.) The yard dog, as would be expected, had sitting in its seat a typical asshole. A natural ill feeling exists between a road driver and a trailer jockey. Call it jealousy, or envy, or something, but it exists as naturally as the feelings between trucker and cop. Barley was angered by this man's lazy aloofness and lack of respect. The yard dog driver should have said, "Drop it right here and I'll park it." He didn't. He pointed out to the field beyond the gravel lot and said, "We're backed up. There are used trailers all over hell. Take it out there, damn it!"

Barley got out and looked over the ground as the yard dog drove off to another lot. The wet ground had been deeply rutted. Trucks had been stuck. This was a muddy mess. "No way," Barley thought, and then he realized that this trailer already was checked in. He himself would mail the papers tomorrow. "I'll just keep the damn thing until I come back. I know I'll need an empty trailer when I get home. Hell, it would be months before they'd even miss it. I'll have it back here next week." He rather liked the idea of it and headed out of the lot onto the street, and then north. Hobbs took control, and Barley reentered his past, remembering the plan . . .

. . . "What can you do if you get off of the road?" Erika asked, looking stunned that Barley was going to give up his dream truck.

"I don't have a clue, but it will come to me. I know it." Barley believed it.

Erika would wonder and contemplate all night about what Barley was doing. She understood, slowly, how much he must love her. He was giving up his very way of life to be with her.

At breakfast, in a Denny's restaurant the next morning, Barley was reading the local Capital City newspaper. "Breakfast is the most important meal of the day, but one must feed more than just the body. One must feed the mind too to stay healthy." This was a philosophy Barley believed in. All of his adult life, he had used breakfast as his phoenix from whatever abuse his Ruthian ego had demanded of his mind, body, and soul. Reading the paper at a leisurely breakfast was the one absolute luxury an overworking trucker could afford. Barley had burned past exhaustion at night or arose long before sunrise just so he *could* afford that luxury a thousand times. Today was different, though. He would look at the classified section for the first time of his life. And there it was.

Wanted: Owner/Operators to run in a less-than-500-mile radius. Be home most nights and weekends. Call Roy Bird at . . . .

Barley called and then bobtailed the Aerodyne to the location near downtown Capital City. A coal hauling and dump operation company, Blend Trucking, had won the contract for hauling foundry coke from the local coke plant to Midwest foundries using the plant's trailer fleet. Blend Trucking was also to service and maintain the trailer fleet. The home office for Blend Trucking was in the southern tip of the state, and they were hiring 20 owner/operators to begin in 10 days. This was perfect, except that the Aerodyne was too heavy with its big Cat and large cab over design. Barley signed the contract and said, "I'll trade trucks today." With that, he was off to the Kenworth dealer where he had purchased his dream truck. The dealer was just a few miles away on the other side of town.

Barley laid out his plans for the dealer. "I want to trade down. I need some of my equity to start a new life. I'm getting married."

"Okay, we have some nice trade-ins. Take a look," salesman George offered.

Barley walked the lot . . . "There she is. A conventional Peterbilt! Ugly paint and crying for chrome, but it has that long hood, 20 gauges, and a walk-in sleeper." She had a Detroit motor, but he needed a lighter tractor, and this would do.

The deal was struck with a few hitches. Barley wanted $10,000 cash out of his equity, and salesman George couldn't arrange for that large of a check. George made an offer in which the cash would be used to prepare the Peterbilt for its new operation. Barley wanted more. He decided to make this Pete look just as he wanted, as if he were ordering a new one.

Along with the required power take-off and wet kit for operating the end dump trailer, he had her painted black, jet black, with polished aluminum wheels and a new custom chrome bumper added. All of the necessary chrome highlights were ordered to be put on after the painting. The paint would be special and was to be cut and buffed prior to taking final delivery. To finish the deal, the Kenworth dealer included in the trade a VW Rabbit automobile that had been used for parts delivery. ("I'm going to have to have a car for this new life," Barley figured.) In the deal was a purchase of an insurance policy to cover the loan on the Peterbilt. This was a minimal-coverage policy and did not cover any of the improvements. It was limited to the fair market value of the 1979 Peterbilt as she was, a 359 model, not yet 4 years old. The total time taken for the remake would be 13 days, which caused a little rumble from the new company. The time was well spent with Erika and her two daughters until a fateful event occurred.

On a day in which Erika would learn a great deal about the character of this new man in her life, Barley would have his Ruth ego challenged as never before. A call came from the baby's father, and he was demanding to see his daughter. He was lying; he wanted to see Erika, and he was quite a belligerent young man, angry that he had lost his wife. He came to the door and Erika answered. She could sense his anger, and an argument began almost immediately. Barley came to the door and then stepped into the entrance area next to the stairway leading to the second-story apartments. "No need to get violent young man. I'm sure you two can come to some agreement."

The young man was hot, and began spouting off at Barley. Erika had gone back inside and was calling the police. A restraining order had been issued. Barley was sure that he wouldn't be physically challenged by this young man, who was stocky but at least 4 inches shorter and 10 years his junior. Erika returned to the door, announcing that she had called the police. Barley looked back at Erika, seeing a fearful anger in her eyes. WHAM!

A perfectly executed sucker punch to Barley's temple sent him to the floor, out cold. By the time he began to regain consciousness, while struggling to his hands and knees, an officer was talking. "Are you all right? Do you want to press charges?"

Barley shook off the cobwebs and got to his feet. "Nah, I just didn't see it coming. No need to have the law involved. I don't think it's worth missing work over. But I won't let that happen again," Barley stated directly to his attacker. "Just tell him to leave."

"I'm so sorry," Erika said once back inside.

"Well, I think that we should have a little talk while I put some ice on this. I'll bet I'll look real pretty in the morning." Barley laughed as if he had just fallen off of a bar stool.

"Erika, our lives—we come from different worlds. I think I've figured out what has brought you to here and now with me. Tell me if I'm wrong. In contrast to an old, big, ugly guy like me, you have beauty that has brought trouble into your life. Government has dominated my life. I'm *old* enough to have had Vietnam and the government's lies and policies about it dictate my beginnings in adult life. I'm *young* enough to have been saturated with influences that taught me not to accept those lies and policies. You, on the other hand, have lived a life dominated by your beauty, which has attracted men, blind of their own limitations of youth. I've listened to you, and I've figured the ages. You, your daughters and ... what did you say? You said your first husband had *joined* the service? Now if that doesn't contrast with the times! Anyway, as you have said, your parents got divorced when you were in high school. So, it's in the genes."

"What do you mean, in the genes?" Erika responded with a quizzical look.

"Well, you dated, and some young guy fell in love with you, and you were probably hurt by that divorce of your parents. All of which explains your first child. The two of you were not ready for life at 17 and probably had all kinds of financial problems."

"We had to file for bankruptcy," Erika sighed. "Divorce soon followed."

"Well, then you dated again, and some young guy falls in love with you again while you were probably hurting from your own divorce. All of which explains your second child. Only this time, my guess is, there was violence." Barley exposed the swelling and darkening under his left eye. "So, as you can see, it's all in the genes." Barley laughed, and then made a playful advance. "And the way that you fill out those jeans!"

"Anyway, I want you to know that I believe when a child is involved, that it is a lifetime commitment, and at least a 20-year commitment as a couple. I hope you know that I would never hurt you and will do my best to provide for you. This new trucking I'm about to begin should be the perfect compromise for me and for us. I get to keep my dream of being an independent trucker, and I also get to have a family, which I've been dreaming about for quite a while. I want to try this for 30 days to establish what income can be expected, and then buy a house for us that can be affordable with money left over. When the 30 days is up, we'll get married. I think it would be best if we just have a quiet ceremony and enjoy a nice honeymoon, or buy what we need, like a new car. Your truck is a project, and I'm no mechanic."

"And that yellow Rabbit you got in the truck deal is a stick shift." Erika shook her head. "I can't drive a stick." Erika then put her hand on Barley's forearm. "My divorce isn't final yet."

"What?"

"I haven't been able to give John Walter, my lawyer, his fee yet, and the divorce won't be final until then."

"What a lowlife!" Barley shouted. "You are trying to protect yourself from a violent, irresponsible, stalking idiot, and he holds it up for money." Barley pulled his checkbook out. "Pay the immoral son of a bitch tomorrow."

Barley picked up his truck on a Tuesday and was as excited as a kid getting his first bicycle. The Peterbilt had turned out absolutely beautiful. She looked better than a brand-new truck. The cut and buff made the jet-black color look like a show truck. The aluminum was glistening, and the added chrome just made the paint look deep. Barley was overflowing with pride and was thanking God for this chance at happiness. He showed the truck to Roy Bird at the office, and everyone there came out to look at her.

"Holy shit! You're going to pull an end dump with *that* truck! Wow!"

"I'll be ready to roll tomorrow," Barley proudly announced. "I'm having it lettered this afternoon. Can I pick my own truck number?"

"Wow! Damn, that's a pretty truck." Roy shook his head in disbelief. "Any number you want!"

"Seven seven seven," Barley stated. "Lucky sevens." He also would put Erika's name right on the front hood wind deflector—in chrome, of course.

Erika was impressed and excited to see this truck. She now felt at ease with herself. She could see that Barley was beside himself with joy and was convinced that they were doing the right thing for all involved in this destined meeting of two lovers.

Barley went to work and loved it. This was a real man's world. The operation was void of females, from the coke plant to the foundries and the coal mines. The group of owner/operators were cut from the same cloth as Barley: independent and proud of it. The loads only required occasional overnights (no more than three per week), and only on rare occasions would require two nights away in a row. (It was completely up to the driver whether or not he wanted to stay out more than one night, allowing for extra money earned.) Barley was continually being complimented on his truck and quickly made friends with the other drivers. He believed that this was going to work.

At the end of 30 days, Barley sat down to do some calculations and was delighted at the income. It wasn't that it would make them rich, only that he could confidently purchase a house and tell Erika that she would not have to work anymore. She could just raise those kids and get a dog, like she wanted.

Barley bought Erika an almost-new car of her choice, and the two of them set out to find a house. On the following Saturday, they found a brand-new, three-bedroom home outside of the city in a quiet, rural sub-division. It had been used as a model, and had a larger double lot on the corner of the main road to the complex and the entrance. "Plenty of room to make a truck parking space, and plenty of room for kids and dogs," Bar-ley chuckled. The payment would be within the limits he had laid out at the end of the 30 days. Barley left a deposit with the salesman, and the home-buying process began.

That evening, however, when they returned to Erika's apartment, Bar-ley sensed something was wrong with the Peterbilt. "Pull over next to her." Erika was driving the new Monte Carlo. Barley got out, entered the cab, and was angered as he realized that the truck had been broken into. Gone were the C.B. radio, the radar detector, the TV, and, he blurted, "Oh God, my music collection—my Heep! All gone!"

Barley got back into the car and said, "We probably should call the po-lice." Barley then looked directly into Erika's face. "They've taken my Heep and a lot more. Do you think your ex did it?" "Maybe, I wouldn't put it past him," Erika answered.

Two officers came and filled out a report. They wrote down Barley's suspicions about the ex. They questioned him at length about this "parking space" and how often and long this pretty truck sat there. Barley explained, and stated, "We're getting married and are trying to buy a house. I don't know how much longer I need to use this spot, but I hope it isn't long."

One more week went by, and Barley got two speeding tickets before replacing the C.B. radio and radar detector. He ran an extra load and ar-rived back on Saturday evening. He was very tired and slept late.

During the still of the darkest night of Barley's life, a shadowy figure walked up to the Peterbilt. He forced open the vent window and drove off in that truck of dreams. A dark Ford LTD with government plates followed a short distance behind.

On the following morning, Erika drove down to the store but stopped. She turned around and sped back to Barley. "The truck is gone. Did you park somewhere else last night?" Desperation filled her eyes.

Barley got up, pulled on some pants, and ran—barefooted and shirt-less. She was gone! Barley just collapsed onto the ground, and the shock hit like a lightning bolt. "My God, I know I don't have enough insurance to replace her."

And he knew right then and there that all of his hopes of a new life were gone—gone like the strength of Samson without his hair.

CHAPTER 15

Return to Fantasy

Hobbs was still in control, heading in a generally northern direction on the way to Barley's home, his home of a second chance at life. The emotion emitted by the Ruth memory of losing that first black Peterbilt generated a response of Hobbs inventorying the entire music collection to find a song that would combat that shock Barley had experienced so long ago. There wasn't any such song; there were only songs to make matters worse. The confused thoughts of duty and desire to get home versus the intense fear and dread of what he must face upon arriving, combined with those terrible memories that would follow naturally from the truck theft, convinced the Hobbs that Barley's Ruth needed nourishment—liquid nourishment. The safest place, a protective haven, would be a tavern. A two-lane highway would provide one even if it meant drifting a little out of route. The second small farm town had just the place, with an area near the grain elevator to park in the shadows of day's end.

As Barley walked toward the Defiant Lounge he could sense a familiarity with his own hometown, only this town had no impending threat of loss. The tavern was in an old turn-of-the-century building, and the interior was true to its 100-year history. Behind the bar was antique carved wood, with a large mirror that had reflected jolly good times for generations. A double row of spirits extended the full length of the mirror to the matched cabinets on each end. The bar's wooden rail had been worn smooth at intervals where the elbows and forearms of farmers and workingmen had leaned attentively into endless conversations. This place was a shanty Irishman's heaven.

The stools were lined up from the front curved corner, along the 24-foot straight, to the back curved corner. Barley found an open stool near the back corner on the straight—4 feet beyond the mirror and its liquor display.

The group of men drinking at the corner were all men 50 years of age and older. Barley listened avidly to these men bitching about government as if the talk were a symphony. He gradually joined in—subtly at first, until he was dominating the conversation with his opinions, and these men were listening as if he were playing the solo of Tchaikovsky's *Violin Concerto*.

"The government's involvement has not only destroyed the small family farm, but it [the government] is attacking the family itself." Barley was not arguing, but he was nearly approaching a speech: a speech based upon experience and an ever-growing thirst for information—information about the details behind the headlines and the liberal press agenda. He hadn't put any faith in the excuse "It's just about sex." He had read the entire Starr Report. He not only listened to Rush Limbaugh, but to PBS and other shows as far left as Diane Reem. He read newspapers daily, and most importantly he had read the Constitution—all of it. "The federal government has been passing laws and pushing legislation from the bench to bury the Constitution while taking an oath to defend it. And take note, the Constitution is not taught in school systems. How many of you here today have read the Constitution, or have been required in any of your schooling to know its details or its purpose? My guess is you've read only the Preamble." Barley was right, of course. No one there except Barley had read the Constitution, and more than a dozen men were involved in the conversation.

Opinions were offered, and Barley listened. One individual suggested that Barley did not love his country. "I beg to differ. I love all of this country, and most of all I love the principles of individual rights and freedom envisioned by those great men who created our government. However, some politicians crave power in a tyrannical way; they're elitists who pass laws on the common individual, trying to establish a class system with a judicial branch that makes unequal rulings based upon that class system."

"Yeah, remember O.J.? He got away with it by hiring that team of lawyers," an older man, angry at that trial's result, spouted off. "And them politicians can take payoffs from rich men to get laws passed that take American jobs away."

"Absolutely, but worse is the constant growth of government. People *used* to know that *anything* the government runs is all screwed up. All of their programs are filled with waste—waste because of the bureaucracy running the program, whatever it is. Now with this media push, the people, ordinary people, as individuals, are looking for the government to help them or solve their problems, which is ludicrous. One law established for WWII—withholding tax—created this whole mess. Withholding tax is allowing our government to become an absolute power."

"And, absolute power corrupts absolutely," a grizzled man in his late 50s offered. "Is that your assumption?"

"Absolutely!" Barley replied. "What two words go together better than *love* and *marriage*? Not *horse* and *carriage*, not in today's world. It's *politics* and *corruption*. We all know that, or we used to before this constant propaganda by the TV and liberal press. I believe the government learned two things as a result of WWII. One, people *will* accept taxes taken out of their paycheck before they can cash it, and two, women will be willing to enter the workforce. Thus, the government can take even more from the masses—the working-class people. That's why the government allows and promotes the degradation of the traditional family and traditional morals. If a woman would *want* to stay home and raise her kids, she is portrayed as a second-class ignorant."

"Yep, June Cleaver doesn't exist and never will again. And that damn TV always shows the man of the house as a buffoon. I think you're right; it has been calculated," the bartender chimed in.

The oldest man sitting with this group offered, "That's right; Rosie the Riveter did not go back to the home, at least not all of them did. A lot of men did not return from the war, and a lot who did looked to the younger girls for marriage; to girls who were closer in age to theirs when they left for the war. That was the start of it, I mean the beginnings of ..."

"Yes," Barley interrupted, "and all of this fuss about abortion is caused by the change in language and morals. Call it *choice* and the meaning is lost. What today's woman doesn't understand is that she has *lost* the right to choose, to choose to stay home. It all goes back to taxes."

"And the government doesn't tell you about the emotional side effects you'll have after that abortion they are promoting," said a nurse in her 40s, who had just joined this group of men who were reciting political views similar to her own. "The majority of women who have had an abortion say they never would again. It's something that the woman will never forget that she did. Many women develop post-abortion syndrome, even years later, and the relationship that conceived the child more often than not breaks up anyway. And what about that woman in the media who was pro-abortion but who has changed her tune now that she herself is pregnant? Having had children myself, I cannot understand how any woman, for any reason, could have a partial birth abortion when she's already experiencing kicking and other signs of another life from the person growing inside of her."

"Yes, it all goes back to taxes. The promotion of abortion promotes two wage earners in the family, producing more tax revenue," Barley repeated. "Family farms do not produce taxes, so the government passes laws that supposedly help the farmer, but instead the laws only help the corporate farmer. Anybody here question the dealings of Tyson Food and Bill Clinton when he was governor of Arkansas? And what the government is doing to the independent trucker is all-out war. First demonize and demoralize, then regulate out of existence. But, if you run a large trucking company, they pass laws and promote unfair competition to force the independent to give up. Except, because of fuel prices, the rigged foreign competition, and the knowledge of the soon-to-be-opened Mexican border, the devaluation of trucks has created a situation where the independent trucker has to file bankruptcy to quit, even if he has given up. And let me tell you, there is a scheme going on right now, by the government, to buy up all of these leftover trucks and send them to Mexico. Just think of it, if it is true. Taxpayers are going to buy trucks to send to Mexico to take away American jobs. This stuff goes on in all industries—all of it because of the unlimited flow of money created by withholding taxes. And the government will spend it on the most un-American projects. You guys just would not believe what was done to me, but I don't want to get into that right now. I'm wound up enough already!"

"I would just as soon have the government take taxes out of my check," a 30-something man said, who had joined this group halfway into the conversation. "I don't want to mess with sending taxes in, and I got back $1,700 in my tax return check this year."

"Do you have any idea what you make in a year? I mean, what you bring home?" Barley sighed.

"No, I just know I would never be able to save any money during the year, so I claim zero dependents to get a refund so I can buy something. My credit is shot."

"You're a sad case." Barley sighed again. "You've become a sheep, dependent on government because you can't take care of yourself. You are unable to accept responsibility for yourself. Very sad indeed." Barley then looked at the group. "I guess I better shut up before I get thrown out of here, but I'll tell you this. Many Americans are falling for *this* trap. The government is attacking all of our traditions and principles, and Americans just accept it. But not me; I will not be conquered. Not my heart, anyway. I've been beaten before, but there is something in the heart of a man, an individual, that cannot be conquered. I will not wear a seat belt."

"Here, here!" the oldest man of the gathering said. "I know just what you mean. And the Ten Commandments should be allowed to be displayed."

"One more thing," Barley explained. "The government is actively pushing its absolute power on the whole earth and all of its cultures. And just like the nomadic Indians of the Old West after the Civil War, these cultures will strike back. And like the symbol of government's absolute power of those days, General Armstrong Custer, a gaudy symbol, will be defeated. Of course, the *absolute power* was then put into force, and the American Indian was practically wiped out. There just is that *spirit* in the heart to fight back, against all odds, when your way of life is being taken away."

"Holy Jesus, I'm late for supper," the oldest man said, looking at his watch.

With that statement, many of the men got up to return to their homes. Barley began to relax, with his focus now turning to the row of liquor bottles in front of the mirror. His eyes drifted into the rows of glare.

The spots of glare blurred into a white line, and his thoughts returned to that moment of his life when he had realized that the black Peterbilt of dreams had been stolen ...

Erika helped Barley to his feet, and he made no attempt to hide his anguish. They walked back to the apartment to make the necessary calls, even though it was a Sunday morning. The police were called first, then the insurance company, and finally Roy Bird at Blend Trucking.

"Did you have a load?" Roy asked.

"No," Barley slurred. "I dropped the trailer empty at the coke plant."

"Well, let me know if there is anything I can do. I guess you won't be working until this mess gets resolved, but come on down when you can and update me." Roy was genuinely concerned, and his voice expressed it.

The insurance company had no one on duty, except a person who took minimal information and said that Barley would be contacted on Monday morning. "Be sure to notify the police and give them all of the information that they can use. Was there a trailer with freight involved?"

"No, just the tractor."

"Good, you don't need to bother with the federal authorities if there was no theft from an interstate shipment."

The police sent an officer to the apartment within 1 hour of the call, but Barley was curious about their lack of understanding of the gravity of the situation. Barley thought that the police should have arrived within minutes.

The interview was quite aloof and routine. The officer just wasn't listening to Barley's desperation.

"It's my dream truck. I mean, it's all that I have to provide for this family with. Shouldn't you be rushing to find it? It shouldn't be that hard to find. It's a huge, black beauty covered with chrome."

"Sorry Mr. Williams, but it has probably been gone for hours. It *has* been reported to the department and the state patrol, but this is Sunday. The detectives will be on it tomorrow. You have it insured, don't you?"

"Not enough, I'm sure of that," Barley pleaded.

He would not hear from the police detective for weeks.

The insurance representative called on Monday and informed Barley that a private detective agency would be coming by later that day. This interview would also seem strange. The private detective took all of the proper information with pictures of the tractor but seemed to suspect that Barley was involved in the theft somehow. Barley sensed this, and did his best to explain his desperate need to get back to work *with* that truck. He further explained all that he had done to it after the purchase. "It looks like, *and is,* a dream truck."

Barley was notified later in the week that even if the truck were re-covered, it most likely would be a total loss. Barley was stunned when told that the insurance company legally had 90 days to try to recover the unit before offering the final payoff. "And you must realize, Mr. Williams, you had a policy of minimal coverage."

In the weeks that followed, Barley withdrew into a worrisome wreck, unable to think out what he should do, until Erika came to him just before Christmas to say, "Barley, I'm pregnant. What are we going to do?"

Worry became paranoia, and Barley was near a breakdown. He was a trapped and wounded animal. He wanted—so much he wanted—to have this life with Erika. But the dream was now a nightmare. "I'll find a way, somehow," he told her.

Barley called to cancel the house deal. The credit cards were used up. Further shock set in when the truck finance company notified him that even though the truck was stolen, he was still responsible for the payments. He was already two payments behind. Barley began calling the police twice daily and pleaded with the insurance company for a settlement.

Just after the first of January 1983, the insurance company's private detective contacted Barley to inform him that the police had forced an end to his investigation. "They must know where the truck is, but they're not giving up any information. I doubt that there is much left of your truck. Erie Insurance will settle with you soon. Hang in there, guy."

The police detective arrived at the door in mid January with photos of the Peterbilt. It had been completely stripped; engine, transmission, wheels, sleeper, bumper, and even the seats were all gone. "Do you want it back, what's left?" the detective asked in a matter-of-fact tone.

"No, for Christ's sake, haven't I made it desperately clear to you people? I have to get back to work. I'm financially ruined. I . . ."

The detective interrupted, "The prosecutor's office will be contacting you soon. You will be needed to testify. Don't worry, we have a good, tough prosecutor, and he tells me that he is going to get you restitution."

"What does that mean?" Barley was nearly begging.

"Just contact the prosecutor's office after you've seen your insurance people." Again the detective sounded aloof.

The final settlement was a disaster. The total payoff was for $4,000 less than Barley owed on the tractor, not to mention the loss of all of the improvements, equipment, and every single personal possession Barley owned.

The prosecutor's office was in the main city and county building housing the police, all of the courtrooms, and the administration offices. Its 27-story structure was one of the tallest in the skyline of Capital City.

Barley entered this building with a hopeless outlook on life.

A young man introduced himself as an assistant to the prosecutor and gave Barley copies of the truck theft case, including the police report. Barley read the report and nearly exploded in a violent rage! "You mean that the police watched my dream truck be stolen, stripped of parts, and destroyed?"

The report stated that the police were watching from the moment the truck was broken into. They followed the truck as it was being driven away and had an informant at the strip shop.

"Calm down, please, Mr. Williams. This is just police and detective work. There has been an operation of stealing trucks in this area that we needed to bust. Calm down. We're going to get you *RESTITUTION*. All you have to do is testify each time we bring in one of the criminals."

Barley was now in tears and falling apart. "What is restitution? It sounds like a $10 lawyer word. Give me a $5 definition."

"*Restitution,*" the assistant reassured, "is payment of your damages, and your damages will be automatically tripled."

Barley sat there defeated and shook his head. "I don't think I could get myself out of this mess for $100,000."

"If it's $100,000, you'll get $300,000." The assistant then showed Barley where he wanted signatures.

With his too-small payoff check and this promise from the prosecutor's office, Barley headed for the truck dealer. The truck finance company had an office right in the dealership. The salesman just shook his head. "Barley, I'm afraid you're probably just out of luck, but let's go upstairs and talk to the money people."

A deal was made—an impossible deal based on the promise of restitution. To allow Barley to return to work, a used truck was offered if Barley would agree to pay for the Peterbilt.

"But I'm completely broke," Barley pleaded. "I have no money to buy a wet kit or even to buy fuel."

Salesman George offered a truck already equipped and $1,000 cash to get Barley going, but the finances would dictate the deal. Barley agreed without even seeing the truck—he was so desperate to get back to work and keep the dream alive. His desire was to have a chance at life with Erika by providing for her and her family.

"Well, she doesn't look like much, but it's ready to go for the type of operation you were in when your truck was stolen." Salesman George had no clue on how to prepare Barley for what he had just agreed to.

The truck was an old, day-cab (i.e., no sleeper) Kenworth that had long ago passed 1 million miles, and it looked like it—faded blue with ugly stripes.

"Punishment enough for my own stupidity," Barley shrugged . . .

. . . "Hey stupid! Wake up, you old fart." A young, tall, loud man sneered as he shook Barley's left shoulder.

Barley came out of his liquor-bottle glare trance and realized that the Defiant Lounge was now filled with a new crowd of faces, all under 40. "Sorry, just lost in thought young man."

"That'll be 'sir' from you," the loudmouth said as he cocked his head, suggesting he was about to confront Barley with some challenge.

Barley's muscles tightened, and he grabbed the three-quarters full mug of beer in front of him and downed it with one drink. He noticed that the beer had gotten a little warm. "I'll just move down to the end of the bar and stay out of your way." Barley stood up intending to show his size, and the young man backed away.

Barley watched this man carefully and quickly learned that his name was Dan. Dan was drinking whiskey and was an obvious bully. He was loaded, obnoxious, and bothering anyone who caught his eye. Dan seemed to be looking for respect that he had no idea how to earn.

Three cold draughts later, Barley had had enough and asked the bartender, "Do we have to put up with this asshole?"

The bartender had listened to and joined in the afternoon's conversation. He was at ease with Barley, but he just looked at Barley and shook his head while holding up one hand. Barley didn't say more, as he could see a bit of fear and dread in the bartender's face.

Dan had heard Barley. He walked by saying, "I'm going to take a leak, and you better leave before I get back."

The bartender quickly told Barley that Dan was a local cop, a deputy, and that whiskey just made him worse. "He's busted most of my best customers. Be careful."

Dan came out of the bathroom and stood in front of Barley, as Barley rotated the stool to face him. "You're a damn truck driver; that's your truck out back, isn't it?"

"And you are a Clinton cop, one of the 'wanna-bes' of his 100,000 new cops. You're probably part-time, thank God, now that the federal money is drying up on that project." Barley was now just as ready as Dan.

Dan pointed to the door.

"It's obvious that this place isn't big enough for the both of us," Barley responded using his best John Wayne voice. "But I'll tell you what. How about we arm wrestle for it? Loser leaves, and I'll bet a million dollars that I'll take you!"

"You're on, old man."

As they lined up across the bar, other people started to notice. A young man with a Cubs ball hat stated, "I've got $20 on the truck driver."

Three others in the bar offered $10, all on Barley. This angered Dan, and the bartender said he would cover the $50 by betting on the deputy.

Barley wanted this bad. He had arm wrestled countless times as a young man, and sized up his opponent.

Dan was 25 years younger, and taller but slimmer. He looked athletic, and Barley figured that he probably worked out on weights. Barley knew that the young man would get the jump on him.

The bartender said "Go," and Barley was right. Dan had him halfway down before he could recover. Barley held, and his mind searched for stimulus. Barley thought about all of the years of being on the reluctant end of some of the worst frustrations of his life, caused by police. This Dan was like many young cops he had conflicted with. Barley was getting quite red in the face and was breathing heavy, sucking up oxygen to gather strength. He thought of those who were in that damned city county building 20 years ago, and then he made his push. Barley could hear the cheers as he brought Deputy Dan's arm back to upright. Barley could feel the anger in the young man's effort, but Barley held him there straight up.

"Get him! Come on old man, get him!" Barley heard a woman's voice from the other side of the bar.

He didn't dare to look; he must concentrate.

With all that he had in him, Barley made his final effort, and Dan's arm moved down nearly halfway. Barley could hear yells of "Yes!" and "Yahoo!"

He was puffing hard, trying to finish that loud deputy off, when "*AAAAHCH,*" something pulled in Barley's elbow.

Deputy Dan pulled right through and slammed Barley's arm down hard onto the bar. No one in the bar spoke. Dan was angered more.

Barley rubbed his injured elbow and then chugged down his beer. He pulled out his wallet and laid down a commemorative Ronald Reagan $1 million bill. Barley then looked at the group closest to the match. "Damn, I'm sorry. I guess youth will be served."

With that, Barley walked out and got into his bunk in the Peterbilt. He would sleep through sunrise and into mid morning.

When Barley arose, he knew that there was no place nearby to get breakfast, so he just started the motor and headed east out of town. His elbow ached, but he was sure that no permanent damage had been done.

He had traveled less than 3 miles on the two-lane road when the flashing lights caught his eye in the shoulder view. He knew he hadn't done anything wrong and was not speeding. What could this cop want?

Barley pulled over to the side, but the shoulder was not wide enough to get the rig off the road. The police car was approximately 30 feet behind the trailer and was not completely off the road either.

As soon as Barley recognized that this was the same man—Deputy Dan—he felt pain, a stabbing, explosive pain coming from deep inside his skull. Barley was overwhelmed, leaned forward, and closed his eyes. Hobbs took control, scanning for an opening—an escape.

The opportunity came as the young deputy was still sitting in the police car's driver's seat: an oncoming cement-mixer truck. Hobbs rocked his head to judge the timing and then put the gearshift into high-range reverse. While releasing the clutch pedal, Hobbs gave the wheel a three-quarter turn to the right, sending the trailer into the passenger side of Deputy Dan's front grill.

The impact spun the car directly into the path of the cement-mixer truck, with the police car driver's side door being struck by the overhanging steel bumper just above the bottom of the window. Hobbs observed the large, wide eyes of terror in the instant before the young deputy's death. The driver of the cement mixer hadn't even had time to hit his brakes.

Hobbs casually put the Peterbilt back into forward gears and disappeared into the eastbound wooded two lane. He then doubled back and to the north until connecting with Highway 421, not stopping until reaching a truck stop at the intersection of Interstate 194 near Gary, Indiana.

There was now a witness. The cement-mixer driver was uninjured. He was almost in shock, but uninjured.

CHAPTER 16

I'll Keep on Trying

Linda Wright and her team were the first to arrive, via helicopter, and she had footage of the accident scene and the mangled remains of the local police car. Her report already was airing on the local area TV station when Arnie Benson and his investigators arrived to compile the analysis.

Bill Jackson drove directly to the hospital, where Hugh Cauley, the cement-mixer truck driver, was being held and counseled. Hugh also had been given a shot of Valium to calm him down.

When the attending physician gave Bill Jackson permission, he began his interview as casually and reassuringly as he could. Then Bill asked the most important question, before asking Hugh Cauley to relive the details of the crash: "Can you describe the truck?"

"It was a Peterbilt, a fancy brand-new one," Hugh offered. "I noticed it just before the son of a bitch backed into the cop car, sending it right in front of me." Hugh Cauley's voice began to break up. "I didn't even have time to hit the brakes. I . . ."

Bill stopped him with as soothing a voice as he could. "I just need you to tell me what the truck looked like. There was nothing you could have done. Did you see any markings, door signs, or company names on the trailer? What model and color of Peterbilt was it, and what type of trailer—refer?"

"It happened so fast. It was a Peterbilt. I saw the emblem and grill," Hugh replied sternly.

Arnie Benson then entered the room. Bill introduced him as the re-gional director of D.O.T. Hugh Cauley looked down as if he didn't want to make eye contact with the D.O.T. man. Bill said softly, "Go on Hugh, just tell us what you saw of that truck."

"Okay, like I said, it was a fancy new Peterbilt. It looked like it had just left the showroom. I saw the emblem, the Peterbilt emblem, and the grill. It was really shiny, with a lot of chrome. I don't remember any markings or company names. The trailer was white, but I don't know if it was a refer or just a box."

"And what color was the Peterbilt? Did you see what model type?" Bill asked again, gently.

"I'm not sure if it was a 379 or a 377, but it was a conventional, with the stand-up sleeper behind it."

"And the color?" Bill again asked.

"I dunno," Hugh said, looking down.

Arnie Benson was having none of this. He was too close to being a patrol officer, and his kind was being killed. He butted in with an angry tone, "How the hell can you not know the color of the damn thing?"

"I guess it doesn't matter anymore. But I don't want to get anyone in trouble. I plead the fifth. Ah . . ."

"You're not in trouble, Mr. Cauley, and you're not going to get anyone in trouble for telling us what color that truck was, trust me," Bill reassured.

"I'm color-blind, sir. I'm sorry."

Arnie then demanded, "How did you get your CDL? You do have a CDL, don't you?" (A CDL is a commercial driver's license as mandated by the Commercial Motor Vehicle Safety Act of 1986.)

"My doc, my doctor knew I needed the job, and I just drive that mixer here in this county. He said it's a dumb law."

"Okay, Mr. Cauley, don't worry. You're all right," Bill said kindly, as he motioned to Arnie for the two of them to leave the room.

"We didn't get much," Arnie shrugged. "You think this is the same guy as Nebraska and Michigan?"

"Yes, it fits my profile," Bill acknowledged.

"Okay then, we'll have the research people list all Peterbilts of 379 and 377 models, registered by state, and trace as many as we can—process of elimination. That mixer driver said it looked brand new, but I think we better start by going back 5 years," Arnie suggested.

"Yeah, some of these drivers love their trucks and keep them looking good. I sure wish we had a company name, though." Bill shook his head. "At least it's a start."

Linda Wright was updated privately, as had been arranged for in the secret deal that stopped any lawsuits from being brought by Azmath's lawyer. The large money settlement was hush money paid jointly by the TV network and the government.

Linda had survived that mistake and was becoming a nationally recognized face, a celebrity. She was replacing her thirst for vengeance with a thirst for this status; the celebrity status created by the Road Rogue name she had coined. Linda Wright also was becoming curious; it was the instinctive curiosity of a reporter to understand why—what caused this monster.

Curious, too, was the nation—the C.B. chatter of truckers, the talk radio world, and the newspaper editorials. The Long Riders were in Nashville, Tennessee, at a recording studio, putting the final touches on a song. It started with a low guitar like an old Johnny Cash tune.

Running with the Road Rogue
Rolling into the night...
We're tired of being hassled
And watched at every turn.
Running with the Road Rogue ...

A legend had been born, and it was growing every day with something of a Billy the Kid appeal.

As the government turned up the search at weigh stations and portable scale inspections, drivers being delayed turned up the resentment. Loads were late and incidents occurred. Investigation agents were flying all over. Soon copycats would surface. Frustrated men would erupt ...

Barley had stopped at the small truck stop on 421 and 194 only to grab a bite to eat and then to continue on. Hobbs had regressed into the unaware, and Barley was feeling the pain in his right elbow along with a terrible ache in his lower back. He had tried too hard to win that arm-wrestling match and was angry that he had aggravated an old injury in his lower back. He had no memory of what had happened earlier with the cement mixer.

Barley began to lapse into a memory of how his back was injured, but then he shook off those thoughts with, "I know I need to walk ... to walk off this pain, or my back will go into spasms that could lay me up."

Barley pulled off the interstate and parked at a Speedway mini truck stop. He was in a small town, and he walked slowly toward the main street area. Nothing in this little downtown interested him. He just needed to walk.

A sign pointed east that read Village Park. Barley headed in that direction, trying to pick up the pace to force his lower back muscles to align and relieve the pain.

The park was small, with a swing set, a little league ball yard, and a few picnic tables. Barley sat down at the table closest to the road.

Across the street was a semi tractor parked in the driveway of a cute Cape Cod bungalow, with two young girls playing in the front yard. A young man, probably in his late 20s, was finishing washing his Freightliner. Barley sat watching this wholesome scene with an uplifted spirit.

The young man opened the driver's side box and pulled out a dairy crate. He put his polishing kit on the ground near the passenger's side front wheel. He turned the crate over and began the tedious task of polishing his aluminum wheels.

Barley had done the same countless times, but this was different. Such a wonderful scene—a young man polishing his dream with pride while his two daughters, one about four and one a toddler, played in front of this lovely, well-kept home. Most likely, the mom was inside preparing supper.

Barley's left eye watered a little as he got caught up in the emotion of this picture of America. Barley looked skyward and said with an audible whisper, "Thank you, Lord. Thank you for letting me see this. To know that this can still happen in America. That it is still possible. Thank you."

Barley looked back across the street as the young man stood up, looked at his own handiwork, and then eyed over his machine. He turned and smiled at his two daughters with love. He moved the dairy crate to the front of his fuel tank and started again, polishing the tank in 1-foot-diameter sections.

And then they came—a two-tone brown sheriff car with two officers followed by a large tow truck. The sheriff car stopped in the road in front of the yard with the two little girls playing. The tow truck stopped on the other side of the driveway, with its nose partially blocking the driveway. The young man rose off his dairy crate and planted his feet about shoulder width apart, knuckles flexing, and his jaw setting. Both of the officers exited the car, with one standing near the front at the curb, hand near his pistol in a show of force and authority. The other handed the repossession papers to the young man and motioned to the tow-truck driver. The tow truck moved into position, and its driver hooked up quickly. The two little girls were crying, with the oldest repeating, "Daddy, Daddy, what they doing? Daddy!"

The youngest just wailed away until their mother came out, apron on, and picked up the toddler and held her on her shoulder. She took the older girl by the hand and went back inside. The young man just stood there, left hand holding the papers, right hand in a clenched fist around his polishing rag. With a nod, the tow truck and its captured prey drove off. Convinced that no fight was left in the young man, the two officers got back into their car, and they drove off.

The young man sat back down on his stolen dairy crate, putting his elbows on his knees and his face in his hands. Barley tried to prepare himself for what he knew would come next—the sickening sound of a defeated man weeping. From across the street, Barley cried with him and for him, wanting somehow to console. And finally the young man's wife, who somehow knew he had cried enough, came outside and gently put her hand on her husband's slumping shoulders. "The children are waiting for you. Please come inside. Supper is ready."

Barley stood up and began walking back to his truck, saying aloud, "Yes, thank you Lord for showing me this scene. This scene can still happen in America. It happens every day. Many thousands have lost their dreams because of the government's attack on the individual. By next week that man will be driving a company truck somewhere with no pride, and the government will get their damn withholding taxes. Government just can't let a common man use the tax breaks or write-offs of the rich man. No, they have to get their taxes from the workingman before he is paid. I think I remember reading somewhere that one of the sins that cry out to heaven for vengeance is to rob the workingman of his wages . . ."

[I (the author) am the absolute power within the pages of this world, and I am dictating that you (the individual who has entered into my world) must stop reading. If you read on, you are subject to penalty and fine. The absolute power of the federal government passed a law that requires a truck driver to stop after driving 10 hours. The driver must take an 8-hour break. The government knows best. Of course, the law was written long ago, before freeways and when driving a truck required huge forearms (like Barley Bill has).

A driver heading west from Michigan to Wisconsin must drive through Chicago, but his 10 hours are used up in Gary, Indiana. He wants to push on, maybe to his home. Just another 45 minutes and he can miss the rush-hour traffic. Thus the dilemma; go on break the law (subject to penalty, fine, and shutdown), or wait 8 hours and then fight through 4 hours of hellish frustration. Only this rush hour is not just typical; federal highway funds are at stake (i.e., your dollars, extracted in withholding taxes). The governor and the mayor are both eyeing that huge amount of cash. The money must be appropriated. The governor has control. The mayor fights back by shutting down half of the highway lanes available, and only half of the usual number of tollway workers are called in. The result is what the military calls a cluster fuck. People respond with rage, both physical and political. With total disregard for the common individual caught in the mess, the mayor wins the lion's share of the prize. He will win reelection, because he has delivered for the city. A few individuals might even die as a result of the rage, delay, and frustration that was caused.

And in Detroit, a snowstorm hits. The mayor orders the snowplow trucks to stay parked. The governor resists the blatant attempt to win the money prize. Another cluster fuck is created. Individuals die.

This is how the government operates. This struggle for appropriation money is over 25 cents of each dollar extracted from Americans through withholding tax. The rest of the money stays in Washington s bureaucracy.

I (again the author), therefore, as the supreme absolute power of this world, command that you stop reading. What lies ahead is a Chicago rush hour of hell that you should prepare yourself for. I know best!

To prepare, while on your 8-hour break, you should take a ride. Drive if you can, and listen to one song. It is a long song *not* written as a hard rocker. The song is written as if it were a symphony with several distinct movements. The powerful poetry of its words perfectly describe the anguish of the human heart fighting a battle of emotion, ranging from love and duty, to pain and angry hate. Its music includes a heavenly chorus and a cry from hell. The song is "Paradise/The Spell" by Uriah Heep, written by Ken Hensley. You will find it on side two of "Demons and Wizards" or on the re-mastered 30-song collection "Classic Heep, An Anthology". However, you probably will not be able to find it at all, certainly not at your local Wal-Mart. You *will* find mountains of garbage rock and roll with mindless lyrics, but no Heep. Why?

Uriah Heep was popular for a short time (in America). The original band with singer David Byron produced nine albums of original music, with an additional Best Of and a Live album, and finally the classic Anthology. But you won't find their music easily. It was controversial. The music was considered mesmerizing and hypnotic, the lead singer was described as a dictator, they were very popular in Germany, and so on.

"Paradise/The Spell" is not my favorite song; it is too painful. But it is the world's greatest song. I will hear no argument! And it best describes the emotion of Barley Bill's world of his third million miles.]

CHAPTER 17

"Paradise/The Spell"

Watching the repossession of the young family's truck was dominating Barley's thoughts as he climbed back into his cab and fired up the motor. At first he longed to get home as quickly as he could. The Ruth ego could drive home in less than 4 hours, but the Hobbs of him was affected by the turmoil of emotion that was created from that scene. Barley had cried with that man, feeling that defeat as if it were his own. The dread of what he would face at home threatened the Hobbs. This separate thinking entity was growing in strength daily. Hobbs was extending his presence beyond the world behind the wheel, beyond just protecting. Hobbs was becoming defensive of his own existence. If Barley went home to lose his truck, Hobbs would have no life, no existence. In less than 30 miles, with the heavenly chorus of "Paradise/The Spell" capturing Barley's ever-weakening conscious mind, Hobbs took control. Hobbs exited the freeway, turned left, crossed the overpass, and reentered the freeway heading west.

Barley was convinced by Hobbs that this was his last ride. Why not just go around Lake Michigan through Wisconsin and see the Upper Peninsula? He could go home from the north. Just one last ride. Barley drifted back in time, back to accepting his fate with that old, ugly, worn-out Kenworth day cab ...

The old, blue day cab wasn't much, but if he could just survive with it until he got his restitution. That is how Barley would explain it to Erika. "All will be okay. I'll truck us out of this mess!"

Barley used $400 of the cash to rent a house in the country 25 miles outside of Capital City. The house was in the adjacent county west. Erika's pregnancy was beginning to show. A justice of the peace married them in a small office at the county courthouse. A limited gathering was arranged at the house, with just a few friends of Erika's and Barley's brother. Allen was 3 years older but looked much younger. The two of them walked out back to see this new truck. Allen couldn't say much; he didn't have to.

"There is no way I can make this work," Barley sighed. "Unless I get this restitution money, I'm finished!" Barley then tried to put on a more optimistic face. "You're looking good, Allen."

"You, too," Allen replied, while thinking that he had never seen his adventurous brother look worse.

Barley was in so much financial trouble that he was possessed into working beyond reason. The loads of Blend Trucking's operation were varied, with 500-mile maximum one-way hauls, to short hauls across town. Barley would take the long ones whenever possible, but he also would take short runs rather than lay down while waiting for the next long run available. The truck had no sleeper, anyway. Barley would drive beyond exhaustion, then crash on the steering wheel until discomfort forced him to wake up.

The loads all paid by the ton. Barley quickly used a trick of leaving one axle off of the weighing scale at both the tare and gross weighings, allowing him to have a legal ticket while hauling a few extra tons on each load. Of course, he was running overweight and would have to dodge all of the scales (government weigh stations). He just was absolute in his determination to save this dream of having a life with this newly formed family. The stress of the overworking, worrying, and taking chances was clouding his mind.

The prosecutor's office was moving on bringing those involved in the theft to trial, but it would be a slow process. The plan was to bring in the low-level criminals to cut deals for testimony against those higher in the crime ring of the truck-stripping operation. There would be no restitution from the first trials, Barley had been informed. "We have to get to the big boys. Just be patient and come to court when we need your testimony."

Each time, however, Barley would lose a day's work and then attempt to drive all night to make up for it. Barley began complaining and pleading with the prosecutor's office about his plight. "I can't hang on much longer. Don't you guys understand?"

The newspaper sure didn't. Barley went to the first trial wanting to vent some hate—hate for anyone who had contributed to his demise— but that first trial only showed Barley a tall, thin, black man with tombstones in his eyes (Reference: "The Pusher" by Hoyt Axton). The newspaper, however, reported a $75,000 judgment for Barley. They did not report that it was not collectible. The prosecutor gained political clout.

"Who was this guy, the prosecutor?" Barley would question. He was never in sight. Only subordinates were around in cheap suits. Frustration grew.

Weeks became months. Along the way, the old blue Kenworth kept breaking down. She was well past her prime and was now being pushed beyond her limits by this possessed driver, hell bent on trucking himself out of financial disaster. By June, Barley had renegotiated the loan contract twice (for transmission failure and pinion gear). Each time he had to report on the progress of restitution. The loan company was now way out on a limb. This old Kenworth represented only a small fraction of the loan.

The loan officer was lending upon the reputation of Barley's past and upon the hope of a final settlement that would truly restore his formerly solid customer.

By using some clever financial juggling, Barley was able to convince another loan officer that a small, three-bedroom home in a subdivision of homes of similar build was affordable. Again the promise of restitution would allow for completion of the deal. This house would be ready and finalized close to the due date Erika was given.

The old blue Kenworth had provided time—time to put the house deal together and time to use its cash flow to survive. This survival though, had caused great deterioration in Barley's health. He had simply pushed too hard without sleep. He wasn't thinking clearly. With less than 2 weeks before being able to take possession and move into the house, the old Kenworth died. Its motor sent oil and water out the sides of its block. Erika arranged for the family to move into her grandmother's house until they could move into their own house. Barley made yet another deal on a truck. It was a cab-over Peterbilt that did not exist. Actually, it was a truck made of components from wrecked trucks. The cab was a 1978. The rest, well, it didn't matter. At least it had a sleeper and some new paint. Barley could have just a little pride in it. It would be a project that would take 2 weeks to complete, including removing the wet kit from the old blue Kenworth.

A daughter was born, Katherine Rose, 1 week before the family could move into the house. Barley was now a proud father, but pride had to be swallowed before Erika and the baby could leave the hospital. There was no money, no insurance, and not much hope of ever being able to pay the bill, unless the hospital could wait for restitution.

The loan officer of this put-together Peterbilt was as kind as he could be, but he had to say it: "Mr. Williams, this is as far as we can go. You now owe, well, it doesn't matter. You better hope you get your money soon."

Barley called to report his status, his plight, to the prosecutor's office. "I don't have much time left. Please get to the real settlement."

On paper and in the newspaper, Barley was getting restitution. On paper and in the credit report, Barley was getting destitution. On toilet paper, he was passing blood.

Barley had hated every minute spent in the old blue Kenworth and was so ashamed of his financial failure. His heart was filling with anger, frustration, and worry, and his resentment of the unseen prosecutor grew with each passing day. Why hadn't this man even met Barley? Was he so important that he could not even offer some explanation of what was happening? Barley began to understand that he was being used and violated, as if he were being raped of self-respect by a man who was representing those whose job it is to protect and to serve.

The "component" Peterbilt offered a little hope. To an uninformed eye, she looked pretty good. Erika's spirits were lifted, as were Barley's. If he could just get a year out of this truck, things would be better. Surely restitution would arrive soon. Barley even received a couple of "Not bad" compliments from the men at work.

Of course, holding that brand new baby girl was heavenly. Precious and perfect, Barley could only think of how important it was that he become financially stable again. Barley pulled on, dragging the anchor of his debt across an ocean floor with his titanic dream and determination.

In the first 30 days, Barley had pulled more loads and had run more miles than any of the other men of the operation had in 6 weeks, and more than most had pulled in 2 months. Barley spread the money out the best that he could. All creditors got something. It was a start, a glimpse of what life would have been for Erika and Barley had the black Peterbilt not been taken. Barley and Erika felt a moment of calm.

The moment of calm, healing peace brought them together on a Sunday evening of love and passion as they had not had in months, long months of worry, stress, and struggle. Erika did not want the night to end. "Won't you stay here with me just a little while longer?" she asked, her voice and eyes flush with love that had been taken, taken by an unseen enemy.

Barley sighed from deep within, "You are beauty; I am burden. For a beast of burden not to be working at sunrise would be like a beauty refusing a rose from God Himself. I must go."

The transmission gave out later that day. Barley had sent out every available dollar to the list of creditors. He couldn't possibly negotiate the contract. He called Roy Bird with the news. "I'm afraid it's over. There is just nothing left to fix it."

Roy Bird called back. "Damn it! I don't want to lose you. You've worked harder than anyone I've ever had. We have a mechanic here who is a transmission specialist. He'll fix it, and the company will take the repair bill out of your weekly settlements, $200 a week. Now get down here, and you can use the old dinosaur to pull loads until the damn transmission is rebuilt."

This was another bitter pill for Barley to swallow. But his pride in being independent was a wounded soldier now, and he jumped at the chance. Barley just had to laugh at what he was going to drive. This would be the first truck he would drive that wasn't his, but he had to admire it for what it was—a 1967 Autocar, with a four-by-four (i.e., two gearshifts) transmission and a Cummings motor of unknown origin, unknown horsepower, and unknown miles. "I think I'll rather enjoy this, but I don't think you should send me too far away."

Barley did enjoy working the four-by-four, even though he could see the ground rolling by (i.e., there was no boot covering the opening in the floor for the two gearshifts). It *was* a dinosaur. It roared through the floor and rattled everywhere. She died before the first day ended. Luckily, Barley was only across town. He returned home to spend some quality family time while a rebuilt transmission was found and installed in the component Peterbilt.

Barley returned to the road as determined as he had ever been, "To truck myself out of this mess."

The week brought only disappointment from the prosecutor's office. He pulled a load up to Michigan, with a delivery in Ludington at its foundry. Autumn colors were in their glory as he rolled on the smooth highway through the landscape of beautiful western Michigan. Ludington is such a picturesque town. His delivery was near the Great Reservoir Project, a 5-mile long, 900-foot (above sea level) tall swimming pool that is used to generate electricity. The principle is to fill the pool from Lake Michigan, then drain it, producing electricity in peak usage periods.

Barley pulled over onto the parking lot and walked the paved pathway to the observation booth on top of the rim. The view is one of the most awe-inspiring comparisons available in the world. God made the great lake in His time, and man made this marvel of a swimming pool to use God's gift for man's time. "I wonder why man can't use this technology in tune with God's nature? Why not drop a dam across the Golden Gate and use San Francisco's Bay to generate electricity by using the tides," Barley pondered. "That's it! Maybe that's my get-rich quick scheme." He chuckled at the thought.

The reload was not available until the following day, and it was on the other side of the state. "Great, a chance to see the folks and maybe even Earl," Barley planned. Later, in the early evening hours, Barley and Earl were guzzling draught beer at a local tavern. Reminiscing about their road adventures brought roaring laughter of the kind Barley hadn't felt since before his July morning. It was so good to laugh once again. With a gripping handshake and a serious tone, Barley said good-bye with a finality that made Earl wonder if he would ever see the world's greatest truck driver again.

The motor of the component Peterbilt died with a loud metal-against-metal moan just north of Capital City on that return trip. The Frankenstein's monster carcass was towed into the dealer for its last rites, and no new deal was possible. Barley broke the news to Erika. "It's over. I can't go further into debt. No one believes in the restitution anymore."

Erika's response took Barley by surprise. She was crying, but with anger—anger at Barley. "You've given up! You've given up the dream!"

"I have no choice. I'll just drive a truck for someone else until ..." Barley was stopped in midsentence.

"I don't want to hear it—that WORD again," Erika nearly shouted. The downward spiral of her and Barley's life was beginning to fracture her once-solid belief that love is all you need.

Barley was out looking for work on the second day after giving up as an owner/operator. He first called the list (creditors) and then pleaded with the prosecutor's office. There was no news or estimation of settlement yet.

Barley quickly learned how damaging the speeding tickets were to his driving record. Getting a driving job was nearly impossible. Although there were no serious violations (he had never been caught above 15 miles per hour over 55), the habitual traffic offender law had caused many of the best drivers to be forced into new trades, because insurance companies forced driver-record standards onto trucking firms. Barley ended up taking a driving job with an otherwise-respectable businessman who owned a few extra trucks not used in his main business. It was as close to being an owner/operator as Barley could find. He would earn 25 percent of whatever revenue he could generate in a flatbed operation that the tractor was leased to.

"What a truck," he remarked sarcastically.

It was an F model Mack. Barley would quickly learn what the F stood for. A steel cabover with only five forward gears, this tractor was completely worn out, trashed (used by many drivers), and had absolutely no class.

The first load began in Cleveland with delivery of steel pipe in Minneapolis, Minnesota. It was early December 1983, and a frigid cold front swept in from the Arctic. There was some type of electrical problem in the Mack, and the heater would not work. Barley could not track down the problem. The owner would not allow Barley to take the truck into a repair shop. "Just get it back to the yard, and I'll have it fixed here," the owner said.

The owner, Bob Thompson, was unwilling to pay for any road repairs. He had given Barley a sheet of paper with instructions listed including "No road repairs" and "Do not cross weigh stations." Barley nearly froze to death and had to scrape frost off the inside of the windshield continuously to be able to see enough to drive. The cold front produced temperatures below zero for several days. When Barley returned to the yard, he was sick from the exposure to the cold and had to take 3 days off to recover. Bob Thompson repaired the heating unit himself. It was a cobble job, but the heater did work. There was a terrible smell, though, generated each time the heater was turned on.

While on a run from Pennsylvania to Chicago, the tractor just shut off on the freeway near Toledo, Ohio. It was still terribly cold, and Barley had stayed up long hours in a vain attempt to make some money. Nothing would work. The electrical system had failed completely. The truck was on an exit ramp off the driving lane, and Barley just had to lie down and gather himself before walking to a phone. That terrible smell seemed worse, and Barley luckily noticed a flicker of flame in the right-side mirror. He got out of the cab only moments before the old F model Mack burst into flames.

Barley marveled at the intensity of the fire. The fire department's men and equipment had no effect. Every nonsteel part of that old truck burned away, including the tires.

Bob Thompson did not want to reimburse for the bus ticket home.

Christmas for the Williams family was as humble as its origin. Just after the holiday, Barley was called by the prosecutor's office. "We are about to charge one of the perpetrators who has money. You will need to be ready to testify when we go to court. We will notify you of the date."

Barley responded with anger at the further delays, and said, "Do you people even understand what my family's Christmas was like? Instead of greeting cards, all we have are threatening letters from creditors and constant phone calls."

Bob Thompson offered Barley another truck. "Just run this one until I get my insurance money from the fire."

It was an 11-year-old cab-over White Freightliner.

"My God, it has an old 71 series Detroit. I didn't know there were any of these left on the road," exclaimed Barley. "Listen, 25 percent of nothing is nothing. I can't make you or me any money in a junk truck."

Bob Thompson repeated, "Just until I get my insurance money."

Barley took the truck and attempted to make some money, but that old Detroit kept losing its prime (i.e., losing fuel flow). It was extremely frustrating. Each time the prime was lost, the cab would have to be jacked up, and the fuel filters had to be removed and dipped in diesel.

On a crisp Monday morning in mid January 1984, Barley had Erika drive him to the yard to make another run with this old White Freightliner. He kissed Erika good-bye and said, "I'll probably stay out 2 to 3 weeks to earn as much as I can, but I'll need you to notify me as soon as a court date is decided on."

The truck would not start. Barley was furious and frustrated. He jacked the cab to get at the filters but did not put the safety bar in place. The hydraulic line had a hole. Barley did not notice the cab settling back down until it reached his back. He tried to get out, but his coveralls caught on something, and it was then too late. He was pinned. The side of the cab's metal began crumpling as the 3,000-pound cab settled onto Barley's back.

He was pinned with his chest on the fuel tank, feet on the ground, with his arms in a useless position for lifting. With every bit of his strength stimulated by the rush of adrenaline, he was able to lift, using only his back, to get just one last breath of air. He managed a weak "Help."

He held that last breath as long as he could, knowing there would be no chance for another.

Bob Thompson heard the cry for help, signaled to the other men in the yard, and they tried to lift the cab. They couldn't, but they were able to ease the crushing enough for Barley to inhale once more.

Two more men ran up to the cab, and with a "One, two, three," Barley slid out. He attempted to walk away but couldn't. He wasn't able to stand, and he collapsed, unconscious.

Barley opened his eyes in a bright white room. Erika was there. There were two IVs in his left arm. Oxygen was being fed to him. Monitors were next to the bed. "Kind of looks like Star Trek," Barley smiled. "I'm all right. What am I doing here?"

"Mr. Williams," the doctor stated, "you've been in an accident. You've damaged four vertebrae—two high and two low, in your back. You've also suffered a heart attack. You're going to be here awhile. Can you move your legs?"

"Aaaaghhh," Barley grunted in great pain. "No. If I try it feels like a knife in my back."

"Well, that's good you still have feeling," the doctor offered, then continued his exam.

The accident had damaged the two upper vertebral disks, right at the point where the cab itself had settled onto his back. They would heal over time. The two lower disks, along with various lower back muscles, would never be the same. The heart damage was minimal, but Barley would never have the great strength that he had had before.

Within 2 weeks Barley was able to stand painfully, and within a month he was able to walk. One day after being released from the hospital, Barley climbed back into that White Freightliner. Its crumpled side remained a horrible reminder of its crushing moment.

The first run was to Texas, and the pain in his lower back increased with steady throbbing until just before approaching a tollbooth near Tulsa, Oklahoma. There the pain vanished, but Barley lost control of his legs. There was no feeling. He pulled the trailer hand valve and stopped the truck on the shoulder. A call for help on the C.B. radio provided someone's codriver to park the truck in a truck stop on the east side of Tulsa.

Barley arranged for a driver to bring him some whiskey. He drank the fifth quickly and passed out in the bunk.

The next morning Barley was able to move his legs enough to enter the truck stop and notify his boss that it was over. "I can't drive anymore."

He rode home on a Greyhound bus and checked into a hospital in Capital City, as had been arranged for by the workers' compensation representative.

Thirty days later, Barley was released but was put into 100 percent temporary disabled status. There were numerous pills to take, various procedures to undergo, and attempts made at medical methods to stop the pain in his lower back. Nothing worked.

This was also a legal case. Decisions were being dictated by state law mandates. The doctors would have 1 year to treat the injury. At the end of 1 year, a final determination of percentage of disability would be settled in court. Barley hired a lawyer to handle the legality and to prepare bankruptcy. John Higgins accepted on a contingency fee basis. John was a struggling lawyer in an office with two other lawyers and a shared secretary.

John Higgins reviewed all of Barley's mess of finances and tragic downfall. "First of all, you need to understand that you cannot file bankruptcy with this chance of restitution. All of your creditors have rights to it. You must face the fact that you can never drive a truck for a living again. The workers' compensation claim will probably stop anyone from hiring you. A bad back and trucking do not mix, even if you ever recover. I *can* help you, though. Bring me your last 5 years of tax returns. I will income average and that should get you a refund."

"Anything will help," Barley sighed.

"You can also go back to school on a government grant program because you are disabled. I would suggest something short in time, though. The workers' comp law in this state won't allow for much time in your legal status."

"But if I can't drive, I can't work. It's all I've ever done," Barley pleaded.

"You eventually will end up with some disability and be released for light-duty work. I'll do all I can to delay that status, but the law mandates an end to it," John said strongly to push his point.

Barley found a business college that specialized in computers in a rapid training program. He would use public transportation to get to the campus and return on a daily basis. It was difficult to handle the chronic pain in his back and be able to concentrate, but he knew he had to find some way to become a provider again.

The legal medical case ended before Barley could finish the school and get his associate's degree. The case ended with the court deciding on a 15 percent permanent disability. His back needed more treatment, but workers' comp would not cover any more. The final settlement was a mere $2,300 dollars, of which John Higgins would take one third.

The court date with the prosecutor's office was postponed several times. Barley found a job with a small trucking firm that hauled for a large factory. The firm, Olive Street Trucking, was converting to a computer-based system for dispatch and billing. Barley was hired to do computer backups and to review driver logs and compliance. His shift would be from midnight to 8:30 A.M., but for the first 2 weeks he would work 8:00 A.M. to 5:00 P.M. to learn about the operation. It was an entry-level job that paid a salary equal to $6.50 per hour.

Erika was devastated by the accumulation of disappointments and financial stresses. This job of Barley's was to her a symbol of Barley giving up.

On the eve of Barley going to work for the first day at Olive Street Trucking, Erika came into the bedroom. Barley was lying there. She wanted to comfort him.

Barley was asleep but turning side to side, fighting to get comfortable. He was fighting to relax. She reflected that the back injury prevented him from ever getting comfortable, and the financial woes had destroyed his happy, optimistic personality. Something happened at that moment. Erika looked at her husband, could feel his pain and anguish, and came to a realization. Erika was a natural woman, close to nature. She loved animals, and the law of survival entered into her heart. Erika turned away, walked back into the living room, and began to plan the third divorce of her young life.

[Love is difficult to describe. It must be recognized that the human heart is not unlike the animal world. In the forest, the doe waits as two bucks challenge. The doe has no preference, instinctively knowing that the stronger will win and ensure her species the best chance at survival.

The human heart comes in two forms, man and woman. Love is a meal served in a large dining room with two entrances. One side has an on/off switch. The other side has a dimmer switch.

A man can be cruel, using women with indifference until he falls in love. He then enters the dining room, turning on the light to full brightness to illuminate the meal. A woman enters this room cautiously, turning the light on slowly. When the meal is finished, she exits with a flick of the off switch, not wanting to see the mess. The man leaves on the dimmer side, slowly turning off the light. He looks at the table and does not want to leave, because it was good.]

On the second Thursday, Barley was to receive his first check from Olive Street Trucking. Erika said she would need the car and the check in order to distribute money. She drove Barley to work, and he walked back to the car and handed her the check. She did not want to kiss him before she left. Barley wondered why.

At 2:00 P.M., the sheriff arrived to hand Barley a restraining order. He was shocked, and its contents were an insulting lie.

The supervisor who had escorted the sheriff into the office offered to Barley that he could leave for the day. The papers were clear that he was not to attempt to even contact Erika. Barley walked to the nearest branch of his bank.

He had started the day with $10, but that was before lunch and a pack of cigarettes. He had $2 and change left, that was all. He had no car, nowhere to go, no friends, and he needed a drink. Most of all he needed a drink.

The bank was more than half a mile away. His back was hurting, and his heart was broken. Erika had closed the checking account earlier that day.

Barley walked next to a convenience store. He viewed the display cooler. Less than $3 would not purchase enough beer to help. Liquor was out of reach. "Wine, I'll buy a bottle of wine," he thought.

Barley read the labels, looking for the highest alcohol content. He stood in front of that display case for 20 minutes, carefully examining the bottles. The man behind the counter finally said, "You want Richard's Irish Rose or Mad Dog 20/20. They have the highest alcohol content."

He had seen many winos lost in the same dilemma. Barley took the Irish Rose and had enough left for a Pay Day candy bar.

The back pain was worsening. Barley walked, looking for a safe place in which to fall apart. He knew he had to find somewhere isolated enough to not be picked up for vagrancy. From the factory where his job was located to downtown Capital City was a railroad line. The railroad track offered the shortest route.

Barley started in the direction of downtown. His back was throbbing. Walking the ties of the track was difficult. He just couldn't get the timing right. The track ran behind a General Motors factory and over a river. This area was isolated with no road access. Barley climbed down to the riverbank area under the railroad bridge. This place had been occupied. There was a small stack of wood and a Styrofoam, makeshift bed.

Barley took the last four muscle relaxers he had in his possession and built a small fire. "I hope whoever has been here before doesn't mind," Barley thought. He then broke down completely, weeping until he could cry no more. It was now dark.

The fire felt warm, its heat reflecting off the concrete base of the bridge. It was a crisp, clear night in the middle of March 1985. The sky was brilliant, with stars of infinite number and no visible moon.

Barley opened up the bottle of wine and concentrated on its warm flavor. Each swallow was savored. He felt the warmth of its spirits in his chest. He stared at the motion of the river. He thought of just jumping into its icy grasp and ending his life.

The fire and the wine were warm, though, and there was absolute beauty here under this railroad bridge. Barley's mind drifted. He didn't have to wonder why; he knew. He knew that the prosecutor had caused all that had happened. He had destroyed the dream.

Barley's mind drifted back, back to eyes that had met his eyes long ago. He envisioned the face and eyes of that Houston hooker who had been crushed. The world's greatest hooker had given him the name world's greatest truck driver. It *was* who he *was*.

Barley climbed to the top of the bridge and stared at the skyline of Capital City. From there it just looked like a crowded graveyard. Each building was a monument. He focused on the one housing the prosecutor's office and the courts.

Barley Bill then shouted, "Restitution! I will have restitution! I will return. Like the hooker from Houston, I will return! I will restore my dream!"

[Not, however, with any help from the prosecutor's office.]

Barley planned on throughout that night. Money was the key. "How can I put money together to buy a car and find someplace to live on this minimal salary with a bad back?"

He mulled this question over and over again. Barley looked once more at the beauty of this spot, under a railroad bridge, behind a GM factory, and isolated. "I'll just stay here, collect my paychecks until I have $1,000, and I'll buy a car. I can live in the car, just like being a trucker, and save more until I can rent an apartment. With my midnight shift starting next week, no one will notice me. I can do it!"

It took 5 weeks until Barley was able to buy a car. She was just what he needed. A huge, full boat, 1974 Chrysler New Yorker, big enough to live in and cheap to buy because of its huge, gas-guzzling 440 four-barrel motor. The car was in pretty good shape.

Barley contacted the prosecutor's office soon after moving into the Chrysler and was surprised by a court date with a moneyman caught in the sting operation. He has a criminal record dating back to 1927. He stole bicycles back then. He looks like Santa Claus now.

Barley didn't even bother to ask to whom he was talking; but he knew it was just some cheap suit assistant.

Living in the Chrysler was such an improvement over living under the railroad bridge. No more washing in the cold river. No more scavenging for firewood. The Chrysler gave Barley freedom to travel around town. He used truck stops for showering and Laundromats to take care of his clothes. For the rest of his life, whenever Barley would see a well-creased pair of pants on a man, he would think back to the railroad bridge where he used two saplings tied together to make dress pants look pressed.

When the court date arrived, Barley was in the courtroom 2 hours early. Adrenaline was flowing, and he was ready to hate. The courtroom was quite full with half of the individuals mulling around when *he* walked in—someone of great importance. "Who was he?" Barley thought. "Was this some celebrity or something?"

The man obviously commanded this court. But he wasn't the judge or the prosecutor. He was the defense attorney, Owen Miller. When Barley realized that this center of attention was defending the man Barley was going to get restitution from, his spirits lifted. If that old Santa Claus could hire this superstar lawyer, then he had the money—all of it, maybe even $300,000.

Barley waited for the trial to begin. "Hey, this is going to be like 'Perry Mason,' but where is the prosecutor?" Barley was thinking fast.

It was not to be. Owen Miller simply tipped his hat and walked behind the courtroom. Within 10 minutes they all left: Owen Miller, the defendant, and what looked like plainclothes armed guards. Barley tried to follow them. The strong men separated Barley from the famous lawyer and his defendant at the elevator door. Barley turned around and was confronted by one of the cheap suits. "Come back with me to chambers, and I'll explain," the young man said. He was one of the assistants.

Back behind the court, Barley was stunned at the result of what he had seen. A plea bargain had been made. That old Santa Claus had pleaded guilty to a felony but received a suspended sentence. This subordinate yes man offered, "No one wants Santa Claus to spend his remaining years behind bars."

Owen Miller, during the numerous postponements, also had arranged to have all assets put into Mrs. Santa Claus's name, and they had been divorced. "There is nothing to seize. He has agreed to testify against those who are on the receiving end of the stolen truck parts."

Owen Miller had been paid handsomely. The prosecutor had won felony charges against all involved by testimony bought from suspended or reduced penalties. The press had listed the prosecutor's victories, but the prosecutor had never even been in the courtroom. It was obvious to Barley that whoever this prosecutor was (he knew the name), he was afraid of going to court against the great Owen Miller.

"What was his goal? Justice wasn't involved. All the criminals walked. My life has been destroyed, and for what? Why?" Barley was thinking and evaluating all that had happened in the last 3 years, while two large men seemed to be escorting him out of the building.

The golden boy prosecutor assigned to getting Barley restitution, and who had never shown up in court on Barley's behalf, was elected as mayor of Capital City soon after this Santa Claus case was "tried."

Barley was enraged when he walked into John Higgins's (his workers' comp lawyer) office to say, "I want to go public with what has happened."

John said in response, "It might make the evening news, but that won't buy you a cup of coffee. I've been working on this. I think we can take the city and county to federal court under the Civil Rights law and try to recover your damages."

"My restitution," Barley grunted.

"It will take some time. They will fight this with all of their resources. We are talking 'fighting City Hall' here. Try to keep yourself clean and go to work. Do you want me to represent you in your divorce?" John was talking as if he were a friend, not just a lawyer.

"No! I haven't given up. I want to save my marriage . . ."

Rage burned in Barley's heart as he returned to rebuilding his life. The determination filled his veins with adrenaline as he walked back to his home, the Chrysler . . .

CHAPTER 18

Tears in My Eyes

Barley pulled on westward through Chicago and turned north. Bill Jackson and Arnie Benson were called to Oklahoma near Enid. A confrontation had taken place between a driver of a midnight blue Peterbilt and the state patrol.

The driver had been stopped three times that day and was thoroughly inspected at a Missouri weigh station. His temper had gotten the best of him, and during a scuffle he had been shot. Research from Washington, D.C., F.B.I. headquarters verified that he wasn't the Road Rogue who was creating the now-nationwide search. Another messy lawsuit possibility had been created.

Linda Wright's report of the incident was tailored to create more interest from the public. "Where is this Road Rogue, and where is he going?"

The song recorded by Bobby Long and His Long Riders debuted and was cause for further embarrassment for the government.

Barley was heading north on Wisconsin back roads, and his Ruth was desiring to return to memories of his past. There was one song he usually skipped on his CD, "Uriah Heep Anthology." The song brought the most painful memories to him. It is a song of rage from the worst of emotional pain. The song begins with two double thuds like being struck with heavyweight left-right combinations from a George Foreman ("Big George" of boxing fame). Then the guitarist (Mick Box) plays (no, he tortures!) a riff, symbolic of a man's heart being ripped from his chest by the woman he loves. The angry, powerful words follow ("Look At Yourself", Uriah Heep).

. . . I'm no longer pretending you're mine . . . .

. . . So I have to forget you.
And I don't even know if I can . . . (Ken Hensley)

Barley worked his midnight shift, gathering paychecks, preparing to rent an apartment. Any clue of what hardship or turmoil was befalling Erika was unavailable because of the restraining order. Barley was focused on one item—rebuilding himself. In his mind, that would win her back and restore the dream. Just maybe, he hoped, John Higgins (his attorney) would be able to create restitution. Money, a large settlement would . . .

The long hours of walking during Barley's time living under the railroad bridge and walking the ties built muscles strong enough to counter the permanently damaged ones. He just had to be careful, ever so careful, not to twist or lift improperly. The pain in his lower back never would cease, but it could be managed. Barley only thought of getting stronger any way that he could. The midnight shift was a blessing to this goal.

The financial disaster associated with Barley's name prevented him from renting an apartment, getting a phone, or having electricity in his name. Bills were not being paid, and without bankruptcy, Barley could not start over. Over and over again, Barley struggled with the dilemma of not being able to file bankruptcy. "If only I had just filed for bankruptcy when the truck was stolen," Barley fretted. "Was this restitution just a lie to keep me testifying for the prosecutor's office? Justice, I want justice! All that work! All that I did was make matters worse."

The old Chrysler New Yorker was providing some freedom—freedom to explore Capital City, as long as he avoided any attempt to contact Erika. The summer approached, and one afternoon at a pub on the east side of town Barley met a man who shared a common interest: baseball. The atmosphere of The Court Jester allowed for easy conversation. With no home, Barley began spending afternoons sitting at its square C bar, and allowing some of his former persona out to look for friendship. The baseball fan called himself Red, as he was a devoted Cincinnati Reds fan. Barley had always been an American League home run enthusiast. Barley even liked the designated hitter. Red and Barley talked baseball in detail. The Big Red Machine versus The 27 Yankees was becoming the final inning of each of their draught beer games. It felt so good for Barley to get away from the constant pain (physical and emotional).

On a beautiful sunny day, Barley offered up an old joke in hopes of getting just a little more out of the conversation with Red.

"Did you hear about the truck driver who was laid over in San Diego? He bobtailed down to the beach, and while walking in the sand he came across a bottle."

"With a genie inside, I'll bet," Red chuckled.

"And he rubbed it, but the genie was angry. 'I've already been bothered three times this century, so I'm only granting one wish. Make it a good one.' The driver thought for a moment, and then said, 'I'd like to go to Hawaii, but I want to drive there. I'm a truck driver, and I'm scared to fly or ride in a boat.' 'You are nuts!' was the genie's reply. 'I'm not building a bridge all the way to Hawaii. Ask for something else.' 'Okay, I've always wanted to understand women,' the truck driver demanded. 'And how many lanes do you want on that bridge, damn it!' said the genie."

After the joke, Red said that he was divorced, and so did all six of the men sitting at the bar. Red offered to Barley to go to his apartment building's swimming pool for a party and to listen to a Red's game, while soaking up some sun. This would be the start of a long friendship between Barley and Red.

While at the pool, Barley met another guy who seemed like a real levelheaded man. He was the complex maintenance man. He was divorced, and after some jokes and a good deal of watching the babes at the pool, Neil made Barley an offer. "I don't make much here, but I have a free apartment. If you would like to, you can be my roommate for a couple of hundred a month." (As the day had progressed, Neil had joined in on Barley and Red's conversations. Barley had opened up enough to say that he was living in the Chrysler.)

"When do you want to move in?" Neil asked.

"All I have is a bag of clothes," Barley shrugged.

Neil wasn't what he appeared to be. He was a manic depressive, recovering alcoholic, and shortly after Barley moved in, Neil barricaded himself in the apartment. Neil suffered from ghosts left in his mind that he had carried since Vietnam. Barley arrived in late afternoon to this apartment, now turned into a bunker. Neil was irrational but allowed Barley in through a window. Barley had no idea what to do for this troubled man. Just after sunset, the apartment manager arrived with a Catholic priest.

The priest had been working on rehabilitating Neil for a long time. The priest, Father O'Connell, was an Irish lucky charm. Barley would come to realize in a few weeks that Father O'Connell—a sarcastic, bombastic, tireless, nonpious, ego challenger, and controversial public figure—was the most Christ-like man that he would ever meet. Father O'Connell's business card, "Working To Beat Hell," was Barley's first clue to Father O'Connell's great compassion for the hopeless. Father O'Connell had a gift from God to heal the heart with humor. Barley saw a miracle on that first night, as Father O'Connell saved Neil from the demons within a tortured mind. What life Neil ever could have, he owed to Father O'Connell.

When Barley had his chance, he approached Father O'Connell. "I need a miracle. Can you save my marriage?"

Father O'Connell was taken by surprise by the large man who had observed his work with Neil. The humble, desperate look of Barley's face and eyes must have touched the tireless worker's heart, and from that day onward Father O'Connell would be the rock of Barley's rebuilding. "Saving marriages is not my specialty. I'm not a marriage counselor, but come to the rectory tomorrow and we'll have a beer." Without the offer of a beer, Barley probably would not have made the attempt. Very insightful, this priest was indeed a lucky charm.

Father O'Connell's first miracle for Barley was to arrange for the apartment manager, Susan Star, to forge a little paperwork to allow Barley to rent his own apartment under an alias. Barley was allowed to change his name around to install a phone and have electricity turned on. The plan worked, and after paying the first bills, Barley called the utilities and stated, "Must have been a clerical error; my real name is Bartholomew Levi Williams, not Levi W. Bartholomew."

They never checked his name against the records.

Just prior to meeting Father O'Connell, Barley received a call from Erika while at work. What was said wasn't important; every word from Erika was vile bile from hell. The broken heart creates vicious hate, and all of Erika's hate was directed at Barley. Each word uttered stabbed his own heart, mind, and soul. A court hearing would begin the end of the marriage, with support and visitation as the main topics.

Barley leaned heavily on Red and Father O'Connell in preparation for the stormy encounter. John Walters (Erika's attorney again) prepared a standard agreement, which was presented to the judge and to Barley. Not once did Erika's eyes meet Barley's in front of the bench. Barley objected to every word on that agreement, and with his head bowed he stated, "I love my wife. I want to save my marriage." Tears ran down Barley's cheeks as the judge scolded attorney John Walters for using standard papers. She ordered marriage counseling with a final hearing in 6 months.

Barley could not understand why Erika hated him so much. Hate also filled Barley's heart, but he directed it at that golden boy whom he believed had cowardly orchestrated his demise. The judge did order counseling. That was a positive flicker of hope, the *only* positive moment that would ever emanate from that damn building!

Lack of money was still the most dominating factor in every aspect of Barley's life. Counseling would cost a lot of money. The counselor would have to be licensed and approved by the government. Father O'Connell would help again. Father O'Connell already had offered the use of the rectory as a neutral site. Erika had refused to rescind the restraining order; thus, the "no contact" order was still in effect. But Barley was allowed to have limited visitation with Rose and to pay support. Erika would drop off Rose at the rectory, and Barley could pick her up 15 minutes later (and visa versa for exchange back). Father O'Connell also offered a counselor (a former priest) whom the court would accept.

The first item on the counselor's list was a long compatibility questionnaire. Barley should have recognized Erika's divorce plan after this meeting with the former priest, but love is blind. The counselor's first words to Barley were, "There is no hope. You two are *not* compatible!" Barley was shocked. He believed that they were destined to be soul mates. Barley would not give up hope.

Erika's plan was not working. She had thought that she could break the spell and make Barley stop loving her. That was why she emptied the checking account and used the restraining order. Erika thought that Barley would go back to his home state, and then she would be done with him (i.e., shut off the light in the dining room). When filling out the questionnaire, Erika deliberately answered the questions the opposite of what she thought Barley would. There would be no more counseling.

Father O'Connell was Barley's only hope. His advice was to just stay away completely. "Erika will either come back to you or not, and you have at least 6 months."

Barley followed the advice. The 6 months passed slowly. No new news from the prosecutor's office. No more testifying. It was as if the restitution case was over. John Higgins, Barley's attorney, suggested not making a move (legally, with his civil rights case against the city) until the divorce hearing. Barley managed to buy some weights and tried to get strong again. Work was meaningless, although Barley's duties were shifting to more and more responsibility for safety and compliance for Olive Street Trucking. Red was Barley's only release other than The Court Jester Lounge. The visits with Rose were precious but painful and degrading due to the neutral site arrangement. Father O'Connell was a busy man.

When the dreadful day arrived, outside the courtroom, in the hall, Barley stood waiting. He was desperately hoping to see Erika before entering the courtroom. First he saw John Walters (her attorney), and anger rushed through him. There she was, standing beside the attorney with her back turned toward Barley. It was Erika, but she was dressed in a blazer or sport coat. That was not her style. Barley approached Attorney John Walters, visibly shaking, and blurted out, "May I have a word with my wife, you immoral bastard?"

"You step back, right now, or I'll have you put into a cell," John Walters sternly replied.

Then she turned to him. Their eyes met for the first time in what had seemed like ages. Nothing but hate and anger was in her eyes. Barley bowed his head as he retreated. Erika was wearing a blazer to conceal that she was pregnant. Barley collapsed against the wall and wept. It was now over. Erika was now gone and belonged to another man. The dream was finally void of light.

Not much could be settled that terrible day. State law prohibited divorce in Erika's condition. Barley could not stop shaking before the judge but gathered himself enough to object to the statement prepared by John Walters: "Have been living as man and wife."

For obvious reasons, the final decree could not come before the due date. This time the judge scolded Barley with, "Mr. Williams, do not come before me without your own representation again."

Erika stopped Barley as he walked to the door of the courtroom. Her eyes were now expressive with a look of worry and desperate realization that she had finally succeeded in killing the love she no longer wanted. "Barley ... I'm ... having trouble ... with Rose. Would you be willing to take Rose if things don't work out?"

"To raise her?" Barley questioned in complete surprise. "You have no morals left! Of course I will." Then as threateningly as he could, Barley warned, "I *will* be ready the next time we enter this courtroom."

Barley turned his back without attempting to meet her eyes. He would never attempt that again. There was no more love, only anger and hate. He walked away as if there had never been a serious back injury, determined to create whatever home he could in order to welcome his daughter. Barley drove back to Olive Street Trucking and asked to see his boss.

"I'll be needing to work days now. I'm going to be raising my daughter. There are more than enough safety issues to warrant it full time." There was no room for negotiating. The force of Barley's conviction overwhelmed the boss. This conviction was created by the hate and rage burning within Barley's mind for the golden boy prosecutor who had destroyed the soul of the mother of his child.

Watch out Big George, the World's Greatest Truck Driver has gotten off of the canvas.

CHAPTER 19

Rain

Political embarrassment (ineptitude), public perception, possible lawsuits, and the next coming election pressured the White House to address the growing problem of this Road Rogue who was continuing to elude capture. A specialist was sent to the assistant director of the F.B.I. Dr. Paul H. Lindsey was a criminal psychologist with a reputation well deserved. Although only 36 years old, he was considered phenomenally gifted, possibly psychic. He had an ability to enter the mind of a criminal, think what the criminal thought, and feel what the criminal felt. He was also gay, and most of the men of the department were aware of him and his reputation. Numerous jokes were made about the "Cry Psy," even though most agents had never even seen him.

Dr. Paul was given complete authority to review all material related to the Road Rogue case and make recommendations. Failure to follow those recommendations was cause for severe discipline within the department. As he examined every bit of the documented reports, he wasn't getting any feeling or vibes about the mysterious monster. Dr. Paul *was* feeling something: strong emotion from both William (Bill) Jackson and Arnold (Arnie) Benson. Further, he thought, "Who is this face, Linda Wright, telling the public about the Road Rogue?"

After scratching his head, Dr. Paul ordered for himself the complete F.B.I. list of files on Agent Jackson, Regional D.O.T. Director Benson, and TV Reporter Linda Wright.

. . . The Ruth of him was deteriorating fast. Barley's Ruth could remember and relive all of his life except this last month. The last month seemed to be a blur of severe headaches, chest pains, and nightmares—terrible nightmares. Barley wasn't even sure if it was just a month. Time was becoming irrelevant. He had stopped earlier this day to give a check call to the company, but he could not for the life of him remember the phone number. He concentrated, with only pain, deep pain, as a result. Confused and frustrated, he could not remember to whom he was currently leased.

Hobbs rolled on until . . . "Where is the Ruth?"

No emotion and no memories were present. Hobbs was still a dependent child in development. Without the emotion emitting from the

Ruth, Hobbs had no access to the memories. Hobbs's world existed only behind the wheel. Hobbs could drive, read the gauges, and react to road conditions but had no permanent memories of routes without access to Ruth's memories. Hobbs knew when the truck needed fuel by monitoring the gauge but had no knowledge how to fill up the tank. Hobbs had no method of using muscles not used in driving. The emotions of Ruth opened up the mental pathways. Without the Ruth, there was no destination.

Hobbs pulled the truck off the highway and found a safe place to park in a large parking lot in Green Bay, Wisconsin. Song after song was punched up on the stereo without response from the Ruth. "Where is the Ruth?" Must have the memories. Loud . . . soft . . . more songs . . . no more Heep left . . . try the tape collection . . . no response. The Hobbs of him, who was desperately trying stimuli to spark a memory, looked out through the windshield. Lambeau Field (hallowed ground for any man) brought about a stir in the Ruth. That sight through the eyes of Hobbs woke the Ruth, and Barley was back.

A low growl in his stomach signaled that Barley hadn't eaten in a long while. His lips cracked from dehydration, Barley climbed down from the cab and looked at the site of this shrine of professional football. He remembered the one time he was privileged to enter that stadium. Bart Starr was on the field, not as a player but as the head coach. Barley had wanted Bart Starr to succeed as coach in the same way that he had succeeded as the legendary quarterback. Barley had paid a lot of money that day, so long ago, just to get inside. The Packers had lost that day.

The smell of bratwurst was in the air, Barley was sure of it. As he turned to the large bar and grill to the east, a man over 65 walked up to admire the truck.

"Whew boy, she sure is a beauty! What's a rig like that cost, eh?" the old fellow asked, without expecting an answer.

Barley turned to look at his own truck, momentarily forgetting which of his dreams he was driving. After hesitation, Barley responded with a lighthearted thought by saying, "She didn't cost me a dime. I got her one piece at a time." He almost sang that response, thinking of the great old Johnny Cash hit song. "Hey, does that place sell brats and beer?"

"Yes sir," the old man nodded, "best in the world, eh. Just look at what you can see from the windows. There ain't no better sight from heaven, eh." The Packer pride in him was shining through the wrinkles and twinkling eyes of his once-handsome face. "What's your name, driver?"

"Bart," Barley replied, remembering his school-age nickname that would forever tie him to the Packer glory days. "Let's go up there and I'll buy you a beer. Do they still serve Pabst Blue Ribbon?"

"Nah, thanks, eh. Nobody drinks it anymore since they closed the factory. I gotta go. Better order Old Style or you'll look like a tourist."

Barley entered the bar and ordered two brats and a large draught beer. He savored every bite and let the foam head soothe his cracked lips. He realized that it had been a while since showering and attempted to clean up a bit in the rest room. Upon returning to the bar, he ordered another draught beer and a Packer hat just to cover his hair. While looking at the bar's many signs and memorabilia pictures, he stopped at the rows of liquor bottles. The white glare of the reflecting spots in the row formed a line from where he was sitting at the end of the bar. His focus changed. The spots seemed to move, and they blended into white lines. White lines passing on a freeway, a freeway to the past . . .

Barley's life shifted gears rapidly after leaving the courthouse no longer loving his July morning. As hurt as he was, Barley began to prepare for life as Mr. Mom. The work of John Higgins produced a one-day courthouse appearance in which the divorce would be settled with custody of Rose being transferred to Barley, along with giving in to bankruptcy (thereby giving up hope of the prosecutor's restitution). Barley wanted it all over with, except for the possibility of a lawsuit in federal court against Capital City.

Erika was in some deep trouble Barley thought, because she called to offer a settlement without further argument or delay. The two lawyers worked it out. Barley would pick up his daughter on the Saturday following the agreement.

Bankruptcy court, however, was another matter. The judge went off into a scathing speech belittling Barley to tears. There was something about that court. These people—the judges, lawyers, and all involved—seemed to work a little too well together. Something told Barley that it was wrong for one building to house all five courts, the police, and the prosecutors.

When it was over, Barley first told Father O'Connell the news about Rose and that he wanted to come to talk with him. Then Barley spent a good night with his buddy Red.

"I'll help you any way that I can," Red offered.

Red was as good a friend as Barley would ever have, and Red would help in ways that would leave Barley forever indebted. Without Red, life as Mr. Mom would not have been possible.

In Father O'Connell's office at the rectory, Barley saw pictures on the wall of the Irish priest who had been volunteering at the city's annual sporting event. Television's "The Wide World of Sports" had produced a documentary of Father O'Connell's work. Now Barley realized why this priest had looked so familiar and inviting when they had first met. He was something of a celebrity.

The meeting with Father O'Connell was humbling. Barley spoke as if he were talking to an old friend, while at the same time attempting to confess the sins of his life. The big question for Barley was difficult to ask. "With all that I have done, would it be possible to come back to the church? I was raised Catholic, but I haven't really had anything to do with formal religion almost as far back as when you guys [priests] stopped using Latin. It lost its mystery for me, lost its beauty."

"Sure you can!" Father O'Connell replied. "I'll help you. There is a program called Cursillo that just might make you feel welcome."

"I'll do it. For Rose, I'll do anything."

Barley was filled with hope, the hope of bringing stability to his daughter's life. Barley put all of his love into Rose.

The Cursillo experience was wonderful. Barley came out feeling as if he were loved. It was a minor miracle for Barley to have some sense of self-worth again. The Cursillo also afforded some help in raising Barley's spirits. He joined a group in which 12 Cursillo members would meet weekly at Father O'Connell's rectory. Red would watch Rose.

The Cursillo group had consisted of men from all walks of life, all of them indebted to Father O'Connell's compassion. Through Barley's mind came an outpouring of scenes about the help and guidance he had received from his lucky charm.

And on a night just before the piety of Holy Week, the world's greatest truck driver was witness to the world's greatest miracle. It is a shame the world was not witness.

The group of 12 was to meet for a supper and mass for the last time prior to an annual 2-month break from meetings starting Holy Week and running until Father's Day. A Lenten meal had been prepared. Seven of the 12 were seated including a former jet pilot, a famous aging race car driver, a G-12 government employee, a brooding recently divorced salesman, a postal letter carrier, and a destroyed truck driver (Barley).

Father O'Connell entered the room with his "I'm a horse's ass" Irish eyes and smile. He was a horse's ass, but the members all followed that horse, knowing that he pulled a wagon load full of miracles.

An eighth member arrived just after the meal had been served and the blessing had been given. All except Father O'Connell bowed their heads but not in prayer. Barley felt the same pity for this member as the rest of the group.

The eighth member, Gary, had not made an appearance at the group gathering for a long time. He was a very proud, common, decent man of humble resources. He had been proudest of his two beautiful daughters. Now he lived in anguish and shame. One of his daughters had become rebellious in her teenage years and had run away with a black man. She had returned, alone with a child, and had run again, leaving the child for Gary to raise.

All at the table felt Gary's anguish and responded with sympathy in their silence. Sympathy was exactly what Gary was seeking as he entered the room carrying the child. "Father O'Connell, will you baptize my grandchild?" Gary pleaded, with tears running down both cheeks.

Father O'Connell was quick to respond, "Of course I will Gary [pause], and I'll even put a carp in the baptismal bowl to make it feel at home."

Every one of the men present was stunned and outraged at their leader. Barley actually wanted to knock that horse's ass down for that vicious and cruel insult. Around the table jaws set and muscles flexed. And then there was a giggle from one of the eight as they all looked directly into the eyes of their leader in disbelief. Then Barley put his hand on his head and laughed. They all laughed. Gary began laughing so hard he had to sit for fear of dropping the child—the innocent child.

Father O'Connell had taken that cruel remark right out of the heart of every one of the men there, Gary included. He had taken the ugly demon of prejudice, racist prejudice, out of their hearts and laid its ugliness onto their own table of piety. They all knew it. The lesson was learned. This child was individually innocent, void of the sins the men all had in their own hearts, created by being part of a group, an exclusive group. For the group that scorns the innocent individual has no place in the Kingdom of God. God grants rights to the individual soul, not to the group. Eight hearts had been freed of their ugly fear. It would have been easier to move eight mountains!

. . . The Hobbs was growing ever stronger, and for the first time, while Barley was lost in the endless white lines created by the liquor bottles, he (Hobbs) attempted to use the voice. "Beer, I'll have beer."

The bartender was just about to disturb the daydreaming, and Hobbs understood that the beer was reviving Barley's Ruth. This was more protection being executed by the not-so-subconscious Hobbs. Hobbs was learning; the Ruth had to have this beer and food. It was no different than reading gauges.

The television announced that the next segment to be shown was an update of the hunt for the Road Rogue by Linda Wright. The bartender casually pointed out the window and asked, "Is that your rig? What do you make of this Road Rogue trucker?"

Hobbs regressed as Barley awakened from the daydreaming. "Excuse me, I was lost in thought, I guess."

"I said, what do you think about this Road Rogue guy? That *is* your rig outside, isn't it?" The bartender was a tough-looking, linebacker-sized man growing impatient with this stranger who was staring off into never-never land.

"Well, I don't know much about it. I guess I've heard a little C.B. talk." Barley was still a little groggy. "I . . ."

The bartender held up his hand. "Let's see what this babe has to say today."

With a backdrop of a slow-moving line of trucks at a weigh station, Linda Wright began. "No progress has been announced by the authorities in identifying the Road Rogue today, but as you can see, inspections of trucks are increasing nationwide. There have been reports of further incidents of anger from delayed truckers, some of whom are suggesting a strike. Additionally, three automotive plants had to shut down assembly lines due to parts not being delivered."

"Wouldn't you like to have a little of that? Whew, she's a babe," the bartender said, as if he were in the locker room just west of the bar.

"USDA prime, I'd say from Iowa," Barley offered while looking at the fair, blond TV reporter. "Definitely corn fed," Barley pulled from his own locker-room experience.

"Pretty close. She's from Nebraska and was related to the first cop killed by that Road Rogue." The bartender then turned to wait on a new customer who was seated on the other side of the bar.

Barley got up from the stool and opened his wallet. There was only $5 left. "Do you take plastic? Damn, I've got to get home."

Barley thought about home as he signed the receipt. "The trouble at home. I must get home to my lady in black." Barley started the motor and punched up the song of his second chance in life.

> She came to me one morning
> One lonely Sunday morning
> Her long hair flowing in the midwinter wind . . .
> (Ken Hensley)

When the song ended, Hobbs had the destination and was able to continue. Barley's Ruth tried to remember about home. She had told him about a money problem. What was it? It was something about a loan. He could not remember. He could only see her face. The song could not clear his mind. The Ruth must go back further and retrace life's footsteps to find the memory . . .

There was some connection between his lady in black back to Father O'Connell . . . the Cursillo . . . Rose . . . the old job at Olive Street Trucking . . . hair, long hair . . .

. . . Barley's love of his daughter Rose dominated his every thought. She was a precious princess with long golden hair. At 3 years old, Rose would need constant care. Barley spent long hours lovingly and tenderly untangling and brushing Rose's hair. He had to learn to cook for her, to help her dress, and most of all give her happiness. Father O'Connell helped in every way that he could. His parish had a day care and an elementary school. There were loving parish members to help. And the friendship with Red would hold Barley together to get through the first year.

Erika's life must have continued its downward spiral, Barley thought. She didn't even look like herself when she came for visitation. She looked painted and plastic, with no warmth. Then she quit coming at all. Father O' Connell was a savior for Barley, but no miracle could remove the hate inside Barley for that golden boy who had orchestrated this whole mess. Barley had to have that focus of hate in order to survive.

The work at Olive Street Trucking was a thankless, underpaying prison for the once-proud trucker. The work would soon become an insult. Barley's duties developed into being responsible for all safety compliance, and he studied the regulations as if this could be his only chance at a new career.

The Commercial Motor Vehicle Safety Act of 1986 was a blatant insult to the Constitution of the United States. The years of demonizing trucking had paid off for the politicians. The law was passed without much uproar from the trucking world. When management asked Barley about the effects it would have, Barley quickly replied, "Massive driver shortages and turnover." Barley was right. His duties regarding the qualification and hiring of drivers began dominating his available time. These qualifications included complete driving and background checks, and physical driving tests. At first, the test-drives were pleasant truck rides with established and experienced drivers. As the effects of the driver shortage began, the quality of the recruits quickly dropped. The intended higher standards for drivers mandated by the new law simply lowered standards for every company to fill the seats. Government-subsidized driving schools started up all over the country. These schools preyed on warm bodies that could qualify for government grants to pay for the schools. The driving schools aggressively competed for the possible grants without any stipulations (or morality) for ability or likelihood that these hard luck cases could possibly drive a truck. (Eventually, a federal investigation would follow. Yes indeed, a federal investigation of a federal program provided to promote a federal plan to . . .).

Barley finally demanded more money for risking his life on these journeys with frightened, overmatched pawns in the government's plan. The company unwillingly agreed to $25 per test-drive on top of Barley's salary. Many times Barley would simply pull down the trailer hand valve from the passenger's seat, pull the parking brake, and drive the truck back. It was the only driving of trucks he would do for more than 1 year. Barley kept a driver qualification file on himself, including regular drug testing, to help ease the resentment from the established drivers in the company. (He kept, of course, no record of the back injury. Filling out his own physical form was part of a commonly practiced art.)

Pressure mounted as the driver shortage worsened. Barley would not budge in demanding that drivers could actually drive a truck. (Some were being sent in to be used only for logbook compliance.) Management was tiring of Barley's standards for obvious operational needs. On one occasion, a man was brought in who could drive. He handled shifting and backing very well, but on the road test he did not follow instructions for turns. Upon returning, Barley discovered that the man was completely illiterate. He had an accomplice filling out paperwork. Barley would not qualify this man. (D.O.T. regulations require literacy in English.) Management was furious. "He's just going to be a codriver!" Barley wouldn't budge.

Other company drivers delivering to the plant also continued to demonstrate the falling quality of expertise in the trade. On a Friday afternoon, a young driver came storming into the office. "There ain't no fucking way you can get a trailer into that damn dock." His eyes were red with anger and frustration.

The girls in the office were afraid of him. Barley interceded. "What's the problem?"

Again he repeated expletives and was now shouting.

"I'll put it into the dock for you. Why don't you just calm down." Barley was attempting to save this man from himself. The police would be called soon if his ranting did not end.

"No way." The young driver shook his head, thinking that a white shirt and tie-wearing, clean-shaven office clerk could not possibly know how to back a truck.

"I'll bet you $20 I can, and don't be afraid. I won't hurt your truck. I used to be a driver," Barley reassured.

"I don't give a damn. Nobody can put a trailer into that hole. No way you're using my tractor," the slowly calming driver replied.

"Okay then, you drop, and I'll hook up with one of Olive Street's tractors." Barley then added, "You do have a $20, don't you?"

"Shit. What the hell. Use my tractor, just don't hit anything," he said, shrugging his shoulders.

As the two of them, Barley and the angry young driver, walked to the side dock and his rig, the word spread fast inside the office and loading area. When Barley climbed up into the cab of the orange International cabover, he could see several dock workers and two suits standing at the open dock door. This would be a difficult maneuver. This dock was seldom used. It was on the side of the building, and leftover metal machines and debris piles served as obstacles. There was very little room. An old press machine was to be sent out for scrap, and it was sitting in position to be loaded there. The plant's renovation had sealed this area off from the main loading area.

Barley fired up the tractor, quickly assessed the problems, and put the tractor and trailer at a 90 degree angle, spinning the trailer tandems and trailer into the sloping dock entrance. Then two quick pull ups to straighten the rig combination out and he was able to back straight in. As Barley entered the loading area from the side door next to this dock, the men were laughing, and Barley saw money change hands. The driver called foul, and said, "It's a trick. No fair!" That driver had only been taught to back one way at his subsidized school.

"Trick? Okay, watch this." Barley was riled by the young driver's attitude. Barley jumped back into that rig, pulled out of the dock facing the opposite direction, got out to look the area over, jumped back in, and repeated the maneuver from the blind side. The young driver said, "No more," handed a 20 to Barley, and walked outside to have a cigarette (avoiding the jeering from the dock workers).

Barley walked up to his supervisor who had witnessed the feat and said, "That driver has a point. The yard is a mess. Why don't you let me come in on Saturday mornings and I'll repark all these trailers so this area can be utilized. I can double the capacity of the yard for trailer parking."

The supervisor agreed to pay Barley driver's wages on top of the clerical salary. This was, however, the beginning of the end of his safety office job. From that day forward, management would only consider Barley as a displaced truck driver. They soon would offer trips to Barley when the driver shortage problem left loads with no one available. This was akin to opening a bottle of vodka and setting it in front of a hopeless alcoholic.

Barley hid from sight whenever his back acted up. Each time he took a trip or worked the yard was a chance to get away from that thankless compliance work. He also would take Rose with him on runs without management knowing. These were special experiences for Mr. Mom and his princess. To be discovered would mean termination, but it was a risk well worth taking.

The end of the job at Olive Street Trucking came gradually. With the election of the golden boy as mayor, Barley's resentment and hidden anger grew with each passing day. It had been months since Barley had had any contact with his lawyer, John Higgins. In the last meeting with John Higgins, John stated that the case involving taking the city, county, and those responsible for Barley's violation of civil rights to federal court would be hard fought. John had stated that he would need help. "This will be the biggest case of my career, and if you don't mind, I'm going to seek additional council." Barley decided to drive to John's office and talk face to face about any progress.

As Barley entered the reception area, he was puzzled by the woman's reaction upon seeing him enter without an appointment. She was the secretary for three lawyers who shared the building, and her shoulders slumped while her head bowed down, avoiding eye contact. "I'm here to see John, if he's got a minute to spare," Barley requested.

She looked up, now crying with eyes that looked as if she had been crying a lot. "John . . . John has been disbarred and has left the country."

"My God, what has happened?" Barley was shocked. Then slowly, with a long sigh, "Never mind. You just can't fight city hall. John was not just my attorney; he was a friend." With that final word, Barley turned to walk back to his car. Just before reaching for the door, one of the other attorneys ran up to Barley.

"Mr. Williams, I'll take your case." His voice was strong, as if he wanted vengeance.

Barley just looked down and shook his head, "Nah, enough lives have been ruined by that old black Peterbilt. It's time to realize there can be no justice where politics and politicians are involved. It's just time to forget it."

Barley never would. The hate would grow in him, and alcohol became the only escape from its ugliness. Barley drank himself out of the job at Olive Street Trucking. He found a new position at another trucking company as a safety director, but that company was under attack by the D.O.T. and filed bankruptcy less than a year after he accepted the job.

After a terrible period of desperate financial struggle, in which Father O'Connell would again save Barley with a cash loan, a new job as a loss-control supervisor for an insurance services company would provide an escape from the haunting life in the city being governed by Barley's focus of hate.

After 6 months of reviewing loss-control reports, Barley created his own new opportunity. The commercial reports coming from his home state of Michigan were substandard. The company had no qualified commercial inspectors in Michigan. Barley offered to move to Michigan and become the commercial inspector for the whole state. The company accepted.

The good-byes were good. When Barley pulled out of Capital City with a 12-year-old Cadillac, a U-Haul trailer, and his precious daughter to begin a new life, his mind reflected upon the previous 10 years over a Uriah Heep song.

Rain, rain, rain . . .
In my tears,
Measuring carefully my years. . . . (Ken Hensley)

CHAPTER 20

Lady in Black

Bill Jackson was driving from his home to a congressional hearing in which he would be giving testimony on the investigation and quest to capture the Road Rogue. The previous night, he had discussed with his wife his resentment and fear of the politicians who would be questioning him.

"Nothing will be accomplished by wasting a day in front of these publicity-seeking, arrogant elitists," Bill rationalized to his supportive woman. "They will infer that I am inept and failing to serve the American people. The whole thing will be a staged show to give those politicians face time on TV. They all have the same information that I have, which isn't much."

"Can't you just get off this case?" Lisa, his wife, pleaded in response. "I know this Road Rogue case is eating away at your mind."

"Not possible now. I'm set up as a scapegoat. Damn politicians." Bill Jackson's frustration was growing each day.

As he was entering the beltway, Bill Jackson needed to get his mind off of what he was about to face. He hit the seek button on the car radio to hear a little music. The second song played was the new hit "The Road Rogue" by the Long Riders.

After testifying on camera to the committee, Bill had a meeting with Arnie Benson. Arnie Benson also had testified. "I'm getting tired of running all over the country because of these incidents being created by local law enforcement and the new people that have nothing to do with the Rogue we're trying to catch." Arnie was equally as frustrated as Bill Jackson. "Why haven't the research and records people come up with anything?"

"I know what you mean about all the false leads," Bill agreed. "I wish we weren't looking for a Peterbilt. It isn't that there are more of them. The problem for the research team is that independent truckers like them damn Peterbilts. Most of the independents are not on the satellite system. To verify the whereabouts of individual trucks is a tedious job without satellite tracking."

"And those independents love those trucks," Arnie interjected. "We may have to go much further back in checking registrations. Last week I was fooled into thinking a 6-year-old tractor was a new one. That driver was a very angry man for being held up while we checked him out," Arnie added.

"You know those politicians," Bill shrugged. "They're being pressured by the delay problems. When the factories shut down, the GNP is affected quickly."

"What else can we do?" Arnie grumbled. "Until we know who this monster is, we have to keep inspecting the trucks. There are no facilities to carry out a nationwide inspection."

"Just think what it will be like when the Mexican border opens up," Bill voiced.

Barley was rolling through the Upper Peninsula of Michigan with Hobbs in control. His Ruth was daydreaming of his return to Michigan and a fresh start on life. The scenery and people of the Upper Peninsula represent a step backward in time. Some of the best two-lane highway rides can be found in the undeveloped forests and spectacular shorelines of the Great Lakes in this secluded land. The Ruth of him was soaking up the views and pleasant thoughts of his return to his boyhood home 10 years ago in 1991 ...

Mom, Dad, brother Allen, and his good old friend Earl were there at the apartment Mom had arranged for Barley to rent in 1991 upon his return to live in Michigan. Everything was moved in, and the new home was set up in less than 2 hours. The previous decade of disasters brought feelings of relief so strong that memories of pain would fade, allowing Barley to breathe in the fresh, fair air of the new life of the early spring.

School for daughter Rose would be in the same buildings in which the young independent-minded Bart had developed. The town looked almost as it was when Barley had left so many miles ago. Yes, this was the right thing to do. Coming here would give Rose stability, family, and a safe environment in which to grow up. He would miss his friend Red and the counsel of his lucky charm priest, but this move was the best way, maybe the only way, to escape all of the pain and hate of the last decade.

Lack of money was a continuing problem. Barley had to live in this credit-driven society without credit. There had been six junk cars, including the latest shit-brittle-brown Cadillac with more than 200,000 miles on it. He had little hope of ever being financially stable. He had become a victim, surviving from year to year with the hope of getting a tax refund check large enough to buy the next discarded dream ride. "I would rather drive an old Caddy or Lincoln than a newer, politically correct roller skate," Barley reminded himself.

The loss-control inspection job required long drives throughout the state, and these old cruisers still provided great rides for as long as they would run. Family would help in caring for Rose, who was growing so fast that Barley truly recognized the limits of a lifetime for man and machine. There were occasional opportunities for short truck rides hauling farm products for area farmers in rigs older than rusted thick chrome Cadillacs with tail fins. There wasn't any money involved in these farm truck rides, but a few mugs of draught beer at the town's only tavern was reward enough.

Earl had completely settled down. Married with children, he had even quit drinking beer. Barley was a little envious but not about the beer. In the time after losing his July Morning, there had been a few dates with women, arranged for Barley by others, without Barley liking any of the women. "All so damned liberated and seemingly angry about it." Not one even contemplated a traditional home as Barley envisioned. He was also self-conscious about his nagging back injury and his constant financial burdens. "Never could I be a provider again," echoed in his thoughts. "I'm half a man, but half a life is better than no life. Each day is a gift from God. It could have ended under that Freightliner."

Barley would take to his life in his old hometown an attitude of enjoying as much as he could. As it had been from the first day of custody, Rose was the center of his life. The apartment was within walking distance of the tavern, with familiar faces always seated in positions of receptive conversation. Each day was putting miles between the healing Barley and his haunting memories. The local parish had built a new church, but Barley could see that family facial features of the gatherings were almost as they were a generation ago. A new emotional feeling was replacing pain. It was peace.

Peace, healing peace, brought desire and the ability to dream again. Barley began to look for ways to rebuild and have optimism again. He read an advertisement from a car dealer about rebuilding a good credit rating. He drove to that dealership, which was a "buy here, pay here" small lot with well-used cars.

There she was, Beauty—a midnight-blue, full boat Fleetwood Cadillac with a little less than 100,000 miles. Whoever had owned her before had loved this car. She had dreams embedded in the chrome. Barley was in love. Price did not matter. Under the contract, he would be paying double its worth, but it would fan the flicker of flame of the new hope in his heart if he could complete the contract.

From the first moment behind the wheel of this beauty, Barley's spirits were lifted. He would enjoy every ride and with *pride*. Pride is essential to a man's heart. Pride singularly generates the fire to melt an ice-cold heart. Daily life now was joy from breakfast with his precious princess, throughout the working day, during an after-work beer with friends, and while tenderly tucking in Rose in the evening. It was only at night when the something-is-missing feelings would come.

On a crisp winter morning while at Sunday morning mass, Barley's thoughts wandered while the priest began his sermon. He looked at the familiar families in their traditional pews, and feelings of loneliness and envy nearly overwhelmed him. The destruction of his life and his battles to hold onto that previous life challenged his new optimism, and he thought or prayed, "Why?"

Then he heard a voice—a singing voice that touched him even more than the power of David Byron's lead voice of his always favorite Uriah Heep. This voice had to be straight from heaven. It was the slow, sweet sound of an angel. "The Lord hears the cry of the poor ..." She sang with a voice that brought silence from the congregation, a voice that was more than beautiful. It was holy.

Barley looked at the choir to see a beautiful woman in her early 30s, he thought. Her long hair flowed naturally, without cuts, bangs, or man-made curls. Her face was the picture of goodness and innocence. Tears formed in Barley's eyes, he could see tears forming in her eyes while she sang the song with such feeling.

*The Lord hears the cry of the poor. Blessed be the Lord.**

Barley left mass quickly, not wanting to see what man she belonged to. Right now he did not want to see any more happy family faces. He drove to the Post Office to drop some completed inspection reports into the outside mail drop. Rose was sitting in the back seat. As Barley turned to get back into the car, she was there. The wind was blowing her long, natural hair. Sadness filled her eyes. "You have the voice of an angel," was all that Barley could say as he opened the door of his blue Cadillac.

"Thank you," she said so softly that fear entered Barley's heart as he drove back to the apartment.

At the apartment, Barley walked over to the passenger's rear door to let Rose out. A small car pulled up next to them, and she got out, the winter wind blowing that beautiful hair. "Hello. I guess we're neighbors. I just moved into this building."

And they were married 13 months later—"The Angel and the Bad Man" (John Wayne movie), Barley and his lady in black.

With credit partially restored, Barley would be able to buy a house again. The blue beauty had served him well, and the next car would be a Lincoln Town Car with a real bank loan. That loan in turn established credit. An FHA loan on a three-bedroom ranch completed rebuilding of a new life, new heart, and new hope. He changed his favorite Heep tune to "Lady in Black."

*She came to me one morning,
One lonely Sunday morning.
Her long hair flowing in the midwinter wind....* (Ken Hensley)

*From the collection "Wood Hath Hope." Copyright 1978 by John B. Foley, S.J. and North American Liturgy Resources. Written by John Foley, S.J.

CHAPTER 21

Sweet Freedom

Barley was alert, his Ruth ego concentrating on getting home, as he crossed the mighty Mackinaw Bridge heading south. The dark blue waters on the western side expanded into the horizon in a geometric display of whitecaps marching into the morning sunrise. To the east, the long white porch of The Grand Hotel on Mackinaw Island, Michigan, reflected the new day's brilliance with an electrifying view. This stimulation cleared the memories in his deteriorating mind, just as the air was cleared of the morning mist. It was on a day like this 8 years ago, during this same crossing in a midnight-blue Cadillac, that Barley had decided he *could* offer his lady in black, Marie, a life to share in a second dream of hope and happiness . . .

There was little happiness for agent Bill Jackson, as pressure mounted for an end to the run of the Road Rogue. With ever-increasing effort to inspect and investigate each truck, the resentment and rage of a nation of truckers increased geometrically. Groups of trucks had blocked roadways. Truck stops were becoming sounding boards in which to vent frustration into TV news cameras. Three drive-by shootings occurred, with one causing a major chain-reaction accident in Ontario, California. The driver of a cattle-hauling truck lost control when the driver's side window exploded. The ensuing rollover split the trailer's roof in the center of six lanes of eastbound, afternoon rush hour traffic. Bloody carcasses and half-dead cattle mixed into the melee, creating a horrifying backdrop for the Linda Wright report.

Using Arnie Benson's Department of Transportation report, she explained to a nation: "Two men, convinced that they were passed by the Road Rogue, attempted to stop this cattle truck by showing a shotgun. The truck veered toward them, and the gun discharged. The driver of the semi was killed, along with four other motorists. Twenty-six others were injured. The two men have been arrested and are being held without bail. The driver of the cattle truck had never been east of Texas."

Bill Jackson studied stacks of material at his home as his wife approached him. "I can't take it anymore! You have to get off this case." The tears rolling down her face showed her desperation. "You can't go on without sleep, and you haven't been here in almost 2 months. Even when you do get home, all you do is study those maps and reports."

"I'm sorry, but I don't have a choice," Bill firmly replied. "Something will break soon. I just have to figure out where he is going."

"When you can find the time, maybe you'll figure out where I'm going!" The slamming of the door signaled she wasn't coming back . . .

[Notice: Your reading privileges have been suspended. You have accumulated too many opinions of character, emotion, and pain and must appear before the absolute power of the pages. To continue will result in permanent loss of your reading privileges. This judge has determined that you must bring a symbol of freedom into your mind. Careful now, these words are connected via satellite to the absolute power of the author. I know exactly where you are.

The American flag, Old Glory, you are visualizing right now as a symbol of freedom. But is it? Without question the flag is presented today as the symbol of freedom to Americans by our government. Our government is based upon the United States Constitution. Old Glory predates the Constitution. However, its original symbolic meaning was independence, and it was designed as a result of the Declaration of Independence. The American flag was a defiant enemy of the symbol of absolute power of the world then, the Union Jack. Our government, prior to the Constitution, was based upon the Articles of Confederation. Thirteen independent states were united in defiance of an overtaxing, tyrannical government (England). Old Glory describes the sacrifice of brave men dying for a cause, then believed to be against impossible odds. Perhaps *freedom* needs to be defined in this context. "Freedom's just another word for nothing left to lose" (K. Kristopherson) is inappropriate, you may argue. How about the freedoms listed in the Bill of Rights of the Constitution? Well, this is a story about a truck driver, and those rights don't apply. The truck driver is exempt from numbers I, II, IV, V, VI, VII, VIII, and X and Amendments XIII and XV. The government believes there is legitimate argument for exempting the over-the-road driver. But if *exempt* is an inappropriate word, then replace it with *infringed*. The freedoms of those amendments are exempted by putting the truck driver into an exempted group.

Getting back to the symbolism of the flag may seem a bit more clouded journey now. The reference to the XIII Amendment should be your obvious objection to my assumptions, except involuntary servitude exists in a trucker's everyday life. The symbol of slavery as we are being taught today is the flag of Dixie, the Stars and Bars. However, that flag's original symbolic meaning was exactly as Old Glory's symbolic meaning, against the Union Jack, except that government (the South) promoted slave labor.

Time and language change perception and meaning, you may argue, but then look closely at that American flag you visualized. Up close it says "Made in China." Perhaps Old Glory is now a symbol of a government promoting slave labor, the same as we are being told the Stars and Bars is. Old Glory has replaced the Union Jack as a symbol of world dominance. Angry now?

There it is! The real symbol of freedom—the bird! You have just flipped the author the universal symbol of independent, individual thought. Defiance of the authority of absolute power, perfectly stated with your extended middle finger. *FREEDOM!*

Your privileges are now reinstated. Continue reading at your own free will.]

...And she would not come back. Bill Jackson would receive his first divorce papers within 30 days. The quest to capture this Road Rogue now forced increased anguish and resentful determination onto an already-pressured man. Bill Jackson mulled over what he must do: find the monster to end the politicians' royal demands and win back the love of his life ...

Barley rolled on south into the forest divided by Interstate 75 of the northern Lower Peninsula of Michigan with memories warming his heart, his Ruth allowing Hobbs control as the smooth ride sent him back to the driver's seat of the machine that had provided a spark of pride and the dream of love again ...

The midnight-blue Caddy was taking him home to ask her to spend the rest of their lives together. Surely, she had been heaven sent. Barley would not let anything destroy this second chance. He felt alive and strong again. She had said yes!

A new plan was set into motion. All preparations were made for a real marriage ceremony by a priest in a church. The religion did not recognize the previous marriage by a justice of the peace. They could be married anytime after 6 months if all proper conditions were met. The Caddy's contract was completed, and Barley traded for a 1989 Lincoln Town Car. It was 1993.

The Lincoln was special. It was the last American car made with vent windows and chrome bumpers. Most important, time had passed, allowing the bankruptcy to fade into memory. The Lincoln was purchased with a real bank loan. Within 3 months, Barley and Marie were elated to discover that Barley could now finance a house.

As the wedding date approached, Barley mulled over his choice of best man. Should he choose a brother, Earl, or maybe even Ol' Red? The title determined the choice. "The best man I have ever known was Father O'Connell." So they were married, "Angel and the Bad Man" (with a priest as best man, in a church, with a real reception, including a polka band).

For the honeymoon, they took a trip to Florida in the Lincoln. Just before heading back, Barley and his new bride visited Battleship Park in Mobile, Alabama, to walk the decks of the great ship once more. All was right, Barley was sure of it. This marriage *was* the right thing to do. Rose would have a mother, and loneliness would be conquered for two souls who needed each other. Barley's thoughts were peaceful. Everything within his plan had been put into place for this new life . . .

. . . Barley's Ruth memories began to change from peaceful to full of frustration as he passed Gaylord, Michigan. He decided that a walk in the pathways of the large white pines of Hartwick Pines State Park would ease a stiffening back and prepare him for the final ride to whatever fate home would present to him. After dropping the trailer nearby and bobtailing to the parking lot next to the Welcome Center, he entered the whispering pines on the man-made walkway into Michigan's living tree museum.

From days of being a young boy walking fast to keep up with his older brother to this moment, the pines had provided markers to Barley's stages in life. These old-growth forest trees are not as large as the California redwoods but are impressive, 400-year-old reminders of nature's beauty. Disappointment filled his heart when he came to the largest monarch pine. Lightning had struck the great tree, killing it. The massive trunk still stood as a temporary monument to its past glory.

Barley walked off the path and sat on another huge trunk already lying horizontally on the forest floor. His mind drifted back to the first month of his second-chance marriage . . .

. . . The honeymoon trip was not yet 30 days past when a strange, padded envelope arrived from the federal government. It was March 1994. Barley had quickly analyzed the new President Clinton. The seemingly harmless Good Ol' Boy from Arkansas was exactly as former Governor Jerry Brown had warned America he would be. "If we elect him [Clinton], there will be a scandal every week" was as close to the quote from the primaries as Barley could remember. Actually, Clinton was worse in Barley's view. "President Clinton has a very important job. He seems to have to do something every 24 hours to piss me off!" was one of Barley's favorite bar quotes. Specifically, Barley's observation was that Clinton was a political contribution shakedown thug. The strange, padded envelope from the federal government confirmed Barley's observation. Its contents described consequences attacking his newly formed life.

The federal government had busted the top executives of the loss-control services company that employed Barley. The legalities described in the envelope involved stock manipulation of the employees' 401K plan. Barley understood only one aspect—the result. The stock dropped immediately from the mid $80 dollar range to single digits, and the company was destroyed. For what gain was it destroyed? More than 2,000 workers lost their jobs and their retirement savings. Barley was one of those, and his opinion was then forged in steel. "This Clinton is considered the greatest politician alive, which means he is the most corrupt liar alive. If a company does not contribute to his cause, then the full and absolute power of his government will wage war."

The new chance at life was now as threatened as his first one had been. What could Barley do to provide? This was remote Michigan, and no employer could or should be expected to hire a partially disabled man without a college degree. Any work available would require physical labor that Barley knew he could sustain for only short periods. Further work in the safety and loss-control world would require further education and relocation. His anger increased daily, and no job possibilities appeared through which he could provide for the family.

"I'll go back to driving a truck," Barley stated across the dinner table 60 days later to his wife Marie. "I am much better at managing my back injury, and I'll avoid any job that would require any lifting. I'll do my best to find something local."

"Who would hire you with your back history?" she questioned. "Don't you have to pass a physical?"

"Enough time has passed, and that company is probably out of business by now. I just won't admit to any workers' comp injury. Hell, it's been more than 10 years, and I know how to get around the physical," Barley stated defiantly.

"Get around the physical?" she said with widening eyes.

"All they will know or care is if I can pass the drug test, and I haven't used any illegal drugs in more than 12 years. The physical form is irrelevant. I have a stack of them in my loss-control file cabinet."

"You mean you're going to falsify the form?"

"Yes I am, I'm Dr. Barley Bill. I've filled out the damn forms before. I have had to do quite a bit of fudge work in my safety days." Laughing, Barley said, "Bet you didn't know you married a doctor."

Barley found a job hauling a pneumatic tank that would allow Barley's back to be protected. The job required only 3 to 4 nights a week away, with weekends at home. The tractor was new but a rough-riding plain Jane. The work was dirty. The products hauled were sea coal (finely ground coal), coke breeze (finely ground foundry coke), sand, and a few dry chemical products Barley was unfamiliar with.

Driving a truck full time again was an uplifting experience for Barley. It was his destined trade, just not like this. As an owner/operator, his spirit was fulfilled. As a truck driver, he was reminded of being victimized by the government and its justice system. Justice was what Barley's inner thoughts were always seeking. The O.J. Simpson case was playing on the AM radio gavel to gavel as he drove.

The O.J. trial became an obsession with Barley while driving. He was waiting for some symbolic justice, and also realizing that there was little justice in this job. The government took so much out of each check, and combined with road expenses, the paychecks just weren't covering the bills. The finances of the home pushed Barley harder, only to have more taken out in taxes. The O.J. trial's end was a depressing blow, only to be followed soon by another knockout punch.

Barley had been spending too much time on the road, and Rose was feeling neglected. A surprise call from Father O'Connell caught Barley completely off guard. Erika wanted to have visitation again. Her life had settled down. A visit was arranged.

It had been a very long time since Barley had seen Erika, and she looked much as she had before the word *restitution* had destroyed the dream. She looked healthy and natural again. Her husband was a pleasant, peaceful, and calming presence at her side. Whatever turmoil and struggle she had gone through was obviously behind her. Barley could feel it immediately. Rose, now almost a teenager, went to Erika with that bond that can exist only between a mother and daughter. Barley fought back tears, as if witnessing exactly what he was witnessing. The tears were of joy and fear at the same moment. Rose would leave the custody of Barley to spend the rest of her growing years with her mother. Rose left at the school year's end. Barley knew it had to be, but out of sight he wept from the loss and his own failures.

A new voice entered Barley's world while driving the tank truck and looking for something to fill the void. The O.J. trial had provided long hours of seeking justice. Out of habit, Barley listened to the same AM station as it returned to its previous programming after the trial's infamous outcome. Rush Limbaugh seemed to be speaking directly to Barley and for Barley. "Someone in the media can actually speak for me!" he gushed from within the world behind the wheel. Rush's themes of doing what you love to do for a living inspired Barley into a new plan—a plan void of victimization.

The plan was to put a second mortgage on the house and use the money as a down payment on his own truck again. It would not be easy, but as he explained to his wife, Marie, "They won't finance me easily, but with 20 percent down on a used tractor, I can reestablish my business credit, just like the old blue Caddy did for my personal credit. Then I can trade for a better used truck and complete that contract. I will have real equity in 5 years, and then I can have my dream truck back. A black Peterbilt!"

"Go for it. Live the dream," Marie responded.

"And there will be *no* withholding taxes going to that damn Clinton!" Barley was reborn with a Ruthian dream . . .

... Barley snapped out of the exhilaration still sitting on the fallen giant tree of Hartwick Pines. He looked around and realized that many of the giants had fallen. This haven of memories was becoming a haunted grave-yard. He ran to the truck and pushed on hard to home.

Barley pulled into the parking space of the vacant lot behind his house. It was early spring, but the house looked cold and empty. He walked, and then broke into a trot, around to the front door. A strange lock and some government notice were on the door. Feeling inside his jacket pocket, he realized that his reading glasses were still on the dash. "Damned, if they can lock me out of my own house," he thought as he now ran to the back shed. "I'll just grab one of the old sawhorses and break into the back bedroom window." Strange, there should have been two sawhorses, but there was only one. Stranger still, there at the back bedroom window was the miss-ing sawhorse, and the window was already broken with blood—dried, brownish-red blood drops—on the siding. Barley climbed through and fell onto the floor. The furniture was all gone. He ran through the vacant house, breathing cold stale air. A foul smell was emitting from the second bath-room. A partially full half gallon of whiskey sat upright next to the toilet, and dried vomit was on the floor on the opposite side. Barley turned, walking slowly to the dining room carrying the whiskey and its remaining contents. He stood before the wall where family pictures once protected the paint. Written in dried, reddish-brown blood across the sun-faded space for fam-ily pictures, in angry smudged letters, was the word *RESTITUTION*.

He pulled hard on the whiskey and collapsed on the floor next to the phone jack. He found the papers and the letter from Marie. Barley then dropped his chin onto his chest, and his shoulders slumped into a position of weeping. He had already been home to see this scene 60 days ago, and now he realized it.

The house was repossessed for an unpaid government loan that was supposed to have been a grant—a grant for a disabled truck driver 20 years earlier. The papers were a rejection of that claim. The school had gone bank-rupt, and no further records were available. The second mortgage was for home improvement, and criminal charges were going to be pending as a re-sult of the lack of increase in property value. The lawyer had advised di-vorce to protect the remaining assets from seizure by the government.

Her letter further explained the details of how she had attempted to stop the foreclosure. No one in the government would listen. Her letter also reminded Barley that he had promised to get off the road after the heart attack 2 years ago. It was now too late for "me or the highway." And 60 days ago, Barley had decided to take one last ride, just as he had said 2 years ago.

When he had cried until no more tears would come and drank until the bottle was dry, Barley entered the master bathroom and stood before the wall mirror. Of all the cruelty he had endured, what he saw in the mirror was the cruelest. Age and physical deterioration would prevent any rebuilding of life now. His world was lost. There was no duty, need, or reason to live.

But outside was the ride. One last ride! One last ride without reason, destination, responsibility, or care. All he would need would be money, cash without contract or trace.

Barley called the boat and motorcycle dealer that stored his two hobbies. "Make me an offer; I have to leave." The call back produced $6,000 for both, which was less than half of their value. In the Post Office box was his final settlement check from the truck company and a notice of termination from his carrier for too many speeding tickets. In his truck briefcase was an emergency check for a 24½ percent interest loan, which he cashed. He then emptied what remained on five of the six credit cards at an ATM machine, sending $1,000 to the one card he would keep for emergency or use when a credit card was required. When he was finished, Barley had $23,482 in cash, which he put into a leather replica Crown Royal bag. He pulled his belt through the straps and left his hometown for the last time on his last ride. It was a ride of freedom with nothing left to lose.

Westward . . . west to the big sky.

CHAPTER 22

What Should Be Done

Dr. Paul H. Lindsey, the Cry Psy, was having no luck in the research and records department. None of the registrations of late model Peterbilts had produced a credible lead or any link to felonious conduct from the numerous "might-be-the-Road-Rogue" incidents. He just did not have any feelings or any perceptions about this case, except for the anguish of the lead agent, William Jackson, and the anger of the D.O.T. regional director, Arnold Benson. The F.B.I. file on Jackson clearly justified his anguish, but nothing of Jackson's history would suggest incompetence. Perhaps a meeting with the TV reporter, Linda Wright, might uncover a clue to the identity of this Road Rogue.

They met for lunch to discuss the case, with each hoping for some new bit of evidence from the other. Linda aggressively and ambitiously asked questions without result. She would leave with more questions unanswered. This criminal psychiatrist was not easy to fool. She had used her natural beauty many times to entice information from men in her career, but her prior knowledge of the Cry Psy left her without that edge.

This woman equally puzzled Dr. Lindsey. He had expected some anger and grief from the loss of her brother. He didn't sense any. She was excited and stimulated by her new celebrity status. If anything, she seemed to rather enjoy the mystery of this Road Rogue, and she didn't want the story to end. Dr. Lindsey decided that further investigation with the lone witness, Hugh Cauley, and those who were possible witnesses in that small Indiana town would generate insight into the mind of the monster.

Several interviews were conducted by Dr. Lindsey, which only resulted in confusion and puzzlement. It was clear that Agent Jackson was correct in his assumption of an antiauthority dinosaur, but the witnesses from the bar described a more pleasant man who had avoided an obvious fight. This Road Rogue must have a violent, uncontrollable temper behind the wheel.

The interview with Hugh Cauley netted a serious setback. Not only was he color-blind, but when shown photographs of various trucks, he made identification errors, referring to Freightliner classics and the no-longer-made Autocars as Peterbilts. Hugh Cauley was a high school dropout. Dr. Lindsey sent copies of the report of the problem to Agent Jackson and Arnold Benson.

The report included a physical description of the man at the bar that would only vaguely detail the Road Rogue as a typical, middle-aged truck driver wearing a ball cap and tinted glasses, with a short beard with gray in it. His estimated size was 6 feet tall and 250 pounds. The report also requested additional investigation of witnesses to confirm or refute Hugh Cauley's truck model description.

Bill Jackson read his copy and shook his head. "Might as well start over." The phone rang as he was still holding the report.

"Bill, I'm sorry, but you need to join me out in South Dakota. I know you just got home." Arnie Benson was on his way to the airport and calling from a car.

"I'll be there before the plane takes off," Bill sighed.

On his way to the airport, Bill stopped by the law firm where his wife worked. He wanted to plead for saving the marriage. "You've done lost her, Willie boy. Lisa told me she's going home to Missouri to make babies and have a real life. I'll bet you didn't think she would go, but that time has come. You know that biological clock is running, and . . ."

"Thanks, Yvette," Bill interrupted. "Do you have a number where I could reach her?"

Yvette just shook her head "No."

On the plane, Arnold Benson broke the bad news to Bill Jackson that another officer had been killed and the trail was already cold. The preliminary report was of another trailer swat.

Barley had been bouncing along without paying much attention, Hobbs in control. His destination was Seattle, Washington, for no other reason than that he hadn't been there in a while. If it had not been that the officer had just heard the country song by the Long Riders, he would have just let the truck pass, but a two-lane road in South Dakota can be isolated, and Hobbs was getting rather good at bandit duels. A lone patrol car was no match for the natural. This growing mentality was breaking down the neurological pathways to the library of memory and experience of the man known as Bartholomew Levi Williams. The experiences of 5 million miles allowed Hobbs to understand what the bandit was thinking as a driver. Hobbs could anticipate moves and read facial expressions through a mirror view. He had toyed with the bandit, challenging with speed until an angry overconfidence left the patrol car exposed and taken by surprise.

The Ruth rarely desired the wheel now. The realization of nothing left to lose, and the terrible pain inside the skull each time he had control was leaving that part of the former man as only a stimulus for the body's physical needs. Hobbs responded to these needs without fully understanding them. Hunger, thirst, pleasure, pain, and morality still existed only in the Ruth.

The driving habits of the Rogue began to change. Barley had loved sunrises. Throughout his career, he had risen before dawn and driven until sunset and beyond. The passing scenery of the road was a true love. Hobbs wanted the protection of night and darkness. With Hobbs in almost constant control, the truck driving began just before sunset and continued until sunrise. Each day's new dawning was a signal to find a safe haven parking place. The body needed rest and nourishment. Hobbs understood, but there were other needs of the Road Rogue as more and more of the mind and bodily functions were explored.

After the duel in South Dakota, Hobbs first doubled back and then turned south. A little ZZ Top music changed the destination to warm Texas sun and memories of cold Pearl beer. Sunrise brought Fort Smith, Arkansas, into the search for the day's safe haven. A large parking lot of a closed-down department store provided a place for rest.

[These kind of havens are becoming hard to find. Nearly all parking lots prohibit trucks as if all drivers are terrorists. The government's pronouncements of forcing tired truckers off the road sound good to the public, but all this demonizing has left no place to park. Every truck stop on any major route is full to capacity by 7:00 P.M., and rest areas fill up by dark. Tired truckers are routinely kicked out of available space and forced to continue to drive.]

The signs No Truck Parking in this lot no longer mattered. This business had gone broke. "Perhaps the store would still be open if truckers were allowed to park and shop," he thought. His body was exhausted, and he would sleep until 2:00 P.M. in the afternoon.

The sleep was healing. Barley rose and stepped down out of the cab to scout the area. There was no restaurant close by, but across the street 100 yards past the curb was a bar and grill. The building was run-down looking. A lighted beer sign was plenty inviting. He walked to this bar and was pleased with its atmosphere. This was a manual working-class gathering place with a biker feel. Hobbs was allowing control by the Ruth while learning. The woman behind the bar was sexy looking. Thoughts of pleasure entered his mind.

Barley walked directly to the bar and looked in the mirror. He looked terrible. He quickly turned away and returned to the truck. "I must do something to fix myself up," he thought.

A grocery store on the opposite corner provided a new razor, men's hair color, 2 gallons of bottled water, and elastigen collagen gel from the women's section. An old memory from days spent in too much sun sparked the idea. A woman at the pool from that first apartment back in Capital City had given him this gel to heal sunburn. She had winked at him saying, "It's for stretch marks, but it works for sunburn, too. Try it."

One hour and 20 minutes later, Barley Bill looked and felt 10 years younger. An inside-the-cab cooler bath with a remarkably good hair color job and a clean-shaven face brought a smile. The gel felt so good that he had to voice a loud "Yes" to himself. He dug out his best T-shirt and jeans and headed back to that bar. Hobbs rather liked this euphoria and did not want any painful memories to interrupt it.

He smiled as she brought the first beer, not recognizing him from the earlier walk-in and walk-out visit. She was Arkansas, real Arkansas, without modern political correctness, with the accent and boldness that were once dominant in this state. She seemed to be a throwback to a time when the geographic regions of America had distinct cultures. "Tammy, call me Tammy, not Mame or Barmaid," she instructed.

"Named after Tammy Wynette, I suppose," Barley said, giving away his non-Arkansas speech.

"Whereabouts you from, cowboy?" Tammy questioned, with a little more interest than Barley would have expected.

"From the road. I'm a trucker, originally from Michigan." Barley was hoping to spark more interest.

He studied her. Tammy worked the bar while being watched as if she enjoyed the spotlight of this little stage. She was wearing tight, form-fitting jeans and an "upper" shirt, revealing most of what was being held up by a space-age, carbonic-fiber, superstructure undercarriage with a loose-fitting, unbuttoned, undersized blouse, as if curtains were drawn open on a mountain view. Her long hair was teased, bleached, and falling into a painted face, suggesting she had already been where Barley wanted to go.

The Hobbs of him sent chemical stimulation into areas of the mind, hoping to produce the correct words or phrases with which to tempt her.

"It sure is refreshing to hear your accent." Barley smiled as he gazed at her.

"Accent?" Tammy rebuffed him with a tilted head.

[Strike one.]

"What I meant was, all over the country everything is becoming the same. You sound like you haven't been influenced by television, and you look like you like being a woman," Barley offered.

"Well honey, I am a woman," she stated to all of the men sitting at the bar. "And I don't fall for any cheap one-liners."

"Okay, a spirited woman," Barley said in a John Wayne imitation of Rooster Cogburn, "Out here in the territory, men like a spirited woman—almost as much as a spirited horse."

"One more line like that, and you won't get another beer," Tammy giggled.

[Strike two.]

Barley settled back into the bar stool and did not attempt to talk anymore. The line of liquor bottles provided the glare spots to refocus the Ruth into a memory . . .

When the decision was made to attempt to return to being an owner/operator, optimism filled Barley's heart, along with a defiance regarding paying taxes to a government with Bill Clinton as its leader. The prior bankruptcy limited the choice of trucks to ones costing less than $35,000 of total price. The first tractor was a 5-year-old Volvo/GMC. Barley considered it ugly, but it was plush inside and had an old-style Cat engine with a 13-speed transmission. The Volvo was a good-riding truck, and the first year was successful. The second was not; breakdowns began eating up profit. Barley realized that he just didn't have enough credit and capital to keep going.

"If I can just survive until that Arkansas lowlife is out of office, I would be willing to go back to a regular job," Barley often said as the election of 1996 approached. On his way home, Election Day, it was announced that Clinton had won even before the polls were closed. Barley struggled on in trucking because of it, determined to last long enough to see an end to what he viewed as the most corrupt president of his lifetime. "Losing money has its benefits," was a regular bar quote. "I don't owe taxes to that S.O.B."

Then there was hope. The impeachment saga would show the country, Barley was sure of it. Just maybe Bill Clinton would be forced to leave. The off-year election, of course, saved him. The media was as shameless as the shameless democrats that defended the scoundrel. Barley wanted to see justice. "Please Lord, show me justice!" he prayed.

His prayers were answered in another part of the election. The golden boy prosecutor was defeated in his bid to become a governor. The discovery of this brought new hope and optimism. Barley decided to carry out his original plan, and he traded for a newer truck—a 2-year-old, red classic Freightliner with enough chrome to warm his ego into confidence anew. He would make it happen. "I will survive until Clinton is gone and I replace my dream with a black Peterbilt . . ." Barley said aloud, while still staring at the liquor bottles in the bar. The woman named after Tammy Wynette placed a fresh mug in front of him.

"Oh, you don't like our Billy Clinton, eh cowboy?" She smiled.

"Sorry, I was just daydreaming," Barley sighed self-consciously. "The john, where's the john?"

Tammy pointed to the back corner. On the door was a poster of Bill Clinton smiling in the upper center, just below the word *Bucks*.

"Oh, I forgot. I'm in Arkansas. Sorry," Barley apologized as he pointed to the poster.

"Honey, everything you see isn't always what you think you see," Tammy quipped.

As Barley walked toward the door and its poster, he began to realize that the poster wasn't as he had thought at first. With each step, the face of the smiling "Bubba" became an arrangement of small squares, until only the small squares could be seen, not Bill Clinton. The squares were reduced photos of naked women and female private parts. Barley laughed aloud and marveled at the concept. He returned to the bar and a playfully smiling Tammy.

"That poster is great. Where did it come from?" Barley asked, still half laughing.

"It's from a Penthouse magazine, January of 1999, I believe." Then Tammy looked directly at Barley. "Now do you understand about what you think you see, honey?"

Barley did. Hobbs did not care. Hobbs was exploring within the mind, searching for the clever magic words.

Barley tried an old joke after he guzzled down another mug. "You know, they did a survey in Arkansas, and 40 percent of the women said that they would like to have sex with Bill Clinton. The other 60 percent said 'never again'."

There was no reaction from Tammy, indicating that she had heard that one long ago and many times. "You know," Tammy then said, mimicking Barley, "he's no different than any of the politicians."

"I'll give you that point," Barley replied quickly. "All the politicians are for globalization and social engineering. They want us all to be sheep, a class system that can be controlled."

Tammy turned away, not wanting to hear political talk, and Hobbs could sense the rejection. Hobbs must stop Barley from ruining this encounter. Hobbs must protect. Pain pushed the Ruth into submission. Hobbs searched for magic words, and then as Tammy returned with another mug, he looked intensely into her eyes and in stumbling words said, "You are voluptuous. I need you."

"Okay, cowboy," Tammy said firmly while pointing to the door. "Finish your beer. You're out of here!"

[Strike three.]

As Barley walked toward the exit he heard Tammy's final siren, "Hey cowboy, y'all come back and see me when you pass through again." Barley turned, cocked his head, smiled, and shrugged his shoulders. The beer provided a long sleep of needed healing.

The following day Barley awakened as refreshed as his diseased mind could be. He was hungry on this mid-afternoon sunny day. He drove a short distance, spotting a fast-food burger restaurant with enough room to park the rig past the rear parking area in a gravel lot.

Barley walked inside, noticing an old woman while he waited at the counter for his food order. She was the only other customer. She looked ancient and stared at Barley with fear. "Well, I guess I look a little rough," Barley thought, remembering he hadn't cleaned up from the previous day's drinking and long sleep. A newspaper was on the counter, which Barley picked up to avoid the fearful stare coming from the deeply wrinkled face of the old woman.

On the newspaper's second page was a story summarizing the saga of a mad truck driver. This was the Road Rogue Barley remembered hearing about. As he read, an elevator music song began playing on the restaurant's sound system. The melody sounded familiar. Barley looked up and glanced at the old woman.

She looked changed. The wrinkles were not as deep. Some color appeared in her cheeks, and her eyes were glassy. Fear was no longer being emitted. She was looking up slightly, and her shoulders were not as slumped. He saw her mouth move, and without hearing the words he could see her sing, "I saw the Harbor Lights . . ." Her hands were cupped now, and Barley could see by the twitching of her exposed calves that she was dancing—dancing in her mind with a handsome, uniformed soldier in another world long ago. Fear now struck Barley!

Barley looked at the newspaper article and pictures of wrecked police cars. Fear and anxiety filled his mind. He looked back at her. She was not mentally here. She was reliving a dream! She was oblivious to her physical surroundings, lost in the song . . .

Barley got up and ran to the truck. He examined the trailer. This trailer should have been turned in—damage, tire cuts . . . "Oh, my God, my God! It's me! I'm the Road Rogue!"

Barley struggled to the curb side of the trailer and collapsed . . . vomiting and sobbing until his heart began racing out of control. He forced himself into the cab, took a nitro, started the engine, and collapsed again . . . on the wheel, his heart pounding as he fought to hold on to conscious thought. "I must turn myself in, go to Washington, try to tell them why . . ." Then he passed out—out on the wheel with the vibrations . . .

So you think you've found a way of living . . . (Ken Hensley)

CHAPTER 23

The Park

He awakened from the near-death attack of realization as Bartholomew Levi Williams. The Ruth of him was now aware of the secret evil of his subconscious. He knew *now* that his former talent was a monster—a monster created by years of suppressed hatred. The remaining morality of his deteriorating mind had formed a plan. He would go to Washington, D.C., and confess to the crimes of violence at the national symbol of justice with a statement of his long-held grievances. His plan would be to contact this voice-for-America reporter, Linda Wright. This would be his last ride—his last ride to justice. His Ruth was determined to control the monster, Hobbs. No music, no memories, Hobbs must not be allowed to have the wheel. Bartholomew Levi Williams found Interstate 40 and pulled east. The trailer's damages would be proof enough that he was the Road Rogue.

Linda Wright received a call, but it was from Nebraska. "Hey, this is Jim, Jim 'Dandy' Daniels. Remember me?"

"Hello Jim," Linda sighed. "I know we need to talk."

"Talk hell!" Jim shouted into the phone. "We're supposed to be getting married, and I haven't seen nor heard from you in weeks. Do you remember that you promised to be here for the sales promotion this weekend?" Jim "Dandy" Daniels had a car dealership outside Lincoln, Nebraska.

"That's not possible now. I have another network special to tape." Then Linda Wright forced out the words she had wanted to say for those same weeks. "It's over, Jim. I have a new life now. I'm not coming back to Lincoln, Nebraska."

"Big time celebrity now, aren't you?" Jim angrily shot back. "What happens when they catch that old truck driver?" Click.

Bill Jackson's last call to his wife Lisa (after being given a phone number) was also ended with a click of a phone being slammed into a receiver. "I'll quit, I'll really quit the bureau, just as soon as this case is finished with the Road Rogue!"

Lisa did not want to hear anymore. Her new life was now back in Missouri, near Joplin.

Life for Barley Bill was gone now. All that remained was the last ride to Washington, D.C. The worn out pavement of Interstate 40 from Little Rock to Memphis, Tennessee, helped to keep the Hobbs in the subconscious as its wash-boarded grooves required constant attention from behind the wheel. Once in Tennessee, the road smoothed out, and the rolling hills of heavily forested scenery began to relax Barley physically and mentally.

Barley tried to organize his thoughts. He wanted to make a statement to the public. He still had no detailed memory of the individual crimes of violent rage, only an understanding that what was described in the paper, on the TV, and over the airwaves was a part of him. He pulled over to rest near the junction of I40 and I75 west of Knoxville, Tennessee. Hobbs had been sending impulses, creating painful headaches, in the attempt to take control. Barley had resisted and had held on until the pain was unbearable. "Rest in the sleeper bunk away from the wheel to strengthen the will," Barley thought as he closed his eyes and pulled the covers over himself.

The sleep was shallow and filled with demon dreams that woke him several times. Just before sunrise, Barley sat behind the wheel with a groaning, ill feeling of dread, guilt, and sorrow in his gut. The Ruth of him was still determined to drive to Washington, D.C., and give himself up. The morning sun's rays gave him strength through the windshield as he peered out at the mountainous terrain that Interstate 81 snakes through as the border of Virginia is passed. Hobbs remained in the hidden, allowing the ride to relax the body and ease the mental anguish.

Rolling north on Interstate 81, with the glorious Blue Ridge Mountains off to the west, Barley marveled at the natural beauty of Virginia. "There is no wonder that so many great Americans of our founding history were Virginians, and that those men fought so bravely for their independence," Barley pondered. "Independence and individual rights are what freedom should mean. Those founding fathers understood that and became the driving force of the Revolutionary War for independence from Britain. Is that what part of me has become?" Barley's mind began searching for an understanding of what had happened to him and what had created the hidden monster. Was it the government's march to tyranny and its acts against the individual man and his independent way of life? "I must make a statement to America before its ideals are taken, or worse, more individuals will become like me."

Barley pulled off the Interstate and found a strip mall. An electronics store provided hardware for a plan to turn himself in. He would videotape a statement of grievances and send the tape to Linda Wright, and if her report aired the message, then the Road Rogue would meet justice. Justice would be the main grievance. The lack of equal justice under law undermines the principles of the foundation of the country and created the Rogue.

Barley stood 50 feet in front of the grill, with the Blue Ridge Mountains as a backdrop and two American flags tied to the chrome bumper guides. The video cam was on a tripod pointed at the grill's center. Barley walked into the camera's view wearing dark glasses and a Caterpillar ball cap.

"I am the one—the Road Rogue. The madness and death I have caused, I did not realize until recently. I can only speculate that this violence was during some sort of sleepwalk while driving. I have seen the evidence, and I now am convinced. I am truly sorry for the loss and heartache of the individuals directly involved. I do understand what has caused my madness, and I wish to offer these grievances in the hope that no other rogues are created. The madness of my unknown actions has been defensive. I do believe this. I also believe that . . .

I love America, all of its natural beauty and its founding principles. The government of America is based upon individual rights and the premise that individuals are created with equal opportunity for those basic rights. We are not created *equal* if that word is misconstrued to mean the same as it is by today's politicians. That same is to put individuals into a class system of separate, equal justice under law, based upon class. A political philosophy in America today attempts to remove the ugliness and pain of poverty by removing individual opportunity to be the best or better than the rest. This philosophy will only result in the removal of the beauty and pleasure of success. This class system has at its core the tax system—withholding tax from the working masses, while providing exemptions for those not subject to withholding. Those Americans subject to this withholding are subjects or slaves to the ruling elite. I call for an end to withholding taxes! Ending this class war will end political apathy, government dependence, and injustice.

The justice system must be separate from the political system that promotes this class system. I also call for the resignation of the politician who was from the justice system that has created the monster within me. Politicians engaged in justice seek only political gain, thereby destroying equal justice under law.

With the founding principles of this great country being buried under mountains of politically influenced laws, justice is lost. The government becomes an absolute power, and is corrupted absolutely. The corrupt politician from whom I seek restitution now works in the administration of the White House.

I ask this reporter to investigate how my July morning was taken from me. That should answer her question of Why?

If government continues on its path of destroying individual independent life with its social engineering of tax by class and its globalization, more rogues will rise up here in America and worldwide."

After copying the recording onto a videotape, Barley dispatched the tape and a short, handwritten note to Linda Wright at the TV network. The note stated the title of the golden boy prosecutor at the White House and gave a time when Barley would call to make arrangements to turn himself in. He sent the package by Federal Express from Virginia, and then he drove to Carlisle, Pennsylvania.

Carlisle, Pennsylvania, is a major truck-stop town. Its location at the crossing of Interstate 81 and the Pennsylvania Turnpike, as well as being near the state capital, Harrisburg, makes for a natural distribution point. Several truck stops are located in a row, and at any time thousands of trucks are parked in a virtual truck city. For truckers, any further east and north has increasingly worse conditions, until reaching the nightmares of old eastern cities built without foresight of their future dependence on trucking. Cross-country truckers usually stop here, prepare to complete whatever tasks are required of them in the Northeast, and return to this oasis without stopping. (So much for D.O.T. compliance and safety.) There simply are not enough places in the Northeast for trucks to stop. Near the center of the row of truck stops of Carlisle is a small, overcrowded, wood-frame tavern. This was not just an oasis for Barley; it was a heaven and a safe parking spot to avoid detection. (Even this town of truck stops is completely full by 8:00 P.M.)

Barley entered the tavern at 11:00 A.M. in hopes of easing the gut-wrenching guilt and to see if Linda Wright would air his tape. The beer and trucker talk helped to calm his nerves and encouraged maintained control. Hobbs *was* present, learning, and not combative; Hobbs was in a stealth mode. The Long Riders' song "The Road Rogue" was played twice before noon.

> *Running with the Road Rogue,*
> *No Bears in sight . . .*
> *We're not gonna be hassled—*
> *Smokey must have learned.*
>
> *Running with the Road Rogue . . .*

The TV network mail-room supervisor signed for Barley's package to Linda Wright, and it was screened by security. Linda was contacted at her new midtown apartment. She taxied to the network building and read the handwritten note. Previous letters, had been received from kooks claiming to be the Road Rogue, but something in the video convinced her that this was the real thing. Despite the numerous immediate arrangements necessitated by receipt of the video, she decided to do the right thing and called Arnie Benson to repay the debt she had in her heart. "He [trucker in the video] didn't give his name."

Arnie Benson called Agent Bill Jackson, and a meeting was arranged hastily at the network. Promos were put together quickly and aired by Linda

Wright without showing any of the video. Linda Wright would have a segment on the nightly news program. This would provide a major exclusive,
but Arnie Benson and Bill Jackson were given strict instructions and authority to censor the video. A phone call from the White House convinced
those in power at the network to comply.

The meeting at the network confirmed Agent Bill Jackson's initial suspicions and assumptions of who and what this mad trucker was: an antiauthority dinosaur. Linda Wright *could* use the video for her report, but
only the audio containing "I am the one . . . the Road Rogue." The rest of
her report would be limited to an approved script that used her voice.

Barley and all the drivers in the Carlisle, Pennsylvania, tavern saw the
promo. Much of America either saw or heard the promo on the radio.
Linda Wright's segment would generate great advertisement revenue.

Barley was dressed quite differently and was not wearing the cheap,
wraparound sunglasses as he had in the video. The promo was used to hype
the little information that would be released. The only real identifying fea-
ture from the video was the grill of the truck. Barley was ordinary looking, and he had struggled to voice the first quote—sounding unusual, with
a deep sad tone, forcing the words.

Throughout the afternoon, from the first airing of the promo at 2:00 P.M.
until the start of the evening network news, Barley slowly drank bottled
beer. He savored each swallow, believing that this was the last time he
would have the freedom to enjoy an atmosphere of workingmen in a smoke-
filled, run-down tavern. His belief that he was about to surrender took
away the gut-wrenching guilt. Around him the talk of trucks and how fast
or how well they pulled, the jukebox music, and the occasional sexual in-
nuendos aimed at the barmaid and waitress were heavenly.

An old-fashioned, greasy bar burger dressed up with ketchup, mustard,
pickle, and a thick slice of raw Spanish onion would be his last meal of freedom. His last political conversation was to attempt to inform the younger
drivers of the dangers of the Qualcom satellite system that most were
using. "The satellite is a violation of the Constitution. You must see that!
The Fourth Amendment of the Bill of Rights was written before this technology, but its [satellite system] records can be used against you in court.
They know exactly where you are, and when. If you have driven past that
10-hour rule, you will be subject to a negligence lawsuit. Your company cannot protect you or itself in a case such as an accident with a fatality. You
will be guilty automatically. I hope that you younger drivers will not fall for
the traps being set by the government, as your companies that you pull for
have. They [both the government and company management] want total
control of your lives in the truck. They can't stand, or understand, or are

outright jealous of your freedom. Is convenience and efficiency worth giving up freedom and independence for?"

A young man offered, "Well, as long as I follow the rules and don't break the law or make mistakes, it doesn't matter. I like the system because I don't have to talk on the telephone to get loads."

"God help you." Barley shook his head. "Does that company know you're in here? They will soon." Barley did not offer anymore and simply thought that the government and its media propaganda have destroyed the last world for a common workingman—a cowboy independent individual.

The airing of the censored Linda Wright segment was the end of the visit to this tavern heaven. Barley was angered by it. All I accomplished was to make my own wanted poster, Barley thought. He looked back at the bar as he left. "It doesn't matter if this was the last time. The local government will tear this place down soon anyway." Barley walked to the tractor and lay down in the bunk to rest, contemplating a different way to surrender—without Linda Wright.

The next morning, Barley had no new plan, and he decided that he should get away from the truck to think it out. A car rental company picked him up, and he drove a few miles south to Gettysburg National Park. The words of Ken Hensley's Uriah Heep song from the Salisbury album played in his mind.

Let me walk awhile alone
Among the sacred rocks and stones.... (Ken Hensley)

After parking and refusing the assistance of a guide, Barley walked into the hallowed ground of the most important battle of American history after winning independence. It would become a battlefield again within one man's heart, mind, and soul. Barley had been here before, of course, but he was not then burdened by this internal fight of his Ruth and his Hobbs.

The natural beauty and peace of this land so contrasts with its horrifying past. Barley walked slowly, stopping to read and study the monuments. The sculptures of faces emitted the characters of men who fought until their last breath for a cause. Barley looked at images of leaders, both blue and gray. These were true leaders, real men who led common men into battle from the front of the line. Even high-ranking soldiers died with honor on this field. "Such bravery," Barley thought, "such a different world and society, compared to today."

As the afternoon's brilliant sun began to dim and the shadows from the trees began to extend into the open fields, Barley started to hear the sounds of the great battle in his mind. He sat down on the edge of trees where the men of Picket's Charge had gathered for their ill-fated march into sure death. Barley was feeling the anguish of those brave men, some of whom were mere boys. With his eyes closed, he could picture the battlefield in front of him: the cannon fire and smoke, the troop leaders preparing their men, the nervous adrenaline building.

Barley stood up as if he were with them and marched into the field. He imagined the incredible noise of men charging and screaming . . . cannon fire . . . and then the musket balls everywhere . . . huge explosions of shrapnel . . . men falling. Then, as if from some scene from a movie, Barley could feel musket balls striking his own flesh. A ball hit his left side chest, and he fell hard on his left side. His heart was racing, and he was sweating, but he felt a shivering cold and numbness. He passed out of consciousness.

The setting sun had reached the treetops as Barley regained consciousness and struggled to his feet. He continued walking until he reached the far northwest area of the national park near the barn once used as the field hospital of the Confederate Army. He sat on the edge of the trees, away from the main path, and attempted to collect his thoughts. The two parts of him, of his mind, the Ruth and Hobbs, were now directly confronting each other.

For the first time, Barley was able to remember all that the Hobbs had done. His anger was reaching past the delusions created by the fever his body was enduring. "How could you do this—murderer!" And then tears flowed as he realized that it was himself. "I am only your servant," replied the Hobbs.

Barley then collapsed and passed into a dreamlike status. Again he could hear the cries of the battlefield. Now those cries came from the field hospital, from men and boys who fought for a cause. What was that cause? Why did these men fight so hard and so long—both sides?

In this haunting dream, Barley speculated the way. He saw the face of the stoic, defiant, and beloved General Lee, and he looked upon the face of Lincoln, the president, whose face seemed to show all of the sadness of his times, as if he could see into the future. But the common man fought this battle. No leaders could create this battle without a cause reaching into the heart of the common man. Both sides were armies of men believing that they were right. How could it be?

As Barley's mind neared a complete pass out, he could only think that these men (of both sides) who were calling to him today had fought for the same cause—against tyranny. The only difference was the rhetoric offered by the politicians of those times. The South won the battles until the North found the moral high ground of the slavery issue. The men of the South, the common men, were fighting against a growing, centralized federal government that threatened their independent way of life. The common men of the North fought against a government that allowed slavery by a ruling elite. Could it be that our greatest president could see the future, that he could see that his federal government would one day take the livelihoods of common Americans and promote the use of "slaves" in foreign lands in a new global society (for example, those who make the American flags that are cheap to buy and say "Made in China")? Could Lincoln have envisioned a justice system based upon class or royalty?

Barley thought again of the sadness in the eyes of Lincoln, and he heard the screams of haunted souls who had died in a vain attempt to keep justice for all. Sadness overtook his heart. Barley passed out of thought. He lay there until dawn of the next morning. In his mind's eye, two unseen images appeared: one in the dark shadows of the tree's edge, the other in the morning mist cloaking the battlefield. The image in the shadows held out its left arm, fingers extended, showing the prostrated body of a tortured creature of a man. The image in the mist bowed its head, and unspoken words formed in a gentle rush of wind through the leaves: "Raise your gidden."

The Hobbs of him stood up with adrenaline flowing as a new and complete-in-itself being, feeling all of his body, muscles, lungs, senses, and mental pathways. He walked directly back to the visitor's center with the strength of two men and a mind possessed.

CHAPTER 24

Rainbow Demon

... On his horse of crimson fire.
Black shadows are following closely
On the heels of his desire....

... Possessed by some distant calling ... (Ken Hensley)

The Road Rogue stopped while walking back to the visitor's center parking area and flexed muscles throughout the body. Each limb, joint, cartilage, and ligament was stretched to the physical limit. All flesh, nerves, blood vessels, and organs were flushed with a regenerating rush of awareness. Mental command pathways were explored by the new entity. Antibodies and an aroused immune system were attacking injured muscles, tumors, and damaged cells. The mind and senses lit up as if charged with a mythological force. The complete metamorphosis had created a human flesh android, programmed from the memories, emotions, desires, pain, and dreams of the former being, without fear of consequence.

The watch on the left wrist beeped its alarm, instantly triggering a memory from the night after watching the Linda Wright segment with the video made by Barley Bill. It was time to call the network and read the short response Barley Bill had written on the bar napkin. The Road Rogue walked to a pay phone and made a collect call for Linda Wright.

She was there at a special phone with Bill Jackson, Arnie Benson, and several agent technicians (for tracing) in the prepared room. Intense anxiety filled the room as a pointed finger told Linda Wright to pick up the receiver. "This is Linda Wright."

"Reporter, why did you not play his message? You have asked 'Why?' for America." The Road Rogue coldly questioned her, as if speaking from authority.

"I must be accurate and have all the facts. Are you calling for him?" Linda spoke softly, hoping to gain an advantage. She nodded to Arnie Benson and quickly wrote on a pad, "It's him, the one from the video."

"Did you not investigate?" again spoken with cold authority.

"Yes, I have called the White House and *he* denies having any knowledge of you or your claim. What is your name?" Linda stopped asking more, waiting for a response as she looked at the technician who was giving her hand signals.

"He created me!" The Road Rogue felt anger. "And I have created you."

"Now hold on, you killed my brother!" Linda Wright's own anger removed the soft, sexual tone from her voice, even though the technician tried to whisper instructions to her.

"And how shall you be judged, beauty? The golden boy took my July morning from me because I was an insignificant, political stepping-stone not deserving of justice. You of the media are puppets of all those like him who threw away the principles America was founded on. Lady Justice is supposed to hold her scale with a blindfold over her eyes. And beauty, have you thrown away your July morning for fame?" The phone was hung up before Linda Wright could respond.

A resentful curiosity rushed through Linda's mind as she thought of Jim "Dandy" back in Lincoln, Nebraska. Something in the way the Road Rogue had spoken had gotten to her. She was angry with herself for allowing it, but she turned to the technician.

"Gettysburg. He's calling from the visitor center at Gettysburg National Park." The technician nodded to Arnie Benson and Bill Jackson, signaling his assurance.

"Call the state police! Call the park! Must be a semi truck there somewhere!" Arnie Benson and Bill Jackson called for a helicopter ride to Gettysburg.

The Road Rogue sat back in the rental car driver seat without any emotional aftertaste from the phone call. His only desire was to get back to the truck and to continue on a never-ending last ride. He did not bother to return the car, leaving it parked in front of the truck-stop restaurant. He called the rental car company and said he had to leave for an emergency. The rental car employee spoke of an additional charge for coming to the truck stop to pick it up. The keys were left at the fuel counter, and no special suspicions were aroused. "We'll just add the cost on your credit card."

Once in the familiar, behind the wheel, the Road Rogue headed directly north on the two-lane State Highway 34, up onto Blue Mountain and on to Mahoney Ridge, with the natural forest trees of Little Buffalo State Park providing timeless scenery on this challenging drive used only by old veteran and local drivers. It is not a recommended route for trucks, but it serves as a short cut toward Route 322, bypassing the city of Harrisburg, Pennsylvania. He continued on Route 322, through State College, to reach Interstate 80 westbound. The Road Rogue would be a clever fugitive, fearless but careful not to expose himself.

What remained of his former mind was a memory of all that had happened in the life of Bartholomew Levi Williams, as if that past life were chronicled on a data storage disk. The Road Rogue could access the data in forming a new way to think, decide, and plan.

A cold, evil plan was forming as the setting sun darkened the valleys between the long grades of Interstate 80 in central Pennsylvania. The next destination would be Capital City and its tall building of restitution justice. Speed building, turbo whining, beep-beep-beep-beep-beeeee . . . from the radar detector, and a full-grown Bear entered the westbound lanes from a hidden, shadowy stand of trees.

The Road Rogue's muscles tightened in his neck and shoulders as the Bandit closed in, disco lights not yet turned on. Reaching behind the driver's seat, the calculating mind of the monster pulled a gallon of engine oil up to its lap. The oil container was opened, and just as the Bandit's intentions were confirmed with the flashing command to pull over, oil began spilling out of the vent window, creating a sticky spray. The downgrade into the shadows allowed for the truck to accelerate quickly past 80 miles per hour.

As the Bandit's wipers made their first blinding swipe, the Road Rogue downshifted and hit the engine retarder (Jake brake) while drifting right, exposing the cursing Bandit officer to the violent trailer swat. The patrol car struck the opposite guardrail with such force that it flipped up over the rail and down the steep slope, rolling and spinning, until it reached a death valley 300 feet down in the old rubble of the highway's birth.

Twenty-three minutes later, the state police were notified of their fallen comrade by a private road-paving dump-truck driver who had seen the flashing lights flip over the guardrail and plummet downward. He was struggling along the upgrade and pulled over at the first available exit to call.

Bill Jackson, Arnie Benson, and Linda Wright were still at the Gettysburg visitor's center conducting interviews when they were notified of more carnage. Inspection roadblocks had been set up on I81, the Chambersburg Pike, the Pennsylvania Turnpike entrance, and north of Harrisburg on Route 322/22. Bill Jackson called off the search with the concurring nod of Arnie Benson as they realized that the Road Rogue was out of the area.

Hundreds of angry drivers trapped in the mess of inspection roadblocks around Carlisle, Pennsylvania, and Harrisburg vented frustration on the C.B. radio airwaves. A violent fight broke out near the entrance to the turnpike between two rowdy young men and a truck driver. A stone was thrown at the truck as the line of trucks and cars waited to get through the slow inspection. Others joined in the fight. Four were hospitalized.

Linda Wright gathered more footage and studied for her weekly update. Bill Jackson and Arnie Benson studied the map. In Washington, Dr. Paul Lindsey studied the video and phone recording until morning. Not one was any closer to passing the test of solving this case.

The Road Rogue continued under the cover of darkness and dropped off the Interstate onto the bowels of a southeastern Ohio two lane. Coal-hauling country would be a maze of protection from any organized attempt to stop him. Reviewing the memory of days hauling overweight loads provided routes through this hilly backcountry without Bandit battle until a local sheriff saw the black beauty pass a small general store. He did not attempt to stop the truck. The state police of Ohio were contacted about a black Peterbilt pulling a white, 53 footer out in coal country, heading west and north.

A quickly organized roadblock was set up at a two-lane bridge crossing. Six patrol cars were sent to the location, with four of the six having an extra officer armed with a long gun. Their plan was to use the six cars to block the bridge, and the long-gun officers were to take positions on foot on the shoulder areas to shoot out the tires or the driver if he tried to ram the blockade. A road commission dump truck was dispatched to the location, but it did not arrive in time. A helicopter was ordered, but it was coming from Columbus, Ohio.

The six patrol cars were just finishing the formation of a wedge on the nearest side of the steel-girded bridge when the Road Rogue topped the hill. He could see the four long-gun officers scrambling to take position on the shoulders. In the mirror, he saw the flashing lights of the sheriff's car closing in from behind.

In an impossible maneuver, the Road Rogue instantly assessed the trap and the available space and put the tractor trailer into a jackknife of controlled, out-of-control skidding, like Jimmy Hendricks using feedback as part of his out-of-control music. The rig slid around on the too-narrow pavement . . . with the trailer tandems first sliding in the loose gravel of the shoulder, then squealing onto the pavement while the tractor was given full throttle as it slid onto the opposite shoulder. Then by pushing in the clutch pedal, the trailer's weight and momentum pulled the entire rig back in line, with the rear of the trailer now facing the wedge. The long-gun-armed officers shot, hitting only the rear doors and tires of the trailer. All six officers ran for their cars, believing the truck was pulling the bat turn to head in the other direction. The sheriff's car topped the hill and its driver lost control, believing he was about to have a head-on collision. The car skidded into the ditch. The Road Rogue put the tractor into high-range reverse, and picking up speed with the grade, rammed the wedge of cars, sending the first four into opposite ditches and the remaining two up against the steel girders causing two fiery explosions as the cars spun violently and crashed down onto the riverbanks. The truck continued through the bridge until clearing the opposite side girders, and then the Road Rogue spun the trailer tandems off the shoulder, with the tractor following around, stopping with the trailer blocking the two lanes of pavement. The Rogue jumped out of the cab, pulled the kingpin and glad hands (air-line hookup), and dropped the trailer on its nose.

The black Pete sped off bobtailing as the officers looked on in complete disbelief. Three were injured (one with critical wounds). Only the sheriff's car was not a total loss. The frightened driver of the late-arriving road commission dump truck saw the black demon tractor closing in as if it were a challenging armored knight on horseback. Black-as-coal smoke billowed out its stacks, and an impending head-on collision forced the driver to jump from the seat as the dump truck veered into the ditch. The helicopter came to the scene, but there was no place to land. Its pilot then was dispatched to search the area. Thick trees and the setting sun made the effort fruitless.

The Road Rogue had turned north after the chicken duel with the dump truck. Within 30 minutes, at the intersection with Interstate Highway 70, a truck stop provided the Road Rogue with a different trailer to pull. A loaded flatbed covered wagon was a natural match for the dream truck. Its driver had dropped the loaded trailer and bobtailed home. The Road Rogue and this stolen flatbed blended back into the world of traffic and normal operation, continuing onward to his next destination while planning restitution.

Something else seemed to be calling to the Road Rogue from the distant past on his way to Capital City vengeance. He was nearing a chicken house (weigh station) that had been the site of several nasty inspections. Over the course of his life in trucking, hundreds of dollars had been collected in the name of safety. Years earlier, "safety" had a brother-in-law who ran a truck-repair business with road service. His memory was clear. The inspections put trucks out of service, and the repair-service brother-in-law was the only repair service available.

"All repairs must be made by a certified mechanic, driver. You can fix it yourself, but I have to have a mechanic's certification before you will be released," was the exact quote. Somewhere in the memory was a story about a federal investigation into this matter of the federal inspections, but no money was ever reimbursed to the driver.

The black Pete hauling the stolen flatbed purposely pulled into the weigh station. There was a chase car next to the small 10 foot by 10 foot brick building, and a median-type ditch between the building and the highway. Two uniformed men were inside. "Driver, pull around to the parking area and bring in all your paperwork, including your logbook." The voice from the outside speaker was scratchy and threatening.

The Road Rogue surveyed the available space, swung the trailer slightly to the left toward the building, and then turned to the right toward the rear inspection parking area. With the rear of the trailer perfectly positioned for a double hit from a distance of 40 feet . . . high-range reverse and *SMASH!* The chase car was crumpled in the ditch, and the two walls closest to the scale were knocked in. He jumped out, pulled the kingpin, dropped the trailer, and drove off.

"My God! My God! It must be the Road Rogue!" blared over the C.B. from the astonished trucker next in line to be weighed. "We better see if they're okay in there." Three truck drivers then rushed to the collapsed building to help the two injured men escape from the debris.

The black Pete exited the highway at the next exit and disappeared into the maze of back roads. Off into the night the Road Rogue drove. The glow from 20 gauges lighted up a cold, stoic face on the inside glass of the windshield. It was the face of a demon.

CHAPTER 25

Circle of Hands

Behind a secluded, abandoned old truck garage with rusted parts scattered in tall weeds, the black Peterbilt sat when the morning light was bright enough to awaken the Road Rogue. The physical body was feverish and exhausted. The mind and willpower of a possessed demon using adrenaline to force muscles and senses beyond capacity had to accept the limitations and results of the overuse. The body had not rested from Gettysburg to this place of safe haven. The Road Rogue somehow knew this place would not only be safe, but also exactly the place to assemble a plan for restitution. In the memory of the former man, this place harbored evil cruelty. Twenty years ago, a dream was dismantled here. An ironic, evil smile appeared on the face of the demon as the body returned to a deep sleep of recharging, motionless rest . . .

A nationwide directive to all law enforcement was produced under federal authority. Any officer suspecting a truck to be that of the fugitive Road Rogue must report the position and follow at a safe distance. No attempt should be made to stop the vehicle or to indicate that the suspected vehicle is being followed. Federal authority shall direct all further apprehensions. The state governors were notified to place National Guard units on alert status, specifically to seal off borders.

Bill Jackson and Arnie Benson created the directive jointly. The assistant director of the F.B.I. authorized the plan with the approval of the Justice Department and the White House. The political embarrassment was reaching the extreme.

On television, the news media and an endless line of pundits were asking the same question Barley Bill had asked 20 years ago: "How hard can it be to find a big, fancy semi truck?" The media frenzy was, of course, headed by the national voice and face of the search, Linda Wright. From the time of showing the video, to Gettysburg, to the crash on Interstate 80, to the smashed weigh station, and especially the scene of the failed road blockade at the Ohio steel bridge, the country was given a constant and continuous update. Television, radio, and print were portraying a monster, but a large percentage of the common man, workers, truckers, and even curious women were rooting for the Road Rogue. Linda Wright was quick to understand this phenomenon of reaction to the Road Rogue's escapes. Her reports began to concentrate on the ineptitude of the authorities.

The absolute power of government was now focused on ending the embarrassment. At any possible sighting, Bill Jackson had the ball. He was given authority to call in an air strike, if necessary. Arnie Benson would now be at his side until the end of the game.

"We must have a positive I.D. and then set up a perimeter. Every possible escape route must be blocked with heavy equipment or barriers that a truck cannot break," Bill Jackson stated sternly to Arnie Benson. "We need to have immediate contact available with the governors of each state. We have to limit how far the Road Rogue can go before we stop him."

"Will you actually call in a fighter jet?" Arnie asked carefully.

"God have mercy, no!" Bill replied. "The damn television is making some kind of hero out of this killer. I don't think we want the country to see a fighter jet blow up the truck, or even a helicopter shooting rockets. My God, we aren't even able to identify the bastard yet."

"Then you hope to spot a suspect and force him into a real roadblock and get him alive, if possible?" Arnie was asking this only to hear more of Bill's thoughts.

"I want a copter on him, but just so we don't lose him," Bill answered. "We must take him, from the road if possible. Much of this country looks at this as a game now. One man, an underdog against the powerful government." Then Bill snapped at Arnie, "None of this, of what I have just said, is for the ears of your friend, Linda Wright. Do you fully understand?"

"Yes, sir!" Arnie, for the first time, responded with acknowledgement that Bill Jackson was in command. "You're right. Half of the problem is what is being shown on TV."

On the TV screen in the bunk of the black truck sitting behind the old stripping shop, the news updates were teaching a monster. His body was still recovering, but the mind was completely engaged. "It would be best to leave the truck for a while and let them wonder where he is." The Road Rogue smiled again as he thought about his hiding place, here where that first black Peterbilt was destroyed so long ago. The smile grew wider as he contemplated the focus of the former Ruth's hate, the golden boy, denying any knowledge of destroying the dream of a July morning. The magic energy of a Snickers candy bar provided fuel for a burning plan of vengeful restitution. The city county building of Capital City was less than 30 miles from this spot.

The Road Rogue cleaned himself up as best he could inside the cab and decided to walk. A review of memory found walking to be a cure for stiff and spasming muscles that were rejecting commands. Unlike the childlike Hobbs, this new, complete being was in contact with all body systems. Pain was real and to be avoided. He walked for more than a quarter mile before finding a comfortable pace, muscle rhythm, and correct breathing. At the first mile crossroad, he began to take notice of the surroundings. The paved two lane was narrow and tree lined. Old farm homes with deteriorating barns were staggered each 100 yards, approximately. "Quite peaceful," he said aloud, as the area sparked a memory search. "Almost home," again aloud, but then anger brought a quicker pace. "He who would call this home does not exist."

On the third mile, an old gray Ford pickup was parked near the road, just off the driveway to an old, two-story, wood frame farmhouse. A For Sale sign was posted on the windshield. The Road Rogue walked up to the house. Using memory, he made an offer.

"It don't look like much, but it runs good," the stubborn old farmer said. "And it is a pickup. Won't sell it for less than $1,000, and it has to be cash. Don't need the damn government knowing what I sell it for. Paid my tax on it already."

"I've got cash," the Road Rogue smiled. "That damn government gets enough tax. You know, the government wants to eliminate cash completely. They want to electrify all transactions so they get a piece of everything." The Road Rogue was testing himself, trying to match language with the old farmer to gain advantage. It was working.

"Then we got us a deal?" The old farmer's voice cracked as he wondered if he was going to be able to get a whole $1,000 for the old pickup. "Hey, how'd you get here?"

"My truck broke down, so I'm walking," the Road Rogue replied as he counted out ten $100 bills. "I'm not going to be able to get to the Department of Motor Vehicles today. Do you mind if I leave the tag on?"

"Yah, go ahead. It expires at the end of the month anyway," the old farmer agreed. He trusted the stranger and was pleased to have the $100 bills. "Hey, I should know who you are. I mean, what's your name?"

"I believe we have just made a cash deal," the Road Rogue stated, as if he were now in control. "I don't think you have to know my name. What if I were to tell you something entirely false?"

"I'd guess you're right, stranger," a now-suspicious, squinting-eyed seller replied.

The Road Rogue could sense the change in the old farmer's voice, and then he smiled (if only to himself) as he held out his right hand for a deal-ending shake. "Hobbs, Roy Hobbs, and it's been a pleasure to do business with you." The mind of the monster had searched the memories for that name. Self-preservation dominated the thought processes now. This name, Hobbs, was a protection as well as being part of a formulation of the plan for acting on the memory of the anger, pain, and injustice that had destroyed the mind of the one called Barley.

The Road Rogue *was* the fruition of Hobbs of the subconscious, only with an access to the memories of the Ruth, and no longer needing an emotional link. Self-preservation as an avenger for a lost mind was a new emotion that had dispatched this new, cunning creature. As he drove the pickup away, he began formulating the details of his evil plan of vengeance.

The old gray pickup would provide stealth as materials were gathered. A bomb, using a semi trailer, would be large enough. Using the site of the old truck garage where he had been destroyed would bring satisfaction that would restore him. "Yes," this new Hobbs thought, "this will be the restitution."

An old trailer sat on the premises of the old truck garage. It was not road worthy, but it would serve as storage, along with the building itself, for safe and separate housing of the necessary materials. Memory review brought a vision of a trailer drop lot located on the south side of Capital City, less than 20 miles away. That lot would provide an easy access to suitable trailers. In the cab of the black demon truck was a hazardous materials-handling guide. Hobbs smiled as the thought entered his mind. The Commercial Motor Vehicle Safety Act of 1986 requires truck drivers to have a thorough knowledge of hazardous materials. The Hazmat guide carried as a requirement of law would provide a detailed blueprint for the plan, and stealing would provide the necessary materials. "Yes," he thought aloud. "I will steal a trailer, steal or buy what I need, and watch the tower of injustice fall!"

He went forth gathering, using the pickup and his special forgotten hiding spot. With careful cunning, each theft and purchase was made without regard to time. Time had no meaning . . .

"It's time we get some answers," Bill Jackson demanded on the phone 3 days after the scale house was destroyed at the weigh station. He continued in an aggravated tone with the research agent back in Washington. "What about that trailer that smashed the blockade and was dropped on the spot?"

"That trailer was reported stolen from the manufacturer's plant. It was turned in months ago in a trade-in program from the original carrier. It showed up missing in a monthly inventory in the same month as the first reported accident in Nebraska. The lot it was stolen from has thousands of trade-in trailers parked in an unsecured field." The research agent then offered, "We, here at the department, understand your frustration. You have been given complete authority in this matter." He paused, then he said in an almost whisper, "So the politicians will have cover. Trust me, we are doing everything we can to help. If this mess isn't over soon, heads will fall, towers of power in the Justice Department included."

"Damn!" Bill almost shouted. "Haven't you any clues?"

"The Cry Psy—oops—Dr. Paul Lindsey is studying this case every day. He has an extensive list of suspects based upon individuals in trucking who are in financial distress or having IRS problems, but I'm afraid that list has thousands of names. We are attempting to whittle it down by process of elimination. Dr. Paul is positive the man in the video has lost it all, including his lover. We believe the truck is stolen equipment, and that list is as long as . . ."

"Never mind!" Bill interrupted. "I want to be contacted the moment you people have anything to go on."

"Yes, sir." Click.

Bill Jackson turned to his newly admitted second in command, Arnie Benson. "Study the map. I want unmarked cars at all major crossroads. When, not if, the next incident occurs, we need a tail on him. Helicopters at every major city are to be put on call. We can forget about weigh stations. This Road Rogue isn't going to cross them now, I'd bet my life on that. Once we have a tail, we'll set the perimeter using National Guard. We have to limit the area of search."

"Agreed," Arnie nodded. "And no false alarms. They [the politicians] will crucify you, destroy your life."

"What life?" Bill sighed. "My wife has already divorced me over this case."

"If it's any help, my wife left me years ago," Arnie shrugged. "Kind of makes ya wonder if it's worth it. A nationwide crossroad stakeout—unbelievable. We're entering his world, you know."

"Yes," Bill nodded slowly, "it's a world my father knew well. I wish he were alive right now, but I know what he would say. Something like, what did you people do to that trucker that would cause him to go that crazy?"

"That's why so much of the public is fascinated by all of this, isn't it?" Arnie questioned in agreement. "They want to know why."

"We may never know, but the public can *never* know. He's just a monster. That's all that can be said," Bill stated, as if he knew something very wrong indeed had created this monster. Something or someone from governmental authority could not be accepted. Politicians can play vicious games, and Bill Jackson was becoming more aware of the consequences each day.

On the day Hobbs was satisfied that enough hazardous materials and components had been gathered, stored, and readied, he decided to drive the old pickup to the area just west of downtown Capital City. Perhaps a return to another site of memory would spark the mind of the Ruth. The convenience store where a bottle of special wine was purchased long ago was still there. It looked much the same. The wine was there, as it should be. It was time for a walk. He parked the pickup near *the* railroad track leading to downtown. Within 20 feet of walking the rails, he was able to hit each wooden tie as if only yesterday Barley Bill was looking for a place to fall apart. When he reached the river's bank, he drank from the bottle. Its effect wasn't as it had been before. The old bridge where Barley had camped was gone now. Great development of the land had taken place over the years. The riverbanks were not where they had been. Hobbs could revisit the pain and anguish from the memory but also felt something new. It was a realization that the golden boy had had success here. In front of his eyes there was evidence that the city had prospered. Hobbs did not like this new feeling, and he continued to walk toward downtown—toward the City County Building, wanting to inspire hate. Hate would create the spark to bring back the Ruth, or at least some part of him, Hobbs thought.

As the Road Rogue walked past the City County Building, he scouted the area. A freeway exit was in close proximity. Only a curb separated the base of the building from the street. A truck could easily drive right into that base. The plan would work. The tower of injustice would fall. He just stood there from across the street at the entrance to the parking garage, envisioning an imploding building erasing this monument to injustice.

A young woman exited the parking garage as he stood there. She was carrying an infant and held the hand of a blond-haired little girl. The young woman smiled at him, somewhat fearfully, but with such a soft innocence that he stared back at her. A moment of eye contact hit the Road Rogue as powerfully as the bomb explosion he envisioned. She was heading for the City County Building. She carefully crossed the street, protecting her children. Perhaps she was seeking justice of her own.

The adrenaline rush sparked something inside of him, not what he had expected. "No! The vengeance being sought is against corrupt politicians, lawyers, judges, and police—not innocents," his mind screamed in new anguish. "Knocking down this building would not stop injustice. Those who were here before are gone. The golden boy is in Washington."

His head was bowed, with shoulders slumping, while his eyes darted back and forth and his mind reviewed memory data. "McVey, Timothy McVey," he said aloud to no one. "McVey knocked down a building, but they will never let it be known why. Whatever his message was, it won't be told. There must have been more to it, but what was the result. A madman was put to death because of the loss of innocent lives. My plan won't work."

With a final look from the building's base to the top of it, a defiant monster with clenched fists uttered aloud, "Let it stand as a monument of a grave . . . a grave where a dream died."

The Road Rogue turned away to walk back to the rails, and as he walked toward the pickup, a new plan began to form in his mind. "This fight must be fought in 'their' world, a world of words, words to change laws and bring this government back to its founding principles." He found a quote from memory: "The pen is mightier than the sword."

As the old gray pickup reached the black demon truck, pain from deep inside the Road Rogue's chest signaled that rest was needed. He could plan later. The body struggled to climb into the cab. With head, chest, and shoulders collapsing onto the wheel, the Hobbs of him started the motor to let the vibrations soothe the body. He turned on the music, and just before passing out he heard lines from "Circle of Hands" (Uriah Heep).

> . . . *Searching my land for an enemy*
> *Came across love's sweet cost*
> *And in the face of beauty Evil was lost* (Ken Hensley)

CHAPTER 26

Stealin'

In Washington, D.C., Dr. Paul Lindsey was determined to find the connection from which to identify the Road Rogue. In every other case that he had ever been involved with, he had felt something that eventually solved or at least explained a mystery. His nickname The Cry Psy originated from a case in which a man had been brutally tortured. Two agents witnessed the tearful psychiatrist moaning as if he were being tortured. From that experience, he was able to identify the murderer's face from a large group of suspects, and with the help of a tough interrogator, a confession solved what had been a perfect crime. Over the next 5 years, the Cry Psy became a secret weapon of the F.B.I.

Over and over again, Dr. Paul Lindsey played the video and the recorded phone call from the Road Rogue. That there was pain and a long-held grudge was obvious in the voice of the Road Rogue. At the White House, no obvious connection was felt with the former prosecutor. What did July morning mean? Opportunity? A lover?

Files of every case of the former prosecutor were in front of the Cry Psy. Pictures of everyone sent to jail . . . nothing . . . no link. "It has to be here," he mumbled aloud to himself, just as the phone rang.

"Dr. Lindsey," the secretary said, "it's the TV network calling. They want to use more of the video and phone call of the Road Rogue."

"No!" Dr. Lindsey shouted. "Absolutely not! What do they think this is, a weekly TV drama? Just give them the prepared statement. I guess Linda Wright is disappointed that no cops were killed this week."

As the week passed, Bill Jackson waited with sleepless nights for his plan of "sight and follow" to unfold. Three calls were made to Missouri, to his Lisa. She did not return the calls. He needed her and missed her. A monster had taken her away from him. Bill Jackson's anguish was turning to anger . . .

The Road Rogue lifted himself up off of the wheel as the angry cries of haunted souls rang inside his head. They were the same cries he had heard at Gettysburg. No new plan evolved. A ride would provide a new plan, he thought, but the Hobbs knew protection would be needed to go on a ride. They were shooting at him now, and the whole country's lawmen, the bandits, were chasing.

Before leaving this safe haven, the Road Rogue moved the explosives into the old trailer, and he set the timer for noon. Then he bobtailed to the nearby trailer drop yard and found a trailer with only a few markings. At a pay phone from this yard, he called a local TV station.

"There is going to be an explosion 30 miles south of Capital City ... at noon today. If anyone shoots at me, expect the same with Hazmat 124. I am the Road Rogue! The City County Building should be evacuated!" Click.

West on a two-lane road to a high point approximately 5 miles directly west in the next adjacent county, the Road Rogue drove. At 11:55 A.M., he climbed up to the top of the cab's sleeper. He could see the tremendous explosion and the quickly growing cloud, and smiled. Then feeling as if the world belonged to him, he drove west, contemplating new ways to fight City Hall and government.

The local TV station had a helicopter up in time to capture the explosion, and the words of the phone call were given to the police. The call was recorded. Upon viewing the explosion on tape, the City County Building was evacuated for the remainder of the day while the search for explosives was carried out. Until this Road Rogue was caught, heightened security measures would be required. Old Barley Bill's court of injustice was not stopped, but infringed, causing speculation by those inside.

A 20-foot-deep crater provided excellent footage for Linda Wright's report to the country. It was a terrifying report shown on the evening news.

By nightfall the Road Rogue was well out of the area, and he came to a decision. Reviewing memories brought to mind a place to reflect. Hartwick Pines in Michigan had provided head-clearing peace in the life of Barley Bill; it was a destination at which to plan a battle without the end result of McVey and the loss of innocent lives. Violence was not the answer; no, it was survival until a new plan could be formed.

In Washington, the latest national directive would alter Bill Jackson's plan of capture. "Do not fire at the Road Rogue without direct command of the F.B.I."

"Arnie," Bill stated, "our plan will still work, except I *will* call for an air strike. That footage of the explosion and the bomb threat gives us the cover to blow him away without public outrage. We just have to isolate him in as secluded an area as possible."

"It will be over with soon, Bill," Arnie nodded. "This monster laid low while he built that bomb, but he can't stop driving. He will show up somewhere."

"You're right, Arnie," Bill offered. "I think the son of a bitch is using that explosion and building threat just so he can drive away as far as he can get. We'll comb the area, but he's gone from there. I just hope one of our people reports tailing him."

The truck of the demon was rolling north on back roads and passed into Michigan, picking up Highway 131. The Road Rogue was immersed in thought but was distracted by a growing pain. Deep inside the skull, the cancerous tumor was coming out of remission. The adrenaline of the body's system counteracted it. The Hobbs still within him took control of the wheel, allowing the monster to think, much as if the Ruth were still in control of the conscious mind. There was no Ruth—only a physical shell of Barley, as if cloned from the original—with all of the physical frailties and memory data stored within, but soulless. Hobbs drove on with a growing awareness of another presence.

As if the body of the demon were equipped with an inner radar detector, Hobbs became suspicious of a car that seemed to be following from a distance . . .

"Bill!" Arnie said excitedly as he entered the office. "I think we have a tail. An officer is following a black conventional pulling a trailer that might be stolen. The company that owns the trailer has told us that it should be in a drop yard, and that yard is less than 20 miles away from the Road Rogue's explosion."

"That's him! It's got to be!" Bill exclaimed. "Where is he?"

"Michigan, heading north," Arnie stated, as he pointed on a map to the reported location.

"We've got him!" Bill Jackson was exhilarated, as he nearly shouted into the speakerphone on his desk at an assistant just outside his office. "Get me the governors of Michigan, Indiana, and Ohio. Now, damn it!"

Within 10 minutes, the three governors were in a conference call with Bill Jackson and Arnie Benson. The immediate plan was for the National Guard and state police of Indiana and Ohio to set up a blockade across the southern border of Michigan. Only four entrance/exit points were to be allowed. At those crossings, inspections would stop all trucks, as if going through customs at the Canadian border. In Michigan, the Mackinaw Bridge would be closed until a similar inspection roadblock could be set up. The border crossings with Canada (the Blue Water Bridge in Port Huron and the Ambassador Bridge near Detroit) were to be closed until further notice. Additionally, the governor of Michigan was to mobilize all law enforcement and available National Guard in order to post lookouts at each crossing of Interstate 69, from the border of Indiana to the north side of Lansing. From that point on I69, lookouts were to be posted at each crossing of Highway 27 North through the merge with Interstate 75 to the Mackinaw Bridge, thereby effectively dividing the Lower Peninsula in half.

With the absolute power of the government concentrated on Lower Michigan and with a tail established, it appeared that the end was near. After finishing the conference call to the governors, Bill Jackson barked out one more order. "Get a bird on him, fast!" Then he looked at Arnie and said, "We better get to Michigan. Lansing is about center of the state."

The latest stolen trailer had been the Road Rogue's misfortune. A driver was scheduled to pick up that unit and had reported it missing to his company. However, the eyes of the possessed demon were not missing the threat of the car behind. It looked like a government car. The Hobbs tested with speed first and then exited Highway 131 onto Interstate 94 eastbound.

As the officer reported the new direction, the Road Rogue was awakened and joined with the driving Hobbs. Adrenaline flowed. Convinced a bandit was behind the wheel of the car behind, the black demon truck increased speed. The bandit car followed. Then the black demon truck cut in front of another semi, and hit the brakes and the engine retarder. The bandit was caught by surprise and passed by in the hammer lane.

The officer called in for immediate help as he saw the charging chrome grill coming up fast from behind. "He's after me!" The steel bumper reached the back of the car at 90 miles per hour. He tried to accelerate, but the car had no more speed left to give. This was not a patrol car.

The car was pushed past 100 miles per hour before the officer lost control and the Road Rogue sent the bandit vehicle into the median with a gentle push to the right-rear taillight section. The terrified officer mistakenly hit his brakes as this last touch from the cold chrome steel put his tires into a skid without traction. The car began an intense rotating and flipping airborne ride in a fraction of a second, until returning to earth in an exploding mess of metal and plastic parts.

Several witnesses saw the attack, and two of them would confirm that the black truck exited in the next mile and turned north.

A helicopter searched the area and had only missed the carnage by 10 minutes. Bill Jackson and Arnie Benson were notified while waiting for their plane to take off.

"No question now, Bill," Arnie sighed. "We'll get him before tomorrow is over."

"He can't go far, but damn it. Why did that tail get too close?" Bill said as he shook his head. Bill Jackson then called to the governor, and stated, "Don't lose any more men. Set up the perimeter. We'll take the Road Rogue out with an air strike. Get heavy equipment, any heavy equipment, at perimeter intersections, and . . ."

The Road Rogue doubled back to the west on heavily wooded back roads and then zigzagged on county routes northward. The pain in his skull was increasing, and a burning came from inside his chest. It was after midnight when adrenaline could no longer keep him from seeking a safe haven in which to park and rest. An old fire trail in the thick, tall pines of

Manistee National Forest near Ludington, Michigan, would have to do. He pulled in nearly 100 yards off the paved road, until the trail's turns would not allow further penetration. Something in the memory ... take a nitro ... then, collapsing onto the wheel ... the soothing vibrations of the idling motor ... sleep.

By morning, Bill Jackson's entire plan to entrap was in place. Road graders, wreckers, military trucks, and police cars were ready to block intersections. Helicopters searched.

One helicopter flew low over the crash scene from the night before. Linda Wright and her cameraman videotaped the area and then landed near the airport of Battle Creek, Michigan. Her report for the network was filmed there. This was the second time the saga of the Road Rogue had brought her to this area of Michigan. She interviewed a witness from the crash and floated a theory that the Road Rogue might be from this area. The footage shot during the day also would include long lines of angry, held-up public at checkpoints, amid the massive attempt to blockade the Lower Peninsula.

The Road Rogue slept until afternoon. He did not like the painful aching muscles of the body. Something was wrong with the left side. The lower back injury from long ago signaled the need to walk. Frustration with this deteriorating physical being produced adrenaline, forcing the left arm to respond to commands refused only moments earlier.

The radio was on, tuned to an AM station. Anger filled the Road Rogue as the news report spoke of the massive search in Lower Michigan. He climbed down from the cab and looked around in an attempt to recognize where he was. The mind was not yet fully functioning. Standing erect and stretching, muscles were forced to flex, and he walked away from the rig to the paved road. The walking was needed he realized with more frustration.

Following the paved road west 3 miles, the Road Rogue found an intersection with a numbered sign. "Hartwick Pines is more than 100 miles from here to the east and north," he thought, as this location registered from memory. "Why not just plan from these woods? Why fight the bandits today?" He turned back toward the hidden truck and walked.

As he walked, the mind and muscle found rhythm and blood circulated, but a nagging low pain remained in the head with a growing ache in the gut. The afternoon sun was casting long shadows, making the trail to the truck appear strangely dark, but sunset was hours away.

This darkness was cover. Hobbs, the protector, fully understood the need for darkness, but what could be done to avoid the ever-searching bandits? A new plan for restitution would have to wait. Distance was needed, but escape would be difficult. Then the idea brought relief. There was a way. The Road Rouge had used Hobbs's fear to search memory for that idea. He restarted the motor and backed down the trail and onto the pavement.

Time was available for quenching his thirst and eating. It was the lack of fluid and food that caused the nagging pain. The Hobbs knew the way, following the paved road to Old Pierre Marquette Road and then north, passing slowly by the Dow Chemical factory just south of Ludington, Michigan.

One block past the plant, the Road Rogue parked the truck next to a vacant building on Dowland Street by backing into its old dock area. Just across the street was a small workingmans' tavern.

Buddy's Tap Room was not a tourist stop the way most of Ludington is. Ludington is a picturesque town on the beautiful coast of Lake Michigan. Buddy's Tap Room is off the main drive, next to the ugliness of a chemical plant. It is rather rough looking inside and out, which makes for a real and friendly pub with real local patrons. "Old Barley Bill would have loved this place," the Road Rogue thought aloud as he gazed at the interior's 40-year-old cheap wood paneling nearly covered with beer mirror signs. A lighted gas neon window beer sign was evidence of the bar's history. Michigan politicians had passed a law outlawing those lighted signs years ago. This one was simply moved to behind the bar.

The barmaid was quick to offer, "What'll ya have?"

"A tall cold draught beer and a hamburger with everything." The Road Rogue actually felt joy in anticipation of the much-needed replenishment. The beer's flavor sparked a collage of memory flashes. Dehydrated, cracked lips absorbed the liquid gold and foam. Ice-cold, thick glass numbed any pain, as would have been expected. The flavor of throat-soothing barley pop tasted even better than imagined. The 12-ounce mug was half gone with that first drink. A good shake of salt created a new 1-inch-thick head of foam, and the second gulp emptied the glass. "God's own nectar," the Road Rogue stated aloud.

"I must say, I don't think I've ever seen anyone have quite that expression on their face for a glass of beer." The barmaid turned to a local and suggestively continued, "I *have* seen that look before though."

"Sorry, I guess it's been a while," the Road Rogue replied in a more controlled, low voice.

Again she playfully declared, "That's just what I meant ... like it's been a while."

Laughter broke out around the corner of the bar at that sexual innuendo.

When the burger arrived in plain white waxed paper tightly wrapped, the Road Rogue knew instantly that he was in for a classic treat—a true traditional bar burger, with ketchup, mustard, pickle, and a thick slice of raw Spanish onion. The waxed paper contained all of the distinct flavors from the grill. "There is no scientific way to duplicate a true bar burger from an independent beer garden like this. To call a fast-food offering anything but an insult in comparison would be sinful," the smiling stranger said to anyone who wanted to listen while he savored each bite.

"There, there *it* is again . . . that look, see? Where have you been stranger? Locked up?" a laughing barmaid joked as she scanned the eyes of her regulars.

The Road Rogue smiled again and finished another glass. This was something new for him. Reviewing memory data did not produce true emotion, but sitting in this little tavern with beer and a true bar burger was . . . pleasure, pure pleasure. He could feel it. "This must be what it was like for Barley Bill," he thought, and he wanted more. "What would Barley Bill do here?" he thought. "Drink beer, tell jokes."

"My name is . . ." Barney paused while deciding what name to use. "Bartholomew." He struggled to say it and then added, "Barley for short."

"Because of the way you drink beer," a laughing, strong-looking man in his mid 30s said from the next stool. "Doug," and he held out his hand. "I'm new here, too."

Doug wasn't new today. He had been in the bar for several hours and was half in the bag, loud when he spoke, and trying to impress the barmaid. She wasn't impressed and was ready to cut him off.

"Hey Cheryl," Doug loudly barked to the irritated barmaid. "Do you know why brides always wear white?" Cheryl turned and raised an eyebrow. "Because all household appliances are white." Cheryl didn't laugh, but a couple of the men did as their minds began searching for the latest bar jokes . . .

"Ain't this a joke?" Officer Ted Harding said to his partner for the night. "It's just you and me kid. We get to patrol the whole town of Ludington by ourselves tonight. Everyone else is out on the roadblocks. You're brand new, aren't you?"

"Well, I have been called in to work security at high school football games," the 22-year-old deputy said in response.

"I'd say you need a little experience," Officer Ted grunted. "Why don't we bust a drunk tonight."

The local police car cruised the downtown section, while Officer Ted Harding explained the types of drinking establishments of this summer tourist town. He turned east and slowly passed Buddy's Tap Room. The young deputy saw the truck as Ted was talking about the little working-mans' bar.

"Okay, let's check it out," Ted agreed. "Do you have the information on that Road Rogue truck?"

"Yes sir."

As the two local policemen were out of their car walking around the black demon truck and the stolen trailer, the Road Rogue was just coming out of the bar's front door. Time was just about up for his latest plan.

Adrenaline flowed instantly. He would be caught. "Must think of something quickly." The Hobbs of him was alerted. His senses were heightened. He turned back into the bar and sat down next to Doug again.

"What's the mannnner?" Doug slurred the words.

"My heart, Doug. It's my heart but keep quiet. Will you go to my truck and get my nitro pills. I'm okay if I take one. They're right on the sun visor. Here is a door key. Please? Thank you."

"Okay, you—you gonna be okay?" Doug again slurred. "Bbblack semi right across street, gggot it."

Outside Ted Harding sat in the patrol car with his young deputy.

"Aren't we supposed to call like the directive says?"

"Listen kid," an excited Officer Ted lectured, "the directive says do not attempt to stop the truck. It doesn't say not to stop the driver. That's the trailer they're looking for, but we know there's no bomb in it. Anyway, it's empty. I'll bet he's here to steal a chemical trailer, probably waiting for the wee hours of night. He's in the tavern, I'd bet that too, but we don't want to give him any chance to kill anyone inside. We'll just wait here until he tries to get into his truck."

"But, won't we get in trouble for not calling the feds?"

"Just let me handle this kid. I'll tell you this, you'll be famous. On your first patrol night, you'll help capture America's most wanted man. Wow, unbelievable! And I'll be living in the governor's mansion. Look, here he comes now."

Doug was drunk and staggering as he approached the cab. He did not even notice the two uniformed officers as they walked up behind him. Doug was attempting to put the key into the door lock and cussing under his breath because he couldn't fit the key into the hole. He had been given a wrong key intentionally by the cunning monster.

"Stop, put your hands in the air. You're under arrest!" shouted Officer Ted Harding.

Doug turned with a clenched fist and grunted out, "Aw fuck you." He cocked his arm for a roundhouse right. Officer Ted Harding dropped him with a nightstick blow to the head.

"Cuff him," Ted called to his deputy while waiting for the big drunk to attempt to get up. Doug was finished fighting and offered no more resistance as the two officers pushed him headfirst into the back seat of the patrol car. They then sped off to the city lockup.

The Road Rogue waited until the patrol car turned at the next corner, and then he exited Buddy's Tap Room. Casually unlocking the cab's door with a correct key and grabbing the fifth-wheel pin puller, he walked to the dolly crank, rolled the dolly stand down, unhooked from the trailer, and drove off.

At the city lockup, Officer Ted Harding placed the call to the F.B.I. to report, "This is the Ludington, Michigan, police station. We have the Road Rogue in custody."

The agent taking the call responded with, "Agent Bill Jackson will contact you momentarily."

After establishing phone contact, Bill Jackson instructed the local officer not to make formal charges until he could arrive, and not to attempt to interrogate.

An overconfident Ted Harding responded in an arrogant tone, "We've picked him up on a drunk and disorderly charge, along with assaulting an officer. I'll leave the rest to you. Don't worry; this guy is in no condition to talk. He's drunker than a skunk and is passed out in the drunk tank."

"And the truck? What have you done with the truck?" Bill Jackson's voice carried full authority as he emphasized, "There could be a bomb."

"We checked the trailer out. It's empty. The truck is sitting right where it was. It's about one block from the chemical plant. I figure he was going to try to steal a chemical load, but I can't move the truck. Anything big enough to tow the truck is out on your roadblocks with all of my men. Can you call off the blockade?"

"Not yet," Bill retorted defiantly. "I'll be there in Ludington in ... about 3 hours. I'll talk to you then. Do not allow anyone near him. Do you understand?"

"Yes sir," Officer Ted answered without due respect.

Bill Jackson and Arnie Benson were quick to arrive at the small local airport, almost as quick as Linda Wright and her film crew. Linda had established a new inside contact within the department. She had been notified of the capture moments after Bill Jackson had hung up the phone with the local hero. A disgusted glare at Arnie Benson from Bill Jackson demanded an explanation as the two shocked federal authorities walked into the police station in Ludington to see Linda Wright interviewing Officer Ted Harding. "It wasn't me, I swear it Bill," Arnie pleaded.

Bill Jackson stared at Officer Ted Harding, signaled with a pointed finger passed across his throat to end the interview, and coldly held up his hand when Linda Wright approached.

Arnie Benson just shook his head and then directed two field agents to go to the truck to gather evidence. Linda Wright followed the two agents.

In the drunk tank cell, the young deputy helped Bill Jackson awaken the grumbling and groggy Doug.

"Do you know why you were brought in here?" Bill looked at the young deputy.

"His name is Doug Belinger, sir," the young deputy offered carefully.

"Mr. Belinger, you are about to be charged with the most serious crimes imaginable. Do you understand?" Bill Jackson's voice was as serious as those charges would be.

"All I did was get drunk." Doug then asked sheepishly, "Did I do something I don't remember?"

"How long have you been driving a semi truck?" Bill was still sounding stern.

"Truck? I don't drive truck." Doug then sullenly added, "I've had two drunk drivings, ya can't drive a truck . . . I mean you can't get a C.D.L. with drunk driving charges against you. I'm an operator. I operate dozers and cranes when I work. What's this all about?"

Bill turned away and motioned to Arnie Benson, who was looking at the prior record of Doug Belinger.

"Bill, this isn't adding up," Arnie said while shaking his head. "I think we have another 'Azmath' here. Look at this. This guy just got out of 6 weeks in jail. He's only been out . . ."

"Damn it!" Bill's angry explosion got everyone's attention. "Where the hell is the registration for that truck, Officer Harding?"

"I didn't get it," Ted Harding shot back defiantly. "There was no plate and there were no markings on the truck, just a gold name plate that read 'This unit made for world's greatest truck driver,' or something stupid like that. I must remind you that all our men are out on your blockade. Me and the kid there, and this is his first night, brought that big drunk son of a bitch in. It got a little rough . . . and who called that TV gal anyway? Wasn't me."

Bill's anger was still rising, and just as he started to shout, "You didn't follow instructions," Linda Wright entered the police station.

"The truck is gone!" she announced.

Bill Jackson moved quickly to a desk and began barking orders to field agents and supervisors via cell phone. "Notify all personnel on roadblocks that the Road Rogue is on the loose and moving. Get me a detailed map, damn it. Arnie, how much time has passed?"

Arnie just turned to Officer Ted Harding.

"I arrested the drunk at 7:25 P.M. That truck was there then." Ted Harding bowed his head. "I'm sorry."

Arnie put his hand on Bill Jackson's shoulder. "He can't go anywhere, Bill. Every road is blocked. Hundreds of agents are searching. In the last 2 hours, there have been no reports of any truck attempting to cross Highway 27 or 169 (which divides the Peninsula in half, north to south). The governor authorized an additional stakeout from Port Huron to Muskegon, which divides the state from east to west. Look, the Road Rogue *is* trapped. It's just a matter of time."

"Okay, you're right Arnie," Bill sighed as he calmed down. "Interrogate that drunk and send someone down to that tavern. We can call the governors of Ohio and Indiana to call off the southern border blockade. Here in Michigan we move everything available to the northwest quarter of Lower Michigan and release the rest of the state from the blockade. The area covered will be from here," Bill and Arnie studied the map, "Muskegon to Lansing in the middle, straight north to the Mackinaw Bridge. Right now we'll search every building big enough to hide a tractor and have every fire trail of this forest . . ."

"Bill, we need a command post and a place to rest." Arnie was offering advice to help his partner in this quest to find the monster and end the frustrations of their failures. Arnie Benson was growing to respect Bill Jackson more each day. "The Stearns Motor Inn over on the main drag has the facilities for a practical base. You have to sleep, eat, and take care of yourself, Bill. So do I."

Sunrise's daylight had illuminated the postcard town of Ludington, Michigan, with a brilliant blue sky and endless whitecaps on the shades of green, sandy, shallow shore, to the deep blue horizon of Lake Michigan, when Bill Jackson and Arnie Benson met for coffee in the conference room prepared as a command post in the Stearns Motor Inn. No report of finding the Road Rogue had disturbed either man throughout the night.

"It's only a matter of time now, Bill," Arnie consoled. "I hope you got some sleep."

Bill's eyes spoke in contradiction. "It's like he's a ghost. What are the newspapers reporting?"

Arnie looked out of the room to the check-in desk in the lobby and interjected, "Let's go find out."

The counter receptionist pointed to the front entrance door and declared, "The newspapers are outside in coin machines, except for the local paper, and it hasn't been delivered yet."

The two federal partners walked outside to see a teenage boy filling the coin-operated machines when they suddenly heard air foghorns sound, as if an ocean liner was nearby.

"What the hell is that?" Arnie questioned.

The teen looked up and explained, "Oh, that's the *Badger,* sir. She's a dinosaur. I mean my dad calls it a dinosaur. It's the steamship car ferry just coming in to port. Dad says the libs want to shut it down cuz it pollutes. It's a coal-burning steamer, 50 years old."

"Oh my God!" Bill then grabbed the boy. "How big is it? Where does it go?"

"It's 410 feet long. Hey, what did I do?" The young teen then pointed inside. "They got pamphlets on it. It used to haul railcars."

Both men ran inside and grabbed a tourist pamphlet for information about the *Badger.* The schedules hit them like a hammer on a warning tower bell.

Depart: Ludington MI 7:55 P.M. Eastern time.
Arrive: Manitowoc, WI 10:55 P.M. Central time.

Depart: Manitowoc, WI 12:30 A.M. Central time.
Arrive: Ludington, MI 5:30 A.M. Eastern time.

"He has at least 6 hours from Manitowoc, Wisconsin, to be . . . anywhere." Bill looked at Arnie in exhausted bewilderment.

Yesterday's sunset on Lake Michigan from the bow railing of the Titanic-like car ferry *Badger* brought a cunning smile to the face of the Road Rogue, as he reflected on the words of the Uriah Heep song that had provided the idea for escape.

Take me across the water
Cuz I need someplace to hide . . .

. . . Nothing left to save
But my life . . .
. . . Stealin' . . . (Ken Hensley)

CHAPTER 27

Why?

Something was changing inside the mind of the Road Rogue. He had en-joyed the beer, burger, and conversation at that tavern in Ludington. He felt strong emotional satisfaction from his clever escape on the *Badger* car ferry. While aboard the ship, he visited the upper deck and portside bars, and savored more beers. More conversation was tested. He quickly re-moved any bad thoughts of the fate of the "big Doug" sent out to the wait-ing bandits. Confidence in himself surged as he explored the memories of Barley Bill looking for more—more of the emotion.

"The world is mine," the Road Rogue uttered audibly from the bow of the *Badger* as the ship slowed in preparation for docking in Manitowoc, Wisconsin. He had developed no plan for restitution yet, but there was thirst for satisfaction. A good long ride to think . . . the destination would be Arkansas—the bar at Fort Smith, Arkansas, where the tempting woman had said, "Come back and see me." That just might be satisfying.

Onward into the night the black demon truck rolled. The stimulation within the mind of the monster would fight sleep and fatigue. He stopped at a truck stop south of Milwaukee and stole another trailer for a better ride and more protection. As the night entered its darkest hours, he pulled on, always changing routes in a zigzagging method, as if this truck were a battleship being pursued by submarines in a wartime ocean, an ocean of back road curves, hills, farms, and tiny towns . . . Wisconsin, Illinois, and into Missouri.

By morning's full light, the Road Rogue was traveling in north central Missouri. Bill Jackson was now in the temporary command post room of the Stearns Motor Inn (Ludington, Michigan), plotting possible distances and realizing that the escape was going to be hard to explain. Little useful information would be obtained during the day while questioning those who had seen and talked to the Road Rogue.

Linda Wright filmed a tour of the soon to be nationally famous *Badger* (the car ferry), including an interview with the ship's two bartenders who had served the mysterious fugitive the previous night. The old steamship *Badger*'s paint and design were hauntingly like that of the *Titanic*. The re-port ended with a verbal observation that contrasted with the scene of the huge car ferry disappearing into an approaching fog. "At least we know the Road Rogue is not a ghost. He is just a clever fugitive with a thorough knowledge of our country's transportation system."

Frustration grew in the Road Rogue when muscle cramps painfully distracted memory review and planning as he drove. The body's frail limitations were increasingly burdensome for the rogue of him, independent from mere flesh. All through the night, fatigue had been fought off by using various tricks and stimuli that Barley Bill had used on thousands of all-night pulls. Similar to a Boston marathon runner who pushes on through heartbreak hill and then realizes he *is* going to beat it, the Road Rogue had beaten that fatigue. Like the Ruth before, the Rogue had Hobbs as a codriver. Hobbs began using music to stimulate memories for the Rogue just as he had for Ruth. At the darkest hour, a cassette tape was put into the system as loud as possible. "Ladies and gentlemen, please welcome R . . . E . . . O . . . Speedwagon!" More than 100 miles passed . . . the Rogue visualized the face of Earl, the real codriver so long ago. A review of those carefree days brought joy, *joy* into a monster's mind.

A truck stop was located ahead. At the intersection of this two lane and Interstate 44 northeast of Joplin, Missouri, the body had to be replenished. After parking near the back of the lot, the Road Rogue walked to the restaurant with a frustrating limp caused by dehydrated muscles in both legs.

Inside, sitting at the quick-serve counter, a lone trucker sat sipping coffee. He was a proud but desperate owner/operator. He had spent the entire morning on his C.B. radio attempting to sell his bunk, TV, tools, part of his load, his C.B. radio, and anything else that he could think of, just to gather fuel money to get home. He was 6 weeks overdue on his truck payment, and the repair bill for a new pinion gear on the drive axle had wiped out the last of his credit. Anger filled this proud man's heart as he realized it was over. His dream was played out. He sat there desperate, looking for a miracle.

The Road Rogue finished a large, early afternoon breakfast and read the paper's report about him being captured in Ludington, Michigan. A confident smile was on his face as he approached the cashier next to the counter. Without a second thought, the Road Rogue reached into the leather bag on his belt when he realized there was no cash left in the wallet. He pulled out five $100 bills, gave one to the cashier, and put the rest into the wallet along with the paper bill change.

The desperate trucker at the counter observed this careless handling of money and wondered, "How much could be in that leather bag?" He followed the Road Rogue outside and asked, "Hey driver, could you help me? I have a skid in my trailer that I need to move."

The still smiling Road Rogue replied, "Sure."

The two of them walked to the back row of trucks where the desperate driver said, "This is the one. Just a minute. I'll grab my crowbar in my tractor."

The driver opened the trailer door and climbed inside, then turned and offered his hand to the Road Rogue to help him up. Once inside, the driver pointed toward the front of the trailer, and *thud!*

The desperate driver climbed back down and shut the trailer door. He carried a wallet, leather bag, and his crowbar back to his cab. He started the motor and drove out of the truck stop toward Joplin. He exited the freeway at Exit 6, turning north onto Route 43, and pulled over in the Shaal Creek area. At the back alley of a strip mall parking lot, he pulled the limp body of the Road Rogue out of the trailer, careful not to be seen. "It looked as if the truck was just making a delivery, and three hospitals were located within 2 miles of here. It's the best I can do," the cold, desperate driver thought as he reentered the freeway ...

The telephone rang. "Bill, this is Arnie. Are you awake?"

"Yes, I think so," an exhausted Bill Jackson replied into the phone from the bed of his motel room. "Arnie, it's too early. I'm in no hurry to go back to Washington. They [politicians] want my ass!"

"No, no," Arnie interrupted, "we have the truck. It was found abandoned in Missouri. I was just notified by my regional director. This is it, for real. We're verifying the name on the registration. It's all happening fast. We have to get to Missouri."

"Missouri, that's where my, Lisa, it's where I'm from, Arnie." Bill Jackson was still groggy from two almost-sleepless nights. It had been 72 hours since the *Badger* had signaled the escape with its foghorn.

The Road Rogue woke up in a white room in a bed. An IV was in his left arm. An electronic monitoring device was next to the bed on the right. A pretty, young nurse greeted his now-open eyes.

"Mr. Root, Mr. Bob Root. Is that your name, sir? Do you know where you are?"

The Road Rogue gazed around the room before he spoke, forcing adrenaline into the body, and attempting to recognize and remember. He looked at the monitoring machine and remarked, "Sort a ... looks like Star Trek." His mind realized he was in a hospital.

"You walked into this hospital with a head injury. You probably were rolled and robbed. You did not have a wallet or any I.D." The nurse then turned to the doorway. "The doctor has some questions."

"How do you feel? Dr. Rosenblatt is my name. You have quite a bump on the head, fella. The local police would like to speak to you as soon as you feel up to it, but you look like you still have some cobwebs."

The mention of police brought an immediate defensive rush into the mind of the Road Rogue. He shook his head, signaling he wasn't up to talking much yet and said, "I ... I ... can't remember. How did I get here?" While acting as if he was in worse condition than he was, the Road Rogue analyzed in thought, "I must have slurred Babe Ruth into Bob Root. These people do not know who I am. I must escape." Aloud, he said, "I . . . I need a little . . . sleep." He was hoping the doctor would leave.

"I'll come back later," Dr. Rosenblatt stated as he nodded to the nurse. He gave the on-duty nurse the chart with the prescribed medications and exited the room to study the CAT scan further. It was there, a tumor not related to the immediate head injury. The test results confirmed the diagnosis. This cancerous tumor would be inoperable. This man was dying, a terminal case of maybe . . . "I'm going to need a second opinion, Julie," Dr. Rosenblatt announced to the desk nurse. "We need to identify this patient as soon as possible. I'll be back tomorrow. Just let the poor old guy rest."

By late afternoon, the medications were reviving the Road Rogue enough that he sat up and then stood up next to the bed. The I.V. was on a wheeled stand. He gingerly walked around the room. In a drawer were the only personal items found on him when he had entered. The little bag had one and a half packs of Winston Light cigarettes, a Bic lighter, a wedding ring (gold band), a small Boy Scout pocketknife, and a little more than $2 in change.

The nurse entered the room. "Well there, are you feeling a little better now?"

"How long have I been here?"

"This is your second day," answered the nurse. "Can you answer some questions now? We need to check for allergies and get your insurance information."

"I'll do the best I can, but where's my wallet?" The Road Rogue was acting as if he could not remember their first conversation. "Oh, you said I was without I.D. That's right." He added, putting his hand on his head, "I, I just can't think real straight, but I know I need a cigarette bad. Where can I have one? Maybe a little walk and a cigarette would clear my head. I know I *need* a cigarette."

"Okay, but you have to smoke outside. Down by the emergency entrance is a picnic table where employees and patients can smoke. Smoking is not allowed anywhere in the building. Are you sure you're okay?" The nurse then decided, "Let's try a little walk in the hall."

"Yes, I feel okay, and I can get you all the information you need from work. I have my ink pen. Why don't you give me your forms and I'll fill them out as best I can at that smoking table." (The Road Rogue was already looking for an escape.)

"All right, I'll have Gilbert walk with you." The nurse then nodded at the orderly, who was a good-sized man of at least 200 pounds.

"Here, Mr. Root." Gilbert offered a lab coat that he helped to drape over Barley's shoulders. "I could use a cigarette, too."

On the way down to the outside smoking table, the Road Rogue was able to question Gilbert to find out exactly where this hospital was. "Less than 30 miles from the truck stop," he thought to himself.

While sitting at the table, an ambulance drove up to the door, lights flashing, until the vehicle stopped. Two paramedics got out, one man from the driver's side and a female when the back door was opened. The female paramedic motioned to Gilbert to help, and the three of them removed a bleeding patient on a stretcher and entered the emergency room.

The Road Rogue waited momentarily, then got up, removed the I.V. from its stand, and got into the ambulance. He drove off, casually found Route 43, headed south to Interstate 44, and sped off to the truck stop.

Inside the emergency room, the paramedics were busy with the patient and informing the on-duty doctor. Gilbert answered a call to return to the second floor.

After separating themselves from responsibility for the incoming patient, the male paramedic said, "I've got to hit the rest room. Here's a couple of bucks. Will you get us a Coke before we leave?" In all, 36 minutes had passed since the ambulance disappeared. After an initial check with hospital on-duty employees, the police were notified of the theft of the ambulance. The Rogue had a 1-hour-and-30 minute head start.

Inside the ambulance, the Rogue had found a paramedic hat and covered the bandage on his head with it. When he pulled into the truck stop, a sickening feeling swept through his body. His truck was surrounded. It was circus-like. He saw two TV crews and dozens of patrol cars. An officer held up his hand as the ambulance was making a U-turn to get away.

"I was going to get some coffee officer. What's going on?" the Road Rogue casually questioned.

"It's the truck of the Road Rogue, you know that famous killer truck," the officer answered. "You better not come in here if you need to be somewhere."

"Thanks, I'll just catch the next exit," the Road Rogue gave a little salute and drove away heading east toward Springfield, Missouri. At another truck stop on the south side of Springfield, the Road Rogue took inventory. The female paramedic's purse was next to the passenger seat. She had two credit cards and $42. There was rain gear to put on. He took an emergency medic kit and found a small toolbox containing the necessary items to break into a vehicle.

Angry desperation pushed the Road Rogue. Using the tools available, he removed the ignition switch from the dash of the ambulance. The ambulance was parked with the cars near the restaurant. He walked to the back row of trucks looking ... looking .... He saw a truck sitting some-what out of line, as if it had sat there longer than the rest. The tires were cold, and no one was inside of it. The truck was a conventional International, obviously a company truck. He pried the passenger-side vent window open, reached inside, and opened the door. Quickly he removed the ignition switch and replaced it with the ambulance's switch and key, and within 10 minutes the Road Rogue was rolling down the highway. He pulled over onto the shoulder before he had traveled 10 miles. "The damn satellite!" He jerked the wire off the unit and then turned south at the next exit.

"Distance, must have distance from the dream truck." His thoughts brought the strongest emotion, hatred. "The police, government, they have taken the dream again!" Hatred, and thirst for vengeance filled the mind of the monster. As he drove on Missouri back roads in a generally southwest direction, his mind plotted. Hobbs took control of the wheel.

The last destination in his memory was Fort Smith, Arkansas. Hobbs took back roads toward the Ozarks of Arkansas. He found a secluded spot behind an abandoned building in a small town and dropped the trailer, knowing there would be roads ahead that a tractor trailer would not be allowed on. Pulling a trailer in this area would only be cause for notice. It was a dark, muggy, hot night when the white International tractor pulled into the lot of the closed-down department store across from the biker bar in Fort Smith, Arkansas. Now it was time for the Road Rogue to plan yet another way to find restitution ...

Bill Jackson and Arnie Benson arrived at the truck stop in Missouri to find the circus-like scene: television crews, police cars with lights flashing, angry truck drivers wanting to leave, and general chaos.

"We've got to end this right now, Arnie." Bill Jackson shook his head in disgust. "The Rogue is gone, for sure."

"Yeah, but we have him identified, at least if he's is the registered owner of this truck." Arnie then was handed some papers by one of the D.O.T. agents. "Bartholomew L. Williams. Let's see here, 50 years old ..."

Bill interrupted, held up his hand, and motioned for the agent who was somewhat in command of the scene. After a short conversation, Bill Jackson said, "I'm going to drive that machine to the Joplin Airport, and our people can go over it in a secured hangar."

Arnie nodded. "I'll have my people clear a path through this mess, but I would like to ride with you. My people will provide escort," he said.

With a mutual nod, the two partners approached the black demon truck. It would have created more chaos to bring in a wrecker. Arnie Benson got into the passenger seat. Bill Jackson paused at the driver's door and read the small gold plaque, 3 inches by 5 inches:

This unit custom built for:
THE WORLD's GREATEST TRUCK DRIVER

Bill then climbed into the driver's seat with his mind picturing his father's face. "Damn, what a truck!" Bill looked at Arnie, into his eyes. "My father would have loved this truck. Look at the detail in this dash. Arnie, all of this [pointing with open hands] is custom." He then started the motor. "This engine has been worked on. Damn, Arnie, this Rogue, whatever has set him off, he's not happy about losing this truck. We have to find him."

The black demon truck was secured in a hangar at the airport, but the agent technicians were told not to touch the unit until a specialist from Washington arrived, Dr. Paul Lindsey.

The registration had provided the name of the Road Rogue, and the great machine of the government went to work. Agents were sent all over the country. Every relative, ex-wife, employer, and known acquaintance was contacted, even high school teachers. The life of Bartholomew Levi Williams would be reviewed in every possible detail in order to find clues to where he might be.

Dr. Paul Lindsey arrived on the scene to touch the demon truck. He "felt" the pain, anguish, anger, hate, and love of the monster. His computer search found the name in the files of the former prosecutor. Dr. Paul Lindsey was putting it all together now—the why of The Road Rogue. He called for a meeting in Washington to discuss his findings with all of the top-level officials and the top field supervisors, including Bill Jackson and Arnold Benson. Before Dr. Paul Lindsey would leave to return to Washington, a phone call from Joplin, Missouri, was transferred to him. It was from Dr. Rosenblatt. The stolen ambulance had been traced back to the missing patient with a head injury ...

Thought of no tomorrow
The pain, tears and sorrow
And you never told me why ... (Ken Hensley)

CHAPTER 28

New Heep, New Hope

In Washington, D.C., at the meeting called by Dr. Paul Lindsey through the authority of the assistant F.B.I. director, a gathering of 20 regional supervisors, Bill Jackson, Arnie Benson, two information research agents, a White House chief of staff assistant, and the assistant F.B.I. director sat in a classroom-like setting.

The room fell silent as a huge man entered the room wearing a secret–service type government business suit that did not hide his muscular build. Arnie Benson leaned towards Bill Jackson and whispered, "Bet his tie is 6 feet long to go around that neck."

Bill Jackson returned a whisper, "Isn't that Cory Richards, the all-American tackle from ..."

Bill's whisper was interrupted by the huge agent. "That's right, I am, and I didn't turn pro because I blew out a knee. In college, I studied law enforcement."

Agent Richards continued walking toward the front of the room and sat down next to the small podium. His size and entrance into the room distracted all of them from the entrance of the slim, rather frail-looking, Dr. Paul Lindsey, who followed him in and stood in front of the podium.

"Gentlemen and ladies [two were present], we are here today to discuss information in order to develop a plan to capture the most-wanted man in America—Bartholomew Levi Williams, known as the Road Rogue. I am Dr. Paul Lindsey. Some of you may have heard of me as the Cry Psy [chuckles, smiles, and bent heads throughout the room], and I don't object to using penned names, but please do not refer to my partner as big Dick." (The room exploded in laughter at the audacity of the known-to-be-gay doctor.)

When the room quieted down, Dr. Lindsey continued. "This Road Rogue has eluded and escaped from an incredible effort to capture him. I believe that he is not finished and presents an even more dangerous risk than before we captured his truck and discovered who he is." Bill Jackson nodded visibly in agreement. "He will not give up. He has a long history of not accepting defeat, and he carries a grudge dating back ... well, at least over 20 years. New information has been found that may help to explain what has happened that has created this monster."

Dr. Lindsey produced a blown-up photo of the cat scans of the patient from Joplin, Missouri, who stole the ambulance. He explained about the tumor. Bill Jackson was especially interested and asked, "What would be the symptoms of this cancerous tumor?"

"From the expert advice I have received, he would suffer paranoid schizophrenia, delusions, recent memory loss, and at times severe headaches, even total blackouts, but he may have complete and accelerated analytical thinking—cunning, if you will." Dr. Lindsey then sadly sighed, "A resourceful rogue, deeply wounded. He knows very little now except pain, like a very old dragon."

Arnie Benson then interrupted. "Okay, enough of this. We need information with which to find him."

"Well then, let's look at his history," Dr. Lindsey replied. "There are a couple of ex-wives. Stakeouts should be set up there and at other family members' homes. But understand, we know through interviews that he told his family group that he was leaving and did not expect to return— Alaska, I believe. Of course, he didn't go to Alaska. He went home to the only real home he knows, the open road behind the wheel of a semi truck. Everything else he knew has been taken from him." The Cry Psy was now living up to his reputation. Tears were forming. "I have prepared a written narrative of his history." After the narrative copies were handed out, Dr. Lindsey continued. "Other than your copy" [pointing to the White House chief of staff assistant], "please read and destroy. This information, in regards to the court case history, house seizure, and so on, must never become public information. Gentlemen, it could easily be argued that we, meaning government, created this monster. I will give you all a little time now, and then I wish to allow you to hear directly from some field agents who have gathered some remarkable information, hopefully insightful into where to corner him."

Bill Jackson's reaction to the Cry Psy report was a sickening ache deep in his gut. He completely understood the shoddy police and detective work described in the truck theft case of Bartholomew Williams. With images in mind of politicians mirrored in his own life, he *did* understand why it had happened: for the personal gain of an ambitious politician. The ensuing legal case history of the Road Rogue, divorce, bankruptcy, workers' comp settlement, the failed attempt to sue under civil rights, and then having to face the loss of his home and a second divorce. Yes, this man had been put through hell. Bill Jackson closed his eyes and muttered to himself, "There's probably more, and now he's dying."

When the meeting reconvened, Dr. Paul Lindsey was composed and stoic. "As I'm sure you all now fully understand, this fugitive is as dangerous as anyone here could imagine. Agent Mark Meyers has been to the home of Bartholomew Williams."

Agent Meyers walked up to the podium and began. "I have been to the house that was seized. Inside I found painted on a wall in the dining area the word *RESTITUTION*. It was written in blood. The house had been broken into, without doubt by the suspect. I have contacted his family members and found no reason to question their statements. Bartholomew Williams had not returned to this town in months. All who knew him believed that he would not return. I have copies of my interviews for your reference. Additionally, I tracked down two of his high school teachers. You might be interested in those interviews in particular. I think what they have remembered will demonstrate that this Road Rogue is capable of planning revenge in unique and intricate ways.

- Interview: Mr. Carl Lewis, Teacher

  'He [Bartholomew Williams] was an independent, idealist sort. I had him in a typing class. He was a good student with high marks in every class, but I had to fail him and remove him from my class. During the first marking period, he was top of the class, typing the most words and without mistakes. Then the second period he could not type at all. I was curious, and he told me what he had done. Instead of practicing on the keys and looking at what he was typing, he memorized the test material and then punched out the words while looking at the keys. After the first marking period, the test material changed, and he did not have time to memorize it. This was a defiant attempt not to learn as the rest of the class. He was just scamming me.

  He was also a very good chess player. In another class I taught (our highest-level mathematics course), we used the game of chess to figure probabilities and projections. Bart, that's what he went by, had never played before but learned quickly and was champion of a school tournament.'

- Interview: Mr. Lyn Bolten, Teacher and Basketball Coach

  'For whatever reason, I can't tell you, but in Bart's senior year he decided to go out for basketball. He had not played before, and I cut him from the team. He was a big guy, but rough. I couldn't cut someone else who had been playing for years. Anyway, he would not accept being cut. Bart formed his own team of high school friends and wanted to play in the town's adult city league. He was turned down, of course, but he would not give up. He wrote letters and started a petition— something about paying taxes and having the right to use the public facilities. He won, and his team was allowed to play in that league.' "

Other agents who had conducted interviews with former employers of Barley Bill were called to the podium. Their general consensus was "hardest worker," "safe operator," "can do what seemed impossible." No one contacted had any negative words about how Bartholomew Williams operated a truck.

Dr. Paul Lindsey took the podium again. "I have another report that our research department found, an old F.B.I. file on Bartholomew Williams. In the winter of 1978, January, a sensitive military computer component system was purchased from a Boston defense contractor. A terrible storm hit. All planes were grounded. It was decided to put the system on a truck to transport it to Edwards Air Force Base in California. Mr. Williams was the driver. He was told to get the shipment there as fast as possible. It was a Wednesday afternoon when he left. He arrived at Edwards' gates on Friday afternoon ..."

"Hey, you mean he drove more than 3,000 miles in 48 hours?" Bill Jackson interrupted.

"Yes," Dr. Lindsey nodded, "But no officer was on duty with the authority to accept the delivery. No one expected him until Monday, so the driver was held there until Monday. By Saturday afternoon, he became irritated. He was kept under armed guard until Monday when the commander returned. The driver was allowed to leave after the shipment was removed from the trailer, and he shouted obscenities as he left."

As the proceedings continued, Arnold Benson became annoyed and frustrated. He was red in the face and staring at the floor. White knuckles appeared on his clenched fist, with two of his fingers holding a coffee mug.

Bill Jackson thought of his own father when the story of the 48-hour continental crossing was told. In his mind, he could see his father's exhausted face after making some impossible run. In his own time behind the wheel, Bill Jackson had fought off fatigue. "But to cross the entire country without stopping. The poor bastard probably thought he was doing something patriotic," Bill whispered to himself.

Dr. Lindsey then continued. "I have provided you all here with this information to help explain just what kind of fugitive you seek. As you all know now, the Road Rogue's truck was not what we previously believed. My research team has been trying to identify a new, late-model truck. This truck, although it has many new and customized parts, is a 1979. This is significant. It is apparent, based upon the records we have been able to find, that rebuilding this truck was how Bartholomew Williams was fighting, if you will, to replace what he lost 20 years ago. Please understand, all that we have in evidence now shows that this man is fixated on that truck theft case, but of course he lost more than just his truck."

"My team and I have thoroughly investigated and studied this truck. I was most impressed with this man's music collection." Dr. Lindsey's voice was losing the stoic statement quality, and he was sounding emotional again. "I must tell you, he has a wonderful collection of music of all types, with songs of passion, love, and freedom. He has classical symphonies, tear-jerking country, and rock music from the late sixties to mid eighties. It's a truly remarkable collection indeed, but what I found of real significance was music by a rock group called Uriah Heep. I've never heard this music before. It has beautiful poetry mixed with power rock and . . ."

"Shut up you queer cocksucker!" Arnie Benson had heard enough. He threw his coffee mug toward the front, nearly hitting the Cry Psy, and approached as if he were going to assault the young doctor. "We're tracking a monster who is killing police and anyone else who gets in his way, you damn idiot. We don't need help from a gay who's falling in love with him."

Agent Richards stood up displaying his huge bulk, and Arnold Benson stopped, apologized, and returned to his seat.

The Cry Psy had hit the floor as if a bomb were about to go off. He stood up slowly next to the smiling Agent Richards. Peering over the top of the podium, he looked directly at Arnold Benson, who was red in the face. "I don't love this man, Mr. Benson. If anyone in this room loves the Road Rogue, it is Agent Jackson!"

Everyone in the room turned their eyes to Bill Jackson as the Cry Psy asked, "Just how did your father die, Agent Jackson?"

Bill Jackson stood erect, muscles in his hackles raised. The assistant F.B.I. director then stated with an arrogant command, "Go ahead and tell us."

"My father drove truck all of his life. He was found dead of a heart attack lying across the steering wheel of one of his trucks." Bill Jackson said no more and sat down.

The assistant F.B.I. director then motioned to Dr. Lindsey to continue. "A little patience, please. Everything being discussed here today has its purpose. This music group, Uriah Heep, is very important to our fugitive. We have tested his entire music collection. He listens to this Uriah Heep five times as much as anything else he has."

"You can do that?" Arnie Benson inquired.

"Yes, we have the technology." Dr. Lindsey held up a finger to make his point. "Not only does he listen to this stuff often, he has spare copies of each of the CDs and tapes. This monster will not be without it. Everything presented today suggests that the Road Rogue will return, and he will attempt to rebuild again. He *will* get back into a truck, and he *will* replace this music."

The Cry Psy was getting a little emotional in his tone again. "As I stated earlier, I have never heard this music. It's not easy to find. At one time, I've been told, the music of Uriah Heep was, how would you say—suppressed here in America. It is my belief that we can capture this fugitive when he tries to replace the music."

"What are you proposing?" Bill Jackson asked, now in a calmer mood.

"As quietly as possible, we have ordered Uriah Heep off the shelves." Dr. Lindsey shrugged his shoulders. "This music is not in the open market anymore, anyway. My recommendation is to stake out music stores. We were able to discover from the spare copies found in his truck that he has gone to these music specialty stores and ordered music." Then, raising both hands, the Cry Psy smiled and suggested, "There you all have it. Of course, stakeouts are needed at all of the possible family connections and former homes, but review this material. The Road Rogue will return."

The assistant F.B.I. director walked up to Bill Jackson. "I need to see you privately. Come over to my office in the morning. I want a summary of your recommendations and whatever plans you have . . . in writing."

"Yes sir."

The following morning in the assistant F.B.I. director's office, Bill Jackson handed over his report. "Well Bill, after yesterday's meeting, what is your best guess as to where this Road Rogue will go?"

"The meeting was informative," Bill stated a little doubtfully, "but I don't know about that music stuff. My guess would be that he would attempt to see that first wife. If he is fixated on the past, I would expect that he eventually would go there."

"Good, we'll be sure to cover that." The eyes and voice of the assistant director then seemed aloof. "Bill, this is a political world here in Washington. You've been removed from this case."

"What!" Bill Jackson was shocked.

"I'm afraid you don't understand." The assistant director nodded toward the door of his office. Two secret security agents entered. "Your resignation will be announced this afternoon. Here are the papers for you to sign. Resign, or charges will be brought against you. We have those press leaks, you know. Be sure to stop downstairs. We have a good severance package for you." Bill Jackson grabbed the papers and signed, muttering, "Politicians." His F.B.I. career was over. Then, just after the fired agent left the room, the phone rang. The assistant director answered, "Dinner? Sure, Linda."

Bill Jackson drove to his apartment, repacked his traveling bags, and headed for the airport. He wanted the first available flight to Missouri. At 8 o'clock the next morning, Bill Jackson stood on the porch of a rural home and rang its doorbell. A man answered the door. "May I speak to my . . . may I speak to Lisa?" Bill asked, without assessing the man in front of him holding the opened door.

"Lisa, it's him. Do you wish to speak to him?"

A quiet, cold moment passed, and then Bill Jackson looked at the love of his life's eyes as she appeared in the doorway. Only an icy, angry stare was returned. Bill Jackson bowed his head on slumping shoulders. Lisa was pregnant . . .

The Road Rogue was busy with a new plan in Fort Smith, Arkansas. He knew he had to start all over. The memories of Barley Bill had provided a cunning plan. First, he needed some cash. Barley Bill had started in trucking by lumping freight (household goods). Although he had the injuries, he was able to convince a cross-country mover to hire him to load furniture (covering his head with a hat). The young driver was impressed with the knowledge and tricks of the trade that this old mover showed. In 2 days of hard labor, the Road Rogue was able to earn $200 dollars, plus a $100 tip from a shipper who was impressed with the careful technique this older worker provided. This shipper's wife had a special hutch, and it was handled with great care. She was put at ease in the moving of her home.

With the money earned, the Road Rogue bought a new set of clothes and prepared his plan. He used a local library computer to design an application form and made 50 copies. The Road Rogue's plan was based upon memories from Barley's time as a safety director when he had hired drivers. Clean-shaven with new clothes, the Road Rogue drove to a local truck stop and paid a manager $100 cash to allow him to do a little recruiting from a card table. The computer at the library also provided the graphics to produce a brochure describing a new trucking company that was offering $2 per mile in compensation to owner/operators.

The Road Rogue was careful and cunning. When asked how *any* truck company could offer so much, he responded, "It's a special government contract. You must be able to pass a federal background check, be financially sound, and have a tractor no more than 2 years old."

The plan worked well. By insisting on financial stability, only older drivers could apply. Drivers did apply. In the scheme, the Road Rogue made photocopies of drivers' licenses and social security cards, and the applications required detailed background information. It all sounded logical. Two drivers were so convinced that they left a security deposit.

Within 1 week, the Road Rogue was able to produce three sets of complete ID for himself. He had to drive to the hometowns of the three men to have new birth certificate copies made; then he went to driver's license offices to have duplicate driver's licenses made. The young clerical girls did not observe any noticeable differences between the photocopied driver's license pictures of the three truck drivers, who were similar in size and age to the Rogue.

Using one of the new IDs, "Timothy Owens" purchased a P.O. box in a small town outside of Fort Smith. Timothy Owens's name was a good one. The Road Rogue again visited a license branch and registered an address change to the P.O. box. Always careful using the stolen International tractor, the Road Rogue found secluded parking spots near the biker bar where the tempting barmaid worked.

Tammy took no special notice of the new regular customer and did not remember the previous meeting. This new man was just a quiet loner.

The Road Rogue was quiet. Nothing would detour him from this new plan. Credit applications began arriving at the P.O. box within 2 weeks.

Yes, Timothy Owens was a good name with excellent credit. Very soon after applying, the Road Rogue had a total of six credit cards in that good name and was able to put more than $20,000 cash into the new wallet of the next name of the three, Robert Henry.

"Robert Henry will be my new identity," the Road Rogue sighed to himself. Then, boldly, a new letter was written to Timothy Owens along with $500 cash.

> Dear Timothy Owens,
>
> You have a very good name. I have converted it into a large amount of money. You need a lawyer to protect you from all of this.
>
> P.S. To my pursuers: You have taken my beauty again. Thank you. I am now invisible.
>
> Enclosed: six credit cards.
>
> Sincerely,
>
> The Road Rogue

The plan continued. A nearby trucking company Barley Bill had once worked for had a lot behind the repair shop. In this lot were several totaled trucks. It is common for trucking companies to put wrecked trucks out back because they can't risk filing a claim that would raise or cancel their insurance. The Road Rogue visited the lot under the cover of darkness and gathered more pieces of his plan: a license plate, registration, and a door vehicle information label. "A 3-year-old Freightliner Condo would be perfect," he thought. "There are a lot of them on the road."

Next, the Road Rogue visited a large dealership. [The current times have created massive numbers of used trucks sitting on lots all across the country. Tens of thousands can't be sold. Such is the result of the government's meddling in the trucking industry. Repossessions galore, buyback programs, and a general lack of confidence in being able to survive as an owner/operator have dropped the value of these trucks below loan value.] Using an ignition switch and key from the wrecked Freightliner, the Road Rogue left this dealership with a nice Freightliner Classic Condo of the same year as the wrecked unit. The Road Rogue was back in business with an apparently legal tractor, legal ID, a driver's license, and plenty of cash. Robert Henry would be able to blend into the trucking world.

The new truck wasn't complete, nor was the plan for restitution—a new restitution.

With new confidence, Robert Henry made an effort to experience more of the new pleasure feeling by visiting Tammy, the barmaid. Her rejection resulted in a rush of adrenaline being focused upon his fight against the government.

At the local truck stop, Robert Henry bought a 1,000-watt power converter for the new ride. Then he drove to a large nationwide computer, television, and stereo store. The new ride had a huge sleeper area in an integrated cab, set up as a studio. Nearly $4,000 bought a personal computer with printer, several cases of paper, and a powerful 12-disk stereo system. The young salesman, Shane (knowledge gained from observing the name tag), was intrigued with the cash sale and was curious again when 3 hours later this strange old customer reentered the store. He did not realize that the equipment was being installed right outside in a truck in the parking lot.

The Road Rogue's new plan was to use the computer to produce his own newsletter of grievances against the government, distribute it throughout the United States with his truck, and continue to elude capture. The latest failure with Tammy, the barmaid, in a quest to experience pleasure brought about a desire in the Road Rogue to replace the music that had so dominated Barley Bill's life.

This store also had a large selection of CDs in three aisleways; he figured they would have everything in music. Robert, as the Road Rogue had introduced himself to the young salesman, walked to the CDs and started looking. Frustration set in, and he walked over to Shane. "I can't find any Uriah Heep. Do you have Uriah Heep?"

"Never heard of them, what kind of music?" Shane replied.

"Rock and roll, very good stuff." A still-pleasant-acting Robert Henry continued, "In fact, it's the world's greatest rock and roll."

"Must be old shit," Shane sneered, thinking this old man was past an age to be involved with rock music. "I don't have any listed on the computer." Shane noticed the warning posted on the screen to remove all Uriah Heep from shelves but added with a rather aloof tone, "We have a bin over there in the corner for old garbage music that doesn't sell. You might find some if you dig through it."

Rage, instant rage, flowed through the Road Rogue. He had just spent all that money and this kid with an earring and a fish hook stuck in his eyebrow was insulting the memory of Barley Bill. "You," he barked, "you think Uriah Heep is garbage?"

The Road Rogue stormed out, got into the tractor, drove over to the truck stop, and stole a trailer. Within 10 minutes he returned to that store and backed the trailer into the building at the maximum high-range reverse. Busted glass, smashed bricks, a partially fallen-in roof, and a semi trailer half buried into the building was an adequate start for the Road Rogue to return to fantasy on the open road.

The "Crimson Fire" ride of the demon, this new, stolen, red Freightliner XL Classic, was now complete and rolling west.

The shocked, bruised, scratched, and humbled salesman Shane called the police, and the local TV news had a crew on the scene shortly thereafter. Linda Wright was flown to the scene. It had been 6 weeks since the capture of the black truck belonging to Bartholomew Levi Williams.

In national news, the secret of the Uriah Heep controversy was revealed. Linda Wright had not been told. Her story made "Special Report" interruption status in prime time.

In a cocktail lounge of a hotel near Chicago, Illinois, a well-dressed businessman in his late 50s sat at the bar with a martini glass in front of him. He had had several when he noticed the Linda Wright report. The computer store that had been attacked by the Road Rogue was one of his. George Geils was the CEO of the nationwide computer and electronics chain. He had just come from another disturbingly negative meeting with his top staff about poor sales, a slumping economy, and increasing debt. When he heard about the ban on Uriah Heep, a smile formed on his face. His business had started as an LP album store 30 years ago. After the death of the vinyl LP album, sales diminished and the business was diversified. The chain of record stores became computer stores in the late eighties. The LP sales were only a fond memory now, but he remembered Uriah Heep and the phenomenal sales of the early albums.

He pulled out his cell phone and called his top assistant. "Jerry, get everybody up, now! We're going back to the meeting room, right now!"

"Sir?"

"Make the arrangements, right now!" George Geils was exhilarated. Within 30 minutes, his staff was reassembled, including the corporate lawyer.

"Gentlemen, we have a potential bonanza here in front of us." George Geils then replayed Linda Wright's report.

"I want an exclusivity deal completed to purchase the next 2 million copies of anything produced under the name Uriah Heep." George then waved his hand to all of his staff. "You have only tonight to research this. Find out what was most popular and what is available. Get a T-shirt deal, posters, and the like. Prepare an advertising campaign." Then turning to the corporate lawyer, he ordered, "I want that ban lifted. File tomorrow. This is a free speech suit for federal court."

All in the room were stunned as their CEO continued. "I want you all to think back to the cola war—Pepsi versus Coke? When Coke decided to take away the original, the country erupted into protest. The result was a bonanza for Coke. Tell the people of this country that they can't have something and a new market is created. That is what we have the opportunity for right now! I want Computer City to be *the* place to get the music of the Road Rogue. Just think, we can have a complete monopoly for the length of time it takes to fulfill the exclusivity's volume of the contract." Turning again to the corporate lawyer, CEO George Geils pointed and continued, "This court challenge will be the kickoff of the advertising campaign. We can turn this into a patriotic defense of the Constitution! Once the customers are in our stores, we can sell . . ."

Even before George Geils's Computer City campaign would begin, the advertising had begun. On the following morning, Linda Wright's report was aired again on the network's morning show. Gregory Blanchard watched from his easy chair at home. A recently retired automotive assembly line worker, Greg was 51 years old, overweight, bored with life, and now accustomed to sitting in front of his TV from morning when his wife would leave for her work until late afternoons. He drank beer, stared at that TV, and then would drive to the local tavern to talk to other line workers who had not yet been so lucky as to be offered early retirement. He avoided his wife. Something about no longer being the breadwinner, no longer being a valued employee, no longer having to get to work no matter what, had brought a loss of self-respect or self-worth. Greg Blanchard had worked in the Ford Edison, New Jersey, plant all of his adult life. He had worked inside that prison when men soaked themselves with water to avoid dehydration. Years of long, tedious hours and being subject to mandatory overtime made the plant his life. There *were* good times though: playing cards on break, having a beer with the boys after a shift, and of course, a relatively high salary. He was lucky to have gotten that job, or was he?

The Linda Wright TV report brought back memories about the time before the plant dominated his life. Gregory Blanchard had once dreamed. He had dreamed of cars and racing, and he had once loved Uriah Heep music. He knew that in all of his life, Uriah Heep had been the best music he had ever heard—dreamy. "Most of all," he thought, "I shared the experience with my girl—my wife." Gregory Blanchard closed his eyes as he remembered a July morning and his eyes watered.

A defiant, somewhat loaded, and once-proud man stood up from his easy chair and declared to the authorities and responsibilities of all of his life on the other side of the tube, "You *can't* stop me from listening to Uriah Heep, you bastards!" Gregory Blanchard left the comfort of his living room and marched toward his garage. He marched, not as he had when in the armed service, but with the quick step of 30 years ago as he marched toward his life's destiny on a July morning.

The garage of the Blanchard home was full of a lifetime of discarded keepsakes and items that probably still had value when put into the garage. Greg went to work on the mess. He stacked boxes, bikes, and no-longer-used chairs. When he had cleaned half of the concrete floor, he huffed, wiped the sweat from his brow, and put the ladder at the back corner. He struggled with the large Sears dishwasher box as he carefully removed it from the rafters. The box was marked "Bach. Stuff." It contained treasures from days long before responsibility and the Ford plant call. Inside was a stereo with a turntable, vinyl records, a stained T-shirt, a still-folded kerchief headband, and a wooden stash box. All the memories had been protected by another special memory, a military-style sleeping bag once carried routinely in the trunk of a Mach One Mustang.

Greg Blanchard pleaded aloud as he plugged in the small stereo system and placed an old, worn *Look at Yourself* Uriah Heep album on the turntable. He paused before setting the needle into the groove. "Play, damn it, play!"

No turntable noise or scratches could be heard in the music within the mind of this old dreamer, as the organ solo blended into the guitar of "July Morning." With watery eyes, he continued setting up a memory. He put on the headband as if he still had long hair to tie back, and he tried to put on that favorite lucky T-shirt. The T-shirt was from 100 pounds ago, so he simply ripped the side seams to make it look like a poncho. Greg then opened the stash box and found his old favorite pipe and an incense burner. He laid out the sleeping bag and lit a 30-year-old strawberry incense cone. Using his pocketknife, he scraped the sides of the old pipe and inhaled as he ignored the harsh, bitter smoke.

A car pulled into the driveway, and Greg Blanchard knew it was her, his July morning. He followed her into the kitchen. She turned and laughed at first glance of him . . . but his eyes pierced hers, and suddenly she saw her husband of 30 years as a much younger man.

He walked to the refrigerator, pulled out a bottle of wine and coaxed her, "Come with me." She followed him into a dream inside their garage . . .

All across the states, those who remembered looked for their Heep. A few would find the music, but many were to travel to the nearest store that sold music in a fruitless attempt to find it. Nationwide there were thousands of requests.

In a small Midwest town, a DJ of a local radio station saw the Linda Wright report. Long ago, he was a promising radio personality at a large-market station. "Crazy Kelly," as he was once known, would pull stunts and play requests not in the top 40. He, too, was a Heep fan. When management ordered him not to play Uriah Heep 25 years ago, he scoffed at that authority. He had played Uriah Heep and had challenged management. Crazy Kelly was never a promising radio personality again. He survived as a quiet, noncontroversial announcer. The station where he worked now was like many of today. The DJ does not even control what music plays or when. Management-approved computer selections that have been prearranged dominate radio shows now, even request shows. "Callers who make the air are callers who have chosen the correct and approved songs," was a comment disgusted Crazy Kelly used while describing his own work.

A crazy idea for a stunt entered this once-promising DJ's mind as he thought about a government ban on the sale of Uriah Heep. "Good afternoon, America!" was first heard on that local station in Cedar Rapids, Iowa, at 1:00 P.M. central time on the second day after the first airing of Linda Wright's report about the music store crash. "I'm Craaaaaazy Kelly, and due to the government's ban, I have barricaded myself in this studio, and I'm going to play Uriah Heep until they come to take me away."

Within 4 hours, the phone lines at the radio station were full with angry old "Heepsters," request callers, *and* advertisers. By nightfall, television stations reported that the show by a crazy DJ was now being fed all across the nation. Only a small percentage of generation X had even heard of the once and now-again controversial music, and virtually none of generation Y was familiar with it. All had heard of the Road Rogue by now though. A resurgence of a music group or star had happened before (the Doors, Jim Morrison, and more recently Meatloaf) but not on a scale like what was about to sweep the nation.

Back in Washington, politicians were being swept of all credibility. The new point man assigned to replace the now-disgraced Bill Jackson was a tough, hard hunter. Some within the department considered him an assassin, although he rarely pulled the trigger himself. Agent Ken Worthington and his team were loose cannons and the last resort to end political embarrassment. His real name was habitually kept from the public to prevent further political embarrassment, as he had been responsible for the ugly deaths of innocent individuals during his previous zealous quests to complete missions.

Ken Worthington had put *no* credence in the Cry Psy theory of trapping the Rogue by using silly stakeouts at music stores where an obscure English rock band's music might be found. Agent Ken Worthington instead had read the reports and recommendations of his fellow agent Bill Jackson, whom he respected. Agent Ken did not ignore the psychology of the case; he just did not care. "I'll just find him and eliminate the problem," he had replied matter of factly to the assistant F.B.I. director.

Of all the reports and theories Ken Worthington had read regarding this case, he had placed his money on the Road Rogue attempting to see this woman (the July morning). Worthington believed that *she* tied the monster to the use of the word *restitution*. Stakeouts were set up at the homes of all of the known family and possible friends of the Road Rogue, but Ken Worthington himself traveled to the small farm outside of Capital City where this woman of a 20-year-old story lived.

Ken Worthington studied the F.B.I. file prepared on Erika Knight. He wasn't impressed. He was expecting a woman in her 40s who had four children and was in her fourth marriage. His car pulled up to the small farmhouse, and he indicated to the government car following him to park across the gravel road in a farm tractor access drive to a field. He then walked up to the front door in the old, wooden-floor porch.

She opened the front door, and Ken Worthington was immediately taken by surprise. Something in this woman's eyes looked right into his soul. She was quite pretty, really unexpectedly so. The eyes of her bothered him somehow as he introduced himself. "I'm Agent Ken Worthington of the F.B.I." Then he swallowed and asked, "Would you be Erika Knight, formerly married to Bartholomew L. Williams?"

Erika's piercing eyes dropped to the floor of the porch, and she sighed, "Barley." Erika then looked up with a dreadful stare at this government representative. Her eyes emitted anger and sadness at the same time. She asked, already knowing the answer, "It's him, isn't it? Barley? He's the one, the Road Rogue?"

"Yes, we know it now." Agent Ken Worthington was all the more sure of himself now upon seeing this woman. His mind told him she had that something. "We believe he may come here to contact you." Agent Ken then pointed across the gravel road to the government car with two men in business suits wearing sunglasses inside. "We're going to have 24-hour surveillance here to protect you."

"Protect me?" Erika adamantly replied. "No, you think this is Rose's Cantina of El Paso, and you're going to gun him down as he tries to reach my arms" (referring to the Marty Robbins hit song). Erika then looked at him directly. "You're wrong. He won't come here. You're chasing a ghost if you're chasing the man I married 20 years ago. That man is dead. You people killed him." Erika said no more and turned away to reenter her home.

Another field agent who tracked down Marie (Barley's second wife) in Michigan fared no better. "I've had no contact from him in months. He doesn't even know where I am. He had become cold and distant, and I was frightened. Barley tried so hard and worked so hard." Marie shook her head. "I guess I should have known he was the one. I know you have to kill him, but don't expect me to be a part of it."

The crimson red truck rolled west and then north into the high desert. The Road Rogue and his own Hobbs codriver were full of confidence in the new legal ride. Yes, the beauty was gone, but there was a kind of beauty in being invisible. Just the one problem remained. "Need some Heep in this ride."

The phenomenal commercial machine of America was already in motion by the time the crimson truck pulled into a safe-haven parking spot in Albuquerque, New Mexico, with its master looking for a music store. A nationwide buzz was already rumbling about Uriah Heep. Even the cable TV pundents were offering psychological interpretations of the meanings of the music. People wondered why it was suppressed 25 years earlier. Current music stars spoke of the influences of Uriah Heep on their own work. Many were cashing in.

The small Full Moon record store in a strip mall on the north side of Albuquerque was dealing with the exclusivity contract by buying from the local Computer and Electronic City store and then reselling with a small markup of price to loyal customers. The owner of this independent store figured it might be illegal, but then he wasn't a man that worried much.

The Road Rogue entered the store and stared at this independent businessman who appeared to be a defiant individual. He was over 50, with long graying hair well past the shoulders on his black Harley Davidson T-shirt. He wore a black ball hat with the Vietnam veteran logo. His tiny legs suggested that he had been in his wheelchair since that government police action. He coughed with a watery growl and then offered, "What cha looking for?"

"Driving music." Then the Road Rogue cleared his own throat. "Uriah Heep. I'm looking for all nine albums, I mean CDs."

"You mean the first nine?" The watery cough again signaled something to the Road Rogue. This man carried pain within him, physical and emotional, yet was defiantly independent. He continued, "You're like a lot of us. They wanted us to think Uriah Heep was gone, but hell, the group is still going on. If you're an old Heepster, you're in for a treat. The band has quite a history. You know, they say we got our ass kicked in Nam, and they say Ronald "Ray Guns" ended the Cold War, but did ya know how it all really ended?"

"I don't know if I know what you mean." The mind of the Road Rogue was being challenged, but he felt some kinship with this strange-sounding old hippie-looking character.

"I mean the Soviets; they were beaten by a call of freedom." His heavy cough and narrowing, defiant eyes commanded the attention of his customer. "Nobody sings about freedom like Uriah Heep. Uriah Heep was the first rock band to tour the Soviet Union. That was in 1987. It weren't politics or prayer that ended it. It was Uriah Heep. That's what I believe. Now that I have your interest, do you want me to play you the Uriah Heep you've never heard?"

CHAPTER 29

Box of Heep

[Yes, the World's Greatest Rock Band has a history that parallels the life of the World's Greatest Truck Driver including pain and sorrow, love, great success, bankruptcy, rebuilding, loss of beauty, suppression, ridicule—and from the very start, dominating heavy and humble memories.]

Inside of Full Moon, the Road Rogue discovered another emotional feeling, friendship. This old Heepster who lived by selling music could speak to the monster, and the monster could listen. While the music played in the store, his gravelly voice read from the CD liners to explain how tragedies had changed the composition of Uriah Heep and how the band had carried on. [The World's Greatest Guitarist, Mick Box, must have shared the same inner spirit that drove the former Barley Bill man. Mick Box would not let the dream die. The band lost its voice, David Byron, and then its poet, Ken Hensley, but Mick Box still commands its power . . .]

Two hours into new Uriah Heep, the Road Rogue was caught off guard when he was asked by the store owner (as the complete collection of Uriah Heep's recorded music was put into a box to complete the sale), "What's your name?"

"Ah, Robert." The Road Rogue struggled to remember the name he was traveling by.

"Yeah, right, and I'm Jesus H. Christ." Coughing again, the store owner added, "Know what the H stands for? Handicapped!" Then with a laugh, "My name is Bob, Bob Thielman. But your name isn't Robert." After a serious silent pause, the eyes of these two men met. "You're him, the one this [pointing to the box] is all about. You're the Road Rogue who likes Uriah Heep music, aren't you?"

The Road Rogue stood erect and defensive, and stared coldly at his newfound friend. He did not speak. He did not have to.

"Wow! Holy shit! The Road Rogue right here in my store!" Bob Thielman was excited but not afraid. "You don't have to worry about me." Bob held up one hand. "Man, you got the whole damn government after you, and politicians are having a cow. I love it!" Bob rolled over to the front door and turned the hanging sign to "Closed." He locked the door with an excited invitation. "Will you have a drink with me, I mean a beer? They say you like beer. In my store, I'll be damned! The Road Rogue!"

"Beer?" The Road Rogue relaxed, smiled as best he could, and replied, "Beer good."

With the Full Moon record store closed, the Road Rogue followed Bob Thielman as he wheeled to the store's back room. It was a bit cluttered with a well-used dinner table, a coppertone refrigerator, and an odor suggesting regular incense burning. This room was the private world of an independent individual, unwilling to let his physical limitations create a victim dependent on the government. Bob Thielman stood defiantly tall without legs. The various posters and cartoons randomly displayed included the smiling Bubba (Clinton) from the *Penthouse* magazine, bringing a nod of approval from the Road Rogue. There was also a poster of the photograph used as the CD liner of the Longriders' "Road Rogue" hit country CD.

Bob Thielman rolled over to the refrigerator and pulled out a can of cold beer and a bottle of burgundy-colored wine. He handed the beer to his famous customer, held up his bottle of wine in a toast, and announced, "I like beer too, except it just makes me have to empty the bag more often."

They both drank with long pulls. "Aahhh."

"You ever drink wine, eh? Just what should I call you? Guess you don't even know, right?" Bob cocked his head and then added, "Double R, and you can call me D.B. That'd be for Disabled Bob."

"Okay, D.B.," the newly christened Double R nodded, as he held out his hand to accept the bottle of wine for a taste. Nearly everything was new for Double R. He knew that Barley Bill had consumed wine before, but he could not anticipate the flavor or feeling of drinking wine. He tasted a small swallow, then took a long gulp and remarked, "Wonderful." The taste and warming sensation brought a flashback to the railroad bridge, and for a moment he was no longer in the room with D.B.

D.B. interrupted, "Hey man, anybody ever tell you that you have Hillary eyes?" D.B. shook his head slowly. "I mean, some of the time your eyes are soulless, but just before that you looked like a kid when you tasted my wine. Just what planet are you from? And why don't you call yourself Bartholomew? Hell, the whole country knows your name now." He coughed and cleared his throat.

Slowly, the Road Rogue turned his head and looked directly into the face of Disabled Bob. "He doesn't exist. Can't find him."

"Oh, I get it," D.B. said, then coughed again and relaxed. "I guess I've lost a little of myself along the way, too." He pointed to the shriveled remains of his legs. "Hey man, do you know what I've heard?" D.B. paused waiting for a response, but only a quizzical look was returned. "They're bidding on your truck, the black truck. I mean there are some money guys who want to use it as an attraction. I hear that more than a million has been offered."

"To whom?" a now more relaxed Double R replied. "The government, I suppose. No matter. I have a new beauty now, a red one."

"Red for revenge?" D.B. asked, but not expecting an answer.

"Red for *restitution*," the monster stated coldly and profoundly.

"Would you take me for a ride?" D.B. coughed and continued. "I've never been in a truck, and actually I hardly ever go anywhere. They won't let me drive. I don't have enough of me left, and I've been busted for drinking and smoking weed. Yeah man, they, the damn government, even want to close down my store. I've got a court date next month. They came in here in my back room and found some stash."

"Okay, I'll go get my truck." The Road Rogue stood up and pointed to the back door. "Is there an alley or truck access behind?"

"Yes, sure!" D.B. was excited at the opportunity.

The big red truck stopped at the Full Moon's back door, with the passenger's side cab door within 8 feet of the building. D.B. rolled out next to the steps, first with awe at the size of the rig, and then with sadness as he realized there was no possible way for him to climb in. D.B. sat there in his wheelchair with the box of Heep on the lap of his useless legs.

The Road Rogue climbed out, walked around, and without speaking simply grabbed the box and put it into the cab. He then picked Disabled Bob up out of the wheelchair as if he were picking up a small child and held him over his right shoulder. After opening the cab door he stepped up, placed D.B. into the seat, and hooked up the safety belt.

A new sensation entered the mind of the Road Rogue as he stepped back down. He felt a sad pity, realizing how light this broken man was. No words were spoken during this loading of his passenger; none were needed.

Before returning to the driver's seat, Double R picked up the wheelchair, placed it on the frame rails behind the sleeper, and strapped it down with tarp straps. An idea hit him as he finished securing the wheelchair. He walked to the back of the trailer, opened the doors, and pulled out two load locks.

Load locks are expendable metal poles used to secure partial loads. Double R brought them inside the cab and placed them in a cross, one from above the passenger door to above the driver's door, and the other load lock from the front storage pocket in the cab's inside roof to the back of the sleeper. He tightened them and tested them with his own weight while D.B. watched.

"Oh, I get it man," D.B. realized with absolute glee. "I can use these to move around the cab, like monkey bars. Wow! Well, you drive, and I'll be your Disc Jockey."

They began the ride with "Gypsy," the first theme song of Uriah Heep. It was the favorite of this long-disabled man.

I was only seventeen . . .
I fell in love with a Gypsy Queen. (Mick Box)

Bob Thielman had entered the military at 18 in the height of the worst year of Vietnam. The Tet Offensive began shortly after he had arrived at that jungle, police action war. Riding in this semi truck with the most-wanted man in America brought to mind flashbacks of the most dramatic moments of Bob Thielman's life. The pure excitement rush of emotion created a true bond with this monster, who was giving him the kindest miracle of his life since he had faced the monster in his past that had destroyed him as a man.

Bob Thielman dropped the persona of mental strength he displayed in his store and nearly broke down as he spoke to his new friend. "I never got to, you know, fall in love with a Gypsy Queen or any woman. I've never been with a woman and I never will. The doctor said that I could, but what woman would want half of a man like me?"

They rode on, listening to more music of Uriah Heep, with songs promoting philosophical conversations about life. The Road Rogue mostly listened, while realizing that this man of music was a troubled soul carrying long-held regret, grudges, and desire. In some way, the Road Rogue saw in this man what was lost when the conscious mind of the former man Barley disappeared. A new thought entered from a memory. He saw the face of Earl, the codriver.

The red truck entered a rest area and was parked. The Road Rogue stood up inside the cab, unhooked the seat belt on D.B., picked him up, and placed him in the driver's seat.

"What the hell are you doing?" D.B. demanded, although he was getting the idea.

"Reach down beside the seat. There's a kingpin puller there. It's called the happy unhooker. Now place the handle in your left armpit. Use your hand to guide the other end to the clutch pedal. Lean forward."

"Yeah, I got it. I can push in the clutch with this." D.B. was filling with anticipation.

"Now you can use the cruise control toggle switch as your throttle, and you can use the trailer hand valve as your brake. You only have to use the clutch pedal to start. The rest of the gears can be shifted by simply being in the right RPM range."

The dash, parking brake, gauges, and engine retarder were all explored and identified. As Barley Bill had taught Earl so long ago, the Road Rogue taught Disabled Bob Thielman to drive. No amount of gear grinding mattered. The goal was reached. A broken man was driving a machine in a world he could only have dreamed of.

Once reaching a suitable cruising speed on the interstate, it all soaked into D.B. He was nearly overwhelmed by the emotion of it. "I'M DRIVING A SEMI TRUCK!" he hollered.

As the ride continued, D.B. turned to his miracle provider with a longing to do something, anything, in return. "So man, what are you doing? Where are you going? What is your plan?"

The Road Rogue turned and pointed to the small tabletop above the clothes closet (this closet was less than 3 feet tall). A computer keyboard and screen were strapped onto it. "I want to write a message for America that will be my restitution. I want to stop the politicians from taking freedom from the people." Then the Road Rogue just blurted it out. "I need a voice. Do you want to ride with me to save America?"

"I've never . . . Hell, I've got nothing to stop me." He coughed. "Let's go back to my store. Maybe I can help you. Show me your cause." D.B. pulled down the hand valve, parked, confidently climbed out of the driver's seat using the monkey bar, and sat himself back in the passenger seat. They returned to the Full Moon record store.

While parked behind the store, D.B. read rough drafts of what the Road Rogue was attempting to write. "Oh, I get it, man. This is Star Trek, man." D.B. looked at his friend, "Remember Star Trek? What you are trying to say about taxes is very much like a Star Trek episode, you know, with Captain Kirk and Spock. They went to a world where two worlds were fighting a war only they didn't fight. They just used a couple of war game computers. After a computer attack, the people chosen as casualties had to walk down to an infirmary or something and be killed. Captain Kirk smashed the computer because these people were having a war without the messy and ugly consequences of war. Just like our government is doing with withholding taxes, removing the ugliness of collecting taxes. That's how they're achieving this absolute power you mention, and corruption breeds. If you're from the ruling elite, you don't have to go to the furnace. Just think. In the Vietnam War days, the people started burning draft cards and protesting. But if there were no withholding taxes, the people could have stopped the war by refusing to pay their taxes. If only a few refuse, the war continues. If more than 50 percent refuse, the war ends. Wow, man!"

"You're getting the idea."

D.B. continued. "This would work for any issue. Just think about NAFTA. Not one common man wants NAFTA, but we have no control. The message you want to give to America is accountability. If the withholding tax is repealed, then politicians *will have accountability*. I'll do it. I'll go with you to spread this message. We need a one-page notice to Americans with a flip side designed to send a demand to repeal withholding taxes directly to Congressmen. You're absolutely right. It's unconstitutional to have a two-class system of tax collection and justice. The politicians have an unlimited source of money that allows them to waste without regard for the very people they collect it from. The corporations and rich elite can pay off politicians with campaign contributions to get tax breaks and write-offs, avoiding taxes. These same corporate types move their operations out of the country to use slave labor, and the government doesn't even charge tariffs to cover what they should have collected in taxes."

"I see you agree with me."

"Furthermore," continued D.B., "the government is *destroying* America with this economic and political globalization. Worst of all, if another culture rejects the American influence, our government uses its absolute power to wage war without the actual declaration of war." Disabled Bob Thielman then looked at his own legs, and with an inner anger he coughed out, "Since Vietnam, I've always wondered why I didn't die. I was destined to meet you."

The Road Rogue listened and smiled. This chance meeting with a disabled man would provide the passion to enable him to defiantly fight for a cause. The two of them began making preparations at the Full Moon store for a last ride—a ride of destiny. One was a man searching to be a soul, the other a soul searching to be a man.

CHAPTER 30

You Can't Keep a Good Band Down

In a small, run-down motel outside Joplin, Missouri, former agent Bill Jackson was sleeping off the effects of the previous night's bourbon. He had been staying at this motel for more than a month, having made arrangements with the motel owner to pay weekly. Bill Jackson knew that he needed a plan to start a new life, but he could not, or would not. He was a destroyed man, without pride now. The knocking at his motel door grew louder until it was a disturbing banging. Bill Jackson growled, "I'm coming. Just a minute."

Arnie Benson and Dr. Paul Lindsey stood in front of Bill Jackson, staring for a moment at the former agent who was wearing nothing except boxer shorts, had at least 4 days of beard stubble, and was struggling to open his eyes. It was 2 in the afternoon. Bill motioned for the two men to enter as he slowly recognized their faces. The room was in as much of a mess as Bill Jackson appeared to be.

After sticking his head into the sink and attempting to revive himself, Bill Jackson pulled on a pair of pants and asked, "What could you two possibly want of me?" He looked around the room, found a pack of cigarettes, pulled one out and lit it, inhaled, and looked directly at Arnie Benson.

Arnie turned to Dr. Paul Lindsey for a nod of approval and began. "Bill, we think it stinks, what the politicians have done to you. We have an offer. You know, don't you, that the Road Rogue has disappeared? We have no clue where he is. We know he has access to money and has new stolen identities." Arnie laid out what was known regarding the use of others to obtain new driver's licenses and credit cards. He also related the latest information from the department about reported semi truck thefts.

"Why are you telling me all this? I'm no longer an agent," Bill spat out with disgust.

Dr. Paul Lindsey then spoke. "I have authorization to hire you as a special private agent. The Road Rogue will be eliminated, you must know that. The Hunter, Ken Worthington, and his team have been called in."

"Which means a few poor innocent bastards just might get assassinated along the way. I thought he was only used for foreign affairs now. Isn't he with the CIA?" Bill responded, as he was now beginning to think more clearly.

"Bill," Arnie interrupted, "just listen. Dr. Lindsey has a plan. At least it's a chance to end all of this without a Ruby Ridge scene, if possible. Hear him out. I rather like it, and you could redeem yourself in spite of those politicians."

Dr. Lindsey nodded and continued. "I want you to go undercover as a trucker into his world. You will be provided trucks as you need them, all expenses paid, and I have arranged to pay your previous salary for as long as it takes. If you bag him, you'll also get the reward money as a bonus."

"You want me to be a bounty hunter?" Bill quizzed. "There must be hundreds out there."

"In a way, yes," Dr. Lindsey replied. "You will be a contracted special agent, and we'll provide you with every bit of evidence we find. We'll send you to lead areas."

"You *were* right about that music connection, Dr. Lindsey." Bill shrugged his shoulders. "I'll try it. What do you have since I was fired?"

. . . "They fired him you know, man," Disabled Bob stated to the Road Rogue while the two worked on writing the one-page message pamphlet. "They—producers or whoever they were—fired David Byron, the lead singer of Uriah Heep, way back in the mid-seventies. That's when most American fans lost interest. Of course, there never were any promotions, suppression really, almost a censorship. That band never got much airtime."

"Never saw or heard any Heep past 'High and Mighty'." The Road Rogue paused while his mind reviewed, "No memory."

"There was a little buzz around 1982. What were you up to then?" D.B. paused in his writing while waiting for an answer to his question. "Hey man, I do understand about part of you dying, man. I do, but . . ."

"'July Morning,'" the Road Rogue answered slowly with pain-filled eyes. "That year, 1982, was 'July Morning.'"

"Oh, fell in love, words to 'July Morning,' right man. Ah, Double R, what was she like?"

Pain, increasing pain inside of his skull caused the Road Rogue to cover his eyes from the penetrating light. Pressure was pushing out at the temples. He put both hands up to the temples and pushed inward for a moment combating. "Can't see her."

The recent past weeks without the continual adrenaline rush of bandit battle had allowed the cancer to resume its pursuit of the flesh. The Hobbs defensive and protective mind was at this moment blocking painful memories. The Rogue inside was strong, but no strength of will could defeat the disease. Then the pain was gone, along with the moment before when he'd been asked about her.

"Tax money," a calm Double R stated, "politicians blatantly using tax money to promote themselves and win reelection. I want something in the pamphlet that speaks to that. It should be illegal."

"Whew, man, I don't know where you just were man, but it *is* illegal. It's just that they already have the money, you know, from withholding taxes, hidden taxes, and sin taxes. There is just *no accountability*. Remember what Al Gore said, 'no controlling legal authority.' That's why I'm so excited by what you want to do. This is still the greatest country on earth, as long as the ruling elite can be made to *serve* the people, not *provide for,* as if this country is some kind of kingdom. If withholding tax is repealed, regardless of tax rates, the founding principles of the Constitution can be uncovered from the mountain of laws and court rulings that have rendered it useless. I think you're right on track with your premise about government putting everyone in groups. The rights in the Constitution are individual rights that are being taken from us by the government exempting groups and territory." He coughed again.

"It's illegal for a trucker to have a gun," Double R chimed in. "What's more, trucking unions are almost all destroyed, stopping the truckers' voice. And truckers are not even allowed to convoy. Worse, the satellite communication system is a calculated violation of the Fourth Amendment. It amounts to illegal search and seizure. A trucker *cannot* have a fair trial, of course, in the name of public safety."

"Public safety or not, I'm bringing 'Betsy' along on this ride. Hey man, do you remember *Cannon Ball Run,* a movie about a trucker starring David Jensen?" D.B. held up a sawed-off shotgun. "This is actually Betsy's sister. The cops took Betsy when they busted me. If I weren't a disabled war veteran, I'd be in jail now. You know, something is wrong with that. I'm not in jail because of who I am. The prosecutor doesn't want the bad press of putting me in jail. The S.O.B. must be planning to run for office."

"I don't think they want to put *me* in jail either," Double R said while attempting a smile.

"Jail? No, they want you dead, period." D.B.'s face lit up as he got an idea, then coughed before he started to speak again. "Wow, listen man. The government, cops, F.B.I., bounty hunters, and publicity seekers are all after you. You'll be recognized now and shot on sight unless you have a great disguise."

D.B. then rolled over to a closet and opened the door. He struggled momentarily with a broom, mop, and pail before pulling out another wheelchair. "Try this on for size. No one will recognize you if you're in a wheelchair. No one will even look at you. Trust me, I know, people *avoid* looking at someone in a wheelchair. I guess they automatically think we're going to ask for something."

Double R got up, walked over to the chair, spun it both ways, tested it against his weight, and then sat on it. He rolled it around the room and smiled.

"Oh, by the way, use this plaid blanket across your lap in public. The blanket just adds to their fears. Something about a faded red plaid blanket goes right to the heart. Some liberal do-gooders will want to show they care, but they never treat you as a man or as an individual. No one will be looking for the Road Rogue in a wheelchair."

"Two wheelchairs, two men, a computer, printer, and clothes. We're going to run out of room inside the cab." Double R looked directly into the face of D.B. "You can't take much stuff along."

"Uh, I do need to take a small oxygen tank in case my lungs give me trouble. The body of a man wasn't made to just sit in a chair like this. I'm afraid that more of me doesn't work than I want to admit." D.B. then coughed as if on purpose and sarcastically stated, "It's *not* that I smoke. Anyway, I don't need to bring much more except I would like to bring more of my favorite music."

"You can't bring your whole store's collection," Double R responded, and then cocked his head and made a decision. "We must limit the music to 72 CDs total. Each of those cases holds 24 CDs, and three cases will fill the front storage compartment above the windshield."

D.B. nodded in agreement and added sheepishly, "Hey man, you have 20 Uriah Heep CDs already. That leaves only 52. Okay man, I know just what to do. We'll have a contest. We can go to my favorite pub and play the ABCs of rock and roll. I have some buddies I want to see before we leave. Anyway, you can try out the disguise. We can wheel ourselves over there from here."

Within 2 hours, three men who were long-trusted friends of D.B. joined the two wheelchair-bound new partners at a large, round table. D.B. introduced Double R as an old Vietnam War veteran from his company. D.B. excitedly explained that he was going away on a trip with the just-introduced stranger, without any indication that it would be in a semi truck. He jubilantly announced that his aunt and cousin would run his store. After the second round of drinks, D.B. asked if the five of them could play a game.

"We only have room for 52 CDs, which will allow two for each letter of the alphabet. Each of you can nominate one group or artist, and then vote on two of the five nominated. If it's a solo artist, go by the first letter of the last name. If it's a band name, go by the first letter of the band. That's how I arranged my store's collection."

Seated for the game were D.B., Double R (the Road Rogue), Mike, Randy, and Kurt. D.B. pulled out a pocket-sized notebook and a pen and started the game, "A." D.B. then looked at the Road Rogue and said, "Well, you're new here, you start."

"Alabama."

"Hey, that's country," Kurt objected, then quickly backed off by adding, "I guess they do cross over. Okay, I'm nominating hard core, AC DC."

Randy jumped in with Aerosmith, and Mike with the Allman Brothers Band. D.B. finished the nomination of A groups. "We're going on a trip across America. I'm nominating America."

Mike interjected, "Yeah. Ventura Highway! America gets my vote, along with the Allman Brothers."

D.B. kept score, and after breaking a tie, the winners were AC DC and Allman Brothers. This brought a good-hearted objection from Mike.

Another round of drinks started the next letter round, B. Nominated were: Blue Oyster Cult (Double R), Black Sabbath (D.B.), Black Oak Arkansas, Beastie Boys, and finally, Beach Boys (by Mike, who was quickly getting more involved). D.B. toasted the table and tabulated the votes. For some strange reason, or probably because Kurt tried to imitate the lead singer of Black Oak Arkansas with "I've Never Felt More Like Singing the Blues," the winners were Black Oak Arkansas and Black Sabbath. This started a laughing realization that no one had even nominated the Beatles. Kurt again mimicked the tortured lead voice from Black Oak with "Ah, Beatles, just chick's music anyway. Another round and let's do a shot."

D.B.'s voice was getting stronger, and the alcohol was suppressing the constant coughing as he started the C nominations with Eric Clapton. Randy added Cream, which brought a round of laughter. (Cream was Clapton's group from the sixties.) Mike offered Creed, and then the table was stumped and decided that if they couldn't nominate five for a letter, they'd skip that letter, go on, and then later fill up the 52 slots with votes on letters and groups that didn't get in. D.B. declared, "Another round of drinks."

D was a dogfight. "Too many good ones," D.B. shrugged. The game was getting engaging, as the voting was leaving out personal favorites that each individual identified with: Doobie Brothers, Deep Purple, Charlie Daniels, Doors, and Bob Dylan were the finalists. Another round of drinks was ordered. The discussion ended with a process of elimination resulting in Charlie Daniels and the Doors winning the ride.

Another shot and E didn't produce enough nominations, bringing an almost angry plea from Randy that Elvis had to make the ride or he was going to boycott voting. D.B. got a real kick out of Randy's demand and reminded Randy that solo artists were alphabetized by the first letter of the last name. "Elvis is a P." More laughter, more drinks, and by now the whole bar was involved.

F's nominations were filled quickly. The game now resembled TV's "Price Is Right" with a vocal audience shouting opinions, approvals, and an occasional "Boooo." "That's it," D.B. announced, "it's Foghat and Peter Frampton."

"A shot for the whole bar," a now-enthused Double R proclaimed as he began to rise up out of his wheelchair. D.B. noticed and grabbed his forearm to prevent him from giving away the disguise. G and H were left without enough nominations, despite the urging from several patrons now gathering around the table. Only J. Giels Band, Grateful Dead, Heart, Hendrix, and Hagar could be agreed on as the players were now saving spots for personal favorites that had not been voted in. ("What about Grand Funk Railroad?" was shouted from the bar.) It was as if the whole table and even the whole bar were going on this last ride.

K brought a reluctantly accepted easy winner in Kiss (a large number of rather vocal Kiss fans filled the bar), and as a complete surprise—B.B. King. L was a surprise, also. After everyone agreed that Led Zeppelin was a unanimous choice, no other L groups or artists were mentioned. The whole bar, including the bartender and waitress, toasted Led Zeppelin as "Stairway to Heaven" was played on the jukebox.

M brought Molly Hatchet and Meatloaf, as would be expected. N's reservations were given to Nazareth and Ted Nugent. O's slots were reserved for later. "After all, we already have Black Sabbath," D.B. ruled. P produced Pink Floyd (must be Dark Side of the Moon) and Pearl Jam. Queen's nomination was dropped after another round of drinks could only produce that and Quiet Riot for Q.

Then came R, and just before REO Speedwagon was to be made the second unanimous choice, someone played "Far Away Eyes" by the Rolling Stones. Four patrons, two men and two women in their mid 30s, stood up in a line with arms over shoulders singing and swinging to that slow saloon song's words. By the second chorus, nearly everyone in the bar was singing along and laughing. The Rolling Stones and REO Speedwagon were locked in. S started with too many nominations, but Bob Seger was a cinch. Santana sneaked in on another tiebreaker vote, along with another house round. T was a triumph and a tragedy. If James Taylor didn't make the ride all of the women in the bar were going to leave. D.B. purposely skipped U, passing on to V, and the competition vanished when Stevie Ray Vaughn and Van Halen were nominated. W was only one question: "Who (The), and who else?" After a good amount of lobbying in vain for Hank Williams, Jr., the final vote ended in another tie with White Snake beating out Wishbone Ash. Somewhere in the flashback memory of the dormant monster, a song appeared that was just perfect for this occasion. Before moving on to Y, Double R asked, "Anybody remember a group called White Witch? Ya gotta think of a ragtime piano, now." He then attempted to sing their infamous theme song, with several in the bar following his lead and joining in on the verses.

> *A proclamation was issued today*
> *By the government of the USA*
> *Up to 99 years in jail*
> *For illegal possession and sale . . .*

"Sing along, now," Double R commanded.

> *It's so nice to be stoned*
> *(Yeah.) It's so nice to be stoned*
> *It's SO nice to be STOOONED . . .*
>
> *Breathe deeply.* (White Witch)

More laughter, more drinks; this was a special, spontaneous night.

Not enough Y spelled *no* for Yes, but X, Y, and Z were combined, and Yes joined ZZ Top to finish the run through the alphabet, leaving 16 openings. Then D.B. used those in an open round of yeah or neah as groups were offered. The following were added to the collection: America, the Beatles, Blue Oyster Cult, The Beach Boys, Eric Clapton, CCR, Deep Purple, Bob Dylan, J. Giels Band, Grateful Dead, Sammy Hagar ("I Can't Drive 55"), Jethro Tull, Journey, Rush, Iron Maiden, and Thirty Eight Special.

While several in the bar were still bringing up forgotten favorites, D.B. rolled over to the jukebox. Disabled Bob Thielman was more than this night's master of ceremonies. He was a maestro on his own stage, and from this point on he *was* the voice of the Road Rogue.

"Is everybody having fun?" D.B. hollered out, as if he were a lead singer. "Well man, just when you think ya got it about right, someone spoils it. What about the Moody Blues?"

"Oh shit, we have to do it over!" Mike shouted out.

"Wait a minute now, man," D.B. held his right hand high. "I want to tell you all about the trip. It's not just a trip to see America. Me and my partner over there (pointing to the Road Rogue) are on a quest. We are on a quest to save America."

"From whom?" Randy loudly asked.

"We, starting right this minute, are going to save American freedom from politicians who are waging war against the people's freedoms. Class warfare is in violation of the Constitution. We're going to make politicians accountable by ending their unlimited access to your back pocket. We're going across this great country to gather support for a new political party dedicated to restoring individual freedom, ending globalization, and ending the globalization of America's own culture. We want to stop social engineering through the tax system. We want an end to withholding tax collection. Think about it. Tomorrow I'll leave a pamphlet here that is going to be distributed nationwide. Read it, copy it, and pass it on. Remember man, the whole country now knows about the great music that was suppressed. That music will be our rallying call." D.B. then turned and punched up the numbers on the jukebox for "The Wizard" by Uriah Heep. The now-familiar acoustic guitar opening brought smiles throughout the bar, and the true magic of Uriah Heep's music was realized. The words *can* be heard, the poetry's message can be understood, and the message is delivered with music as free as a dream. Those privileged to be at this beginning of a new political movement sang the words.

He was the wizard of a thousand kings, . . .

. . . And I will dream of my magic night
And the million silver stars that guide me with their light.
(Ken Hensley/Ian Clarke)

When the song was over, the bartender asked D.B., "What's the name of your party?"

"It's the Restitution party."

CHAPTER 31

Come Away Melinda

In Washington, D.C., in a meeting of the highest levels of policy power brokering, the politicians plotted. The game must end, at least publicly. Linda Wright would be a pawn, used to convince the general public of a final chapter concluding the embarrassing saga of the elusive Road Rogue.

The plan included recognition of the need to address the newest, unintended consequences of policy. During the time the Road Rogue was in Albuquerque, New Mexico, preparing for another last ride, an overly aggressive private bail bondsman's bounty hunter had mistakenly shot an innocent truck driver. The resulting televised emotional aftermath created a near-riotous trucker strike and blockade of Cheyenne, Wyoming.

More violence erupted, and the state police were unable to break up the angry, rebellious truckers and sympathizers. Two more dead drivers, three protesting students seriously injured, and another fallen officer precluded an almost-calm standoff. Then the tanks and military helicopters arrived with what appeared as an invasive force to occupy the previously peaceful western capital of Wyoming.

The entire nation watched on television while Linda Wright provided narrative. This wasn't Waco with extremists; this scene was a spontaneous reaction from average, hard-working American truck drivers demanding an end to the madness of persecution.

The new government plan was executed. A staged truck wreck with a burning truck rolling over a rocky cliff and exploding brilliantly at the bottom of a western gorge with the flashing lights of police cars and a helicopter in chase was filmed and given to Linda Wright. A prepared statement giving details, including an F.B.I. DNA analysis of the remains of the driver's body, "proved" that the Road Rogue was dead. All investigations, rewards, stakeouts, and national directives were now null and void. The game was over, and there would be no answer to the haunting question, "Why?"

The public could accept this end but with an ill feeling of mistrust. That mistrust was in the heart of the public's spokesperson, Linda Wright, as well. Linda Wright also had an ill feeling that without the complete Road Rogue story, she couldn't expect her career to advance.

The new career of Bill Jackson was about to begin with a modification. The game *wasn't* over, and Bill Jackson was about to be given the ball again. The government's plan to continue the attempt to capture the Road Rogue would still include the secret CIA hunter and his team, and for bait, the privately contracted bounty hunter, former Agent Jackson.

Another staged event included the sale first and then raffling off of the infamous black truck of the Road Rogue. Bill Jackson under an alias identity and disguise would win that raffle and become the new owner of the truck formerly belonging to the World's Greatest Truck Driver. Television and print media unknowingly played the game. The various destinations of the winning prize truck would be advertised in the *USA Today* paper, various truck-stop magazines, and truck show posters.

> Truckers, See the True Monster Truck
> Just as the Road Rogue Left It!

Also, soon to be advertising was the new Restitution political party. Before leaving on a last ride to spread the seeds of hope to save America from political corruption, the Road Rogue and his voice finished their "Declaration to Restore the Freedom of Individuals." This one-page pamphlet included a backside designed to be folded as an envelope, was labeled with the address of the U.S. House of Representatives, and provided a space for the signature and printed name and address of the citizen sending in the form. On the front of the pamphlet was the following:

A RESTITUTION PARTY

Declaration to Restore the Freedom of Individuals

We, the people of the United States of America as individual citizens, do hereby declare and demand full restitution for the principles of individual equal opportunity, liberty, freedom, justice, and rights as established by the Founding Fathers in the Constitution of the United States of America and the guaranties as fundamentally stated in the original Bill of Rights.

- Congress shall not impose taxation prior to payment of wage, income, profit, or transfer of property, and shall repeal all laws establishing the collection of withholding taxes.

- Congress shall repeal all laws establishing exemption, privilege, infringement, protection, or pardon based upon group status.

- No law, directive, initiative, policy, tax, or religion shall be established by judicial ruling.

- No trade agreement shall be established void of tariffs equal to or greater than taxation rate.

- There shall be no governmental social engineering through taxation and appropriation of funds.

NOTE: The Restitution party will convene on Labor Day weekend in Albuquerque, New Mexico, to begin an end to:

      (1) Globalization by America
      (2) Globalization of America
      (3) Class system tax collection
      (4) Class system justice
      (5) Social engineering through taxation

Signed: , American Citizen

Address:

    As the final preparations were completed and the two individually dis-abled patriots wheeled towards the Crimson Fire rig (name taken from "Rainbow Demon" by Uriah Heep), Bob Thielman had a disabling thought and questioned his partner. "I just have to tell you, we have a problem. I really like what we're about to do, man, but this plan is not including the Internet. How can we ever print up enough pamphlets to distribute the message?"

    The Road Rogue stopped, looked directly at D.B. and answered, "I have a whole case of ink cartridges for the printer. Follow me to the back of the trailer. I was planning before I came to your store." Double R then opened up the trailer's doors and showed D.B. the load. There were pallets of of-fice paper, computer supplies, and various cases of materials originally des-tined for distribution to national Computer City stores (the main competitor of Bob Thielman's Full Moon store). "I figured I would need this kind of stuff, so I just found a trailer full at a drop lot yard."

    "Wow man, this is going to be one hell of a ride," D.B. noted with a cough.

Once inside the cab and rolling, D.B. started the journey with "The best damn guitar rocker I ever heard, man."

I'm gonna be "free and easy"
I know just who I am . . . (John Lawton/Mick Box)

And away they went, heading west into the high desert, rolling and rocking through the land of enchantment with a vision of freedom extending beyond the distant desert horizon.

The Crimson Fire truck rolled on west heading for Flagstaff, Arizona. This would be the fitting first point of distribution of the message calling for the end of withholding tax, the food source of the monster that is the absolute power of government. This on the very same day the news report of Linda Wright would be aired telling the public that the Road Rogue was dead—killed in a crimson fire crash.

A call to the network executive from the White House was made demanding a further report that must be the end of Linda Wright's career. It had been decided that her face would always remind the public of the embarrassment of the government. She would be allowed one more report—a short, casual postscript at a small gathering in Michigan—the funeral of Bartholomew L. Williams. The agent, Ken Worthington, would follow her. Just maybe, he thought, the Road Rogue would show up, especially with a little national notification. The result would create a not-so-small gathering of several TV crews, several hundred curiosity seekers, several newly formed Heepster clubs, and more.

At breakfast, two wheelchair-bound patrons were seated in the corner of the large truck-stop restaurant in Flagstaff. The last good idea of the voice was to buy a *USA Today* paper, along with putting the last 100 copies of "A Restitution Party" for this stop inside the newspaper machine. "Wow man, you've won the game. Look at this. They've declared you dead. They've given up!"

Anger filled the mind of the Road Rogue. "Typical government lie."

"Oh man, there's more," D.B. reported between coughs. "Your truck was raffled off. Some black dude won it and is going to show it off in truck shows around the country. That sure was a beauty, man."

The rogue of him continued to fill with anger, and adrenaline flowed.

"Wait, man, wait." Disabled Bob Thielman grabbed the clenched forearm of his about-to-erupt friend. "Listen to me, hear me. You must never even get near that truck. It's a trap. I know it's a trap. This stuff is just for the public. They'll never stop hunting for you. We'll beat them through our words, your words . . ."

In Michigan, at the former hometown of Bartholomew L. Williams, the crowd began arriving—not as if arriving for a funeral, but as if a festival were starting. This was a small town with no motels, one tavern, and a couple of parks. The largest park became the only logical gathering place. Recorded Uriah Heep played from the main pavilion as charcoal grills were lit to feed the growing crowd.

During the service at the small church, one video camera recorded the event. Linda Wright was convinced that a good report could be extracted from this day's events. A short eulogy was told of an adventurous, fun-loving idealist by Earl the codriver and friend from so long ago.

Then complete quiet engulfed the church as Marie Williams walked to the right side of the altar. She had been his wife before the final fall, and those in attendance who knew of her anxiously waited until one note was played on the church's piano.

"The voice of an angel" then began (in acapella), so slowly and sorrowfully that all heads bowed and tears formed throughout the church. The voice was holy, Ave Maria. The Latin words were largely unknown to those who listened, but those closest knew that she had sung this before at the funeral of Barley's father.

Because so many followed to the grave, Marie sang one more song. It was a song only those close to him would have heard before the public reemergence of his favorite music, Uriah Heep. She sang the ballad "Come Away, Melinda," reversing the words of the missing parent from the recorded version of Uriah Heep's first album. The world's saddest song sung softly by a truly inspired voice brought peace to a precious princess, Katherine Rose, the now-grown daughter of Bartholomew Williams.

That marvelous voice inspired one of the TV crew members. Marie's special talent was discovered. The very reason the government planned to publicly kill off the Road Rogue was defeated by more public interest. When interviewed by Linda Wright, Marie Williams spoke prophetically, "My heart tells me that he is not gone. No one identified the body. Could that F.B.I. DNA report be wrong or falsified?"

Linda Wright did not find peace on this day while listening to Marie's voice. Linda only found suspicion in her own heart. Her mind focused upon the many times that her reports had been censored or fabricated by the government. The ill feeling of having been used brought more suspicion. "My God, look what the politicians did publicly to Agent Jackson," she whispered aloud to no one except herself as she walked away with her camera crew.

The closest camera operator to Linda Wright, who also was her most trusted assistant, overheard the whisper and asked, "You're not buying all of this, are you?" Linda just kept walking, then stopped in her tracks as he reminded her, "You, ah, we . . . once reported that the Road Rogue was *not* a ghost. Maybe now he is."

The whole funeral day brought ill feelings to Agent Ken Worthington, especially. The day's hunt had produced nothing of value. Even if his hunch was correct, too many people were present to even know if the Road Rogue was there. Ken Worthington turned to his assistant and growled, "This publicity has to end. We'll never find him in a crowd. Let's go and follow that black truck and Bill Jackson. I think now that our best chance is to have an eyeball on that truck."

The publicity would not end. Linda Wright's suspicions brought out the true investigative reporter within her. When she got into the van with her crew, she emphatically stated, "What we have is a conspiracy, and not just a government conspiracy. Our own people at the network must be involved. Are you guys with me? We're sitting on a great story here, but to whom, and how do we report it?"

The Evening News Report of the funeral scene was viewed by the still-alive Road Rogue and his voice from inside of the Crimson Fire truck. The short clip, including the sound of Marie singing, brought to the mind of the Road Rogue, sitting in the driver's seat, a flashback memory of painful loss.

D.B. was at the table below the top bunk and interrupted the TV. "Lies man, lies. The politicians are controlling this shit, man. Don't let it get to you. The politicians will say and do anything that promotes or protects them. This isn't public safety; this is just the same old shit. Why does the public believe this stuff? This is just like Clinton bombing another country in order to stop the Monica and Juanita stories. The TV just goes right along with it. Damn government, man. They will never admit to their own wrongdoing, but all of this lying and bombing and self-promotion waste costs billions of dollars—tax dollars taken from the masses *without accountability*. That's why we've got to do this, man—start a movement to stop withholding taxes, stop the bastards from spending our money for their political gain. War man, how many times have politicians waged war for calculated political gain only? War is the only thing government does well, wage war using our wages." He stopped his rant and coughed.

The adrenaline rush within the Road Rogue from the TV report and D.B.'s comments awakened the memory and old political opinions, and allowed for engagement in conversation. "All war is based upon disregard for the individual. Government only regards itself and the ruling class; individual citizens are just the ignorant masses. Individuals are expendable to them. To destroy a few individuals to gain power or to get to the White House is nothing to them."

"Or like with me, a disabled war veteran," D.B. responded, his own adrenaline flowing. "Because I am who I am, a wanna-be politician has protected me. Not because of what I have done for my country, but because he would lose political points for prosecuting me."

Come away Melinda . . .
. . . The answer lies in yesterday
Before they had the war. (Fred Hellerman/Fran Minkoff)

CHAPTER 32

The Hanging Tree

"Hey man, who the hell is driving this truck? Hey!" D.B. coughed as he reached over from the passenger's seat and tapped the Road Rogue on the right shoulder. "Hey man, where are you at?"

Slowly the Hobbs driving mind returned to the current world of D.B. and Double R from somewhere, sometime, a million miles ago. "Northern California, heading north to Oregon," the Road Rogue responded as he observed the surroundings and passing scenery. "That'd be Mount Shasta," he continued, while pointing to the spectacular, snowcapped peak piercing into the crystal blue sky with a seemingly small ring of pure white clouds near the top.

"Okay, man." D.B. relaxed and added between coughs, "Glad you're back. I want to tell you, I'm really getting into this. I mean, I'm feeling the freedom of it. This riding on the open road in this fantastic machine with *the* music. This is truly freedom, man. I think I understand you more now. This road, this freedom feeling, the beautiful country, it's addicting. That's it, isn't it? You're absolutely addicted to the road and driving. You couldn't stop even if you wanted to."

The Road Rogue paused and contemplated a response, then looked directly into the eyes of his rider. "I will not stop. They won't take it away, ever again. I won't let them."

"Yeah right, man." D.B. then strongly pleaded, "Let's ah, let's not get into any of that Road Rogue driving shit, okay? You can't win that way. You're . . . we're doing the right thing now by starting this movement to bring the government back under control. The government system of America is fundamentally sound if it can be returned to the fundamental principles in the Constitution."

"Freedom. Independent, individual freedom!" Double R defiantly stated in reply.

"Yeah man, freedom." D.B. coughed, then philosophically declared, "Can anyone who hasn't done this, this trucking on the open road, even understand how it feels? It *is* addicting. Freedom to dream, and the music, the *Heep*, man. It's as if I've never heard it before, and I have listened to music all my life in my store. You man, you drive like I breathe. No, not like *I* breathe, but like a normal person breathes. I've been watching you. You're like, man, you're like The Wizard. Not Heep's Wizard, but like The

Who's Pinball Wizard. You drive without distraction, you don't hear buzzers or bells, don't see no lights flashing. It's as if this machine is part of you. The gearshift is simply an extension of your arm, like your own fingers are moving the gears in that transmission. There is more to it. I mean, why do you sleep lying on the steering wheel with the motor running? It's not because I'm with you. There *are* two beds available. Never mind, I think I understand. Anyway man, I got to tell you I once thought I was sent to war to fight for freedom, but I . . . we were not fighting for freedom. We were fighting for politicians, damn politicians who could not admit they were wrong. Government politicians who would not even declare war. Ten years, man! Ten years in a killing field while those politicians just kept lying. I'm no expert, but there is a reason the politicians have never declared war since WWII." He gave in once again to the coughing.

With a cold, angry statement, Double R interrupted, "If the politicians declare war, the military controls it. The politicians won't give up that power. If the military controlled the Vietnam War, it would have been over in a matter of months. Thousands of lives were lost and billions of tax dollars were wasted."

"You're right." D.B. shook his head and clenched his fists. "Well, this time I'm fighting for freedom. Fighting with these words here in our little mail-in pamphlet. You know what, man? We've already distributed over 20,000. By the time we stage the Labor Day rally, I'll bet the politicians will be having a cow. If the message *does* start a movement, we're going to need a leader to head up the new political party. It can't be me, and it can't be you."

"I think I know who might be a possibility." Double R cocked his head and smiled. "There's a politician that the rest of the politicians hate. He's corrupt like the rest of them, but he has an independent mind. They keep trying to throw him out of office, but he is overwhelmingly voted in every election. He's kind of throwing rocks at the stupidity of government waste."

"I know who you mean." D.B. paused, coughed, and then added, "He embarrasses the rest of those pompous bastards who think our tax dollars are theirs without accountability. If our project works, he might be interested. We'll just wait to see if the politicians start squirming when our signed pamphlets start showing up in Washington. We could invite him to the rally. With a little luck, they just might have fired him by then."

The network did not fire Linda Wright; however, she was told that the story of the Road Rogue was over. Carefully, it was explained to her by her immediate supervisor, "You're *so* associated with the Road Rogue story that we want you to take a nice vacation away from camera exposure. We'll give you a new assignment in 30 days."

Linda Wright was outraged. "This story is not over yet. Didn't you see the not-so-quiet funeral?"

"That's tabloid journalism, Linda. This is network news. We don't engage in …"

"Censorship!" Linda angrily interrupted. "Or is it just government propaganda?"

Linda Wright would receive written notice that to pursue her Road Rogue theories further would result in termination of her contract. Her contact within the government was aloof and insulted her intelligence with an arrogant, threatening comment, "The Road Rogue is dead, end of story."

Linda Wright and her top field technician would approach the tabloid press as a result. A king's ransom would be paid for proof that the Road Rogue was alive. Two of Agent Ken Worthington's hunter team would be assigned to follow her just in case she was lucky enough to find the monster. In her mind as an investigative reporter, Linda Wright was contemplating who the *real* monster was in this story.

The monster's truck with its demon black paint headed west, driven by the fired, former Agent Bill Jackson. The first advertised showing was to be on the south side of Colorado Springs, Colorado, near Fort Carson. The location would provide only limited escape routes, with plenty of support if needed.

Bill Jackson again marveled at the machine he was driving. It's motor was a caged tiger, ever looking to be turned loose. In the intricate detail of every part of the chromed and rosewood dash display of 20 gauges and 14 jeweled chrome toggle switches was heartfelt individual pride. Bill Jackson kept adding up the story and could not stop himself from understanding that a man can only take so much. The passing flatland of Kansas, the smooth pavement, the deep bellowing of twin 8-inch-diameter-thick chrome stacks, his hands on the wheel—Bill Jackson studied his hands on the wheel. They could be, they were, his father's hands. Oh, how his father would have loved this truck. He looked at his forearms and saw a difference from those of his father. His father had had huge forearms from driving trucks in the days before power steering, and he returned in thought to what could make a man become a rogue. Then Bill Jackson had to smile to himself as the image of big forearms became the cartoon character Popeye, who usually said just before he ate his spinach, "That's all I can stands cause I can't stands no more!"

"I better quit daydreaming," Bill Jackson said audibly to himself. He then turned on the radio. Scanning the FM dial, he came across a music channel. The music wasn't to his liking, but this was Kansas. He drove on, trying to concentrate on the road, but it was so easy to just daydream while driving this machine. Then the D.J. on the radio station caught his attention with: "There were two reported sightings of the Road Rogue yesterday: one in Seattle and one in Georgia. Of course, the sighting in Georgia was in a pizza parlor. The Road Rogue was sharing a pizza with Elvis. So, for all of you out there on the highway, I'm going to play you a special song. This one is from 1977, but I think you'll know who they're singing about. It is 'Hanging Tree' by Uriah Heep, and this is Craaaaaazy Kelly bringing it to you."

> *Cast into the arms of Satan*
> *Reaching for the hands of God ...*
>
> *...And freedom is the horse he rides.* (Ken Hensley)

Bill Jackson listened to the entire song riding west.

The western sighting of the Road Rogue in Seattle was real although ignored. Disabled Bob Thielman had become increasingly ill as the climate had changed on their journey. His lungs required the desert air. As the Crimson Fire truck had headed north, rain began near Eugene, Oregon. D.B. began coughing uncontrollably soon thereafter. They checked into a motel near Tacoma, Washington, with a good view of Mount Rainier if the rain would stop. D.B. lay in bed taking oxygen from his tank while he tried to recover. His blood-splattered T-shirt on the floor next to the bed was an ugly reminder of his physical limitations. His determination was not limited, though, and he pushed his friend Double R to continue distributing the pamphlets.

For 3 straight days, Double R traveled in a small, rented U-Haul truck, putting the pamphlets in 100-copy bundles throughout the area from Portland to Seattle, each day returning to D.B. in the motel room. But he got careless with his own physical limitations and left the wheelchair disguise for a walk around the Space Needle and former World's Fair Park to ease the growing pain in his lower back.

Linda Wright received her first lead as a representative of tabloid journalism ...

"Wow, man. You've distributed damn near 50,000 pamphlets while I've been lying here looking at that mountain," D.B. forced out from his sick bed. "Where have you been putting them?"

"Inside of newspaper machines, shopping centers, parks." Double R tilted his head and added, "It's a lot easier using the little U-Haul."

"Yeah man," D.B. offered. "I've noticed that everywhere we go except truck stops that there are No Truck signs. You know, I've been disabled my entire adult life and I've seen these changes, man. I mean, ramps, handicap rest rooms, special parking spaces, and all. But you truckers, now that's real discrimination. Being disabled never made business and society tell me to stay away. Don't those idiots understand that if you pull into a shopping center, you're intending to buy something? Anyway, I'm ready to leave."

"There is more to the unwelcome discrimination of truckers than you can understand." Something in D.B.'s observations brought mind-clearing adrenaline into the Road Rogue. "The government and the media set out on a campaign to demonize truckers long ago. They want individuals, cowboys, off the road and out of the business. I'll show you what I mean over lunch tomorrow."

In a large truck stop in Portland, Oregon, the two wheelchair-bound men sat at a table in the middle of a large dining room. Tables, booths, and a large half-circle counter service surrounded them. Double R held up his hand, put a finger to his lips, and requested, "Shush, just listen."

D.B. leaned forward and whispered, "I get it, man. Over there are two tables of drivers speaking Spanish. Behind us those four are speaking . . . French, I believe, and to my left that's . . . well, it's Oriental of some kind. And, shit man, I guess over to the right, that's some Arabic, right? At least they're still speaking English at the counter."

"You see, D.B.," the Road Rogue stated without trying to hide his voice, "trucking can't be exported like other industries. So, to find cheap, slave labor, corporations have simply lobbied congress to allow the importation of foreign labor, and they even subsidize it. An American trucker, especially an independent American trucker, cannot compete. Just living in a truck is a better way of life than they used to have."

D.B. shook his head. "This, what we're doing, is even more important than I believed before. Now I must say what I hate to say. You've got to take me back to Albuquerque. The doctors told me that I would live longer in the arid high desert air. I'll just slow you down, and I can do more for our cause from home on the computer and organizing the rally, but I sure want to enjoy this last ride from here to Albuquerque, man. You, you must be careful, avoid the hanging tree. Always ride the wheelchair in public." D.B. stopped talking to give in to another fit of coughing.

"Well, I put the truck in the shop while we were here. I think you'll rather enjoy it. As the two wheeled toward the tractor, D.B. excitedly exclaimed, "Wow man, ghost flames. You had ghost flames painted on." There was also an airbrushed row of clouds on the back of the sleeper with elegant cursive writing above the clouds: Powered by Uriah Heep.

"And I had a mechanic turn the motor loose. There are no longer any electronic computer stops. I'm not sure what this motor will do, but I expect triple-digit speed at 2,150 rpms. I also have a couple of other safety features." Then the Road Rogue icily stared a challenge into D.B.'s eyes as he declared with threatening pride: "Weapons!"

"Weapons?" D.B. questioned.

"Just reaching for my sword and gun." The Road Rogue then relaxed back into the personality of friend, Double R, and lightly added, "Actually, I found an electronic high-wattage linear device. It should knock out C.B., cell phone, satellite, and radar signals when I turn it on."

"Wow man," D.B. gravely acknowledged, "you scared me for a moment. I *do* have Betsy. What kind of range does it have?"

"Don't know for sure, but at least a couple of miles I would think."

D.B. attempted to clear his throat and shook his head. "We've got to get out of here. The air has to be better on the other side of the mountains."

"Next stop: Boise, Idaho." Double R pointed east. "Then south to Salt Lake City and the high desert to Las Vegas."

"Yeah, what a ride!"

CHAPTER 33

Sea of Light

The first showing of the Black Demon truck now driven by Bill Jackson produced only frustration. Bill arrived 48 hours prior to the limited truck show and left the unit exposed, hoping that the Road Rogue would make an attempt to take her back. Several hundred people came specifically to look at this infamous demon, many of whom were active truck drivers. Bill Jackson answered questions and asked questions, but found no one to be suspect.

Agent Ken Worthington and an assistant agent waited and watched from a short distance in a government-plated minivan specially equipped for surveillance. They were heavily armed with pistols, two long rifles, and a small, handheld rocket launcher. Neither Agent Ken Worthington nor Bill Jackson really expected the Road Rogue while the crowd was present. The hope and expectation was that any attempt would be made during the night.

Bill Jackson waited 30 hours after this show was over to no avail, and then headed north to the next advertised stop: the Little America Travel Center in Cheyenne, Wyoming. Here and at each predetermined stop, the truck would be left in a seemingly vulnerable spot in the parking area away from the restaurant or other public buildings to avoid unnecessary collateral damage. Bill Jackson's plan was to be either observing or physically inside the cab at all times as much as possible. Private security was contracted for each of the showing stops to keep surveillance of the truck when Bill Jackson had to be out of view. The private security hired was not aware of the plan for using the truck as bait; they were told only of the necessity of protecting this unit from theft due to its inflated value. Bill Jackson was not aware of the additional surveillance of Agent Worthington.

At 3:00 p.m. on the second day of display in the Little America Travel Center lot, the plan was nearly destroyed. A large, burly driver walked up to the black unit. He was laid over without a load and had consumed a few beers after he realized it would be at least tomorrow before he could load. He got in and foolishly started the motor. Bill Jackson dropped the Styrofoam coffee cup he was carrying as he saw the security guard holding his pistol in a firing position pointing at the driver's seat. He ran to the truck with his own pistol drawn. Agent Ken Worthington's assistant, who was a sniper, had a scoped rifle aimed directly at the driver's door of the black truck waiting for a clear shot and an okay from his supervisor, Ken

Worthington. Bill Jackson blocked the shot unknowingly. Agent Ken Wor-thington shook his head and whispered, "Jackson has this under control; let's just let this play out. Be ready."

A local patrol car arrived, and the astonished driver was hauled down to the police station. Bill Jackson was forced to show his Special Papers to be allowed access to the local station's background records. After verify-ing that this driver was nothing more than a curious and careless driver, Bill attempted to minimize any charges against the now-terrified man.

When Bill returned to the lot, he closed up the display and left, head-ing west for the next stop, which was to be a 24-hour showing at a truck stop on the west side of Salt Lake City. From there, the next truck show-ing would be in Las Vegas, Nevada.

Linda Wright arrived in Seattle, Washington, and tracked down the in-dividual who had reported the sighting of the Road Rogue. She did not get much, just a feeling that it was a true sighting. Linda Wright spent 3 days in search of additional clues. She found one strangely while having an early dinner at a family restaurant in a strip-mall parking lot. Her cameraman bought a newspaper to read and catch up on the baseball scores. Inside the paper's sections was the pamphlet. He handed it to Linda. "What do you make of this?"

Linda Wright immediately got an eerie feeling as she read of the "de-mand for restitution." She remembered the video from the Road Rogue and being censored from using its contents. She realized who these words could have been written by . . .

"Hey, what's wrong, Linda?"

"It's got to be . . ." Linda waved the pamphlet. "This is from him, the Road Rogue or someone he has been in contact with. Back at the network, I wish I had a copy to show you. He *has* been here. Look at what this says. Back at the network, in the video message from the Road Rogue, he wanted restitution and justice, equal justice."

"All it says is that there will be a rally in Albuquerque, New Mexico, on Labor Day weekend." The cameraman, Gene Parker, then quizzed, "Isn't it strange that there is no address or even a computer site. Just this flip side to mail it into Washington."

"Of course, Gene," Linda analyzed. "He can't give away his location. We've got to find more of these pamphlets. They'll lead us to him or who-ever is helping him. He's been quite resourceful, you know."

"Wait a minute, Linda. I'll be right back." Gene the cameraman left the restaurant and returned in 10 minutes with several more of the pamphlets. "He's putting these in paper machines, and there was a stack of them over by the mailbox and Federal Express drop."

"This is a big country. Labor Day is more than 2 months away." Linda shook her head. "We've got to get ahead of him or we won't be able to prove he's alive before Labor Day in Albuquerque. I'll call the editor. There are reporters all over the country. We just need for all of them to look for this pamphlet. Maybe we can figure out where he is or is going."

"If not, Linda," Gene suggested, "there has to be someone in Albuquerque who is going to organize this rally."

Disabled Bob Thielman was recovering in the arid desert air enough to do a little driving between Boise, Idaho, and Salt Lake City. He marveled at the stunning views on Interstate 84. Idaho's snowcapped mountains, valleys of crystal clear air, and the general rugged beauty of the landscape inspired him to ask, "Can you take me off the main road? I'd like to see some of this land away from the interstate?"

The Road Rogue paused momentarily, reviewing memory, and with the voice and personality of Double R, he replied, "Out in this territory, the road can get pretty hairy, but we can find a spot in Twin Falls to drop the trailer and then take a tour. We can make a circle and come back for the trailer."

"Alright man," D.B. said excitedly. "And we can drop off some pamphlets in some of these little towns." D.B. looked closely at the atlas. "Wow man, there's a town called Magic City. We have to stop there. How about a little magic music? Let's see . . . *Sea of Light*. In my opinion, it's the best whole album Uriah Heep has done in 20 years."

After dropping the trailer, the Crimson Fire truck headed north to Magic City for a ride that was truly magical. The roads taken on this circle detour included a stop at the Craters of the Moon National Monument in the early afternoon and an overnight stop in Idaho Falls. D.B. was exhilarated by the day's ride, and the two found a good tavern in which to celebrate and pass along the word of saving the American way of life from politicians. One man promised to make copies and distribute them on a sales trip from Idaho Falls to Butte, Montana; Spokane, Washington; and on his return to Salt Lake City.

The following day after picking up the trailer, D.B. concentrated on printing as many of the pamphlets as he could in the bunk of the truck while Double R drove and stopped to distribute. The day finished in Provo, Utah, with a plan to drive straight through to Las Vegas for a concentrated effort to distribute as many pamphlets as possible. D.B. explained his plan. "People come to Las Vegas from all over. Las Vegas will give us our best exposure yet. I've added a line to the pamphlet after that salesman gave me an idea. I've added a request for those who want to help to copy it and give it to friends. I've also added a line to look for a Web site page next month for details. After Las Vegas, we can hit Phoenix, Arizona; Tucson;

then El Paso, Texas." D.B. then sighed and added, "From El Paso you can just head north to Albuquerque and drop me off. I'll organize the rally and advertise on the Internet. Damn I hate the Internet. I can't sell records, I mean CDs, to people on the Internet. They just make their own."

"It's part of the government game," the Road Rogue angrily stated with adrenaline stimulating his mind. "The government promotes the Internet because they want to prepare the country for the elimination of cash. Once cash is eliminated, every possible transaction will be taxed. It's just a matter of time. The people do not even understand what is being taken from them by the convenience and so-called security of the computer."

"I do, man!" D.B. shot back. "Creativity, independence, and individual freedom. In a very short time, maybe just a generation, people will be totally dependent on government and computers."

"And the Constitution will be hung on a wall in some museum with no more meaning than if it were written in Greek. Man will not need to be able to add or even read. What a bunch of sheep we will be then." The Road Rogue reached over the gearshift and touched the shoulder of his voice. "Whatever happens to me ..."

"I know, man, I know."

A desert sunrise provided endless happiness for the two men who were being made whole again. As the hours rolled by, D.B. looked out and contemplated his future. The Road Rogue, with Hobbs driving, looked in and contemplated the past. The Heep played, mixed with other tunes on the random selection, 12-disk CD player. Each song brought a memory review for each of them. The Road Rogue listened to the newer Heep tunes, past the poetry of Hensley to the confusion and turmoil of the band's loss of direction and angry years, to the rejuvenation of *Sea of Light*. He compared the music with the memories of the lost soul. He could almost feel the presence. Disabled Bob Thielman was also almost feeling a presence—a presence of importance and pride, as if he were a whole man.

The hidden quiet of inner thought while the rock and roll pounded from the beat of a different drummer (Lee Kerslake) was interrupted by a slumping Road Rogue who put both hands on his temples, trying in vain to stop the pain. D.B. noticed and tried to get the attention of his friend. "Hey man, what's wrong, man? You've got to drive!"

The Road Rogue returned to the wheel with an angry stare, and without speaking he pointed to a minivan less than 300 feet in front of the truck. He then spoke, "Government plates, and it's following the truck up ahead. It has been for a long time. I'm going to pass it and run up beside that other truck. When we get next to him, hold up the C.B. radio mike and motion two two. I want to warn him without talking on channel 19. That van has a C.B. in it."

The Crimson Fire's stacks pushed a little smoke into the rushing air as it moved into the hammer lane. As the minivan came into view from D.B.'s passenger-side window, D.B. shouted, "Holy shit man, there's two of them and there's a rifle between them. I don't like this!"

The Road Rogue pushed forward, reaching the end of the other truck's trailer, which was in the driving lane. Then he backed off the throttle as the momentum revealed the black dream truck. Its small gold plaque verified the now-present nightmare. Without a hesitation and oblivious to D.B.'s pleas, the Road Rogue turned on the high-voltage linear, hit the engine brake, and fell back without hitting the brakes, avoiding the warning signals of brake lights.

Agent Ken Worthington was taken by surprise, and before he or his assistant could react, the trailer tandems struck the side of the minivan sending it off onto the desert floor spinning, then flipping over onto its roof and skidding into sandy, rocky terrain.

Bill Jackson caught some of what had happened in the mirror views and backed off the throttle. Before he could think of what to do, the Crimson Fire truck rushed past in the hammer lane. In a frozen instant he saw the back of the cab and its words written on top of painted rows of clouds: Powered by Uriah Heep.

Bill Jackson instantly knew that the Road Rogue was in that truck. He tried the cell phone and the C.B. radio. Neither one would work. "Damn!" He then dropped the hammer. Two billowing clouds of black-as-coal smoke signaled to the fiery beast ahead of him that the chase was on.

D.B. finally was able to get the attention of the monster. "Holy shit man, I think I know just what the hell is going on here. You've got to get away man. That was your truck, wasn't it? And, and, that van was ... bounty hunters. Oh shit, man!"

"I don't know what she'll do. I guess we'll find out." The Crimson Fire roared away. Its 85-mile-an-hour speedometer was useless. The needle was pointing past straight down. The tachometer showed a little over 2,100 rpms.

The Road Rogue studied his shoulder view. The black dream truck was a mile behind but gaining. "Damn it!" The Road Rogue turned to D.B. "I can't outrun her. I'm going to have to hurt her." Angry eyes looked for escape.

Bill Jackson was driving faster than he ever had. The speedometer's needle reached 108 miles an hour. As he slowly gained, he said aloud to himself, "What do I do when I, if I, catch him?"

At speeds above 100 miles an hour, the few vehicles on the freeway were startled and astonished as the two semis streaked past. The Road Rogue was cursing to himself that he hadn't tried to block the road by hitting another vehicle before the black dream truck had reached to within

100 feet. He swayed the trailer back and forth threatening, then he remembered his other weapon. D.B. looked on, not knowing what to do. He grabbed his Betsy. Then the Road Rogue pulled out a dairy crate from the compartment behind the driver's seat. It was filled with jagged metal. He struggled to lift its weight up to his lap. In a noisy wind rush of high speed, the jagged metal was poured out.

Bill Jackson could see the reflecting metal as it bounced onto the pavement and into the tires as he struggled to back off and avoid as much as he could. When the right front steering tire blew, the race was over. Bill Jackson was lucky to manage the deceleration without jackknifing or losing control. The Road Rogue jumped off the freeway on Route 56 at Cedar City, Utah, and headed west into the setting sun. Under cover of darkness, the Crimson Fire arrived in Las Vegas from Route 93. After 3 hours of distributing the pamphlets, the exhausted Road Rogue pushed on with D.B. asleep in the bunk, crossing the Hoover Dam at sunrise.

A dumbfounded Bill Jackson waited on the side of the road until across the C.B. radio came the voice of another trucker asking if he needed help. The spilled metal on the freeway would stop that driver's truck less than 10 miles from the black dream truck. There, after two tires failed, he tried the cell phone again and was delighted that it now worked. The Road Rogue had nearly an hour into the darkening desert before any search was started.

Agent Ken Worthington would survive his crash with a broken arm and a few minor injuries. His assistant did not.

CHAPTER 34

Keep on Riding

The news reports on television, radio, and print suggested a new copy-cat rogue truck driver. Linda Wright brewed an angry, frustrated stew of realization that the media was merely a pawn of government propaganda. She felt used, as if she had been raped of self-respect. Guilt filled her heart, as well. She *had* played in their game.

"What has happened to the First Amendment?" Linda Wright exclaimed to her cameraman Gene, not expecting or wanting an answer as she threw the newspaper onto the restaurant table. Gene Parker flinched to protect his coffee and nodded his agreement.

Gene scanned the story and then opened his briefcase. He pulled out an atlas, spun it around, and pointed. "Look, from Seattle to where this crash was. What would be the logical route taken to spread this pamphlet? I'd bet we would find these pamphlets all along that route."

"Yes!" Linda gleefully nodded. "The Road Rogue is leaving a trail, and that trail will end in Albuquerque, New Mexico."

"Linda, I have to . . . well," Gene paused and then looked directly at Linda's eyes, and he finished what he needed to say. "I have to go home to spend some time with my family. Why don't you follow this route for clues and call me when you get to Albuquerque? I will, of course, fly to meet you anytime you call. I do need to make some immediate money for my family. I can go back to the network, maybe even do a little spying for you. I'll leave my equipment with you and you can use a tripod to record and film with along the way. It might make a great documentary."

"I want to thank you, Gene," Linda replied. "You've been with me through all of this. I've depended on you so much. I'll do just that. I'll go alone from here to Albuquerque. Do you think anyone will actually mail these pamphlets to Washington?"

"I already have." Gene smiled.

"Then someone in Washington will figure it out, too. Dr. Paul Lindsey and 'him.' Dear God, I've been so used." Linda Wright now burned with a passion of strong emotion, as if scorned not just by the last man she had shared a bed with to get information, but by the corrupt, absolute power of politicians who she now realized were destroying her trade. "Journalism," she stated, "without integrity for truth; to push an agenda or to hide the truth to protect politicians is not right. It's how the Nazis gained their absolute power!"

Linda Wright was now truly filled with passion—a passion of hate compelling her to relentlessly pursue the truth and expose a monster attacking her heartfelt core belief that the true America cannot exist without the founding principle of the First Amendment. With tears of patriotism running down her cheeks, she said, "I must find a way to speak to the American public without being censored. I need a plan, and I have to find the Road Rogue before they do."

Agent Ken Worthington's plans had been correct. He still believed that his best chance to kill the Road Rogue was to follow the black truck. He was positive of it. He could not or would not understand that the attack and crash that had killed his assistant was a chance meeting. While still hospitalized for treatment and observation in Cedar City, Utah, Agent Ken Worthington was visited by Dr. Paul Lindsey and Arnold Benson.

Arnold Benson spoke first, knowing that the injured, loose-cannon agent had little respect for the Cry Psy: "Can you tell us what happened out there, Ken?"

"Yes," Ken Worthington replied in a tone filled with disgust and a vengeful scowl. "It's my fault Brad is dead. I was driving, and I guess I was a little bored. I didn't see him coming. I wasn't expecting an attack out in the desert. I should have been, though."

"Maybe just a little white-line fever, Ken," Arnie tried to console. "Did you get an eyeball on the truck that attacked you?"

"Nah, not really." Ken Worthington clenched his fists and cried, "Ow, damn it." His broken arm rejected the gesture. "All I saw was the back and side of the trailer. That's what pisses me off the most. I can't picture the truck as it passed us. What about Jackson? What did he see? Do you have a tail on him?"

Dr. Paul Lindsey then spoke, "Yes, we have two of your team ready. Arnie and I are on our way now to meet with Jackson. The black truck sustained some damage after your crash."

Agent Ken Worthington stared at Dr. Lindsey with an icy cold anger, proclaiming as if possessed, "I will get him! The Road Rogue is going down. Send me your report from Jackson, Mr. Benson. I'll be out of here today."

On the way to meet with Bill Jackson, Dr. Lindsey worried about possible unintended consequences of the hate-filled assassin Ken Worthington, who's reputation as a businessman was now complicated by his zeal.

Arnie Benson felt the same and asked, "Can't he be taken off this case? He's injured."

"I don't know if even the president could stop that man now. He's never been beaten before, and he is not concerned with collateral damage."

Dr. Lindsey, Arnie Benson, and Bill Jackson met over a quiet dinner for an update, strategy session, and review of the desert attack. Bill Jackson was cooperative and described the attacking semi, but he did not mention the mural of clouds on the back of the cab or the ghost flames. Bill Jackson wanted an advantage. He would continue driving the black truck, no longer just as bait but as a hunter.

Linda Wright continued hunting, also. She followed the path of the pamphlet. That path was leading to Albuquerque, New Mexico. All along the way, she stopped and recorded messages with glorious scenes of the American West as backdrops on the way to the land of enchantment.

When the Crimson Fire truck pulled behind the Full Moon record store, Bob Thielman was down in spirit. He did not want the ride to end, but he knew he could best help the cause by organizing from here, his home. "You, Double R, you have given me . . . I don't know how to say it. Freedom, I guess, and purpose. I'll do everything I can to wake this country up to your cry for freedom. It's going to take money though for the rally. I'm going to put up my store. This project is my July morning, and I'm going all out for it. I'll risk my own life."

"Maybe I can help with the money, D.B."

The Road Rogue's possessed analytical mind was racing in high gear from the adrenaline rush being created by the emotional buildup to this good-bye. "I also think I can help you walk again. I was once disabled, and I wondered and planned back then about how I could live without my legs. I have an idea I'd like to try out on you. The wheelchair disguise gives me freedom to move around in public. I think my idea will give you freedom to move around in public without the chair."

"It's impossible, man." D.B. bent his head. "Everything was tried, everything. If you're referring to crutches or some kind of arm braces, well man, they just don't work. It's like riding a bicycle. Once you stop moving, you fall."

"I understand that, but let me try. I'll see you tomorrow before I leave to head east." Double R smiled and nodded, "I think you'll be surprised."

"Okay man," D.B. shrugged his shoulders. "I'll tell you what I'm going to do. I'm going to put some bars up in my store and the back room. The way I've been able to move around the cab of the Crimson Fire has made me feel free. Maybe we could have a little party, drink some beer tomorrow night, and then you can go and spread the message in the East. Here, I want you to take this cell phone. I'll call you using a friend's card number so it can't be traced to me. Hey man, I just realized something. You just talked about yourself. Do you know what that means?"

"I'm not sure." Double R tilted his head in a momentary memory search. "I'll see you tomorrow afternoon."

Nothing blocked the memory of the monster as he prepared a farewell gift. He could feel the fear and pain of Barley Bill's disabling injury of nearly 2 decades ago. The fear of never being able to use his legs had sparked an idea then that he would carry out now. Along with a newly pur-chased set of crutches as the basis, metal pipe, bolts, two rubber truck wheel chocks, and some exercise weights provided material for crutches that would stand on their own. The wheel chocks were attached as feet, with extra 2-inch pipe extending their base to prevent tipping over. On each of these bases, a third ½-inch pipe was attached to allow for metal weights to be added as ballast. As a final touch, a large mechanic's jump-suit would cover the invention to provide disguise.

On the following day at 3:30 in the afternoon, the gift was unveiled to the curious Bob Thielman. Bob had already called one of the buddies from the rock and roll ABC contest to help him put up some monkey bars in his back room. Already he was enjoying the added freedom of moving without his chair. He looked at his soon-to-be-leaving friend. "Double R, just what man, do you have in mind?"

Double R set up the altered crutches with the bases inside the baggy pant legs of the coveralls. He then simply grabbed Bob Thielman as he had when he took him on the first truck ride and hung him by the armpits on top of the crutches.

"Put your hands in the pocket openings and grab the hand grips after I pull up the coveralls." Double R then zipped up the coverall front. The crutches were completely hidden along with Bob's shriveled legs and feet inside the baggy coveralls. Double R left the room for a moment and re-turned from the truck with a full-length mirror, which he put in front of Bob Thielman.

A smile came to D.B.'s face, and he sarcastically stated, "Looks like I'm just hanging out down at the car shop with the boys." The image of him-self standing with his hands in his pockets began to seem miraculous.

"Now, just like using the happy unhooker to push in the clutch pedal in the truck, lean on one crutch and try to pick up the other and move it forward," Double R coaxed.

The first step was small, moving the crutch only an inch forward. D.B. then got into the swing of it, taking several steps of 2 to 3 inches.

Double R then added, "I've put removable weights at each of the feet, which you can remove as you get better balance. Where you go with this is up to you, but I thought you . . ."

Bob Thielman coughed a little in interruption and defiantly said, "I can go to the john and stand and piss like a man!" His eyes watered and red-dened as he looked at this man, wondering how he could have become a killer?

The red, tearful eyes of Bob Thielman gave away exactly what he was thinking, and the Road Rogue's mind returned to combat the flashback scenes of smashed patrol cars, buildings, and the faces of fallen policemen now being pictured inside of his skull. Then pain—deep pain, as if the head was going to explode. He closed his eyes from the now-piercing light and held his head between his hands, pushing inward at the temples. A moment that could have been a lifetime passed. The Road Rogue looked back at Bob Thielman, who was still standing. No words were spoken. The red, road-mapped eyes of the Road Rogue emitted hate from the fires of hell, and he turned away from the compassion and returned to the truck.

Bob Thielman heard the motor start and waited for the sound of released air brakes.

A cold, staring Road Rogue reentered the room with a large bag. He sat the bag down in Bob's wheelchair, and then he left on yet another last ride.

Bob Thielman "walked" over to the wheelchair. The bag was full of cash along with two letters intended for two men whose identities had been used by the Road Rogue. Bob Thielman read the names. Then he stated aloud to no one and to all, "May the names Robert Henry and William Patrick be recorded as history's most unwilling patriots."

The Road Rogue wanted to keep on riding, but the ever-deteriorating flesh would force a pull over onto an entrance ramp for a regeneration from vibration, a dream on the wheel.

...And I know you say I'm drifting in a dream ...
... I just can't shake this feeling here inside
This heart of mine just keeps telling me to ride, ride.
(Ken Hensley/Jack Williams)

The ride would continue on an irregular route throughout the eastern half of the country. The destinations for stopping to distribute the pamphlet were chosen by the dreams of the dying monster.

CHAPTER 35

Wise Man

Bob Thielman established a Web site and began organizing a rally with the idea of having an outdoor concert as a method to maximize the gathering. He believed that the concert would generate more funds to begin the real process of creating a new political party and a national movement. Using the cash left by the Road Rogue, Bob Thielman established a legal fund and secured a concert site. Using his own connections, his own reputation as a disabled war veteran, and his own defiant confident spirit, he was able to generate publicity—locally at first, and later some growing national interest. Bob Thielman continued to gain confidence and continued to practice with the miracle legs. His close friends would be helpful in finding the right coordination of both his physical legs and the legs to organize the rally.

In Washington, D.C., a coordinated group of high-ranking politicians organized a truly bipartisan meeting with their close friends from high-ranking media outlets. What had begun as a few meaningless pamphlets was becoming a threatening story with legs. A plan to respond to the growing volume of signed demands would require more than elitist denial. This challenge to the formerly temporary, now permanent tax collection method, "May create a need for a crisis as fearful as World War II" when the system was put into place. No one in the meeting associated the pamphlet with the previous crisis of the Road Rogue. A new investigation team (a Blue Chip Committee) would be formed to locate the source and extinguish the fire.

Reports from the tabloid paper's investigative field reporters began to indicate that the trail being left by the Road Rogue no longer followed a path. Linda Wright decided to stay in Albuquerque. She would attempt to find the source of the pamphlet and whoever was teaming with the Road Rogue. Linda Wright had interviewed many individuals who had talked with the famous fugitive. The one common link was beer and taverns. Whenever someone had spoken directly to him, it seemed that it was at a tavern.

On a late July morning, Linda Wright drove to the Full Moon record store with the most promising tip she had been given. She had been in Albuquerque 4 days visiting taverns for clues when she found the site of the ABCs of Rock and Roll game. A copy of the pamphlet was proudly displayed in a frame on the wall next to the jukebox. She had just about given up and was ready to leave for her home. The thought of home had brought sadness. Home was nothing more than road hotels now.

Linda Wright ignored the Closed sign and banged on the door. She had been told that he would be here and to go to the back door if he did not answer. As she walked around the strip mall to the back truck access alley, she heard the sound of a bird, and she prepared herself to meet a disabled war veteran. Linda Wright took a deep breath, practiced a smile as she always had before meeting someone, and knocked at the door.

"It's open," a masculine, gravelly voice answered.

Linda Wright entered. "Excuse me, I'm looking for . . ." Linda looked up at the tall, rugged man with long hair reaching past his broad shoulders onto the dark blue coveralls. He just stood there with his hands in his pockets. He had piercing eyes signifying a wisdom far beyond his years.

He recognized her and realized that the television beauty was older than she looked on the screen, but he found her absolutely stunning. "You must be looking for Disabled Bob Thielman, Linda Wright." Bob Thielman smiled, and with a twinkle in his eyes he added, "I'm just hanging out here waiting for him. You might as well join me. Have a seat."

Linda Wright was strangely affected by this man in front of her. Not frightened, but there was something in the way he looked at her. She had been undressed by men's eyes all of her life but not like this. It was as if he was looking right into her heart, knowing what was in her mind and soul.

Bob Thielman gripped the left crutch top pad underneath the coveralls with his upper arm and shoulder at the armpit without any expression of strain, freeing his right arm to pull out a cigarette, place it on his lip, and light up, taking a casual drag. He reached back into his pocket, pulled out the pack, and offered it with a shake that exposed a filter.

Linda stood up and took the cigarette. She was unable to stop a genuine smile as she looked up into his eyes after he lit it. Linda Wright was attracted to this man. There was something in those eyes of his, an intelligent understanding of hidden pain, desire, and a confident peace. She was comforted by his presence.

"You're here to see ol' D.B. because of the pamphlet and rally. Pretty good detective work." D.B. then added before Linda could answer, "But you're really here to find the Road Rogue. You know he's still alive, unlike you reported on television."

An angry pain emitted from Linda's eyes. "I don't work for television anymore. They aren't interested in the truth, at least not if . . ."

"The powerful politicians of government are involved," D.B. interjected. "They made a fool of you, didn't they? And you want to prove them wrong, to expose their real purpose."

Linda bowed her head. There was something special about this man and she wanted to tell him. She wanted to expel the pain in her heart. "They used me to fool America and they ..."

D.B. interrupted Linda by reaching down after taking a small step toward her and gently touching her soft face, "Well, I won't fool you." As Linda looked up from a magical moment, she watched as D.B. first leaned left pulling his right arm out of the coveralls, and then leaned right repeating the disrobing of his shoulder and left arm, exposing the crutch tops. He finished unzipping the coverall front and then reached up directly and grabbed the bar that extended from one side of the room to the other near the corner where another bar was installed from each corner wall at a lower level. A wheelchair sat underneath the second bar.

Linda Wright softly sighed aloud as she watched Bob Thielman using his hands and arms as if he were a boy using playground monkey bars to reach the wheelchair and maneuver himself into it. Linda looked at the tiny shriveled legs and feet, and tears began to run down her cheeks. She stood up and slowly walked to him, knelt, placed her head on his chest, and held him as he held her.

Without words, two souls found each other, each feeling the other's pain. Tears flowed, and then Linda Wright returned a touch to the face of Bob Thielman and they kissed.

Linda Wright completed what had been started by a monster. Bob Thielman was no longer a disabled man, and he gave to Linda Wright what had been missing her whole life: pure, uncalculated love. He understood the fire that burned within her now. All through the night they talked of desires, the heartfelt desire to make a difference, to help mankind, and to save the ideals of the American way of life based upon freedom.

Bob Thielman explained the cause and plans he was making for the rally. Linda Wright explained how as an idealistic college student she had chosen journalism, which brought an idea to Bob.

"As a journalist, your job was to report the facts after the fact." With a smile and an intriguing twinkle in his eyes, Bob Thielman offered, "If you really want to make a difference, you must get into the political system of our government. Neither the Road Rogue nor I want anarchy. We just want the government to return to the founding principles of the Constitution. We want government out of the daily lives of Americans. They're trying to take over everything, control every bit of our lives and exploit slave labor all over the world. That is why our goal is to stop withholding taxes. By taking money from the working masses before they can cash their paychecks, the government politicians have unlimited power without accountability. They allow our corporations to seek out slave labor overseas, then the products are brought back and put into K-Marts and the like. It's no different than the Romans with their bread and circuses. The whole process strips us of individuality and eventually of freedom. We'll all be sheep, subject to the ruling authority. Withholding tax has created apathy. The people just don't see what's coming."

"No one in the free press is reporting about this," Linda replied. "They wouldn't dare, would they?"

"Control of the media allows for control of the masses." Bob then continued explaining the beliefs he shared with the Road Rogue, but he stopped to get back to his point. "Linda, you can make a difference. You can be the face of our new political party. You are already nationally known."

"I think I know how," Linda was agreeing without directly saying so. "If I can prove to the country that the Road Rogue still lives, that would expose them, if he *is* alive."

Bob pulled out a cell phone, punched in the coded numbers, and asked, "Hey man, Double R, how are you doing? This is D.B., man."

"Hello." The Road Rogue paused momentarily, coming out of a dream and reviewing memory until he could see the face of D.B. in his mind. "I'm heading north on my way . . ."

"Whoa man, I don't need to know." D.B. was speaking excitedly. "I'm doing great with those legs you gave me, man. Listen to me. There is someone here with me. I want you to talk to her. It's alright, man, talk to her." He handed the phone to Linda with a nod.

"Hello, this is Linda Wright."

A rush of adrenaline flowed through the body of the Road Rogue as he heard the unmistakable voice. "Reporter, why do you still spread government lies?"

A cold chill ran down Linda's spine as she remembered her last conversation with the monster who had killed her brother, but thoughts of the fraudulent funeral snapped her back into the moment. "You're right, I have, but I don't anymore. I want to help, and I want to tell America the truth. I want to know what happened to you. I met your last wife. I want your story."

"The story is with D.B. He is my restitution."

Linda looked at Bob with eyes signaling she did not know what more to say, and Bob took the phone. "Hey man, it's me. Listen, I think you need to find a safe place to park. I'll call you tomorrow with some new plans. Okay man?"

"Okay, D.B."

"Bob, he killed by brother," Linda sadly sighed. "He's a madman, a monster."

"Yes," Bob nodded with his own sadness. "He is a monster, or he has one within him. I've seen it. I can't tell you why, but it's not what you're thinking. He has that monster in him from pain. When he strikes, it's no more than a wounded animal striking, like rabies or something. He has taken life, and he has given life to me and to our cause. It took a monster to expose a monster—a monster that threatens our very way of life."

"The pamphlet!" Linda touched the arm of her new and first love. "I found you because of the pamphlet. It's only a matter of time before they find him and you following the pamphlets. Washington will figure it out. There was a video statement. The Road Rogue spoke of these principles before. The word *restitution* will give it away. You must stop him from distributing more of them. I have an idea. I know someone, my cameraman, who could set up a remote satellite link. If I did a live interview with the Road Rogue on your rally stage, it could not be censored."

"What a way to start a political speech!" Bob laughed. "We have work to do."

Bob Thielman and Linda Wright found themselves organizing, planning, and writing for the rally. They shared in the feeling of purpose and were becoming a team pulling together. Their results were greater than the sum of the two; they completed each other. As each day passed, their respect and love grew. With only 5 weeks remaining before the Labor Day rally, Linda noticed a long limousine parking in front of the Full Moon record store as she was practicing a speech.

"Bob," Linda exclaimed fearfully, "there's a limo outside. Two very well-dressed men are coming to the door. I don't recognize them. Could they be government?"

Bob interrupted Linda. "Quick, put on that ball hat and those sunglasses. You don't want to be recognized. Let me handle this. Bob was in his wheelchair and rolled over to the entrance as the two men wearing expensive tailored business suits opened the door and entered the store. One was in his mid 40s and was an obvious subordinate of the other, who was a temple-grayed, confident-looking man with an aura of great wealth. He spoke before Bob could even finish asking "How may I help ..."

"I'm looking for Mr. Bob Thielman." He looked directly at Bob and his tone suggested that he already knew who he was talking to. With a nod to his subordinate, a copy of the pamphlet was offered to clarify what the two men were here for. "My name is George Giels. I'm the chairman and CEO of Computer City Electronics. I came here to see what I might be able to do to help you with this rally you're setting up."

"Wow man." Bob Thielman was somewhat in shock. "Do you mean you want to donate?"

"Let me explain." George Giels smiled as he continued, "I began my career with one little record store, much like yours. I have some fond memories of those days. Selling music was exactly what I wanted to do then. Of course, I soon started to think about the future, financial security, being successful and all. Let's just say I've taken a different road than you, Mr. Thielman, but I know quite a lot about you and your sacrifice for this great country of ours. But I have never had to sacrifice as you have. I don't want to see more of our freedom taken."

"Well, Mr. Giels," Bob interjected, "a different road indeed. I've never really thought much about the future. I've lived each day as if it is my last until now. I believe that what I," Bob turned to Linda and nodded, "what we are attempting now is to save America, not the ground but the freedom."

George Giels gestured in respect, then he smiled with an expression from long ago. "I always believed if you live each day as if it's your last and then live through it, there will be hell to pay. I understand you're planning a little music with your rally."

"Yeah man," Bob said. "I've got some local bands lined up and a contractor to build a temporary stage next to a rise in the desert just outside of town." Again Bob looked at Linda and continued, "We have a tentative agreement with the band Bobby Long and the Long Riders to headline the concert if we can raise enough money."

"The Long Riders, hmmmm . . . that would be their song about the Road Rogue. Very good." Again, George Geils smiled as if he were a younger man. "I think I can guarantee that you'll have them. How about as an opening act? This Road Rogue fellow, you probably heard, destroyed one of my stores. That incident opened the door for a great opportunity for my company." Looking at his companion, George Geils said, "We've made quite a bit as a result. How big of a crowd do you expect?"

"I guess that depends. With the Long Riders, maybe 20,000 to 30,000." Bob's look suggested that he did not have a clue.

"Which is why I'm here to help." George Giels then dropped his pretense. "With all that has happened because of that Rogue character, I believe it is time for Uriah Heep to have a new American tour starting here with you. How about it? I'll hire people to handle everything except your political message."

"We will fill the desert, man!"

"Shoot for the moon, Bob Thielman," George Geils was genuinely smiling. "We'll have the contractual papers ready tomorrow. If your organization has representation, have them here tomorrow afternoon. It is my intention to donate all of the first gate of your gig's profit to your cause. Let me tell you, my first love will always be selling music. Now my business is mostly selling computers, but even I do not like what's happening to the music business because of the downloading of music. Eventually, the individual creativity of music will vanish. The creative artist must make a profit. By the way, I believe Uriah Heep has been the most creative music of our time. I guess over time I forgot about them. I don't know if I ever would have even found the success of my life without first having those idealistic dreams back when I listened to Heep." He then turned to Linda, who was sitting in the corner trying not to be noticed.

"I think I read in the newspaper yesterday that 38 percent of the country believes that the Road Rogue is still alive. What do you think, Ms. Linda Wright? And can I assume there will be television coverage of this event?" A now almost-cocky George Giels snickered. "When you find him, tell him thank you for me."

Linda took off the cheap sunglasses and ball hat, and stood up to confront the wise man directly, "My answers would be 'yes' and 'no,' respectively."

"I think a little TV buzz can be generated," nodded the exiting executive.

Linda then confidently attempted to get in the last word. "You won't be disappointed. We have some newsworthy topics."

"That is what I figured. Nothing like free advertising through the news."

CHAPTER 36

Fear of Falling/Fires of Hell

[Excuse me (the author again), I have given this chapter two names (titles of songs by Trevor Bolder) for a reason. "Fires of Hell" will be obvious. However, "Fear of Falling" has no special significance or symbolism. In the rock and roll world, there can come a time in the life of a band when something truly magical happens. The music gels and more. Just when the band is hitting on all cylinders and the music has reached an ultimate peak, they find more . . . some kind of overdrive that probably never can be duplicated again. Such a moment of music can be found in the recording of "Fear of Falling." When it happens you, as a listener, know that the band members are giving it all—every last bit of energy—to the song. Want to enjoy it? You can find it on the *Sea of Light* album (1995).]

The news of a corporate sponsor for an event being staged in Albuquerque that included the antiwithholding tax, antiglobalization, antisocial engineering call of "restitution for the Constitution," combined with the return of Uriah Heep, began sweeping the nation and the world. Politicians in America and abroad condemned the event. Common people in America and abroad rejoiced. Within 2 weeks, it was obvious that the event would be the largest of its kind in history. The logistics would require an enormous effort, but the team of professionals hired by Computer City and Electronics Corporation would ensure that the event would not become another unorganized Woodstock. George Giels was determined that order and profit would be top priority to ensure a successful national tour, maybe even extending the tour into other countries. George Giels was indeed a shrewd, cunning businessman, always hunting for new markets.

Although frightened politicians had not yet made the connection to the Road Rogue, the shrewd, cunning hunter, Agent Ken Worthington, had, as had Bill Jackson. A call was placed to Bill Jackson to meet with Dr. Paul Lindsey and D.O.T. representative Arnold Benson. Bill Jackson was in San Diego, California, just finishing a showing of the Black Demon truck.

The next scheduled stop was Tucson, Arizona, at the famous Triple T Truck Stop. The meeting was arranged by Agent Worthington. The four would meet in Yuma, Arizona, for a secluded dinner in a hotel.

Bill Jackson knew now that he was being followed as he drove the beautiful and powerful machine. That beauty and power was casting the machine's spell on him as he watched the spectacular scenery of the mountain pass ascent and descent of Interstate 10 from San Diego heading east to the open desert south of the Salton Sea. The truck handled the grade as if it were Kansas. The rock terrain looked as if he was traveling on another planet. The continual powerful song of the mighty engine bellowed through the thick chrome stacks. Bill Jackson now understood what it was all about—the feeling of pride and freedom. He also understood, for the first time in his life, who his father really had been. As the thudding engine brake sounded his exit from the freeway at Yuma, Arizona, he already had made a decision.

The dinner began quietly, as the four were unified in their suspicion of the pamphlet's origin. Quickly, however, the dinner was deteriorating into a snowcapped volcanic mountain of emotion about to erupt. This stemmed from the zealous vengeance of Ken Worthington and Arnold Benson's frustration and resentment of political involvement. Bill Jackson had his own anger and hidden secrets, and the Cry Psy was nearly overwhelmed with fear.

Ken Worthington laid out a new plan based upon his belief that the Road Rogue would be at the political rally and concert. "The black truck must be left in a vulnerable but prominent spot." Dr. Lindsey did not like the idea and started to voice his objection because of the obvious crowd problem. "Do you want to gun him down in front of thousands?"

One angry stare ended any more opinions being expressed by the Cry Psy without his usual personal body guard. Arnold Benson sensed the visual assault on the frail doctor and tried to speak for him. "Ken, you just can't do it there. Someone could get hurt or for Christ's sake, a riot could erupt. Remember Cheyenne, Wyoming?"

"Let's get something straight right now!" Ken Worthington pointed with the index finger of his left hand, looking a little uncoordinated doing it. His right arm was still in a cast and sling. "I'm calling the shots now, and until this is over, your job is just to analyze the results."

The usually quiet Bill Jackson stood up with a challenging show of physical superiority, commanding attention. "Hold on just a minute here! I've about had it with all of you. My name has been destroyed. My career has been destroyed. I've been lied to and am now being used as bait. Let me tell all of you how this ends for me." Bill Jackson sat back down. "I agree with you, Ken. The Road Rogue will be at Albuquerque. He has something to say there or someone to say it for him. I will finish my part of this my way. I'll go to Tucson, Arizona, for the truck showing that's already been advertised. Maybe we'll get lucky there. If not, I'll drive to Albuquerque and park my Black Demon truck wherever you want, but 48 hours after the event, it's over. If you have him by then, fine. If not, I leave with that truck and my new name. Remember, my name is legally Richard Morris now, and that truck legally belongs to me. It ends in Albuquerque or I'll blow the whistle on this whole ball game—publicly. Are we in agreement on this?"

Arnie Benson smiled slightly in understanding and nodded. Dr. Paul Lindsey just sat there in awe. Ken Worthington sighed and offered his left hand, "It's a deal."

The professionals now enlisted in putting on the show in Albuquerque would not cooperate with the plan to use a live satellite feed. "It would not be worth the risk. If the stunt failed, the whole show would be ruined. Just tape it and we can run the tape on the big screens."

Bob Thielman would have to call the Road Rogue to set up a location. Flagstaff, Arizona, would provide an excellent backdrop for the taping, with the shot being taken looking west at the majestic mountain.

Less than 48 hours before the show, Bob Thielman, Linda Wright, and her ever-loyal cameraman Gene were set up and waiting anxiously when the Crimson Fire rig pulled into the prearranged fire trail location. Bob Thielman was adamant about wanting to greet his friend from atop the miracle legs to show off how well he was doing with them (Gene helped him). The miracle legs also were producing another miracle. By spending as much time in the legs as was practical, Bob was getting stronger. With his body in a more natural position, he was breathing better and not coughing as much. He felt better than he ever had since Vietnam. The newfound love that he shared with Linda Wright and his thrill at having a true purpose made Bob as optimistic, confident, and fun loving as Barley Bill had been in that first dream truck so long ago.

As the Road Rogue climbed out of the cab, Bob knew something was very wrong. The Road Rogue used only his right arm getting down, and the obvious limp signaled further physical deterioration in the famous fugitive. Even the hair on his head seemed lifeless. The speaking voice of the Road Rogue was chilling, weak, and two octaves higher. The cancerous tumor had been growing and now was affecting Double R's speech.

One look from Bob to Linda, and she understood. This image before them more resembled the Jethro Tull Aqua Lung album cover than a powerful monster that had battled the absolute power of government. Without adrenaline stimulus, the cancer had battered easily at the will of what was left of the flesh.

After Gene set up the scene, Linda Wright with Bob Thielman "standing" beside her conducted her interview with the Road Rogue to fulfill her obligation to the tabloid paper. What was increasingly clear was the pain in the monster, both physical and emotional. Beyond proving who he was, Linda wanted to record the *why*. Linda was surprised and befuddled when she asked him, remembering the video he had sent to her and the conversation from Gettysburg, "What is a July morning? Why did you refer to it?"

The Road Rogue paused, fighting the pain inside his skull, and then he drank from the beer can that Bob had provided. "I will tell you of my July morning if you will tell me of yours . . . if you have had one. A July morning is that one moment in time, that only moment in time when you give away your heart—freely without any restrictions, worrying about consequences, or any kind of holding back for defense or protection. Nothing else in the world matters. You walk out on the limb and give your heart, mind, and soul away. You never can again. There will always be a self-defense stopping you from ever doing it again, and you know it when it happens. So, beautiful woman, tell me of your July Morning."

With a camera focused upon Linda Wright's face, she paused and answered, "You can't ask me that. You are asking to rape my mind."

"And so it is, within every private soul. You are an individual. Let no one, king, priest, lover, relative, friend, or foe take away that essence. You *are* an individual soul, unique. That is what separates man from the domestic beast or the slave. This is what I fight, to stop the absolute power of government from taking away being an individual, lest we simply become sheep to be herded, bred, fed, and cared for as a group without individual dreams. That is what government seeks to remove, that essence of individual freedom. Individual freedom is a threat to absolute power. Politicians fear it. They have taken my essence, but now they fear me."

Linda Wright was shocked and bewildered by the words and emotion emanating from the Road Rogue. She was struggling for words with which to respond and to ask additional questions. Then she focused again on the previously censored video and asked, "Tell me about the one you once said you sought restitution from?"

The Road Rogue bowed his head, covering his eyes from the penetrating light. Then he held his own head, pushing in at the temples. When he looked up again at Linda, he was dazed and unaware of what she had asked. Linda noticed that his left eyelid was not blinking with the right and that his left cheek seemed to droop. "Bell's palsy," she thought.

Bob Thielman interrupted, having seen that lost look upon the face of the Road Rogue before. "Hey man, you just have to believe. We have your restitution. It *is* this rally and the start of a political movement that will prevent politicians from casually wasting money in order to promote themselves. It may take 50 years to undo what 50 years of withholding tax has allowed for, but it will be undone! The politicians *will* be held account-able. The only way that they can be made to understand is by threatening an end to their unlimited money supply. No more class warfare, social en-gineering . . . we will all be individuals again, and the Constitution and its freedom will emerge from the wall of group laws and judicial rulings that have hidden it. Ronald Reagan said, 'Tear down this wall,' and now we are going to say 'repeal this law.' Tomorrow night you, with what we film today, here, are going to introduce the music of freedom that will tear down the wall again."

After the filming, a subdued peace was emanating from the eyes of the Road Rogue. Bob Thielman could see that peace and understood that he would not likely ever see this face again. Bob tried to engage in small talk but realized that the mind of the Road Rogue was drifting off into some other place and time.

Linda Wright approached, bringing some sandwiches and snacks from the van they had arrived in. She looked first at Bob, seeing his concern, and then she looked at the monster. "What would you like?"

The Road Rogue turned his head south and weakly sighed, "Cherry pie, cherry pie à la mode." Without hearing or speaking another word, the Road Rogue got up, walked to the Crimson Fire, and drove away.

Bill Jackson drove on after the dinner meeting in Yuma, Arizona, on the following day, stretching the legs of his dream truck, causing much cringing by the driver of the van following him. The 250-mile ride was completed in less than 4 hours. It was a relaxing, peaceful ride. Bill Jackson was look-ing forward to the end of the game. He thought, "I can go to Missouri, lease on to that little truck company my father started, and maybe even . . ."

Again, the thudding of the engine brake through the thick chrome stacks snapped Bill Jackson into consciously concentrating on the next task of parking the rig and meeting with the Triple T Truck Stop manager to set up the display. "Arid or not, it's hot," Bill thought as he walked through the entrance to the fuel desk, purposely avoiding the approaching wheelchair-bound man. "He's probably looking for a handout," Bill thought. "Why else would a crippled man be in a truck stop?"

The Road Rogue wheeled toward the rows of trucks, feeling the burning sun on his shoulders. He stopped for a moment and removed the sunglasses, looking back directly at the radiating heat source, somehow hoping the burning sun would kill the pain inside his head. As he stretched his head side to side to relieve the tight soreness in the back of his neck, he saw her!—his black Dream Truck parked at the end of the front row of trucks, exposed one tractor length from the line of bumpers, vulnerable, still running.

The Road Rogue left the wheelchair 50 feet from his beauty and walked stiffly and deliberately. As the rage within him increased with each step, he focused upon the back of the sleeper. They had defiled her. She represented 5 million miles of sweat, dreams, and most of all independence! That ugly white satellite receiver was bolted onto her paint. He reached up and yanked the connecting lines off. Then he moved to the driver's door, stepping up onto the first rung. It was time to take her back!

Time abruptly shifted to super-slow motion in that instant, as he felt the sting of a blow high in his left shoulder. As the spent bullet bounced off of the 3-inch by 5-inch gold plaque, he saw blood and pieces of flesh almost floating up to and bouncing off the driver's door, which seemed to be rising off of the ground. He heard the sounds: first of "Halt", and then the loud bang bouncing off the cab and into his ears. He was falling. He always had had a fear of falling, and in one motion as the truck rose, he instinctively grabbed his tire Billy from the leg pocket of his coveralls and snapped through it at his assassin. The 2-foot-long bat with its steel weighted end hatcheted directly at the approaching agent, striking his forehead and knocking him down with a split-open skull.

On the ground, the Road Rogue rolled on his back over and over, stopping directly underneath his black dream truck between the fuel tanks, with its old fuel system design of having a line attached to the cross-member stabilizer bar. Using strength from adrenaline and shock, he ripped off the fuel line, allowing diesel to flow freely onto the paved lot. He rolled out from underneath the cab and struggled to his feet. Then he pulled off the diesel- and blood-soaked shirt, lit it, and threw it under the cab. Without looking back, he staggered away from the black dream truck toward the Crimson Fire red truck of revenge.

With the entrance door to the fuel desk open, Bill Jackson heard the loud bang that his trained ear told him was a gunshot, and not just a regular gunshot. Its sound was distinctive, that of a World War II German-made Luger. Bill Jackson, as well as most of the field agents, knew who carried that piece. Bill Jackson was running toward the echoing sound. He saw the fallen agent with the arm cast pointing skyward. He could see the growing flames from underneath "his" black truck. Reaching the sprawled-out agent with blood pumping out of his open skull shocked Bill Jackson into indecision that, became a decision to move the body away from the growing flame. "Must hurry, before it explodes." Bill Jackson dragged the delirious agent, Ken Worthington, 100 feet away from the burning rig. Then the explosion knocked him off his feet. He looked up and could see the fire underneath the next truck in line while hearing Ken Worthington mumbling, "I got him. I got him."

Bill Jackson then looked in anguish at the now-lifeless face of Agent Worthington. Bill looked around and saw a man running toward him. The roar of a diesel at high rpm made Bill look back, and he saw the red truck with ghost flames leaving the lot. The young agent who had been Worthington's newest lieutenant now stood looking at his gruesome dead boss, then froze. Bill Jackson gently set the head of the victim down, and he stood up. The damn cell phone would not work. There was another huge explosion from the next truck ...

The Road Rogue exited the truck stop and found a street that he knew would take him out of town into the desert. The survival instinct told him that he must stop the bleeding, and he pulled over, fighting dizziness. He reached into the closet and pulled out a jacket, then opened it up to expose the lining. He grabbed a large tube of silicone and squeezed its contents onto the left side of the jacket and folded the front into place, then opened the jacket and slid it over his nearly useless left arm. Once the jacket was on, he leaned back into the driver's seat, forcing the silicone into the wound. Then he used his right hand to force silicone into the front exit wound. He pulled down the safety belt and put it on, holding the jacket tight to his chest. Then he released the air brakes and headed into the desert looking for nothing more than distance. Distance was protection ...

CHAPTER 37

Come Back to Me

On Saturday morning of Labor Day weekend, the crowd began arriving at the rally site in the desert just outside of Albuquerque in "The Land of Enchantment." Workers and volunteers handed out information booklets that outlined the long history of the government's waste of tax dollars; infringement of individual liberty; disregard for the human life of the working class; their push for power; class warfare; corruption; payoffs; agenda justice; class justice; legislation from the bench; social engineering; the multiculturalism of America; and the political and media attacks on tradition, morality, and individualism. Examples for each of these were included for clarification. Short, powerful paragraphs warning about the government's ruling elite being unified in their pursuit of globalization and *why* were printed under bold headings of Pursuit of Slave Labor and Absolute Power Corrupts Absolutely (funded, of course, by average apathetic Americans subject to withholding tax, sin tax, hidden tax, double taxation, and so on). The booklet ended with a plea to join in the new organization of individual Americans under the banner of the Restitution party, with a registration form and a goal: Restore the individual rights, liberty, justice, opportunity, and freedom intended in the Constitution by repealing withholding tax. Only then can this great country be governed by the people, for the people, and of the people.

The now nationally recognized DJ, Crazy Kelly, acted as the master of ceremonies while local bands played during the early afternoon. He recounted his own experience of governmental interference in a subtle buildup to the headline act. During the local bands' breaks and setups, several testimonials were given by individual Americans who had been forced to give up businesses, homes, farms, trades, and dreams due to government meddling, taxation, fines, zoning, IRS audits, and bureaucratic red tape. There was no shortage of formerly proud independents from all walks of life willing to share their experiences with the crowd.

One of the most compelling descriptions came from a medical care giver whose angry frustration summed up the crowd's growing resentment of government's agenda pushing at the expense of individual Americans. "The care and treatment that I can or should give is being controlled by politicians and the insurance executives who are in their back pocket. I spend more time trying to diagnose what I am *allowed* to treat and *how,* than in actually treating patients. Furthermore, the required government forms, insurance forms, and legal requirements more than double my workload. This, of course, simply drives the cost of care higher because I can't treat as many patients. Routine procedures *can* and *do* result in me being dragged into court, again raising costs and taking more time away from the actual treatment of patients. All of this mess has only one result. Government bureaucracy grows like a cancer."

The angry medical care giver was followed by a former welfare mother who added to the theme. "Politicians are eager to claim that welfare rolls have been reduced by 50 percent since the reforms. Has anyone heard that welfare's government workforce has been reduced by 50 percent? I want to tell you that as a welfare mom, great anger was pointed at me because of supposed waste and fraud. For anyone who has hated desperate moms like I was, I wonder if you were ever told how much of the tax money actually got to the recipients versus how much stayed with the government, and still does."

The day moved on until early evening when the decorated Vietnam War veteran Bob Thielman was introduced. As he "walked" onto the stage in an obvious waddle with his hands in the pocket openings, he had to stop. The size of the crowd was awe inspiring. A sea of people, colorful beach umbrellas, balloons, flags, and banners extended to the top of the distant rise, truly painting this enchanted desert. Thunderous applause erupted when it was announced that Bob Thielman was the organizer of this event. When Bob reached the podium, he was overwhelmed by the moment, and he attempted to balance himself solely by his armpits in order to hold up his fingers in a victory V. Bob Thielman collapsed into the coveralls and down to the stage floor, with one of the crutches ripping through the shoulder of the coveralls. Stage hands rushed to help him as the crowd was shocked into silence. With a ball hat, sunglasses, and loose-fitting shirt, Linda Wright was among those helping Bob out of the mess and into a wheelchair. He looked at Linda, smiled, and winked, whispering, "I think I got their attention."

Bob Thielman then rolled over to the mike stand and lowered it to his wheelchair height. "Hey man, what a party! How about it!" The crowd cheered in relief. Bob then held up his hand and began speaking. "Let me tell you about the worst kind of government waste: war! Waging war with our wages and lying about why. Government's politicians have been waging war all over the world since World War II, but war is no longer formally declared. There is a direct connection to World War II. Withholding tax was started because of World War II, or so the people were told. It was supposed to be temporary. In a time of national patriotism, the

American public gave up the only true method of holding politicians accountable. The Constitution is ignored by politicians today. Even after Pearl Harbor, President Roosevelt had to ask Congress for a Declaration of War. Before Pearl Harbor, nothing Roosevelt's government could do would sway public opinion from remaining neutral. Pearl Harbor was a terrible event, a crisis. Today politicians have learned to use crises and even create crises to take more control and eliminate more freedom and liberty in their zealous quest for absolute power and how they lie about it. Vietnam, well I guess we all know about Vietnam now. What about the Gulf War? More lies. Let's look at what was behind that mess—oil."

Pictures flashed onto the large screens as Bob Thielman spoke: scenes of the Arab world, the oil fields, and the individual kings and dictators. Then the large screens showed scenes from Alaska and the pipeline. Bob Thielman continued, "There once was a great debate about that pipeline. It was finally approved by attaching legislation that guaranteed that the oil would only be used by Americans. That sounded good. Guess what, man? That oil goes to the Orient to fuel slave labor sweat shops. It's all part of globalization. How many times do Americans have to be subject to whatever is going on in the Arab world? Who in America cares if someone called king, or someone called dictator controls the oil? There is absolutely no difference between a king or a dictator for that matter. America's founding principles do not recognize royal blood. Blood is blood. But the politicians in Washington today spill the blood of common mankind as if they are of royal blood. After all the tax dollars extracted from us to make nuclear bombs, why don't they use them? Because the nukes would kill the rich and royal along with the ignorant masses that they think we are."

"America's principles of individual rights, liberty, justice, and freedom are just like our most precious resource: fresh water. Our government in its push for a one-world government is pouring that fresh water, all of it, from the great lakes and great rivers into the salty sea. When every drop has been used, there will be only the salty sea. The end result of globalization will be a two-class system of the rich, royal, ruling elite and a vast sea void of individual desire. *I do not want to be thrown into that sea!*"

"Let me make one final point; hear me." Bob Thielman's passionate speech was about to exhaust him. He coughed violently and closed his eyes. Tears were running down both cheeks; they were easily visible on the large screens. He opened his eyes and the crowd listened. "We don't want to overthrow the government of America. We want our government to live by its own rules: the Constitution of the United States of America. It can and will happen, if we can take away the source of today's politicians' absolute power: withholding tax."

Bob Thielman then looked at the stage manager and nodded. "I have met many men who have been turned into monsters by politicians." While Bob spoke his final word, the low guitar opening signaled that music was about to start. "I've even ridden with one." The guitar's slow, steady beat broke into the familiar hit country song of Bobby Long and the Long Riders. The stage spotlights of the early evening illuminated the band members.

Running with the Road Rogue
Rolling into the night . . .

Over the intercom speakers, the voice of Crazy Kelly the DJ announced, "Ladies and gentlemen, please welcome the Long Riders."

Bobby Long and his band played their hearts out as would be expected, and the crowd was thoroughly entertained as the last of daylight disappeared. Cheers of more brought Bobby Long to the microphone to address the crowd. "Whew! What a party! To get you all ready for . . ." Bobby Long did not say the name and waited for a moment as chants of "Heep, Heep, Heep" filtered up to the stage. "All right! By special permission and with a very special guest, me and my boys are going to do our last song for tonight. How about a hand for Marie Williams!"

Marie Williams did not expect such a large crowd, nor was she prepared for the thunderous applause out of recognition for being the wife of the Road Rogue. She looked at Bobby Long, who smiled and urged, "Sing from your heart, girl." She smiled back at the man she had rehearsed with for the past week. Somehow though, in her heart she felt something new today, something sad and final. The song was also to have special meaning in connection with the headline act, as if Marie Williams was the voice of Americans who were long-time fans of Uriah Heep. Tears flowed as the soft sweet voice of an angel sang with such feeling, touching every soul listening.

Alone again
I feel so alone again . . .
. . . Can't we try it one more time
Come back to me . . . (Lee Kerslake/Ken Hensley)

The sadness of the song subdued the crowd into a quiet standing ovation, and the stage emptied. A lone spotlight focused upon the beautiful blond walking to the microphone at center stage. Linda Wright was easily recognized as her face was shown on the large screens.

"Good evening, ladies and gentlemen," spoke Linda Wright with the voice of the reporter that had been heard throughout the saga of the Road Rogue. "The Constitution of the United States of America was passed in 1787 after a long political battle. It could not pass without the original Bill of Rights—the first Ten Amendments. The Founding Fathers of our great country inspired wisdom. They recognized the threat of absolute power to individual rights. Their wisdom and foresight created America. The Bill of Rights states the founding principles that guarantee freedom of individuals and prevent our government from becoming a kingdom. The importance of those guaranties cannot be diminished if America is to survive. Most important of the Bill of Rights, and listed as the First Amendment is the principle of free speech. Without free speech, there is no America. If government controls speech, then it is not free. I am here tonight to warn you and all of America that government *is* controlling the speech in much of the media. And much of the media is playing along out of laziness and to push an agenda. It has become a game of high-level stakes and players. I know," Linda said as she bowed her head. "I have been part of it. I, and others like me, have routinely reported government statements and political statements as fact to push an agenda. The news story of the Road Rogue was officially over. That's what we were told and shown. Now, I want to *tell* you and *show* you the real facts about that monster the Road Rogue, who has been cause for great embarrassment for the government."

"When I was young I wanted to make a difference to society. I became a journalist. Yesterday I was still a journalist. Today I have finished my last report. You can read that complete report Monday. Just go to your local supermarket. My last job was a challenge to find the Road Rogue. That challenge was driven by hate. He killed my own brother, and the road I followed to find him passed through dark lies. The monster has led me to the truth, and I have found purpose and love. Tomorrow I hope you will support me in truly making a difference. I am going to run for Congress as the first Restitution party candidate." Applause filled the air.

"If you will look now at the screen." The large screens lit up, showing a majestic mountain reflecting the morning sun. Then a red semi tractor pulled into view. Out stepped the Road Rogue, and he held up a newspaper with a headline visible:

Desert Rally, A "Heep" of Enchantment?

The camera then zoomed to a close-up of the Road Rogue standing directly in front of the shining grill and bumper as he stated, "America, I give you the world's greatest rock band—Uriah Heep!"

A fireworks rocket exploded the desert air, then it was filled with the sound of Mick Box blistering the opening of "Free and Easy."

Cuz I know just what I am ... (John Lawton/Mick Box)

The huge crowd knew as well. Mick Box *is* the world's greatest guitar player.

In keeping with the spirit of the rally, the great band followed with "Spirit of Freedom," showing off its more contemporary sound and featuring the long-established current lineup of founding member Mick Box, vocalist Bernie Shaw (since 1986), Trevor Bolder (bass), Phil Lanzon (keyboards), and the full body drummer Lee Kerslake (who has been with the band since the recording of "Demons and Wizards" in 1972).

Cry freedom ...

Sweet freedom ...
... Free me.

The crowd was enchanted with the spirit of the night. It was a special moment in time. The band reacted with one of its best rockers, fully energized.

Won't you take a chance my brother
Follow me to a time of revelation ...
... Now our journey is just begun. (Mick Box/Phil Lanzon)

As the crowd gathered itself after the powerful performance of "Time of Revelation," the stage lights dimmed and a single spotlight focused upon the lone figure walking across the stage dressed as if he were the Charles Dickens' character namesake of the band. The cheering began as Ken Hensley sat down in front of the Hammond organ and began playing the hypnotic opening to "July Morning." Mick Box strolled over beside the organ, and power was reunited with poetry. The large screens showed a cloud bank as the two played in a slow, melancholy style. Just as everyone was expecting the lyrics, an image appeared upon the screens out of the clouds. It was a still photo shot of the late David Byron mesmerizing an audience decades ago. As Hensley moved into the opening of "Circle of Hands," another still shot blended into view behind the image of David Byron—the image of Gary Thain (whose tragic death ended a brilliant career) on the bass guitar. Ken Hensley continued in a medley of short, familiar song openings from the early days of Heep as a tribute. The crowd was mesmerized ... until the complete band joined Ken Hensley in a violent shift in the organ music, immersing the crowd in the best-ever rendition of "Easy Living," Heep's most-recognized song in America.

After this exhilarating highlight, Ken Hensley stood up, bowed, and left the stage. The band bounced back into the present with "Universal Wheels" and played with pride until the climactic end. The crowd wanted more of course, and for an encore the band returned with Hensley in tow to play "The Wizard." As the song neared its ending line, the lights dimmed, showing off the night sky. In darkness, without instrumentation, Bernie Shaw slowly repeated the last line ...

And the million silver stars that guide me with their light ...
(Ken Hensley/Mark Clarke)

CHAPTER 38

Illusion

February 2001

A s he rolled over onto his side, placing his feet onto the floor next to the sleeper bunk, he could feel every aching muscle. His head was pounding ...! He was cold ... but sweating profusely ... and his left side felt numb. It was dark or dark again, he did not know which. Forcing himself into the driver's seat and to the door he attempted to climb down out of the cab ... but the muscles would not move correctly ... The left side of his chest now burned, and his left leg was not able to hold the dead weight of his large body ... He fell hard onto the left shoulder, luckily not breaking his collarbone. Painfully, he struggled to his feet, stood at the back side of the fuel tank in front of the tandem drives, and emptied himself.

Using what little strength his iron will could summon, he climbed back into the cab, moaning from the effort of it. He sat in the driver's seat and leaned heavily on the wheel. Reaching behind the seat, he found the coffee thermos ... It was filled with cold, bitter poison ...! Straining further, he was able to grab the cooler handle and pull it close enough to open. Fumbling, he found a can of beer. He managed to open the can, only to taste warm, ugly foam. "How is it possible for coffee to get cold and beer to get warm at the same time?" he cursed to himself.

He next attempted to get a pack of Winstons from his coat pocket, but all he found was that tiny brown bottle containing the nitro that had been prescribed 2 years ago. He put two of the tiny pills under his tongue. With a long sigh of exhaustion, he settled his head, chest, and shoulders onto the wheel ... Slumbering, with eyes closed and breathing irregular and labored, his right arm instinctively grabbed the gearshift ... his left foot pushed in the clutch ... and his left hand somehow found first the key ... then the start button ... While completely unconscious, he checked for neutral and pushed the start button ... Five hundred horsepower of Caterpillar diesel engine sputtered, shook, and came to life ...

The engine's massive size vibrated the entire rig, and the vibrations sent the engine's own life force through the wheel into the chest cavity and heart of its master ...

As the big Cat's cylinders, pistons, and internal metal components were being massaged with their lifeblood oil, smoothing out the vibrations, evening the flow of diesel into the injectors, and gradually bringing the legendary motor to normal operating temperature, so too were the blood circulation and heart rhythms evening in the driver's body. Muscles relaxed to normal ... breathing was no longer labored ... Engine, body, mind, mechanics, and the entire combination of man and machine were reaching perfect harmony ...

And then the engine stopped. His thoughts told him that the computerized engine was being shut down by some timer. "Must restart the motor," he pleaded with himself. The calling of thousands of voices of haunted souls who had died in vain attempts to fight tyranny were calling, urging him to restart, to be the champion, the vengeance. "Must have restitution! Fight." The left hand somehow started moving toward the start button.

Then the voices were silenced as the Ruth of him appeared to stop the attempt. No more, no more hate ... no more fighting. A peaceful light calmed and relaxed the flesh. In his mind's eye, he could see the light of dawn. It was the sunrise on a surreal lake from long ago ... long before black Peterbilts and his July morning. Barley Bill was looking out the windshield of a dream at a small lake ... it was surreal.

Sunrise ...
Bless my eyes
Quench my soul
And make me whole again. (Ken Hensley)

... In Wendover, Nevada, February 2001, at a local police station, the sergeant on duty ordered, "Hey you two. I need the both of you to go out to the freeway entrance ramp. We got a call that a truck is parked there, and it's been there for a while."

"Probably just some worn-out trucker sleeping, sergeant," the young officer surmised. "Okay, we'll go get him moving."

The local patrol car was parked behind the trailer with its lights flashing. As the two officers approached the cab, they noticed that the motor was not running but the beat of rock music could be heard thumping from inside the cab. The young officer tapped the window of the driver's door, but the driver slumped over the wheel did not move ... The second officer asked, "Is the door locked? If he can sleep through that noise, we might have a hard time waking him."

They opened the driver's unlocked door ... "Damn, rigor mortis is already set in. Poor old bastard died on the wheel. That's a bottle of nitro there on the floor. Jesus! Let me shut that damn noise off."

Thirty six hours after Bartholomew Levi Williams had started the motor on the entrance ramp near Wendover, Nevada, the fuel tanks were exhausted. He died shortly thereafter. "Barley Bill" had once been the World's Greatest Truck Driver, and in the last 36 hours of his life, God had granted him one last ride. It was a ride of pain and life's reflection, where heart attack followed by stroke had created a fantasy. The fantasy was a gift to cleanse his soul from hate, greed, and vengeance. The fantasy was born out of a confused mix of living a life once full of hope, optimism, dreams, and desire, destroyed by the political ambitions of a government that had forgotten its principles.

Barley Bill had refused defeat and for 20 years had struggled in vain to rebuild his life. There just had not been enough time before his heart succumbed to the pain . . . the haunted souls of defeated men crying for a champion would have to find another.

. . . You'll reach the river of desire . . .
. . . While the valley of love keeps avoiding you
Because it's only an illusion . . . (Ken Hensley)

The 5-year-old red Freightliner would not start, and the Wendover police called for a wrecker to haul the unit away to an impound yard being run by a local salvage operation. The young officer admired the truck, wondering why that old driver would obviously put so much effort into polishing an old truck not worth the money still owed on the loan contract. The sergeant at the police station had gone through the procedure of notifying all concerned parties, and he just shrugged his shoulders when the young officer had asked why. "You would never know by looking at that truck that it was 5 years old with damn near a million miles on it."

The sergeant then suggested, "Well, that old driver was divorced. Maybe he just didn't have anything else."

"What are they going to do with it? Who would want it if they knew?" the young officer asked without expecting an answer.

"By tomorrow we should know," the sergeant smiled smugly. "I sent your report to the loan company and insurance people in Dallas. With what we're charging for storage, they'll be sure to get back with us soon."

In Dallas on the sixth floor of an office building, a pretty data entry girl was typing reports into the computer. She was nervous. An aggressive vice president had been making advances, and she wanted no part of it. Each time he came by, the situation worsened, bordering on sexual harassment. He was more than flirting, and she made a mistake. The report of a stolen Peterbilt that had been completely stripped of parts and was a total loss was combined with the report of Bartholomew Levi Williams's Freightliner. The vice president read the computer printout and called the insurance representative. They decided together that the truck wasn't worth even looking at, and they cut a deal for its disposal. The title was cleared and sent to the police station in Wendover, Nevada. The phone call to the surprised salvage yard owner was an offer to take the truck free if the storage bill was paid. (As the contracted impound yard, half of the bill was his.)

A dark-eyed young man of 23 arrived at the police station to pick up the title. The truck was to be a present to him from his mother and stepfather, who owned the salvage yard. The stepfather wanted the angry, young, rebellious, bastard son out of his life. The mother was a proud woman who had often told her son of his heritage, that he was a descendant of a "wounded spirit on the wind" (Ken Hensley), a great warrior. He walked up to the sergeant's desk for the title.

The police sergeant arrogantly sneered, "What is the likes of you going to do with that pretty red truck? And just what does the Q stand for in your name, Billy Q. Lake? Queer?"

"Quartermoon." His dark eyes darkened more, and what he said was absolutely foreign. It was not like French or Spanish, or German, but was a chant, an ancient chant . . .

[Illusion? you may ask. Or possible, present, past? How much of it is fantasy, fiction, fact? The clever mind will know. Could this music of freedom be suppressed or even censored? In America! Nah, that would be unconstitutional. Yet it seems that constitutional freedom is to join the "proud words on a dusty shelf" (Ken Hensley). My friend found more than 30 album (CD) listings including critically acclaimed recent releases of Uriah Heep on the Internet. Why are they not in stores? I personally will *not* enter the Internet world. Government now has given itself the right to monitor and use as evidence any electronic transaction. But isn't that unconstitutional as well, justice by class, tax-based social engineering, globalization?

. . . Against the odds
I fight for my survival . . .
. . . For my survival. (Uriah Heep, 1995; Mick Box/Phil Lanzon)

Rest in peace, Barley Bill. May the independent individual rest in peace, be he the World's Greatest Truck Driver, the family farmer, the independent butcher, baker, or candlestick maker. They're just names. And rest assured, my friend, the name Barley Bill *was* found at the bottom of a mug. What about *that awful name*—the real name of the golden boy prosecutor? You know his name. Would resignation become restitution? No! Resignation would be anarchy, for his real name is *a typical politician.*

Now, if you are willing, search your heart, mind, and soul for the real name of Barley Bill. Isn't it *the American dream?*]

TV News Flashes

Thousands of protesters today rioted in Seattle in opposition to globalization at the economic summit for the World Trade Organization ...

...Several thousand police, royal Mounties, and military personnel have secured the perimeter of the complex housing the world's leaders in Montreal, today at the economic summit for ...

...The Italian government assures world leaders, today, the 5-mile- square fortress to house the economic summit ...

...Apparently, a commercial jet has flown into the World Trade Center this morning ...

...The government of Iceland welcomes world leaders for the World Trade Organization economic summit today, and accepts the use of the U.S. Seventh Fleet, the Royal Air Force, 10,000 German ground troops, the Russian antiballistic missile submarine fleet, 5,000 United Nations' peacekeepers, China's 100,000 strong Kung Fu fighting division, and Mayberry's Barney Fife to secure the island nation from the expected uprising of the native Eskimos from the Arctic, whose barbaric culture includes the hunting of whales ...

"Bartender, I think I'll have another beer."

"Sorry, your government electronic satellite link transponder embedded in your forehead indicates that you have reached the F.D.A. limit ..."

Final Comment

Please understand, America is *not* purple majesties. "Purple majesties *can* be destroyed by the rogue. America *is* a political system of government based upon individual freedom, and only politicians can take away our freedom. Americans, you have nothing to fear about the political system except fear of the politicians themselves.

Author's Encore

Writing this book began easily, and the words flowed from a burning passion to tell the story of Restitution. I expected to have it completed before October 1, 2001. Then, the terrorist attacks of September 11, 2001, occurred, and what I wrote originally became a nightmarish premonition of reality. During the months following September 11, and after deciding to rewrite this book, another premonition unfolded into a reality. The great rock band Uriah Heep staged a concert in London, England, on

December 7, 2001. For the first time in 21 years, an original member, Ken Hensley (who wrote many of Heep's greatest songs), rejoined the group on stage to perform. This concert is now a DVD movie entitled "The Magician's Birthday Party." I ardently recommend it (but I didn't want to rewrite again because of it).

Constitution for the United States of America

We the People of the United States, in Order to form a more perfect Union, establish Justice, insure domestic Tranquility, provide for the common defence, promote the general Welfare, and secure the Blessings of Liberty to ourselves and our Posterity, do ordain and establish this Constitution for the United States of America.

Article. I.

Section. 1. All legislative Powers herein granted shall be vested in a Congress of the United States, which shall consist of a Senate and House of Representatives.

Section. 2. The House of Representatives shall be composed of Members chosen every second Year by the People of the several States, and the Electors in each State shall have the Qualifications requisite for Electors of the most numerous Branch of the State Legislature.

No Person shall be a Representative who shall not have attained to the Age of twenty five Years, and been seven Years a Citizen of the United States, and who shall not, when elected, be an Inhabitant of that State in which he shall be chosen.

Representatives and direct Taxes shall be apportioned among the several States which may be included within this Union, according to their respective Numbers, which shall be determined by adding to the whole Number of free Persons, including those bound to Service for a Term of Years, and excluding Indians not taxed, *three fifths of all other Persons* [Modified by Amendment XIV]. The actual Enumeration shall be made within three Years after the first Meeting of the Congress of the United States, and within every subsequent Term of ten Years, in such Manner as they shall by Law direct. The Number of Representatives shall not exceed one for every thirty Thousand, but each State shall have at Least one Representative; and until such enumeration shall be made, the State of New Hampshire shall be entitled to chuse three, Massachusetts eight, Rhode-Island and Providence Plantations one, Connecticut five, New-York six, New Jersey four, Pennsylvania eight, Delaware one, Maryland six, Virginia ten, North Carolina five, South Carolina five, and Georgia three.

When vacancies happen in the Representation from any State, the Executive Authority thereof shall issue Writs of Election to fill such Vacancies.

The House of Representatives shall chuse their Speaker and other Officers; and shall have the sole Power of Impeachment.

Section. 3. The Senate of the United States shall be composed of two Senators from each State, *chosen by the Legislature thereof* [Modified by Amendment XVII], for six Years; and each Senator shall have one Vote.

Immediately after they shall be assembled in Consequence of the first Election, they shall be divided as equally as may be into three Classes. The Seats of the Senators of the first Class shall be vacated at the Expiration of the second Year, of the second Class at the Expiration of the fourth Year, and of the third Class at the Expiration of the sixth Year, so that one third may be chosen every second Year; and if Vacancies happen by Resignation, or otherwise, during the Recess of the Legislature of any State, the Executive thereof may make temporary Appointments until the next Meeting of the Legislature, which shall then fill such Vacancies [Modified by Amendment XVII].

No Person shall be a Senator who shall not have attained to the Age of thirty Years, and been nine Years a Citizen of the United States, and who shall not, when elected, be an Inhabitant of that State for which he shall be chosen.

The Vice President of the United States shall be President of the Senate, but shall have no Vote, unless they be equally divided.

The Senate shall chuse their other Officers, and also a President pro tempore, in the Absence of the Vice President, or when he shall exercise the Office of President of the United States.

The Senate shall have the sole Power to try all Impeachments. When sitting for that Purpose, they shall be on Oath or Affirmation. When the President of the United States is tried, the Chief Justice shall preside: And no Person shall be convicted without the Concurrence of two thirds of the Members present.

Judgment in Cases of Impeachment shall not extend further than to removal from Office, and disqualification to hold and enjoy any Office of honor, Trust or Profit under the United States: but the Party convicted shall nevertheless be liable and subject to Indictment, Trial, Judgment and Punishment, according to Law.

Section. 4. The Times, Places and Manner of holding Elections for Senators and Representatives, shall be prescribed in each State by the Legislature thereof; but the Congress may at any time by Law make or alter such Regulations, except as to the Places of chusing Senators.

The Congress shall assemble at least once in every Year, *and such Meetings shall be on the first Monday in December* [Modified by Amendment XX], unless they shall by Law appoint a different Day.

Section. 5. Each House shall be the Judge of the Elections, Returns and Qualifications of its own Members, and a Majority of each shall constitute a Quorum to do Business; but a smaller Number may adjourn from day to day, and may be authorized to compel the Attendance of absent Members, in such Manner, and under such Penalties as each House may provide.

Each House may determine the Rules of its Proceedings, punish its Members for disorderly Behaviour, and, with the Concurrence of two thirds, expel a Member.

Each House shall keep a Journal of its Proceedings, and from time to time publish the same, excepting such Parts as may in their Judgment require Secrecy;

and the Yeas and Nays of the Members of either House on any question shall, at the Desire of one fifth of those Present, be entered on the Journal.

Neither House, during the Session of Congress, shall, without the Consent of the other, adjourn for more than three days, nor to any other Place than that in which the two Houses shall be sitting.

Section. 6. The Senators and Representatives shall receive a Compensation for their Services, to be ascertained by Law, and paid out of the Treasury of the United States. They shall in all Cases, except Treason, Felony and Breach of the Peace, be privileged from Arrest during their Attendance at the Session of their respective Houses, and in going to and returning from the same; and for any Speech or Debate in either House, they shall not be questioned in any other Place.

No Senator or Representative shall, during the Time for which he was elected, be appointed to any civil Office under the Authority of the United States, which shall have been created, or the Emoluments whereof shall have been encreased during such time; and no Person holding any Office under the United States, shall be a Member of either House during his Continuance in Office.

Section. 7. All Bills for raising Revenue shall originate in the House of Representatives; but the Senate may propose or concur with Amendments as on other Bills.

Every Bill which shall have passed the House of Representatives and the Senate, shall, before it become a Law, be presented to the President of the United States: If he approve he shall sign it, but if not he shall return it, with his Objections to that House in which it shall have originated, who shall enter the Objections at large on their Journal, and proceed to reconsider it. If after such Reconsideration two thirds of that House shall agree to pass the Bill, it shall be sent, together with the Objections, to the other House, by which it shall likewise be reconsidered, and if approved by two thirds of that House, it shall become a Law. But in all such Cases the Votes of both Houses shall be determined by yeas and Nays, and the Names of the Persons voting for and against the Bill shall be entered on the Journal of each House respectively. If any Bill shall not be returned by the President within ten Days (Sundays excepted) after it shall have been presented to him, the Same shall be a Law, in like Manner as if he had signed it, unless the Congress by their Adjournment prevent its Return, in which Case it shall not be a Law.

Every Order, Resolution, or Vote to which the Concurrence of the Senate and House of Representatives may be necessary (except on a question of Adjournment) shall be presented to the President of the United States; and before the Same shall take Effect, shall be approved by him, or being disapproved by him, shall be repassed by two thirds of the Senate and House of Representatives, according to the Rules and Limitations prescribed in the Case of a Bill.

Section. 8. The Congress shall have Power To lay and collect Taxes, Duties, Imposts and Excises, to pay the Debts and provide for the common Defence and general Welfare of the United States; but all Duties, Imposts and Excises shall be uniform throughout the United States;

To borrow Money on the credit of the United States;

To regulate Commerce with foreign Nations, and among the several States, and with the Indian tribes;

To establish an uniform Rule of Naturalization, and uniform Laws on the subject of Bankruptcies throughout the United States;

To coin Money, regulate the Value thereof, and of foreign Coin, and fix the Standard of Weights and Measures;

To provide for the Punishment of counterfeiting the Securities and current Coin of the United States;

To establish Post Offices and post Roads;

To promote the Progress of Science and useful Arts, by securing for limited Times to Authors and Inventors the exclusive Right to their respective Writings and Discoveries;

To constitute Tribunals inferior to the supreme Court;

To define and punish Piracies and Felonies committed on the high Seas, and Offences against the Law of Nations;

To declare War, grant Letters of Marque and Reprisal, and make Rules concerning Captures on Land and Water;

To raise and support Armies, but no Appropriation of Money to that Use shall be for a longer Term than two Years;

To provide and maintain a Navy;

To make Rules for the Government and Regulation of the land and naval Forces;

To provide for calling forth the Militia to execute the Laws of the Union, suppress Insurrections and repel Invasions;

To provide for organizing, arming, and disciplining, the Militia, and for governing such Part of them as may be employed in the Service of the United States, reserving to the States respectively, the Appointment of the Officers, and the Authority of training the Militia according to the discipline prescribed by Congress;

To exercise exclusive Legislation in all Cases whatsoever, over such District (not exceeding ten Miles square) as may, by Cession of particular States, and the Acceptance of Congress, become the Seat of Government of the United States, and to exercise like Authority over all Places purchased by the Consent of the Legislature of the State in which the Same shall be, for the Erection of Forts, Magazines, Arsenals, dock-Yards, and other needful Buildings;—And

To make all Laws which shall be necessary and proper for carrying into Execution the foregoing Powers, and all other Powers vested by this Constitution in the Government of the United States, or in any Department or Officer thereof.

Section. 9. The Migration or Importation of such Persons as any of the States now existing shall think proper to admit, shall not be prohibited by the Congress prior to the Year one thousand eight hundred and eight, but a Tax or duty may be imposed on such Importation, not exceeding ten dollars for each Person.

The Privilege of the Writ of Habeas Corpus shall not be suspended, unless when in Cases of Rebellion or Invasion the public Safety may require it.

No Bill of Attainder or ex post facto Law shall be passed.

No Capitation, or other direct, Tax shall be laid, unless in Proportion to the Census or Enumeration herein before directed to be taken.

No Tax or Duty shall be laid on Articles exported from any State.

No Preference shall be given by any Regulation of Commerce or Revenue to the Ports of one State over those of another; nor shall Vessels bound to, or from, one State, be obliged to enter, clear, or pay Duties in another.

No Money shall be drawn from the Treasury, but in Consequence of Appropriations made by Law; and a regular Statement and Account of the Receipts and Expenditures of all public Money shall be published from time to time.

No Title of Nobility shall be granted by the United States: And no Person holding any Office of Profit or Trust under them, shall, without the Consent of the Congress, accept of any present, Emolument, Office, or Title, of any kind whatever, from any King, Prince, or foreign State.

Section. 10. No State shall enter into any Treaty, Alliance, or Confederation; grant Letters of Marque and Reprisal; coin Money; emit Bills of Credit; make any Thing but gold and silver Coin a Tender in Payment of Debts; pass any Bill of Attainder, ex post facto Law, or Law impairing the Obligations of Contracts, or grant any Title of Nobility.

No State shall, without the Consent of the Congress, lay any Imports or Duties on Imports or Exports, except what may be absolutely necessary for executing it's inspection Laws; and the net Produce of all Duties and Imposts, laid by any State on Imports or Exports, shall be for the Use of the Treasury of the United States; and all such Laws shall be subject to the Revision and Controul of the Congress.

No State shall, without the Consent of Congress, lay any Duty of Tonnage, keep Troops, or Ships of War in time of Peace, enter into any Agreement or Compact with another State, or with a foreign Power, or engage in War, unless actually invaded, or in such imminent Danger as will not admit of delay.

Article. II.

Section. 1. The executive Power shall be vested in a President of the United States of America. He shall hold his Office during the Term of four Years, and, together with the Vice President, chosen for the same Term, be elected, as follows:

Each State shall appoint, in such Manner as the Legislature thereof may direct, a Number of Electors, equal to the whole Number of Senators and Representatives to which the State may be entitled in the Congress: but no Senator or Representative, or Person holding an Office of Trust or Profit under the United States, shall be appointed an Elector.

The Electors shall meet in their respective States, and vote by Ballot for two persons, of whom one at least shall not be an Inhabitant of the same State with themselves. And they shall make a List of all the Persons voted for, and of the Number of Votes for each; which List they shall sign and certify, and transmit sealed to the Seat of the Government of the United States, directed to the President of the Senate. The President of the Senate shall, in the Presence of the Senate and House of Representatives, open all the Certificates, and the Votes shall then be counted. The Person having the greatest Number of Votes shall be the President, if such Number be a Majority of the whole Number of Electors appointed; and if there be more than one who have such Majority, and have an equal Number of Votes, then the House of Representatives shall immediately chuse by Ballot one of them for President; and if no Person have a Majority, then from the five highest on the List the said House shall in like Manner chuse the President. But in chusing the President, the Votes shall be taken by States, the Representation from each State having one Vote; a quorum for this Purpose shall consist of a Member or Members from two thirds of the States, and a Majority of all the States shall be necessary to a Choice. In every Case, after the Choice of the President, the Person having the greatest Number of Votes of the Electors shall be the Vice President. But if there should remain two or more who have equal Votes, the Senate shall chuse from them by Ballot the Vice President [Modified by Amendment XII].

The Congress may determine the Time of chusing the Electors, and the Day on which they shall give their Votes; which Day shall be the same throughout the United States.

No Person except a natural born Citizen, or a Citizen of the United States, at the time of the Adoption of this Constitution, shall be eligible to the Office of President; neither shall any Person be eligible to that Office who shall not have attained to the Age of thirty five Years, and been fourteen Years a Resident within the United States.

In Case of the Removal of the President from Office, or of his Death, Resignation, or Inability to discharge the Powers and Duties of the said Office, the Same shall devolve on the Vice President, and the Congress may by Law provide for the Case of Removal, Death, Resignation or Inability, both of the President and Vice President, declaring what Officer shall then act as President, and such Officer shall act accordingly, until the Disability be removed, or a President shall be elected [Modified by Amendment XXV].

The President shall, at stated Times, receive for his Services, a Compensation, which shall neither be increased nor diminished during the Period for which he shall have been elected, and he shall not receive within that Period any other Emolument from the United States, or any of them.

Before he enter on the Execution of his Office, he shall take the following Oath or Affirmation:—"I do solemnly swear (or affirm) that I will faithfully execute the Office of President of the United States, and will to the best of my Ability, preserve, protect and defend the Constitution of the United States."

Section. 2. The President shall be Commander in Chief of the Army and Navy of the United States, and of the Militia of the several States, when called into the actual Service of the United States; he may require the Opinion, in writing, of the principal Officer in each of the executive Departments, upon any Subject relating to the Duties of their respective Offices, and he shall have Power to grant Reprieves and Pardons for Offences against the United States, except in Cases of Impeachment.

He shall have Power, by and with the Advice and Consent of the Senate, to make Treaties, provided two thirds of the Senators present concur; and he shall nominate, and by and with the Advice and Consent of the Senate, shall appoint Ambassadors, other public Ministers and Consuls, Judges of the supreme Court, and all other Officers of the United States, whose Appointments are not herein otherwise provided for, and which shall be established by Law: but the Congress may by Law vest the Appointment of such inferior Officers, as they think proper, in the President alone, in the Courts of Law, or in the Heads of Departments.

The President shall have Power to fill up all Vacancies that may happen during the Recess of the Senate, by granting Commissions which shall expire at the End of their next Session.

Section. 3. He shall from time to time give to the Congress Information of the State of the Union, and recommend to their Consideration such Measures as he shall judge necessary and expedient; he may, on extraordinary Occasions, convene both Houses, or either of them, and in Case of Disagreement between them, with Respect to the Time of Adjournment, he may adjourn them to such Time as he shall think proper; he shall receive Ambassadors and other public Ministers; he shall take Care that the Laws be faithfully executed, and shall Commission all the Officers of the United States.

Section. 4. The President, Vice President and all civil Officers of the United States, shall be removed from Office on Impeachment for, and Conviction of, Treason, Bribery, or other high Crimes and Misdemeanors.

Article. III.

Section. 1. The judicial Power of the United States shall be vested in one supreme Court, and in such inferior Courts as the Congress may from time to time ordain and establish. The Judges, both of the supreme and inferior Courts, shall hold their Offices during good Behaviour, and shall, at states Times, receive for their Services a Compensation, which shall not be diminished during their Continuance in Office.

Section. 2. The judicial Power shall extend to all Cases, in Law and Equity, arising under this Constitution, the Laws of the United States, and Treaties made, or which shall be made, under their Authority;—to all Cases affecting Ambassadors, other public Ministers and Consuls;—to all Cases of admiralty and maritime

Jurisdiction;—to Controversies to which the United States shall be a Party;—to Controversies between two or more States;—*between a State and Citizens of another State* [Modified by Amendment XI];—between Citizens of different States;—between Citizens of the same State claiming Lands under Grants of different States, and between a State, or the Citizens thereof, and foreign States, Citizens or Subjects.

In all Cases affecting Ambassadors, other public Ministers and Consuls, and those in which a State shall be Party, the supreme Court shall have original Jurisdiction. In all the other Cases before mentioned, the supreme Court shall have appellate Jurisdiction, both as to Law and Fact, with such Exceptions, and under such Regulations as the Congress shall make.

The Trial of all Crimes, except in Cases of Impeachment, shall be by Jury; and such Trial shall be held in the State where the said Crimes shall have been committed; but when not committed within any State, the Trial shall be at such Place or Places as the Congress may by Law have directed.

Section. 3. Treason against the United States shall consist only in levying War against them, or in adhering to their Enemies, giving them Aid and Comfort. No Person shall be convicted of Treason unless on the Testimony of two Witnesses to the same overt Act, or on Confession in open Court.

The Congress shall have Power to declare the Punishment of Treason, but no Attainder of Treason shall work Corruption of Blood, or Forfeiture except during the Life of the Person attained.

Article. IV.

Section. 1. Full Faith and Credit shall be given in each State to the public Acts, Records, and judicial Proceedings of every other State. And the Congress may by general Laws prescribe the Manner in which such Acts, Records, and Proceedings shall be proved, and the Effect thereof.

Section. 2. The Citizens of each State shall be entitled to all Privileges and Immunities of Citizens in the several States.

A Person charged in any State with Treason, Felony, or other Crime, who shall flee from Justice, and be found in another State, shall on Demand of the executive Authority of the State from which he fled, be delivered up, to be removed to the State having Jurisdiction of the Crime.

No Person held to Service or Labour in one State, under the Laws thereof, escaping into another, shall, in Consequence of any Law or Regulation therein, be discharged from such Service or Labour, but shall be delivered up on Claim of the Party to whom such Service or Labour may be due [Modified by Amendment XIII].

Section. 3. New States may be admitted by the Congress into this Union; but no new State shall be formed or erected within the Jurisdiction of any other State; nor any State be formed by the Junction of two or more States, or Parts of States, without the Consent of the Legislatures of the States concerned as well as of the Congress.

The Congress shall have Power to dispose of and make all needful Rules and Regulations respecting the Territory or other Property belonging to the United States; and nothing in this Constitution shall be so construed as to Prejudice any Claims of the United States, or of any particular State.

Section. 4. The United States shall guarantee to every State in this Union a Republican Form of Government, and shall protect each of them against Invasion; and on Application of the Legislature, or of the Executive (when the Legislature cannot be convened), against domestic Violence.

Article. V.

The Congress, whenever two thirds of both Houses shall deem it necessary, shall propose Amendments to this Constitution, or, on the Application of the Legislatures of two thirds of the several States, shall call a Convention for proposing Amendments, which, in either Case, shall be valid to all Intents and Purposes, as Part of this Constitution, when ratified by the Legislatures of three fourths of the several States, or by Conventions in three fourths thereof, as the one or the other Mode of Ratification may be proposed by the Congress; Provided that no Amendment which may be made prior to the Year One thousand eight hundred and eight shall in any Manner affect the first and fourth Clauses in the Ninth Section of the first Article; *and that no state, without its Consent, shall be deprived of its equal Suffrage in the Senate* [Possibly abrogated by Amendment XVII].

Article. VI.

All Debts contracted and Engagements entered into, before the Adoption of this Constitution, shall be as valid against the United States under this Constitution, as under the Confederation.

This Constitution, and the Laws of the United States which shall be made in Pursuance thereof; and all Treaties made, or which shall be made, under the Authority of the United States, shall be the supreme Law of the Land; and the Judges in every State shall be bound thereby, any Thing in the Constitution or Laws of any State to the Contrary notwithstanding.

The Senators and Representatives before mentioned, and the Members of the several State Legislatures, and all executive and judicial Officers, both of the United States and of the several States, shall be bound by Oath or Affirmation, to support this Constitution; but no religious Test shall ever be required as a Qualification to any Office or public Trust under the United States.

Article. VII.

The Ratification of the Conventions of nine States, shall be sufficient for the Establishment of this Constitution between the States so ratifying the Same.

The Word, "the," being interlined between the seventh and eighth Lines of the first Page, The Word "Thirty" being partly written on an Erazure in the fifteenth Line of the first Page, The Words "is tried" being interlined between the thirty second and thirty third Lines of the first Page and the Word "the" being interlined between the forth third and forty fourth Lines of the second Page

Attest William Jackson
Secretary

done in Convention by the Unanimous Consent of the States present the Seventeenth Day of September in the Year of our Lord one thousand seven hundred and Eighty seven and of the Independence of the United States of America the Twelfth In witness whereof We have hereunto subscribed our Names,

Go. WASHINGTON—Presidt
and deputy from Virginia

New Hampshire {
    JOHN LANGDON
    NICHOLAS GILMAN

Massachusetts {
    NATHANIEL GORHAM
    RUFUS KING

Connecticut {
    WM SAML JOHNSON
    ROGER SHERMAN

New York . . . .
    ALEXANDER HAMILTON

New Jersey {
    WIL: LIVINGSTON
    DAVID BREARLEY
    WM PATERSON
    JONA: DAYTON

Pennsylvania {
    B Franklin
    Thomas Mifflin
    Robt Morris
    Geo Clymer
    Thos FitzSimons
    Jared Ingersoll
    James Wilson
    Gouv Morris

Delaware {
    Geo: Read
    Gunning Bedford jun
    John Dickinson
    Richard Bassett
    Jaco: Broom

Maryland {
    James McHenry
    Dan of St Thos Jenifer
    Danl Carroll

Virginia {
    John Blair—
    James Madison Jr.

North Carolina {
    Wm Blount
    Richd Dobbs Spaight
    Hu Williamson
    J. Rutledge

South Carolina {
    Charles Cotesworth Pinckney
    Charles Pinckney
    Pierce Butler

Georgia {
    William Few
    Abr Baldwin

In Convention Monday, September 17th, 1787.

Present

The State of

New Hampshire, Massachusetts, Connecticut, Mr. Hamilton form New York, New Jersey, Pennsylvania, Delaware, Maryland, Virginia, North Carolina, South Carolina and Georgia.

Resolved,

That the preceeding Constitution be laid before the United States in Congress assembled, and that it is the Opinion of this Convention, that it should afterwards be submitted to a Convention of Delegates, chosen in each State by the People thereof, under the Recommendation of its Legislature, for their Assent and Ratification; and that each Convention assenting to, and ratifying the Same, should give Notice thereof to the United States in Congress assembled. Resolved, That it is the Opinion of this Convention, that as soon as the Conventions of nine States shall have ratified this Constitution, the United States in Congress assembled should fix a Day on which Electors should be appointed by the States which have ratified the same, and a Day on which the Electors should assemble to vote for the President, and the Time and Place for commencing Proceedings under this Constitution. That after such Publication the Electors should be appointed, and the Senators and Representatives elected: That the Electors should meet on the Day fixed for the Election of the President, and should transmit their Votes certified, signed, sealed and directed, as the Constitution requires, to the Secretary of the United States in Congress assembled, that the Senators and Representatives should convene at the Time and Place assigned; that the Senators should appoint a President of the Senate, for the sole purpose of receiving, opening and counting the Votes for President; and, that after he shall be chosen, the Congress, together with the President, should, without Delay, proceed to execute this Constitution.

By the Unanimous Order of the Convention

GO WASHINGTON—Presidt
W. JACKSON Secretary.

Amendments to the Constitution

CONSTITUTION OF THE UNITED STATES ARTICLES IN ADDITION
TO, AND AMENDMENT OF, THE CONSTITUTION OF THE UNITED
STATES OF AMERICA, PROPOSED BY CONGRESS, AND RATIFIED BY
THE LEGISLATURES OF THE SEVERAL STATES, PURSUANT TO THE
FIFTH ARTICLE OF THE ORIGINAL CONSTITUTION

Article I.

Congress shall make no law respecting an establishment of religion, or prohibit-
ing the free exercise thereof; or abridging the freedom of speech, or of the
press; or the right of the people peaceably to assemble, and to petition the
Government for a redress of grievances.

Article II.

A well regulated Militia being, necessary to the security of a free State, the right
of the people to keep and bear Arms, shall not be infringed.

Article III.

No Soldier shall, in time of peace be quartered in any house, without the consent of the Owner, nor in time of war, but in a manner to be prescribed by law.

Article IV.

The right of the people to be secure in their persons, houses, papers, and effects, against unreasonable searches and seizures, shall not be violated, and no
Warrants shall issue, but upon probable cause, supported by Oath or affirmation, and particularly describing the place to be searched, and the persons or
things to be seized.

Article V.

No person shall be held to answer for a capital, or otherwise infamous crime,
unless on a presentment or indictment of a Grand Jury, except in cases arising
in the land or naval forces, or in the Militia, when in actual service in time of
War or public danger; nor shall any person be subject for the same offence to
be twice put in jeopardy of life or limb; nor shall be compelled in any criminal
case to be a witness against himself, nor be deprived of life, liberty, or property,
without due process of law; nor shall private property be taken for public use,
without just compensation.

Article VI.

In all criminal prosecutions, the accused shall enjoy the right to a speedy and public trial, by an impartial jury of the State and district wherein the crime shall have been committed, which district shall have been previously ascertained by law, and to be informed of the nature and cause of the accusation; to be confronted with the witnesses against him; to have compulsory process for obtaining witnesses in his favor, and to have the Assistance of Counsel for his defense.

Article VII.

In Suits at common law, where the value in controversy shall exceed twenty dollars, the right of trial by jury shall be preserved, and no fact tried by a jury, shall be otherwise reexamined in any Court of the United States, than according to the rules of the common law.

Article VIII.

Excessive bail shall not be required, nor excessive fines imposed, nor cruel and unusual punishments inflicted.

Article IX.

The enumeration in the Constitution, of certain rights, shall not be construed to deny or disparage others retained by the people.

Article X.

The powers not delegated to the United States by the Constitution, nor prohibited by it to the States, are reserved to the States respectively, or to the people.

Article XI.

The Judicial power of the United States shall not be construed to extend to any suit in law or equity, commenced or prosecuted against one of the United States by Citizens of another State, or by Citizens or Subjects of any Foreign State.

Proposal and Ratification

The eleventh amendment to the Constitution of the United States was proposed to the legislatures of the several States by the Third Congress, on the 4th of March 1794; and was declared in a message from the President to Congress, dated the 8th of January, 1798, to have been ratified by the legislatures of three-fourths of the States. The dates of ratification were: New York, March 27, 1794; Rhode Island, March 31, 1794; Connecticut, May 8, 1794; New Hampshire,

*June 16, 1794; Massachusetts, June 26, 1794; Vermont, between October 9, 1794
and November 9, 1794; Virginia, November 18, 1794; Georgia, November 29,
1794; Kentucky, December 7, 1794; Maryland, December 26, 1794; Delaware,
January 23, 1795; North Carolina, February 7, 1795.
Ratification was completed on February 7, 1795.
The amendment was subsequently ratified by South Carolina on December 4,
1797. New Jersey and Pennsylvania did not take action on the amendment.*

Article XII.

The Electors shall meet in their respective states, and vote by ballot for President and Vice-President, one of whom, at least, shall not be an inhabitant of the
same state with themselves; they shall name in their ballots the person voted
for as President, and in distinct ballots the person voted for as Vice-President,
and they shall make distinct lists of all persons voted for as President, and of all
persons voted for as Vice-President, and of the number of votes for each, which
lists they shall sign and certify, and transmit sealed to the seat of the government of the United States, directed to the President of the Senate;—The President of the Senate shall, in the presence of the Senate and House of
Representatives, open all the certificates and the votes shall then be counted;—
The person having the greatest number of votes for President, shall be the President, if such number be a majority of the whole number of Electors appointed;
and if no person have such majority, then from the persons having the highest
numbers not exceeding three on the list of those voted for as President, the
House of Representatives shall choose immediately, by ballot, the President. But
in choosing the President, the votes shall be taken by states, the representation
from each state having one vote; a quorum for this purpose shall consist of a
member or members from two-thirds of the states, and a majority of all the
states shall be necessary to a choice. And if the House of Representatives shall
not choose a President whenever the right of choice shall devolve upon them,
before *the fourth day of March next following, then the Vice-President shall act as
President, as in the case of the death or other constitutional disability of the President.*—The person having the greatest number of votes as Vice-President, shall
be the Vice-President, if such number be a majority of the whole number of
Electors appointed, and if no person have a majority, then from the two highest
numbers on the list, the Senate shall choose the Vice-President; a quorum for
the purpose shall consist of two-thirds of the whole number of Senators, and a
majority of the whole number shall be necessary to a choice. But no person
constitutionally ineligible to the office of President shall be eligible to that of
Vice-President of the United States.

Proposal and Ratification

*The twelfth amendment to the Constitution of the United States was proposed
to the legislatures of the several States by the Eighth Congress, on the 9th of
December, 1803, in lieu of the original third paragraph of the first section of the*

second article; and was declared in a proclamation of the Secretary of State, dated the 25th of September, 1804, to have been ratified by the legislatures of 13 of the 17 States. The dates of ratification were: North Carolina, December 21, 1803; Maryland, December 24, 1803; Kentucky, December 27, 1803; Ohio, December 30, 1803; Pennsylvania, January 5, 1804; Vermont, January 30, 1804; Virginia, February 3, 1804; New York, February 10, 1804; New Jersey, February 22, 1804; Rhode Island, March 12, 1804; South Carolina, May 15, 1804; Georgia, May 19, 1804; New Hampshire, June 15, 1804.

Ratification was completed on June 15, 1804.

The amendment was subsequently ratified by Tennessee, July 27, 1804. The amendment was rejected by Delaware, January 18, 1804; Massachusetts, February 3, 1804; Connecticut, at its session begun May 10, 1804.

Article XIII.

Section. 1. Neither slavery nor involuntary servitude, except as a punishment for crime whereof the party shall have been duly convicted, shall exist within the United States, or any place subject to their jurisdiction.

Section. 2. Congress shall have power to enforce this article by appropriate legislation.

Proposal and Ratification

The thirteenth amendment to the Constitution of the United States was proposed to the legislatures of the several States by the Thirty-eighth Congress, on the 31st day of January, 1865, and was declared, in a proclamation of the Secretary of State, dated the 18th of December, 1865, to have been ratified by the legislatures of twenty-seven of the thirty-six States. The dates of ratification were: Illinois, February 1, 1865; Rhode Island, February 2, 1865; Michigan, February 2, 1865; Maryland, February 3, 1865; New York, February 3, 1865; Pennsylvania, February 3, 1865; West Virginia, February 3, 1865; Missouri, February 6, 1865; Maine, February 7, 1865; Kansas, February 7, 1865; Massachusetts, February 7, 1865; Virginia, February 9, 1865; Ohio, February 10, 1865; Indiana, February 13, 1865; Nevada, February 16, 1865; Louisiana, February 17, 1865; Minnesota, February 23, 1865; Wisconsin, February 24, 1865; Vermont, March 9, 1865; Tennessee, April 7, 1865; Arkansas, April 14, 1865; Connecticut, May 4, 1865; New Hampshire, July 1, 1865; South Carolina, November 13, 1865; Alabama, December 2, 1865; North Carolina, December 4, 1865; Georgia, December 6, 1865.

Ratification was completed on December 6, 1865.

The amendment was subsequently ratified by Oregon, December 8, 1865; California, December 19, 1865; Florida, December 28, 1865 (Florida again ratified on June 9, 1868, upon its adoption of a new constitution); Iowa, January 15, 1866; New Jersey, January 23, 1866 (after having rejected the amendment on March 16, 1865); Texas, February 18, 1870; Delaware, February 12, 1901 (after having rejected the amendment on February 8, 1865); Kentucky, March 18, 1865 (after having rejected it on February 24, 1865). The amendment was rejected (and not subsequently ratified) by Mississippi, December 4, 1865.

Article XIV.

Section. 1. All persons born or naturalized in the United States, and subject to the jurisdiction thereof, are citizens of the United States and of the State wherein they reside. No State shall make or enforce any law which shall abridge the privileges or immunities of citizens of the United States; nor shall any State deprive any person of life, liberty, or property, without due process of law; nor deny to any person within its jurisdiction the equal protection of the laws.

Section. 2. Representatives shall be appointed among the several States according to their respective numbers, counting the whole number of persons in each State, excluding Indians not taxed. But when the right to vote at any election for the choice of electors for President and Vice President of the United States, Representatives in Congress, the Executive and Judicial officers of a State, or the members of the Legislature thereof, is denied to any of the male inhabitants of such State, being twenty-one years of age, and citizens of the United States, or in any way abridged, except for participation in rebellion, or other crime, the basis of representation therein shall be reduced in the proportion which the number of such male citizens shall bear to the whole number of male citizens twenty-one years of age in such State.

Section. 3. No person shall be a Senator or Representative in Congress, or elector of President and Vice President, or hold any office, civil or military, under the United States, or under any State, who, having previously taken an oath, as a member of Congress, or as an officer of the United States, or as a member of any State legislature, or as an executive or judicial officer of any State, to support the Constitution of the United States, shall have engaged in insurrection or rebellion against the same, or given aid or comfort to the enemies thereof. But Congress may be a vote of two-thirds of each House, remove such disability.

Section. 4. The validity of the public debt of the United States, authorized by law, including debts incurred for payment of pensions and bounties for services in suppressing insurrection or rebellion, shall not be questioned. But neither the United States nor any State shall assume or pay any debt or obligation incurred in aid of insurrection or rebellion against the United States, or any claim for the loss or emancipation of any slave; but all such debts, obligations and claims shall be held illegal and void.

Section. 5. The Congress shall have power to enforce, by appropriate legislation, the provisions of this article.

Proposal and Ratification

The fourteenth amendment to the Constitution of the United States was proposed to the legislatures of the several States by the Thirty-ninth Congress, on the 13th of June, 1866. It was declared, in a certificate of the Secretary of State dated July 28, 1868 to have been ratified by the legislatures of 28 of the 37 States. The dates of ratification were: Connecticut, June 25, 1866; New Hampshire, July 6, 1866; Tennessee, July 19, 1866; New Jersey, September 11, 1866 (subsequently the legislature rescinded its ratification, and on March 24, 1868, readopted its resolution of rescission over the Governor's veto, and on Nov. 12, 1980, expressed support for the amendment); Oregon, September 19, 1866 (and rescinded its ratification on October 15, 1868); Vermont, October 30, 1866; Ohio, January 4, 1867 (and rescinded its ratification on January 15, 1868); New York, January 10, 1867; Kansas, January 11, 1867; Illinois, January 15, 1867; West Virginia, January 16, 1867; Michigan, January 16, 1867; Minnesota, January 16, 1867; Maine, January 19, 1867; Nevada, January 22, 1867; Indiana, January 23, 1867; Missouri, January 25, 1867; Rhode Island, February 7, 1867; Wisconsin, February 7, 1867; Pennsylvania, February 12, 1867; Massachusetts, March 20, 1867; Nebraska, June 15, 1867; Iowa, March 16, 1868; Arkansas, April 6, 1868; Florida, June 9, 1868; North Carolina, July 4, 1868 (after having rejected it on December 14, 1866); Louisiana, July 9, 1868 (after having rejected it on February 6, 1867); South Carolina, July 9, 1868 (after having rejected it on December 20, 1866).

Ratification was completed on July 9, 1868.

The amendment was subsequently ratified by Alabama, July 13, 1868; Georgia, July 21, 1868 (after having rejected it on November 9, 1866); Virginia, October 8, 1869 (after having rejected it on January 9, 1867); Mississippi, January 17, 1870; Texas, February 18, 1870 (after having rejected it on October 27, 1866); Delaware, February 12, 1901 (after having rejected it on February 8, 1867); Maryland, April 4, 1959 (after having rejected it on March 23, 1867); California, May 6, 1959; Kentucky, March 18, 1976 (after having rejected it on January 8, 1867).

Article XV.

Section. 1. The right of citizens of the United States to vote shall not be denied or abridged by the United States or by any State on account of race, color, or previous condition of servitude.

Section. 2. The Congress shall have power to enforce this article by appropriate legislation.

Proposal and Ratification

The fifteenth amendment to the Constitution of the United States was proposed to the legislatures of the several States by the Fortieth Congress, on the 26th of February, 1869, and was declared, in a proclamation of the Secretary of State, dated March 30, 1870, to have been ratified by the legislatures of twenty-nine of the thirty-seven States. The dates of ratification were: Nevada, March 1, 1869;

West Virginia, March 3, 1869; Illinois, March 5, 1869; Louisiana, March 5, 1869; North Carolina, March 5, 1869; Michigan, March 8, 1869; Wisconsin, March 9, 1869; Maine, March 11, 1869; Massachusetts, March 12, 1869; Arkansas, March 15, 1869; South Carolina, March 15, 1869; Pennsylvania, March 25, 1869; New York, April 14, 1869 (and the legislature of the same State passed a resolution January 5, 1870, to withdraw its consent to it, which action it rescinded on March 30, 1970); Indiana, May 14, 1869; Connecticut, May 19, 1869; Florida, June 14, 1869; New Hampshire, July 1, 1869; Virginia, October 8, 1869; Vermont, October 20, 1869; Missouri, January 7, 1870; Minnesota, January 13, 1870; Mississippi, January 17, 1870; Rhode Island, January 18, 1870; Kansas, January 19, 1870; Ohio, January 27, 1870 (after having rejected it on April 30, 1869); Georgia, February 2, 1870; Iowa, February 3, 1870. Ratification was completed on February 3, 1870, unless the withdrawal of ratification by New York was effective; in which event ratification was completed on February 17, 1870, when Nebraska ratified.

The amendment was subsequently ratified by Texas, February 18, 1870; New Jersey, February 15, 1871 (after having rejected it on February 7, 1870); Delaware, February 12, 1901 (after having rejected it on March 18, 1869); Oregon, February 24, 1959; California, April 3, 1962 (after having rejected it on January 28, 1870); Kentucky, March 18, 1976 (after having rejected it on March 12, 1869). The amendment was approved by the Governor of Maryland, May 7, 1973; Maryland having previously rejected it on February 26, 1870. The amendment was rejected (and not subsequently ratified) by Tennessee, November 16, 1869.

Article XVI.

The Congress shall have power to lay and collect taxes on incomes, from whatever source derived, without appointment among the several States, and without regard to any census or enumeration.

Proposal and Ratification

The sixteenth amendment to the Constitution of the United States was proposed to the legislatures of the several States by the Sixty-first Congress on the 12th of July 1909, and was declared, in a proclamation of the Secretary of State, dated the 25th of February, 1913, to have been ratified by 36 of the 48 States. The dates of ratification were: Alabama, August 10, 1909; Kentucky, February 8, 1910; South Carolina, February 19, 1910; Illinois, March 1, 1910; Mississippi, March 7, 1910; Oklahoma, March 10, 1910; Maryland, April 8, 1910; Georgia, August 3, 1910; Texas, August 16, 1910; Ohio, January 19, 1911; Idaho, January 20, 1911; Oregon, January 23, 1911; Washington, January 26, 1911; Montana, January 30, 1911; Indiana, January 30, 1911; California, January 31, 1911; Nevada, January 31, 1911; South Dakota, February 3, 1911; Nebraska, February 9, 1911; North Carolina, February 11, 1911; Colorado, February 15, 1911; North Dakota, February 17, 1911; Kansas, February 18, 1911; Michigan, February 23, 1911; Iowa, February 24, 1911; Missouri, March 16, 1911; Maine, March 31, 1911; Tennessee, April 7, 1911; Arkansas, April 22, 1911 (after having rejected it

*earlier);Wisconsin, May 26, 1911; New York, July 12, 1911;Arizona,April 6, 1912;
Minnesota, June 11, 1912; Louisiana, June 28, 1912;West Virginia, January 31,
1913; New Mexico, February 3, 1913.*
Ratification was completed on February 3, 1913.
*The amendment was subsequently ratified by Massachusetts, March 4, 1913;
New Hampshire, March 7, 1913 (after having rejected it on March 2, 1911).
The amendment was rejected (and not subsequently ratified) by Connecticut,
Rhode Island, and Utah.*

Article XVII.

The Senate of the United States shall be composed of two Senators from each
State, elected by the people thereof, for six years; and each Senator shall have
one vote. The electors in each State shall have the qualifications requisite for
electors of the most numerous branch of the State legislatures.

When vacancies happen in the representation of any State in the Senate,
the executive authority of such State shall issue writs of election to fill such vacancies: *Provided,* That the legislature of any State may empower the executive
thereof to make temporary appointments until the people fill the vacancies by
election as the legislature may direct.

The amendment shall not be so construed as to affect the election or term
of any Senator chosen before it becomes valid as part of the Constitution.

Proposal and Ratification

*The seventeenth amendment to the Constitution of the United States was pro-
posed to the legislatures of the several States by the Sixty-second Congress on the
13th of May, 1912, and was declared, in a proclamation of the Secretary of
State, dated the 31st of May, 1913, to have been ratified by the legislatures of 36
of the 48 States. The dates of ratification were: Massachusetts, May 22, 1912;
Arizona, June 3, 1912; Minnesota, June 10, 1912; New York, January 15, 1913;
Kansas, January 17, 1913; Oregon, January 23, 1913; North Carolina, January 25,
1913; California, January 28, 1913; Michigan, January 28, 1913, Iowa, January 30,
1913; Montana, January 30, 1913; Idaho, January 31, 1913;West Virginia,
February 4, 1913; Colorado, February 5, 1913; Nevada, February 6, 1913;Texas,
February 7, 1913;Washington, February 8, 1913;Wyoming, February 8, 1913;
Arkansas, February 11, 1913; Maine, February 11, 1913; Illinois, February 13,
1913; North Dakota, February 14, 1913;Wisconsin, February 18, 1913; Indiana,
February 19, 1913; South Dakota, February 19, 1913; Oklahoma, February 24,
1913; Ohio, February 25, 1913; Missouri, March 7, 1913; New Mexico, March 13,
1913; Nebraska, March 14, 1913; New Jersey, March 17, 1913;Tennessee,
April 1, 1913; Pennsylvania,April 2, 1913; Connecticut,April 8, 1913.*
Ratification was completed on April 8, 1913.
*The amendment was subsequently ratified by Louisiana, June 11, 1914.The
amendment was rejected by Utah (and not subsequently ratified) on February 26,
1913.*

Article XVIII.

Section. 1. After one year from the ratification of this article the manufacture, sale, or transportation of intoxicating liquors within, the importation thereof into, or the exportation thereof from the United States and all territory subject to the jurisdiction thereof for beverage purposes is hereby prohibited.

Section. 2. The Congress and the several States shall have concurrent power to enforce this article by appropriate legislation.

Section. 3. This article shall be inoperative unless it shall have been ratified as an amendment to the Constitution by the legislatures of the several States, as provided in the Constitution, within seven years from the date of the submission hereof to the States by the Congress.

Proposal and Ratification

The eighteenth amendment to the Constitution of the United States was pro- posed to the legislatures of the several States by the Sixty-fifth Congress, on the 18th of December, 1917, and was declared, in a proclamation of the Secretary of State, dated the 29th of January, 1919, to have been ratified by the legislatures of 36 of the 48 States. The dates of ratification were: Mississippi, January 8, 1918; Virginia, January 11, 1918; Kentucky, January 14, 1918; North Dakota, January 25, 1918; South Carolina, January 29, 1918; Maryland, February 13, 1918; Montana, February 19, 1918; Texas, March 4, 1918; Delaware, March 18, 1918; South Dakota, March 20, 1918; Massachusetts, April 2, 1918; Arizona, May 24, 1918; Georgia, June 26, 1918; Louisiana, August 3, 1918; Florida, Decem- ber 3, 1918; Michigan, January 2, 1919; Ohio, January 7, 1919; Oklahoma, Janu- ary 7, 1919; Idaho, January 8, 1919; Maine, January 8, 1919; West Virginia, January 9, 1919; California, January 13, 1919; Tennessee, January 13, 1919; Washington, January 13, 1919; Arkansas, January 14, 1919; Kansas, January 14, 1919; Alabama, January 15, 1919; Colorado, January 15, 1919; Iowa, January 15, 1919; New Hampshire, January 15, 1919; Oregon, January 15, 1919; Nebraska, January 16, 1919; North Carolina, January 16, 1919; Utah, January 16, 1919; Missouri, January 16, 1919; Wyoming, January 16, 1919.
*Ratification was completed on January 16, 1919. See **Dillon v. Gloss,** 256 U.S. 368, 376 (1921).*
The amendment was subsequently ratified by Minnesota on January 17, 1919; Wisconsin, January 17, 1919; New Mexico, January 20, 1919; Nevada, January 21, 1919; New York, January 29, 1919; Vermont, January 29, 1919; Pennsylvania, Feb- ruary 25, 1919; Connecticut, May 6, 1919] and New Jersey, March 9, 1922. The amendment was rejected (and not subsequently ratified) by Rhode Island.

Article XIX.

The right of citizens of the United States to vote shall not be denied or abridged by the United States of by any State on account of sex.

Congress shall have power to enforce this article by appropriate legislation.

Proposal and Ratification

The nineteenth amendment to the Constitution of the United States was proposed to the legislatures of the several States by the Sixty-sixth Congress, on the 4th of June 1919, and was declared, in a proclamation of the Secretary of State, dated the 27th of August, 1920, to have been ratified by the legislatures of 36 of the 48 States. The dates of ratification were: Illinois, June 10, 1919 (and that State readopted its resolution of ratification June 17, 1919); Michigan, June 10, 1919; Wisconsin, June 10, 1919; Kansas, June 16, 1919; New York, June 16, 1919; Ohio, June 16, 1919; Pennsylvania, June 24, 1919; Massachusetts, June 25, 1919; Texas, June 28, 1919; Iowa, July 2, 1919; Missouri, July 3, 1919; Arkansas, July 28, 1919; Montana, August 2, 1919; Nebraska, August 2, 1919; Minnesota, September 8, 1919; New Hampshire, September 10, 1919; Utah, October 2, 1919; California, November 1, 1919; Maine, November 5, 1919; North Dakota, December 1, 1919; South Dakota, December 4, 1919; Colorado, December 15, 1919; Kentucky, January 6, 1920; Rhode Island, January 6, 1920; Oregon, January 13, 1920; Indiana, January 16, 1920; Wyoming, January 27, 1920; Nevada, February 7, 1920; New Jersey, February 9, 1920, Idaho, February 11, 1920; Arizona, February 12, 1920; New Mexico, February 21, 1920; Oklahoma, February 28, 1920; West Virginia, March 10, 1920; Washington, March 22, 1920; Tennessee, August 18, 1920. Ratification was completed on August 18, 1920.

The amendment was subsequently ratified by Connecticut on September 14, 1920 (and that State reaffirmed on September 21, 1920); Vermont, February 8, 1921; Delaware, March 6, 1923 (after having rejected it on June 2, 1920); Maryland, March 29, 1941 (after having rejected it on February 24, 1920, ratification certified on February 25, 1958); Virginia, February 21, 1952 (after having rejected it on February 12, 1920); Alabama, September 8, 1953 (after having rejected it on September 22, 1919); Florida, May 13, 1969; South Carolina, July 1, 1969 (after having rejected it on January 28, 1920, ratification certified on August 22, 1973); Georgia, February 20, 1970 (after having rejected it on July 24, 1919); Louisiana, June 11, 1970 (after having rejected it on July 1, 1920); North Carolina, May 6, 1971; Mississippi, March 22, 1984 (after having rejected it on March 29, 1920).

Article XX.

Section. 1. The terms of the President and Vice President shall end at noon on the 20th day of January, and the terms of Senators and Representatives at noon on the 3d day of January, of the years in which such terms would have ended if this article had not been ratified; and the terms of their successors shall then begin.

Section. 2. The Congress shall assemble at least once in every year, and such meeting shall begin at noon on the 3d day of January, unless they shall by law appoint a different day.

Section. 3. If, at the time fixed for the beginning of the term of the President, the President elect shall have died, the Vice President elect shall become President. If a President shall not have been chosen before the time fixed for the beginning of his term, or if the President elect shall have failed to qualify, then the Vice President elect shall act as President until a President shall have qualified; and the Congress may by law provide for the case wherein neither a President elect nor a Vice President elect shall have qualified, declaring who shall then act as President, or the manner in which one who is to act shall be selected, and such person shall act accordingly until a President or Vice President shall have qualified.

Section. 4. The Congress may by law provide for the case of the death of any of the persons from whom the House of Representatives may choose a President whenever the right of choice shall have devolved upon them, and for the case of the death of any of the persons from whom the Senate may choose a Vice President whenever the right of choice shall have devolved upon them.

Section. 5. Sections 1 and 2 shall take effect on the 15th day of October following the ratification of this article.

Section. 6. This article shall be inoperative unless it shall have been ratified as an amendment to the Constitution by the legislatures of three-fourths of the several States within seven years from the date of its submission.

Proposal and Ratification

The twentieth amendment to the Constitution was proposed to the legislatures of the several states by the Seventy-Second Congress, on the 2d day of March, 1932, and was declared, in a proclamation by the Secretary of State, dated on the 6th day of February, 1933, to have been ratified by the legislatures of 36 of the 48 States. The dates of ratification were: Virginia, March 4, 1932; New York, March 11, 1932; Mississippi, March 16, 1932; Arkansas, March 17, 1932; Kentucky, March 17, 1932; New Jersey, March 21, 1932; South Carolina, March 25, 1932; Michigan, March 31, 1932; Maine, April 1, 1932; Rhode Island, April 14, 1932; Illinois, April 21, 1932; Louisiana, June 22, 1932; West Virginia, July 30, 1932; Pennsylvania, August 11, 1932; Indiana, August 15, 1932; Texas, September 7, 1932; Alabama, September 13, 1932; California, January 4, 1933; North Carolina, January 5, 1933, North Dakota, January 9, 1933; Minnesota, January 12, 1933; Arizona, January 13, 1933; Montana, January 13, 1933; Nebraska, January 13, 1933; Oklahoma, January 13, 1933; Kansas, January 16, 1933; Oregon, January 16, 1933; Delaware, January 19, 1933; Washington, January 19, 1933; Wyoming, January 19, 1933; Iowa, January 20, 1933; South Dakota, January 20, 1933; Tennessee, January 20, 1933; Idaho, January 21, 1933; New Mexico, January 21, 1933; Georgia, January 23, 1933; Missouri, January 23, 1933; Ohio, January 23, 1933; Utah, January 23, 1933.
Ratification was completed on January 23, 1933.
The amendment was subsequently ratified by Massachusetts on January 24, 1933; Wisconsin, January 24, 1933; Colorado, January 24, 1933; Nevada,

January 26, 1933; Connecticut, January 27, 1933; New Hampshire, January 31, 1933;Vermont, February 2, 1933; Maryland, March 24, 1933; Florida, April 26, 1933.

Article XXI.

Section. 1. The eighteenth article of amendment to the Constitution of the United States is hereby repealed.

Section. 2. The transportation or importation into any State, Territory, or possession of the United States for delivery or use therein of intoxicating liquors, in violation of the laws thereof, is hereby prohibited.

Section. 3. This article shall be inoperative unless it shall have been ratified as an amendment to the Constitution by conventions in the several States, as provided in the Constitution, within seven years from the date of the submission hereof to the States by the Congress.

Proposal and Ratification

The twenty-first amendment to the Constitution was proposed to the several states by the Seventy-Second Congress, on the 20th day of February, 1933, and was declared, in a proclamation by the Secretary of State, dated on the 5th day of December, 1933, to have been ratified by 36 of the 48 States. The dates of ratification were: Michigan, April 10, 1933; Wisconsin, April 25, 1933; Rhode Island, May 8, 1933; Wyoming, May 25, 1933; New Jersey, June 1, 1933; Delaware, June 24, 1933; Indiana, June 26, 1933; Massachusetts, June 26, 1933; New York, June 27, 1933; Illinois, July 10, 1933; Iowa, July 10, 1933; Connecticut, July 11, 1933; New Hampshire, July 11, 1933; California, July 24, 1933; West Virginia, July 25, 1933; Arkansas, August 1, 1933; Oregon, August 7, 1933; Alabama, August 8, 1933; Tennessee, August 11, 1933; Missouri, August 29, 1933; Arizona, September 5, 1933; Nevada, September 5, 1933; Vermont, September 23, 1933; Colorado, September 26, 1933; Washington, October 3, 1933; Minnesota, October 10, 1933; Idaho, October 17, 1933; Maryland, October 18, 1933; Virginia, October 25, 1933; New Mexico, November 2, 1933; Florida, November 14, 1933; Texas, November 24, 1933; Kentucky, November 27, 1933; Ohio, December 5, 1933; Pennsylvania, December 5, 1933; Utah, December 5, 1933. Ratification was completed on December 5, 1933.
The amendment was subsequently ratified by Maine, on December 6, 1933; and by Montana, on August 6, 1923. The amendment was rejected (and not subsequently ratified) by South Carolina, on December 4, 1933.

Article XXII.

Section. 1. No person shall be elected to the office of the President more than twice, and no person who has held the office of President, or acted as President, for more than two years of a term to which some other person was elected President shall be elected to the office of the President more than once. But this

Article shall not apply to any person holding the office of President when this Article was proposed by the Congress, and shall not prevent any person who may be holding the office of President, or acting as President, during the term within which this Article becomes operative from holding the office of President or acting as President during the remainder of such term.

Section. 2. This article shall be inoperative unless it shall have been ratified as an amendment to the Constitution by the legislatures of three-fourths of the several States within seven years from the date of its submission to the States by the Congress.

Proposal and Ratification

This amendment was proposed to the legislature of the several States by the Eightieth Congress on Mar. 21, 1947 by House Joint Res. No. 27, and was declared by the Administrator of General Services, on Mar. 1, 1951, to have been ratified by the legislatures of 36 of the 48 States. The dates of ratification were: Maine, March 31, 1947; Michigan, March 31, 1947; Iowa, April 1, 1947; Kansas, April 1, 1947; New Hampshire, April 1, 1947; Delaware, April 2, 1947; Illinois, April 3, 1947; Oregon, April 3, 1937; Colorado, April 12, 1947; California, April 15, 1947; New Jersey, April 15, 1947; Vermont, April 15, 1947; Ohio, April 16, 1947; Wisconsin, April 16, 1947; Pennsylvania, April 29, 1947; Connecticut, May 21, 1947; Missouri, May 22, 1947; Nebraska, May 23, 1947; Virginia, January 28, 1948; Mississippi, February 12, 1948; New York, March 9, 1948; South Dakota, January 21, 1949; North Dakota, February 25, 1949; Louisiana, May 17, 1950; Montana, January 25, 1951; Indiana, January 29, 1951; Idaho, January 30, 1951; New Mexico, February 12, 1951; Wyoming, February 12, 1951; Arkansas, February 15, 1951; Georgia, February 17, 1951; Tennessee, February 20, 1951; Texas, February 22, 1951; Nevada, February 26, 1951; Utah, February 26, 1951; Minnesota, February 27, 1951.
Ratification was completed on February 27, 1951.
The amendment was subsequently ratified by North Carolina on February 28, 1951; South Carolina, March 13, 1951; Maryland, March 14, 1951; Florida, April 16, 1951; Alabama, May 4, 1951. The amendment was rejected (and not subsequently ratified) by Oklahoma in June 1947, and Massachusetts on June 9, 1949.

Certification of Validity
Publication of the certifying statement of the Administrator of General Services that the amendment had become valid was made on Mar. 1, 1951, F.R. Doc. 51 092940, 16 F.R. 2019.

Article XXIII.

Section. 1. The District constituting the seat of Government of the United States shall appoint in such manner as the Congress may direct:

A number of electors of President and Vice President equal to the whole number of Senators and Representatives in Congress to which the District would be entitled if it were a State, but in no event more than the least populous State; they shall be in addition to those appointed by the States, but they shall be considered, for the purposes of the election of President and Vice President, to be electors appointed by a State; and they shall meet in the District and perform such duties as provided by the twelfth article of amendment.

Section. 2. The Congress shall have power to enforce this article by appropriate legislation.

Proposal and Ratification

This amendment was proposed by the Eighty-sixth Congress on June 17, 1960 and was declared by the Administrator of General Services on Apr. 3, 1961, to have been ratified by 38 of the 50 States. The dates of ratification were: Hawaii, June 23, 1960 (and that State made a technical correction to its resolution on June 30, 1960); Massachusetts, August 22, 1960; New Jersey, December 19, 1960; New York, January 17, 1961; California, January 19, 1961; Oregon, January 27, 1961; Maryland, January 30, 1961; Idaho, January 31, 1961; Maine, January 31, 1961; Minnesota, January 31, 1961; New Mexico, February 1, 1961; Nevada, February 2, 1961; Montana, February 6, 1961; South Dakota, February 6, 1961; Colorado, February 8, 1961; Washington, February 9, 1961; West Virginia, February 9, 1961; Alaska, February 10, 1961; Wyoming, February 13, 1961; Delaware, February 20, 1961; Utah, February 21, 1961; Indiana, March 3, 1961; North Dakota, March 3, 1961; Tennessee, March 6, 1961; Michigan, March 8, 1961; Connecticut, March 9, 1961; Arizona, March 10, 1961; Illinois, March 14, 1961; Nebraska, March 15, 1961; Vermont, March 15, 1961; Iowa, March 16, 1961; Missouri, March 20, 1961; Oklahoma, March 21, 1961; Rhode Island, March 22, 1961; Kansas, March 29, 1961; Ohio, March 29, 1961.

Ratification was completed on March 29, 1961.

The amendment was subsequently ratified by New Hampshire on March 30, 1961 (when that State annulled and then repeated its ratification of March 29, 1961).

The amendment was rejected (and not subsequently ratified) by Arkansas on January 24, 1961.

Certification of Validity

Publication of the certifying statement of the Administrator of General Services that the amendment had become valid was made on Apr. 3, 1961, F.R. Doc 61 093017, 26 F.R. 2808.

Article XXIV.

Section. 1. The right of citizens of the United States to vote in any primary or other election for President or Vice President, for electors for President or Vice President, or for Senator or Representative in Congress, shall not be denied or abridged by the United States or any State by reason of failure to pay any poll tax or other tax.

Section. 2. The Congress shall have power to enforce this article by appropriate legislation.

Proposal and Ratification

This amendment was proposed by the Eighty-seventh Congress by Senate Joint Resolution No. 29, which was approved by the Senate on Mar. 27, 1962, and by the House of Representatives on Aug. 27, 1962. It was declared by the Administrator of General Services on Feb. 4, 1964, to have been ratified by the legislatures of 38 of the 50 States. This amendment was ratified by the following States: Illinois, November 14, 1962; New Jersey, December 3, 1962; Oregon, January 25, 1963; Montana, January 28, 1963; West Virginia, February 1, 1963; New York, February 4, 1963; Maryland, February 6, 1963; California, February 7, 1963; Alaska, February 11, 1963; Rhode Island, February 14, 1963; Indiana, February 19, 1963; Utah, February 20, 1963; Michigan, February 20, 1963; Colorado, February 21, 1963; Ohio, February 27, 1963; Minnesota, February 27, 1963; New Mexico, March 5, 1963; Hawaii, March 6, 1963; North Dakota, March 7, 1963; Idaho, March 8, 1963; Washington, March 14, 1963; Vermont, March 15, 1963; Nevada, March 19, 1963; Connecticut, March 20, 1963; Tennessee, March 21, 1963; Pennsylvania, March 25, 1963; Wisconsin, March 26, 1963; Kansas, March 28, 1963; Massachusetts, March 28, 1963; Nebraska, April 4, 1963; Florida, April 18, 1963; Iowa, April 24, 1963; Delaware, May 1, 1963; Missouri, May 13, 1963; New Hampshire, June 12, 1963; Kentucky, June 27, 1963, Maine, January 16, 1964, South Dakota, January 23, 1964; Virginia, February 25, 1977. Ratification was completed on January 23, 1964.

The amendment was subsequently ratified by North Carolina on May 3, 1989.
The amendment was rejected by Mississippi (and not subsequently ratified) on December 20, 1962. Certification of Validity Publication of the certifying statement of the Administrator of General Services that the amendment had become valid was made on Feb. 5, 1964, F.R. Doc. 64 091229, 29 F.R. 1715.

Article XXV.

Section. 1. In case of the removal of the President from office or of his death or resignation, the Vice President shall become President.

Section. 2. Whenever there is a vacancy in the office of the Vice President, the President shall nominate a Vice President who shall take office upon confirmation by a majority vote of both Houses of Congress.

Section. 3. Whenever the President transmits to the President pro tempore of the Senate and the Speaker of the House of Representatives his written declaration that he is unable to discharge the powers and duties of his office, and until he transmits to them a written declaration to the contrary, such powers and duties shall be discharged by the Vice President as Acting President.

Section. 4. Whenever the Vice President and a majority of either the principal officers of the executive departments or of such other body as Congress may by law provide, transmit to the President pro tempore of the Senate and the Speaker of the House of Representatives their written declaration that the President is unable to discharge the powers and duties of his office, the Vice President shall immediately assume the powers and duties of the office of Acting President. Thereafter, when the President transmits to the President pro tempore of the Senate and the Speaker of the House of Representatives his written declaration that no inability exists, he shall resume the powers and duties of his office unless the Vice President and a majority of either the principal officers of the executive department or of such other body as Congress may by law provide, transmit within four days to the President pro tempore of the Senate and the Speaker of the House of Representatives their written declaration that the President is unable to discharge the powers and duties of his office. Thereupon Congress shall decide the issue, assembling within forty-eight hours for that purpose if not in session. If the Congress, within twenty-one days after receipt of the latter written declaration, or, if Congress is not in session, within twenty-one days after Congress is required to assemble, determines by two-thirds vote of both Houses that the President is unable to discharge the powers and duties of his office, the Vice President shall continue to discharge the same as Acting President; otherwise, the President shall resume the powers and duties of his office.

Proposal and Ratification

This amendment was proposed by the Eighty-ninth Congress by Senate Joint Resolution No. 1, which was approved by the Senate on Feb. 19, 1965, and by the House of Representatives, in amended form, on April 13, 1965. The House of Representatives agreed to a Conference Report on June 30, 1965, and the Senate agreed to the Conference Report on July 6, 1965. It was declared by the Administrator of General Services, on Feb. 23, 1967, to have been ratified by the legislatures of 39 of the 50 States. This amendment was ratified by the following States: Nebraska, July 12, 1965; Wisconsin, July 13, 1965; Oklahoma, July 16, 1965; Massachusetts, August 9, 1965; Pennsylvania, August 18, 1965; Kentucky, September 15, 1965; Arizona, September 22, 1965; Michigan, October 5, 1965; Indiana, October 20, 1965; California, October 21, 1965; Arkansas, November 4, 1965; New Jersey, November 29, 1965; Delaware, December 7, 1965; Utah, January 17, 1966; West Virginia, January 20, 1966; Maine, January 24, 1966; Rhode Island, January 28, 1966; Colorado, February 3, 1966; New Mexico, February 3, 1966; Kansas, February 8, 1966; Vermont, February 10, 1966; Alaska, February 18, 1966; Idaho, March 2, 1966; Hawaii, March 3, 1966; Virginia, March 8, 1966; Mississippi, March 10, 1966; New York, March 14, 1966; Maryland, March 23, 1966; Missouri, March 30, 1966; New Hampshire, June 13, 1966; Louisiana, July 5, 1966; Tennessee, January 12, 1967; Wyoming, January 25, 1967; Washington, January 26, 1967; Iowa, January 26, 1967; Oregon, February 2, 1967; Minnesota, February 10, 1967; Nevada, February 10, 1967.
Ratification was completed on February 10, 1967.
The amendment was subsequently ratified by Connecticut, February 14, 1967;

Montana, February 15, 1967; South Dakota, March 6, 1967; Ohio, March 7, 1967; Alabama, March 14, 1967; North Carolina, March 22, 1967; Illinois, March 22, 1967; Texas, April 25, 1967; Florida, May 25, 1967.

Certification of Validity
Publication of the certifying statement of the Administrator of General Services that the amendment had become valid was made on Feb. 25, 1967, F.R. Doc. 67 092208, 32 F.R. 3287.

Article XXVI.

Section. 1. The right of citizens of the United States, who are eighteen years of age or older, to vote shall not be denied or abridged by the United States or by any State on account of age.

Section. 2. The Congress shall have power to enforce this article by appropriate legislation.

Proposal and Ratification

This amendment was proposed by the Ninety-second Congress by Senate Joint Resolution No. 7, which was approved by the Senate on Mar. 10, 1971, and by the House of Representatives on Mar. 23, 1971. It was declared by the Administrator of General Services on July 5, 1971, to have been ratified by the legislatures of 39 of the 50 States. This amendment was ratified by the following States: Connecticut, March 23, 1971; Delaware, March 23, 1971; Minnesota, March 23, 1971; Tennessee, March 23, 1971; Washington, March 23, 1971; Hawaii, March 24, 1971; Massachusetts, March 24, 1971; Montana, March 29, 1971; Arkansas, March 30, 1971; Idaho, March 30, 1971; Iowa, March 30, 1971; Nebraska, April 2, 1971; New Jersey, April 3, 1971; Kansas, April 7, 1971; Michigan, April 7, 1971; Alaska, April 8, 1971; Maryland, April 8, 1971; Indiana, April 8, 1971; Maine, April 9, 1971; Vermont, April 16, 1971; Louisiana, April 17, 1971; California, April 19, 1971; Colorado, April 27, 1971; Pennsylvania, April 27, 1971; Texas, April 27, 1971; South Carolina, April 28. 1971; West Virginia, April 28, 1971; New Hampshire, May 13, 1971; Arizona, May 14, 1971; Rhode Island, May 27, 1971; New York, June 2, 1971; Oregon, June 4, 1971; Missouri, June 14, 1971; Wisconsin, June 22, 1971; Illinois, June 29, 1971; Alabama, June 30, 1971; Ohio, June 30, 1971; North Carolina, July 1, 1971; Oklahoma, July 1, 1971.
Ratification was completed on July 1, 1971.
The amendment was subsequently ratified by Virginia, July 8, 1971; Wyoming, July 8, 1971; Georgia, October 4, 1971.

Certification of Validity
Publication of the certifying statement of the Administrator of General Services that the amendment had become valid was made on July 7, 1971, F.R. Doc. 71 099691, 36 F.R. 12725.

Article XXVII.

No law, varying the compensation for the services of the Senators and Representatives, shall take effect, until an election of Representatives shall have intervened.

Proposal and Ratification

This amendment, being the second of twelve articles proposed by the First Congress on Sept. 25, 1789, was declared by the Archivist of the United States on May 18, 1992, to have been ratified by the legislatures of 40 of the 50 States. This amendment was ratified by the following States: Maryland, December 19, 1789; North Carolina, December 22, 1789; South Carolina, January 19. 1790; Delaware, January 28, 1790; Vermont, November 3, 1791; Virginia, December 15, 1791; Ohio, May 6, 1873; Wyoming, March 6, 1978; Maine, April 27, 1983; Colorado, April 22, 1984; South Dakota, February 21, 1985; New Hampshire, March 7, 1985; Arizona, April 3, 1985; Tennessee, May 23, 1985; Oklahoma, July 10, 1985; New Mexico, February 14, 1986; Indiana, February 24, 1986; Utah, February 26, 1986; Arkansas, March 6, 1987; Montana, March 17, 1987; Connecticut, May 13, 1987; Wisconsin, July 15, 1987; Georgia, February 2, 1988; West Virginia, March 10, 1988; Louisiana, July 7, 1988; Iowa, February 9, 1989; Idaho, March 23, 1989; Nevada, April 26, 1989; Alaska, May 6, 1989; Oregon, May 19, 1989; Minnesota, May 22, 1989; Texas, May 25, 1989; Kansas, April 5, 1990; Florida, May 31, 1990; North Dakota, March 25, 1991; Alabama, May 5, 1992; Missouri, May 5, 1992; Michigan, May 7, 1992; New Jersey, May 7, 1992. Ratification was completed on May 7, 1992.
The amendment was subsequently ratified by Illinois on May 12, 1992.

Certification of Validity

Publication of the certifying statement of the Archivist of the United States that the amendment had become valid was made on May 18, 1992, F.R. Doc. 92 0911951, 57 F.R. 21187.

[Editorial note: There is some conflict as to the exact dates of ratification of the amendments by the several States. In some cases, the resolutions of ratification were signed by the officers of the legislatures on dates subsequent to that on which the second house had acted. In other cases, the Governors of several of the States "approved" the resolutions (on a subsequent date), although action by the Governor is not contemplated by article V, which required ratification by the legislatures (or conventions) only. In a number of cases, the journals of the State legislatures are not available. The dates set out in this document are based upon the best information available.]

ACKNOWLEDGMENTS

I acknowledge my wife, who *is* my *Lady in Black* and has *not* left me due to government threat, hardship, or my own outbursts of emotion. She, in fact, has taken the hand-scribbled, block-printed outpouring of emotion from my heart, mind, and soul and brought this work into readable form. Every word was originally born on the wheel—while waiting to load or deliver, or while being laid over on the road. In my own 5 million miles, I have rarely observed such faith, and she does truly possess the voice of an angel.

Many friends also had to endure the long months while this work dominated my life. I apologize. Bob, I don't think I could have completed this work without your encouragement and attention while bouncing ideas off the wall in front of our bar stools.

Public figuratively speaking, I wish to thank Mick Box for keeping the legend of Uriah Heep alive. Had you simply formed a new band under your own deserving name, the Heep would have disappeared completely into the void. You are the best there has ever been. *Sea of Light* and *Sonic Origami* clearly demonstrate that you can lead a band to where only Heep has gone.

Ditto to Rush Limbaugh. I do like your show, but no, I don't always agree. From what I have written, I would guess that you would want no part of me. Something tells me you're not a Heepster.

Of course, I cannot forget Bill Clinton. No one has ever shown better what it takes to be a politician. He is inspiring, depending on your definition of inspiring!

[UPDATE: Effective January 2004, in typical political arrogant ignorance, Congress has passed legislation changing the Hours of Service Laws of The Federal Motor Carrier Safety Regulations. Specifically, a driver will be required to take a ten hour break between driving shifts (previously 8 hours). This will cause even more congestion and confusion. A government windfall in fines and further infringement of individual freedom will result.]

A RESTITUTION PARTY

Declaration to Restore the Freedom of Individuals

We, the people of the United States of America as individual citizens, do hereby declare and demand full restitution for the principles of individual equal opportunity, liberty, freedom, justice, and rights as established by the Founding Fathers in the Constitution of the United States of America and the guaranties as fundamentally stated in the original Bill of Rights.

- Congress shall not impose taxation prior to payment of wage, income, profit, or transfer of property, and shall repeal all laws establishing the collection of withholding taxes.

- Congress shall repeal all laws establishing exemption, privilege, infringement, protection, or pardon based upon group status.

- No law, directive, initiative, policy, tax, or religion shall be established by judicial ruling.

- No trade agreement shall be established void of tariffs equal to or greater than taxation rate.

- There shall be no governmental social engineering through taxation and appropriation of funds.

NOTE: The Restitution party will convene on Labor Day weekend in Albuquerque, New Mexico, to begin an end to:

      (1) Globalization by America
      (2) Globalization of America
      (3) Class system tax collection
      (4) Class system justice
      (5) Social engineering through taxation

Signed: _____, American Citizen

Address: _____

_____

_____

Order Form

Name:_____

Mailing Address: _____

_____

City & State:_____

Zip Code: _____

Telephone: _____

Fax: _____

E-mail: _____

Please send _____ copy (copies) of **Restitution by K.W. Clark** @ $14.99 per copy.

Please bill my credit card.

Credit card: Visa ❑   MC ❑   Amex ❑

Card No:_____

Exp date:_____

Signature of cardholder:_____

Code: _____

Please mail your order form to:

BookMasters, Inc.
30 Amberwood Parkway
Ashland, OH 44805
800-247-6553

You may fax your order to: 419-281-6883

Email your order to: order@bookmasters.com

Order through our website: http://www.atlasbooks.com